Other Novels by Gary Braver

Elixir

WRITING AS GARY GOSHGARIAN

Atlantis Fire
Rough Beast
The Stone Circle

Gray Matter

GARY BRAVER

TOR®

A TOM DOHERTY ASSOCIATES BOOK
NEW YORK

This is a work of fiction. All the characters and events portrayed in this book are either products of the author's imagination or are used fictitiously.

GRAY MATTER

A Tor Book
Published by Tom Doherty Associates, LLC
175 Fifth Avenue
New York, NY 10010

www.tor.com

Tor® is a registered trademark of Tom Doherty Associates, LLC.

Grateful acknowledgment is made for permission to reprint the following material:

Excerpts from "The Snow Man" and "The Emperor of Ice-Cream" from *The Collected Poems of Wallace Stevens* by Wallace Stevens, copyright © 1954 by Wallace Stevens and renewed of Alfred A. Knopf, a division of Random House, Inc.

Excerpt from "The Hollow Man" in Collected Poems 1909–1962 by T.S. Eliot. Copyright © 1936 by Harcourt, Inc., copyright © 1964, 1963 by T.S. Eliot, reprinted by permission of the publisher.

On page 356, lyric excerpt from "There Is Nothin' Like A Dame" by Richard Rodgers and Oscar Hammerstein II. Copyright © 1949 by Richard Rodgers and Oscar Hammerstein II. Copyright Renewed. WILLIAMSON MUSIC owner of publication and allied rights throughout the world. International Copyright secured. Reprinted by Permission. All Rights Reserved.

ISBN: 0-812-57006-5

First edition: September 2002
First mass market edition: March 2004

Printed in the United States of America

0 9 8 7 6 5 4 3 2 1

For Kathleen, Nathan, and David

ACKNOWLEDGMENTS

I would like to thank the following people for providing me with medical, forensic, and other technical information.

From Northeastern University: from the Department of Counseling and Applied Psychology, Carmen Armengol; from the Department of Psychology, Joanne Miller and Harry MacKay; from the Department of Sociology, Jack Levin.

For their very generous time and expert insights, a special thanks to James Stellar, Professor of Behavioral Neuroscience and Dean of the College of Arts and Sciences, and John F. McDevitt, Assistant Professor, the College of Criminal Justice, Northeastern University.

I am also grateful to Drs. Regis deSilva, Jason McCormick, David Urion, and Gary Fischer.

In addition, I am grateful to Dr. James Weiner, Associate Chief Medical Examiner of Massachusetts; Kenneth Halloran, Clerk Magistrate, Plymouth County, Massachusetts; Lt. Richard W. Sequin, Massachusetts State Police; Lt. Thomas J. Gelson and Chief John Ford, Bourne Police Department; Sgt. Peter Howell, Sandwich Police Department; and Dr. Carl M. Selavka, Director of the Massachusetts State Police Crime Lab.

Thanks also to Jean Hagen, Pamela and Malcolm Childers, Kemmer and Martha Anderson, George and Donna Megrichian, Alice Janjigian, and Kathryn Goodfellow.

I also want to thank Charles O'Neill and Barbara Shapiro for the brainstorms that made this a better story.

A very special thanks to my agent, Susan Crawford, my editor, Natalia Aponte, and my publisher, Tom Doherty, for their great support. You made this possible.

We should take care not to make the intellect our god; it has, of course, powerful muscles, but no personality.

—ALBERT EINSTEIN

PROLOGUE

Mom, do clams have eyes?"

"I don't think so, hon," Jane replied, without glancing up from her magazine.

Her three-year-old daughter, Megan, was on her knees a few feet away, digging quahog shells out of the sandbar. Her back was to her, but Jane could see the impressive pile she had collected. If they were a smoking family, there would be big, white ashtrays in every room in the house. Megan had even found three intact quahogs, which sat underwater in her yellow pail. Jane's husband, Keith, now asleep under an umbrella, would use the guts for bait. He liked to surf-cast for stripers and blues. And August was the season.

"You sure?"

Jane looked up from the magazine. The only other people within half a mile were a man with some kids on boogie boards skimming across the flats in the wavelets. Otherwise, the place was an open stretch of empty sandbar and beach under an outrageously clear blue sky. Except for some sailboats out at sea, the horizon made an unbroken azure arc across her field of vision.

"I'm pretty sure."

The vastness was a wonderful relief from the claustrophobic clutter of their lives, which seemed to be spent in a series of boxes—house, cars, trains, and offices. And far from the horrors of the world that filled the pages of her magazine. One article told of a Pennsylvania teenager who had committed suicide because he was unhappy with his SAT scores.

God in heaven! How far from that they were, she thought.

The water was warm, and the tide was going out and exposing the huge flats of smooth featureless sandbar—featureless but for bright white shells.

"Well, I think this one's different," Megan declared. "It has eyes."

"It has?"

Sagamore Beach. One of the best-kept secrets on the Cape. Not only were there no bridge traffic jams to contend with, but the beach was a strip of cozy postwar cottages that hugged grass-swollen dunes above the beach, stretching five miles from the White Cliffs east to the Cape Cod Canal. Not a motel, clam shack, or self-serve in sight. Just five miles of white beach with rarely more than a handful of people. The public beach, at the canal end, drew a crowd on weekends. But the rest of the strip was always wide open, and Jane loved it like that. It was their one concession to private living. They rented the same cottage for a week each year.

Even more special was how the beach was growing. While the rest of the Cape suffered perennial erosion, Sagamore Beach had become a natural shoring area for what washed down from the north. With every nor'easter, countless tons of sand washed up, expanding the bar and burying the ancient granite jetties that used to segment the beach.

"It's a special clam."

According to the article, the boy had been an excellent student—straight As, his teachers reported. "What's that, honey?"

"I said, this one's *special*. It's big and has eyes."

Jane glanced over her shoulder. Megan looked so cute in her pink two-piece and floppy pink hat. She was digging away with her hands now. Someplace behind them, a bunch of seagulls squawked over a dead fish.

Because of prevailing currents, the beach was a dumping ground of all sorts of "surf kills," as Keith called them. Some mornings they'd wake up to find stripers and small sharks washed up with the night tide. About ten years ago, a forty-foot humpback whale was deposited in a storm down near the canal. Nobody was sure if it had beached itself or died at sea, but the Coast Guard had to come and haul it out to deep waters, because after four days the stench was unbearable.

"Guess I was wrong," Jane said.

Apparently the pressure of college entrance exams caused the poor kid to underperform. His parents found him hanging in the garage. The sad irony was that his test scores could have gotten him into most colleges in the country.

"Does that mean they could see?"

The piece went on to argue that the growing number of student suicides can be linked to the pressure of standardized tests such as the SATs and AP exams.

"I didn't think they could," Jane said, half-consciously.

"We live in a stratified society, characterized by a tremendous and growing gap between the rich and poor, the successful and unsuccessful," one educator lamented. *"Not only do these kids equate SAT scores with IQs, but they see them as a forecast of how they'll do in life . . ."*

"I think this one is blind."

"That's too bad," Jane said.

She yawned, as some child psychologist commented how the use of standardized tests was getting out of hand; how some top preschools even require admission tests for four-year-olds; how U.S. parents spend a billion each year for SAT prep courses.

Jane felt herself grow sleepy.

"And it's bigger," Megan continued.

Jane folded the magazine across her lap and closed her eyes. "That'll make Daddy happy."

"I think it has a nose, too."

"Uh-huh." Jane raised her face to the sun. The gentle lapping of the wavelets made an irresistible lullaby that seemed to be in cadence with her own heartbeat. In a matter of moments, she felt herself fade into the warm sac of sunlight encasing her body.

"AND TEETH!"

Jane's eyes snapped open.

Megan was standing just inches away. Jane let out a hectoring scream.

In Megan's hand was a human skull.

1

Dylan was in the middle of the chorus of "Bloody Mary" when Rachel Whitman turned into the lot of the Dells Country Club. Martin, Dylan's father, loved show tunes and Dylan had learned many by heart.

" 'Now ain't that too damn bad?' "

"Darn," Rachel said and pulled into the shade of a huge European elm, trying to shake the sense of grief that had gripped her for the last several days. "Too *darn* bad."

"But the song says *damn*, Mom."

"I know, but *damn* is not a polite word for six-year-old boys."

"How come?"

"It just isn't." She was not in the mood to argue.

"There's Mrs. M'Phearson Jagger," announced Dylan.

There was a time when she found the way he said things adorable—sweet baby-talk artifacts that she'd let go by. But the specialist had said that they had to work at this together, even if it meant correcting him every time.

"You have to keep after him. He has to hear the rules in action so they'll sink in."

"Jag-WHAR," she corrected. "And it's Mrs. MacPhearson's Jaguar." She emphasized the *s*.

"Jag-WHAR, but I like *Jagger* better. 'Now, ain't that too damn bad?' " he sang.

Rachel parked next to the green Jaguar alongside of the clubhouse, a sprawling and elegant white structure that appeared to glow against the emerald fairways that rolled away to the sea.

For a moment, Rachel stared through the windshield at the dappled sunlight playing across the gold-lacquered hood. Sitting in her big shiny Maxima, dressed in her white DKNY sundress and Movado watch and Ferragamo sandals, her sculpted raven hair and discreet black glasses, she would, to the casual observer, appear to be a woman who had it all—a woman blessed by fortune, a woman of rare privilege, a woman who saw nothing but endless blue skies above her head. And Rachel Whitman did have it all—health, a successful marriage, money, a beautiful new home in one of the flossiest North Shore suburbs, and an adorable little boy. Or almost all . . .

It wasn't as if they'd found a dysfunctional kidney. Just a setback that they would make the best of.

"Mom, do I have to go?"

Dylan looked up at her with those gorgeous green eyes. So full of depth.

"But you like DellKids."

"Yeah, but I don't like her. I don't wanna go." His mouth began to quiver as he fought back tears.

"Who?"

He looked out his window and took a couple deep breaths to control himself.

"You mean Miss Jean?" Rachel asked. Miss Jean was one of the day-care counselors. Her yellow VW Bug was parked nearby.

"No, Lucinda. I don't like her." His eyes began to fill up.

"Lucinda MacPhearson?"

"I hate her. She's mean."

Lucinda was Sheila's seven-year-old daughter—and one of the twelve kids in DellKids, a day-care center located in a separate wing of the clubhouse. Since school let out last week, Dylan was attending it full-time now. Because the waiting list for full club membership was years long, Rachel and Martin had purchased a social membership which allowed them dining, pool, and tennis privileges, as well as DellKids. That was fine with Rachel who didn't play golf.

"How is she mean?"

Dylan didn't answer nor did he have to. Rachel knew and felt the heat of irritation rise. Lucinda was a very bright child, but she was bossy and a know-it-all. Like an intolerant schoolmarm, she would hold forth with Dylan and the other kids on operating computer games or fashioning Play-Doh. Dylan was too proud to admit how the little brat had humiliated him.

"Do you want to tell me what she said?" It crossed her mind to speak to Sheila, though it would be awkward since Sheila had sold them their house and sponsored their Dells membership.

But Dylan didn't respond. Something out the window had caught his attention. "What's that man doing?" he asked.

One of the waiters, a big kid in his teens, was standing half-hidden behind a tree outside the kitchen and staring through field glasses at a girl sunning herself on a poolside lounge chair. While Rachel watched, the boy suddenly slapped himself in the face.

For a moment Rachel thought she was seeing things. But he did it again—he slapped himself in the face. Then again and again—all the while peering through the field glasses at the girl by the pool.

"Why he hitted himself?"

But Rachel didn't have an answer. Nor did she correct Dylan. Nor was she sure if she should do something. She thought about getting out of the car and approaching him, but then what? *"Gee, young man, you really shouldn't be whacking your face like that."* What if he suddenly turned on her? The kid clearly looked disturbed.

And yet, there was something bizarrely purposeful in his behavior—the way he kept studying the girl between slaps, as if waiting for a reaction from her. Or maybe punishing himself for Peeping Tom thoughts. "I don't know," Rachel muttered and got out.

The sound of the closing doors alerted the kid. He shot them a look as they moved toward the clubhouse, then disappeared into the kitchen, leaving Rachel and Dylan wondering what that was all about.

"Is he a crazy man, Mom?"

"I don't know, but I think we better get inside before we're late."

She hustled Dylan to their entrance, hoping that the waiter would be confined to the kitchen and not wander into the day-care center.

"You know what I think?" he said as they moved inside. "I think he a *dummy*."

"Don't use that word."

Sheila was at their usual table beside the one-way windows through which they could watch their kids. The playroom was a large colorful open area with small tables and chairs scattered about, computer terminals, plants, books, posters, and cages with turtles and a huge brown rabbit. It had been carefully designed for a bright nurturing atmosphere. Miss Jean, like her assistant, was a former elementary-school teacher who had been hired full-time by the club. Together they made of DellKids an enlightened center for members' children. And three years ago it was awarded full day-care licensing by the state.

Rachel watched through the window as Jean gathered the children around one of the several computers. While she explained the particular program, the kids listened. All but Dylan, that is. He was making faces at another boy to get him to laugh. A couple of times Miss Jean had to ask Dylan to stop his antics and listen up. After a few minutes, they broke up into groups of twos and, thankfully, he was teamed up with a sweet little girl named Shannon.

The boy from out back stepped through the kitchen door carrying a tray of food for people at another table. "I see we've got a new waiter," Rachel said.

"Oh, that's just Brendan LaMotte," Sheila said. "His grandfather used to be the club plumber and got him a job as a caddy, but they moved him inside because they needed an extra body."

Brendan was a large sullen-looking kid, probably from one of the local high schools. "Is he . . . okay?"

"What do you mean?"

"Well, he seems rather weird. As we were coming in, he was out back slapping himself in the face."

"What?"

Rachel described the scene with the girl and field glasses.

"Hormones," Sheila said with a dismissive gesture. "Actually he's kind of a sad case. His parents were killed in a car accident a few years ago, and he's living alone with his grandfather. He's a little strange, but he's perfectly harmless. So, how's Martin's new business venture doing?"

Rachel took the invitation to change the subject. "Fine, but I hardly ever see him." Over the last two years, Martin's recruitment business had expanded phenomenally, moving out of a cramped office in Hanover to a fancy suite just off Memorial Drive in Cambridge.

Out of the corner of her eye, Rachel saw Brendan approach their table. He was a tall, somewhat pudgy kid with a pimply round face, a shiny black ponytail, and intense black eyes.

"Hey, Brendan. How you doing?" Sheila chortled, trying to warm him up.

"F-fine," he said curtly.

"Do you know Mrs. Whitman? She's a recent member."

He glanced at Rachel with those laser eyes. "I know who she is."

Something about his wording sent an unpleasant ripple through Rachel.

"I'll have the usual," Sheila said.

"Whole wheat English m-muffin, split, toasted medium-well, a half-pad of margarine, fruit cup—no maraschino cherries—decaf hazelnut with skim milk, small glass of vanilla-flavored soy milk." His slight stuttering disappeared as he rattled all that off, while the braces on his teeth flashed, adding to his robotic delivery.

Sheila smiled. "You got it."

He turned to Rachel. "You?"

His manner was so blunt and his expression so intense that Rachel was momentarily thrown off. "I'll have a cappuccino and a bagel, please."

He made an impatient sigh. "We have p-plain, sesame, raisin, poppy seed, sunflower seed, salt, egg, sun-dried tomato, onion, garlic, four-grain, and everything which includes garlic, onion, poppy and sesame seeds, and salt but not the other ingredients." It was like being addressed by a machine.

"Raisin."

"Cream cheese?"

"Yes, please, on the side."

"Regular or fat-free, which is thirty calories for two tablespoons versus a hundred for regular, and five milligrams of cholesterol, but of course you get the xanthan and carob-bean gums plus potassium sorbate and sodium tripolyphosphate and all the artificial flavors and colors. Suit yourself."

Rachel began to smile, thinking that he was joking—that he was doing some kind of Jim-Carrey-waiter-from-hell routine the way he rattled that off with edgy rote. But nothing in his expression said he was playacting. His face remained impassive, the only thing moving was his mouth and that bizarre tic: While he spoke his left eyelid kept flickering as if trying to ward off a gnat. Rachel also noticed that he had no order pad or pen to record the orders.

She preferred the fat-free but didn't want to set him off. "I'll have the regular."

"Toasted?"

"Yes."

"Light, dark, or medium?"

She did not dare question the options. "Medium."

"Orange juice?"

"Yes, please."

"It's fresh squeezed, not from concentrate, but it's Stop and Shop not Tropicana premium. You still want it?"

"I guess. Yes."

"Is that all?"

"Yes, please, thank you," Rachel gasped.

He then turned on his heel and slouched back into the kitchen.

Rachel saucered her eyes. "My God! I feel as if I've just been interrogated."

Sheila chuckled. "He is a tad intense."

"A tad? Someone get him a straitjacket."

"It could be worse. He could be your caddy. Ask him for advice on a club and he'll cite everything from barometric pressure and dew point to the latest comparative test data on shaft technology. He's a walking encyclopedia. He also has a photographic memory."

"I noticed he didn't write down our orders."

"He never does."

A kid with a photographic memory who smashes himself in the face while ogling girls through field glasses.

"He can also recite Shakespeare by the pound. In summer stock last year they did *Romeo and Juliet* and he ended up memorizing every part. He's amazing."

"Where does he go to school?"

"He dropped out."

"Lucky for his teachers," Rachel said, and looked over Sheila's shoulder through the one-way glass.

Her stomach knotted. Lucinda had wandered over to

Dylan and Shannon's computer and parked herself at their desk, explaining something that they apparently couldn't get right. As she watched, Rachel felt a wave of sadness flush over her resentment. While she wanted to go in there and shake Lucinda, the girl's confidence had clearly left poor Dylan in the shadows. While eager to be *with it,* his frustration had reduced him to making goofy faces and sounds to deflect attention—a measure that pained Rachel for its desperation. Some of the nearby kids laughed, but not Lucinda, who chided Dylan so that Miss Jean had to come over and ask him to settle down. She then took Dylan and Shannon to a free terminal and reexplained the procedure.

Rachel tried to hold tight, but she could feel the press of tears. Dylan was out of his league in there. He had a great singing voice, and she had thought someday to enroll him in a children's choir, but he was not one of those "cyberbrats," as Martin called them. Dylan was adorable and sociable and funny, but he lacked the focus of these other kids. Yes, she chided herself for making comparisons even though every other parent did the same thing—gauged their own against the competition: OPK, as Martin labeled them— "other people's kids." Yes, she reminded herself that what mattered was his happiness.

But in a flash-glimpse down the long corridor of time, she saw how hard life was going to be for him, especially being brought up in a community that thrived on merit.

"Was it something I said?" Sheila asked, noticing tears pool in Rachel's eyes.

"No, of course not." Rachel paused to compose herself as Brendan delivered the coffees then moved off to adjust the dinnerware at a nearby table.

She took a sip. "It's Dylan. He's fine . . . just fine . . . healthwise, thank God. It's just that he's got some learning disabilities."

"He has?"

Rachel had known Sheila for only a few months, but she

felt comfortable confiding in her. It was Sheila who had helped them get settled in town. Besides, all of Rachel's old friends were fifty miles or more from here; and her mother lived in Phoenix, and her brother Jack, in San Diego. "He's having difficulty reading," she said. "He tries, but he has problems connecting written words to sounds."

"Give him a break! He's only six years old. Some kids start later than others."

"I guess, but he's a bit behind." The reality was that the other kids in his class were miles beyond him. She and Martin had hoped to get him into Beaver Hill, a well-respected private elementary school where Lucinda was enrolled, but he didn't pass the entrance tests. So they enrolled him at Marsden Public Elementary. Only a month into the school year, and his teacher had alerted Rachel to his language difficulties and problems following simple instructions.

"Have you tried those phonics books and tapes?" Sheila asked.

"We've got all of them—books, tapes, videos. You name it. We even have a language therapist. He's got some kind of blockage or whatever. He doesn't get it."

"But he will. All kids do. He's just a late bloomer. In ten years he'll probably be a published author like Vanessa Watts's son, Julian. Didn't talk until he was four, and at age thirteen he wrote a book about mazes. I don't know anything about them, but I guess there's a whole bunch of maze freaks out there. Whatever, he got it published and had all this press."

Rachel nodded but felt little consolation.

"You know, you could have him evaluated to see what his skills and problems are."

"We did all that already." She had even arranged an MRI scan the other day, although she did not mention that to Sheila. In fact, she hadn't even told Martin.

"I see."

Rachel could sense Sheila's curiosity, wondering how he

had tested. But Rachel would not betray him. Although Rachel questioned the validity of IQ tests, there was something terribly definitive about them—like fingerprints or Universal Product Codes. Once the number was out, a person was forever ranked. *Hi, my name is Dylan Whitman and I'm an 83, seventeen points below the national average.*

"I know I'm being foolish," Rachel said, struggling to maintain composure. "It's not like he has some terrible disease, for God's sake."

"That's right, and you keep telling yourself that. Test scores aren't everything."

Easy for you to say with your little whiz kid in there, Rachel thought sourly.

Sheila was right, of course—and were they still living in Rockville, she wouldn't have been so aware. But this was a town of trophy houses and trophy kids—a town where the rewards for intelligence were in-your-face conspicuous. Hawthorne was an upscale middle-class community of professional people, all smart and well educated. To make matters worse, Dylan was now surrounded by high-pedigree children, bred for success by ambitious parents who knew just how clever their kids were and where they stood against the competition: which kids were the earliest readers, who got what on the SATs, who ranked where in their class, who got into the hot schools.

Suddenly Rachel missed Rockville with its aluminum-sided Capes and pitching nets, tire swings, and kids who played street hockey until they glowed. Where the only scores that mattered were how the Sox, Bruins, and Celtics did, not your verbal and math; where the pickup trucks sported Harley-Davidson logos and bumper stickers that said KISS MY BASS and SAVE THE ALES unlike all the high-end vehicles outside with stethoscopes hanging from the rearview mirrors and windows emblazoned with shields from Bloomfield Preparatory Academy, Harvard, and Draper Labs, and Nantucket residency permits.

She looked out the window onto the splendidly manicured course with its two pools and tennis courts and showplace clubhouse. She felt out of place. The Dells was one of the most exclusive country clubs in New England; and now that Martin's company had taken off they could afford the privileged life for their son. How ironic it seemed, given their expectations and presumptions. Rachel and Martin had both graduated from college so Dylan's limitations were as much of a surprise as they were distressing. Even worse, they made her feel that the perimeters of their lives had been irrevocably altered.

You did this to him, whispered a voice in her head.

No! NO! And she shook it away.

Outside a green Dells CC truck pulled up with two greenskeepers. The men got out. They were dressed in jeans and the green and white DCC pullovers. One of them said something that made the other man break up. As she sipped her cappuccino and watched them unload a lawn-mower, Rachel could not help but think how she was glimpsing her son's destiny—a life of pickup trucks, lawn-mowers, and subsistence wages.

"I guess I just didn't do enough," Rachel said.

"Like what?" Sheila said.

"Like when he was a baby. I guess I didn't give him a rich enough environment. But I tried. I read all the zero-to-three books about brain growth and early childhood development. I talked and sang to him, I read him stories when he was two months old—all that stuff." They had bought him JumpStart Toddlers and other computer games, Baby Bach, Baby Shakespeare and Baby Einstein toys. When he took a nap, she played classical music. From his infancy, she read him poetry because the books said how babies learn through repetition, and that repeated rhymes, like music at an early age, are supposed to increase the spatial-temporal reasoning powers. She breast-fed him because of a *Newsweek* story on how breast-fed babies scored higher on intelligence tests than those formula-fed—as silly as that had seemed.

Newsweek. The very thought of the magazine made her stomach grind.

No! Just a coincidence, she told herself. *Not true.*

Tears flooded Rachel's eyes. "And now it's too late. He turned six last month."

Sheila laid her hand on Rachel's. "Pardon my French, but those first-three-years books are bullshit. All they do is put a guilt trip on parents. I bet if you took twins at birth and played Mozart and read Shakespeare around the clock to one for three years and raised the other normally you wouldn't see a goddamn difference when they were six. You didn't fail, Rachel, believe me."

Rachel wiped her eyes and smiled weakly. "Something went wrong."

"Nothing went wrong."

Something terribly wrong.

Rachel nodded and looked away to change the subject. They were having two different conversations. Sheila did not understand.

Through the window, Lucinda was explaining something to the girl next to her. Sheila took the hint. "By the way, Lucinda's having a birthday party a week from Saturday. It's going to be an all-girl thing—her idea. But, in any case, I'm getting her a kitten."

"Oh, how sweet."

"It'll be her first pet. I think kids need pets—don't you? Something to, you know, love unconditionally?"

"Yes, of course. Dylan has gerbils and he's crazy about them."

At a nearby table, Brendan was arranging the dinnerware. To distract herself, Rachel watched him without thought. He was putting out dinnerware, all the time muttering to himself just below audibility—his mouth moving, braces flashing, his eye twitching. He looked possessed. "The poor kid's a basket case," she whispered to Sheila, thinking that it could be worse. At least Dylan was a happy child.

"I guess," Sheila said vaguely. She checked her watch. There was another hour and a half of day care, so Sheila was going to go to her office in the interim, while Rachel would sit outside with a book until Dylan was out.

As they left the building, Rachel's cell phone chirped in her handbag. The call was from Dr. Rose's office. The secretary said that Dylan's MRI results were back. "He'd like to make an appointment to see you and discuss them."

Rachel felt a shock to her chest. *Discuss them?* "Is everything all right?"

"I'm sure, but he can see you tomorrow at ten."

"Can I speak with him?"

"I'm sorry, he's out of the office on an emergency and probably won't be back for the rest of the day. Is ten tomorrow good for you?"

"Yes, ten's fine," she gasped and clicked off.

Oh, my God.

2

It was only three-thirty when Martin Whitman left the office. He had canceled two meetings and let all the calls and e-mails go unanswered because he wanted to buy some flowers on the way home as a prelude to taking Rachel to dinner at the Blue Heron—a chichi restaurant perched majestically on the cliffs overhanging Magnolia Harbor. Wine-dark sea, sunset dinner, candlelight, and a bottle of Veuve Clicquot. Just the kind of romance-shock they needed.

Because something wasn't right. Martin couldn't put his finger on it, but for the last few weeks Rachel had lapsed into a black funk. She was distracted much of the time—moody, as if plagued by a low-level anxiety. She would become petulant when he questioned her and lose patience with Dylan when he misspoke or had trouble doing things. Without warning, she'd tear up, then withdraw. He hadn't seen her like this since her hysterectomy which, three years ago, had left her in a dark malaise, like a slow-acting poison.

His first thought was that something was wrong with her—that her doctor had discovered a lump in her breast. But, surely, she would have told him. Then he wondered if there was another man—that while he spent up to fourteen hours a day at the office, Rachel had found somebody else. She was attractive, witty, warm, and easy to be with. But there had never been any reason to suspect her of cheating. Not until her recent shutdown—sex, of course, being a foolproof barometer. Overnight she had lost all interest in intimacy, going to bed early and falling asleep by the time he slipped beside her. When he brought it up, she said that it was just a phase she was going through—that it would pass. But so far it hadn't.

Perhaps it was the move to Hawthorne. But she seemed to have adjusted well, making new friends and joining the Dells. They had a great house, and Dylan was a happy and healthy kid. He had some learning problems, but he was probably a late bloomer as Martin had been.

No, it was something else, he told himself. Maybe she needed to go back to work. For six years she had been an English editor of college textbooks at a Boston publishing house. She enjoyed it and had done well. Now she was housebound. More space was what she needed—and to get back into life.

Martin pulled the black Miata down Massachusetts Avenue and onto Memorial Drive heading north to Route 93, which would connect him to Interstate 95. Across the Charles River, a thick underbelly of clouds made a rolling black canopy over Boston, lightning flickering through it like stroboscopes. The forecast was for afternoon showers that would clear out by evening.

This particular strip of Memorial from Massachusetts Avenue to the Sonesta was his favorite sector of Cambridge—even more than scenic Brattle Street with its august six-generational mansions or funky Central Square, or even Harvard Square which, unfortunately, had lost its renegade soul to mall franchises—the Abercrappies and Au Bon Pain in the Asses. Across the river lay Boston in red brick stacked up against Beacon Hill and surmounted by the gold dome of the State House. On the left were the grand old trophy buildings of MIT—interconnecting classical structures in limestone that emanated from the Great Dome, designed after the Pantheon of Rome and forged with the names of the greatest minds of history. He loved the area.

By the time he reached 95 North, the rain was heavy and remained so until he reached the Hawthorne exit. Just outside of Barton, a couple towns southwest of Hawthorne, the rain stopped and the clouds gave way to blue. The streets were puddled, but it would be a clear night after all. Dining under the stars.

Barton was a working-class town, the kind of place that tenaciously held on to reminders of its fisher-family heritage. The houses were mostly modest Capes and ranches, a few trailer homes that had intended to move elsewhere but had burrowed in. The center was a strip of fishing-tackle shops, a small used-car dealership, a marine-engine-repair place, doughnut and pizza shops, a dog-clipping service, and Ed's Lawnmower and TV Repair.

Halfway down Main Street, Martin shot through a puddle that was a lot deeper than it appeared. Instantly, he knew he was in trouble. Water had flashed up under the hood and doused the wires. Thinking fast, he turned into the lot of Angie's Diner and rolled into a parking space just as the car stalled out. He tried starting it, but the engine didn't turn over. There was no point calling Triple A since jumping the battery wouldn't do any good. In half an hour the wires would dry out and he'd be on his way. And a wedge of apple pie and a coffee would go down well.

Angie's Diner was the epicenter of Barton—a greasy spoon with homemade panache whose brash owner was part of its no-nonsense charm. Martin headed across the lot, which consisted of pickup trucks and some battered SUVs, and a Barton Fire Department car, probably from an off-duty firefighter heading home.

The place was half-full, some people in booths, a few at

the counter including the fireman, a middle-aged guy still in uniform. Martin took a seat at the elbow of the counter at the far end, giving him a full view of the booths against the front windows and the staff working the counter. He liked the blue-collar ambiance. The booth radio boxes, red Naugahyde spin-top stools, the gleaming stainless steel and Formica—the place was a 1960 tableau.

In a booth across from him sat a pretty teenage girl and an older guy with bushy hair, talking intensely over cake and coffee. In the next booth, another kid in a baggie black pullover and ponytail thumbed through a book of cartoons while picking on a garden salad. He was probably an art student somewhere.

Martin ordered pie and coffee and opened his copy of *Wired.* He was partway through an article when he noticed the ponytail kid shift around in his seat. At first Martin thought he was trying to get more comfortable, until it became clear he was craning for a better view of the couple, whose conversation had taken a turn for the worse. The bushy-hair guy was quietly protesting something, while the girl, a cute blonde in a black tank top, coolly pressed her case.

Meanwhile, Ponytail slid left and right for a better view. At one point, he got up to go to the toilet—or pretended to—and walked by them without taking his eyes off the girl. When she looked up expectantly, he marched off. A few minutes later he returned still staring intensely at her. She caught his eye and he scooted into his booth. The girl whispered something to her companion, and they got up and left as Ponytail tracked them through the window to their car.

Martin went back to his magazine, thinking that maybe Ponytail was Blondie's former suitor. Whatever, a few moments later, a small commotion arose when the boy asked for pancakes and the waitress said that they were no longer doing breakfast.

"Can you m-m-make a special order?"

"I'll ask Angie," the girl said and went into the back.

A moment later Angie came out. She was a short blocky woman about forty-five with a wide impassive face and a large head of red frizz held in place by jumbo white clips. She was not smiling. "We stop serving breakfast at eleven," she declared.

"You can't m-m-make a s-s-special order?"

"No, we can't."

The kid dropped his face into the menu pretending to find an alternative, but it was clear there was nothing else he was interested in.

"You want more time?"

He shook his head. "I r-r-really wanted p-pancakes."

Martin began to feel bad for the kid. Not only was he getting the cold shoulder from the proprietor, but also he was a stutterer. Martin had stuttered painfully in grade school.

"Then come back in the morning." She yanked the menu out of his hand. "We open at s-s-six." She winked at the fireman at the counter and started away.

"What's the big deal?" he asked good-naturedly. "Cup of mix, some milk, and a pan. It's not like he asked for a turkey dinner from scratch."

"Freddie, do I tell you how to put out fires? Huh? Right! So don't tell me how to run my diner."

"Take you two minutes, Angie. Give the kid a break," Freddie said in a low voice.

Then he added, "Looks like he just woke up anyway."

Angie glowered at Freddie, then appeared to soften. She turned to the kid. "It's gonna have to be plain," she hollered. "No blues or strawberries. They're back in the freezer."

"That's f-fine," the kid said in a thin voice, and returned to the cartoons.

Martin watched the kid. The book was a large hardbound tome of Walt Disney animations, and he was flipping through the pages rapidly as if trying to find something.

A few minutes later, Angie delivered the pancakes and a small rack of syrups. Out of the corner of his eye, Martin noticed the kid remove the tops of the syrups and sniff each one. He was not casually taking in the aromas but deeply inhaling and processing the scents like a professional perfume tester. Dissatisfied, he then poured a little of each into his coffee spoon and continued smelling then testing each with his tongue. It was bizarre.

This went on until Angie took notice and marched up to the kid's booth, her large red face preceding her like a fire truck. "You got a problem here?"

The kid looked up, startled. "Oh, no. N-no problem."

"So what are you doing with the syrups?"

"Well, I'm just trying to find the . . . I'm just w-w-wondering if . . . Do you have any others . . . other syrups?"

"You got five different syrups right there. What else do you want, tartar sauce?"

"Do you have any ma-ma-ma-maple syrup?"

She pulled one out of the rack and turned the top toward him. "Whaddya think *this* is?"

"Well, I meant, you know . . . *real* maple syrup?" He sniffed the small carafe. "This is actually corn syrup with water and artificial f-f-flavors. Also, c-caramel coloring. I mean real *m-maple* syrup, one h-hundred percent, no additives."

Angie took a deep breath and let it out very slowly, working to steady herself, aware that the whole place was watching and wondering if she were going to blow. "No, I'm sorry, sir," she said in a mock-apologetic whine. "We don't have *real* m-m-maple syrup, so I'm afraid you're gonna have to settle for the cheap imitation shit." She spun around and huffed away.

The kid looked around to notice everybody staring at him. He put his hand to his brow and began nibbling on his pancakes, pretending to lose himself in the cartoons. He only ate a mouthful, occasionally sniffing the different syrups when Angie wasn't looking.

He was clearly disturbed, Martin told himself, and operating on another level of reality. Every so often he would snap his head around as if picking up a stray scent like an animal. When he got up to go to the toilet, Martin could see that he was a tall overweight kid with a boyish face and a confused lumbering manner. He loped his way as Angie stood behind the counter wiping coffee mugs and watching him with that flat red face. On his return, he rounded the far end of the counter when something stopped him in his tracks: Blondie's half-eaten cake in the next booth. In disbelief, Martin watched the kid slip onto the seat and lower his face to the dish, sniffing like a dog screening leftovers on the dinner table.

"Shit!" Angie muttered as she rolled past Martin toward the kid. "You gonna eat my garbage now, huh?"

The kid straightened up, and the whole place held its breath. "What kind of cake is this?" His face was intense, his pupils dilated. The earlier deferential manner had hardened into some weird purpose.

She pulled the dish away and walked around the counter and dumped it into a bin without a word.

"I said, what kind of cake is that?" The kid rose from the booth. His eyes were fixed on the woman.

The fireman at the counter sat straight up. Everybody in the place was now looking at the big bear-bodied boy pressing Angie for an answer. She seemed taken aback by his intensity. "Butter almond cake."

"Butter almond cake," he said as if taking an oath. "Like real almonds?"

"Yeah, *real* almonds and *real* almond extract," she said sarcastically.

"Do you have any more?"

Angie looked over her shoulder. "Yeah, one piece."

The kid's eye clapped on the display case where the cakes sat. "I'll have it."

"What about your pancakes over there?"

"I'm finished. I want some butter almond."

"You want it with a fork, or you gonna inhale it?"

"A fork," he said. "And a knife."

The kid returned to his booth, not taking his eyes off Angie as she got the cake, walked to his booth, and clanked the dish down in front of him with a fork and knife. Then she left, moving her mouth in wordless anger.

Like rays in a magnifying class, all lines of awareness had focused on the kid, who appeared to be in a trance, looking at the cake as if it were a strange and wondrous specimen.

Carefully he scraped off the white icing, then with the knife slit the cake down the middle and butterflied it open as if he were performing surgery. With a little gulping "ahhh" he lowered his face to the splayed-open piece until his nose appeared to disappear into it. From where he was sitting, Martin could hear the kid inhaling deeply and letting out little moans and gasps, then inhaling deeply again and again. Then, incredibly, he closed his eyes tightly and testing the cake with the tip of his tongue he whispered: "Almond, almond, almond . . ." Then with little gasps: "Almost . . . almost . . ."

That was all Angie needed. "Aw, shit!" she cried and stomped the length of the counter and shot around to the kid's table. "You're outta here!" She grabbed the kid by the collar and yanked his head up.

His eyes were wild. "Almond," he said as if coming out of a dream. A piece of cake was stuck to his nose. "Almond!" he repeated, his eyes beaming as if he had just had a beatific vision.

"Get the hell out of here!" She yanked him to his feet.

Freddie got off his stool. "Okay, cool it," he said.

But the kid didn't struggle as Angie pulled him bodily out of the booth.

"Cool nothing," Angie said. "He's a friggin' sicko!"

The boy struggled against Angie's arms to get his hand

into his pants pocket, but she pushed him toward the door, probably fearing he had a knife or a gun.

Freddie tried to separate them. "What do you have in there, son?"

"I want to pay," the kid said, suddenly snapped into the realization that she was throwing him out.

"I don't want your friggin' money, and I don't want you in my place again. Got that?" Her face huge and red, Angie pushed open the door with her foot, still holding on to his shirt. "I know who you are, kid. I know about you. And I'm telling you, I don't want to see you in my place again, or I'll call the cops. Now beat it!" And she shoved him through the inner door.

But the wet from the outside made a slick floor, and the kid tripped over a newspaper dispenser and came down headfirst against the glass of the outer door.

"Shit! Now the bastard broke my door."

The kid's head had hit the glass squarely, instantly splintering the panel in a starburst. He fell on his knees, holding his head as blood seeped through his fingers.

"Nice going," Freddie said to Angie and went to the kid's aid.

"He tripped," she protested. "I didn't push him."

Martin pulled a wad of napkins out of the dispenser and pushed his way to Freddie who was kneeling beside the kid with his arm on his shoulders. "I've got a first-aid kit in the car," Martin said.

"I'm all right," the kid said. He looked at his hand and groaned at the blood.

Freddie dabbed the kid's head. "I'll take him to the ER."

"I d-don't want to go to the hospital."

"Just to make sure you don't have a concussion. You also got some splinters that'll have to come out," Freddie said, inspecting the bloody scalp.

The boy got to his feet, holding the napkins on his head. He looked around but he didn't seem dizzy or confused. He looked at the glass door. "S-s-sorry . . ."

"Nothing to be sorry about," Freddie said and opened the door to take the kid to his car. Before he left, Freddie turned to Angie and gave her a damning look. "I should report you for this."

"For what? He slipped."

"For assault."

Angie was about to protest, but she thought twice. When Freddie left, she turned to the rest of the patrons staring at her in stunned silence. "He did that himself," she said. "He threw himself into the glass because he's a schizo creep, is all. Someone should put him in a nuthouse where he belongs. And now I got a freakin' busted door." And she clopped her way into the kitchen.

Martin had no clue what the history was between Angie and the kid, nor what his problems were, but he was certain the kid had not been playacting to put down Angie, her cake, or her diner. Nor had he thrown himself into the door.

It was getting late, and Martin had to find a florist. He laid some money on the counter and left, thinking how he and Rachel were worrying about Dylan's reading problems. Here was a kid who was clearly disturbed, maybe psychotic. Probably had the crap beaten out of him as a kid and was now hopelessly messed up on drugs, living in a cartoon world, making love to cakes.

Jesus! Life's hard, but it's harder when you're stupid . . . or crazy, Martin thought. *Always someone worse off.* And he headed for his car, which started on the second try.

3

T he good news is that you're going to live. The bad news is that we're going to have to shave off some of your pretty hair."

Cindy Porter was just finishing her shift at the Essex Medical Center when Hawthorne off-duty fireman Freddie Wyman brought the kid in. The bleeding had stopped, but there were glass splinters in his scalp.

The boy's name was Brendan LaMotte, age eighteen, from Barton. He lived alone with his grandfather. Cindy called the man to say that Brendan was being treated for a head bruise, but that it didn't look serious and that Brendan would most likely be home in a couple of hours after they took X rays. The accompanying firefighter had said that he had lost his footing and fallen headfirst into the storm door of a diner.

"I don't think you have a concussion, but we're gonna send you to Radiology to make sure just how hard a head they gave you."

She tried to get the boy to smile. But he seemed distracted, not by the bruise but being in a hospital. Because the injury was on the top of his head, they had put him on a chair in one of the ER bed bays and drawn the curtain for privacy. But something about the space bothered him. He kept inspecting the oxygen nozzles in the wall, the X-ray plug, the sink, cabinet, box of surgical gloves, cotton swabs, containers of alcohol, et cetera. And he got up and sniffed everything like a drug dog.

"But first we're gonna clean you up, okay?" She spread the hairs above the cut with her gloved hand. The cut was not deep so he wouldn't need stitches, but there were splinters that had to be removed. "Boy, that must have hurt."

"Wasn't too bad," he mumbled.

"The bleeding stopped, and we got most of the dried blood cleaned up."

" 'The cold in clime are cold in blood, / Their love can scarce deserve the name.' "

"What's that?"

The kid shook his head to say it was nothing.

"Okay," she continued. "What we're going to do is just pick out the shrapnel, so sit tight, and I promise to do my best not to hurt. Okay?"

"H-how much hair you gonna cut off?" he asked.

"Maybe about an inch. I won't shave on the cut itself, just around it to make sure we get it all."

Cindy was of the school that you keep a running commentary to distract patients from unpleasant matters, especially kids. Brendan wasn't chatty, although he muttered to himself as if having a private conversation.

She clipped the hair around the wound, which had crusted over. Unfortunately, the glass from the door was the standard fare, not the shatterproof stuff that came apart in chunks. So she had to use tweezers. All the time the kid sat perfectly still. Whatever he was muttering, she detected some kind of rhythm. "Is that some kind of rap you're doing?"

"Unh-uh."

"So you're not going to tell me?"

"Tell you what?"

"What you're saying."

"Just a p-p-poem."

"Oh. What poem?"

"S-Shakespeare. Sonnet Twenty-nine."

"How does it go?" When he shook his head, she nudged him. "Come on, this place could use a little poetry."

Finally he consented. " 'When, in disgrace with fortune and men's eyes, I all alone beweep my outcast state . . . ' " And he recited the whole poem.

"Wow! How about that. Are you an English major?"

"No."

"That's right, you just turned eighteen so you're still in high school. Wow! You must be a pretty good student."

Brendan did not respond.

"Well, I used to like Shakespeare in school. My favorite is *Romeo and Juliet*." And she recited a few lines. " 'But soft! What light through yonder window shines? It is the east, and Juliet is the sun . . . ' "

"*Breaks.* 'What light through yonder window *breaks*?' "

"Oops. That's why I'm in here and not on stage," she said. "By the way, did you get attacked by a porcupine or something?"

"What do you mean?"

She began inspecting his scalp. "You've got some funny little scars," she said. She handed him a mirror. "If I didn't know better I'd say you had some kind of hair implant."

He stared intensely into it but said nothing.

"Whatever, we got all the glass out and cleaned you up."

The kid continued to study his scalp in the mirror as she pulled open the curtain and announced that Radiology was ready for him.

"Sorry about the hair," she said, walking him toward the waiting room. "But if you comb the other way nobody will notice. Wait a sec." She went behind the reception desk and returned with a baseball cap. On the front it said ELIXIR. "Promo hats from one of the pharmaceutical vendors. We got a whole box of them."

"Thanks," he said, still in a funny daze. He tucked the hat in his back pocket.

She walked him down the hall to Radiology and stayed with him while the technician took several shots of his head from different angles. The kid obliged, turning this way and that when asked. When it was over Cindy led him back to his cubicle. "So, you don't have any headaches?"

"No."

"Dizziness, disorientation, confusion?"

"No."

"Who's the president of the United States?"

Brendan looked up at her to see if she was joking.

"Just checking."

He told her.

"How about the last one?"

"George W. Bush."

"Keep going."

"William Jefferson Clinton."

Then on a hunch she asked, "Do you know any more?"

For a strange moment he locked eyes with her. Then he said simply, "All of them."

"Beg pardon?"

"George Bush, Ronald Reagan, Jimmy Carter, Gerald Ford, Richard Nixon . . ." He stopped for a moment, his eyes taking on an odd cast. "Nixon, Nixon, Nixon . . ."

"That's pretty good," Cindy said to snap him back. Then he looked at her and shook his head as if trying to dispel something. And without a moment's hesitation he began to recite: "Lyndon Johnson, John Kennedy, Dwight Eisenhower, Harry Truman . . ." And he named presidents all the way back to George Washington.

Cindy did not know all the names or proper order, but she had a strong suspicion that this wondrous teenage kid had them exactly right. "Holy cow!" she said in pure awe. "That's amazing." *The kid's a savant,* she said to herself. She looked at the clipboard. Where it asked for occupation he had entered *waiter,* not student. "How come you're not in school?"

He shrugged. "It d-d-didn't work out."

He looked at her with deep penetrating eyes that locked onto her own. He stared at her with such intensity that she had to look away. *God, what a strange boy.*

"Can I go?" he asked.

"Pretty soon. The doc has to check your films first."

A few minutes later, the resident physician, Dr. Adrian Budd, came by to say that he had read the scan and found no signs of a concussion. When he left, Cindy handed Brendan a couple sheets on head injuries. "If there's any sign of swelling, pain, headaches, or dizziness, you give us a call. The number's on the top of the page."

Just then, Freddie Wyman returned with an older man in baggy pants and an ill-fitting shirt. The fireman introduced him as Richard Berryman, Brendan's grandfather.

"He's going to be fine," Cindy told him.

"Hard heads run in the family," Mr. Berryman said and winked at her. Then he turned to Brendan. "How you doing, Brendy?"

Brendan glanced at the old man. "Okay." Then he moved to a sink where he studied his scalp in the wall mirror.

"Maybe it'll knock some sense in him," Mr. Berryman said to Cindy. "He quit school to work as a waiter, would you believe."

"That'll get old fast," Cindy said, seeing the disappointment in the man's face. "He's seems like a smart kid. While we were cleaning him up, he was reciting Shakespeare."

The old man humpfed. "What he needs is a girlfriend, not Shakespeare."

"That'll happen soon enough," Cindy said.

"Watch out for glass doors," Cindy said to Brendan. As she handed his grandfather some ointment and a box of gauze pads for the cut, the air was filled with shouting.

The next instant, the double doors burst open with paramedics pushing in a teenage girl on a gurney, trailed by several others including what looked like her parents crying. The girl's body was covered with blood, and the paramedics were holding a mask on her face and an IV drip to her arm.

Cindy had heard the radio report when she had left for Radiology. Instantly, the ER team was in action. Interns and nurses swarmed around the girl, directing the paramedics where to take her. One tech shook his head at Cindy. The girl was critical. She needed immediate intubation, but somebody shouted that the operating rooms were occupied, they'd have to go to number four where Brendan had been.

While Cindy moved out of the way, she heard Richard say, "Isn't that Trisha Costello?"

Brendan, who was still at the mirror, glanced at the battered girl on the gurney. "Yes," he said, momentarily fascinated. Then returned to the mirror and his scalp.

Someplace amid the commotion, an intern shouted for the defibrillator. The girl had gone into cardiac arrest. Nurses were running and shouting as the girl was hooked up. Cindy was not part of the team because she had been working on Brendan when the dispatch came in. But from across the room she could see the electric pads come crashing down on the girl and the body jolt in place. But a few moments later, another nurse said, "Again . . . No pulse, no pressure. Nothing . . . Again . . . Hang on, Trisha. HANG ON!"

It wasn't long before Cindy could read the signs from the team around her that the girl was dead.

A wail of horror went up from the mother who was at the bedside with the interns, nurses, and technicians.

Like several of the other nonstaffers, Richard was stunned in place. "I think she died," he said to Brendan.

Brendan looked over at the clutch of people through the open curtain. "Mmm," he said. Then he turned to Richard and parted his hair. "Where did I get these?"

"For cryin' out loud, a girl you know just died and you're asking about some goddamn scratches on your head." Richard's voice was trembling.

Across from them, doctors were trying to comfort the parents who sobbed in grief.

Richard pulled Brendan from the mirror. "I can't take this," he said, and they left the emergency room, with Brendan still puzzled and feeling his scalp.

4

The fax report sitting on Detective Greg Zakarian's desk that morning was to the point:

Greg,
Human remains pulled up in scallop net 12 miles off Gloucester 2 months ago. Has similar specs & markings to your case #01–057–4072. Positive ID. I think you might want to take a look.

Joe Steiner

Joe Steiner was head pathologist at the medical examiner's office in Pocasset.

Same specs and markings. Positive ID.

It was the first break in three years. Three long, frustrating years.

Greg sipped his coffee and looked at the two pictures pinned to the corkboard next to his desk: a photo of his wife Lindsay; and a pastel portrait of a young boy.

People no longer asked about Lindsay, because two years ago she was killed in a head-on collision on the Sagamore Bridge by some drunk who swerved into her lane. It had happened a little after midnight. She was returning from a too-long day at the Genevieve Bratton School, a residential treatment center for troubled girls in Plymouth where, for eight years, she had been a social worker. The drunk was returning from a stag party in Barnstable. She died instantly. He walked away with a broken collarbone. Lindsay had been the fundamental condition of Greg's life, and in a telephone call, she was gone.

But people still asked about the boy in the other picture. Those who didn't know wondered if he was Greg's son. He'd say no, which was the literal truth. But to his colleagues in the department—from the dispatchers at the entrance to T. J. Gelford, his supervisor, to Norm Adler, the chief—the boy was his. Greg's Boy. The Sagamore Boy. His own Boy in the Box.

For the last three years, Greg had tried to determine the child's identity—ever since his skull was dug up in a sandbar on a local beach. As the responding officer, Greg had worked with CPAC, the state police, DA's office, the medical examiner, the FBI, and missing children organizations. What they knew from forensic calibrations was that the skull belonged to a six- or seven-year-old white male. But they didn't know who he was, where he came from, or how he had died. From the condition of the skull, it appeared to have been in the ocean for at least three years, and was probably washed up on the Sagamore Beach by storms. From where, nobody knew.

Two years ago, the state police abandoned the investigation since they had no leads, no tips, no cause of death, no evidence of a crime, no dental matches with anybody in the Missing Children Network's files, no identity. Today, it was officially a cold case.

But Greg had kept the file open, regularly checking the databases of the Missing Children Network as well as the daily NCIC and CJIS broadcasts of missing persons from law enforcement agencies all over the country. His file was fat with old broadcasts. Because the Sagamore PD had no cold-case unit or funds, Greg did this on his own, in his spare time or at home, often pursuing out-of-town leads out of his own pocket because the department budget could no longer cover him. He had even hired a forensic anthropologist from Northeastern University to do an artistic reconstruction from the skull resulting in the drawing on his wall.

Greg knew that his colleagues saw the case as a private obsession. And that was true, since, from day one, Greg had had a gut feeling that there was something odd about this case: that it wasn't just some hapless child who had fallen off a raft and gotten swept out to sea. Call it cop instinct, or intuition, or ESP, but Greg sensed something darkly disturbing. And, in spite of the years that had passed, he maintained his solitary investigation against the diminishing odds of resolution. He kept it up in part to take his mind off Lindsay's death and to rescue himself from bitterness and self-absorption. A shrink would probably say that his obsession was rooted in a quest for his lost family—a need to find closure. Maybe so.

Lindsay was seven months pregnant when she was killed. The little boy she was carrying died with her.

Greg took Joe Steiner's fax and walked down the hall to the office of Lieutenant Detective T. J. Gelford, his supervisor.

T. J. was on the phone, but he waved Greg in. When he hung up, he said, "That was Frank. He's at CCMC with a cracked ankle. What else can go wrong?" He looked up at Greg. "What's up?"

Greg handed T. J. the fax.

Gelford, who was in his late fifties, was not a large man. But he possessed a powerful presence. His hair had been buzz-cut so close to his scalp that it looked like a shadow. He had a roughly hewn rawboned face and gray implacable eyes that could with a microflick go from neutral to withering scorn. Gelford looked at the fax then looked up at Greg. "So?"

"It may be something," Greg said. "I want to check it out."

"What's to check out?"

"He says there are similarities. I want to see what they are."

Gelford took in a long scraping breath of air and let it out through his teeth in a hiss. "Greg, a dozen times I've told you to leave that case alone, there's nothing there."

"I hear you, but it's the first time we've got something on the markings."

Gelford looked at him with that flat, chastening glare. "Yeah, and what you got is coincidence. Natural coincidence."

"That's what I want to check out."

Gelford leaned forward the way he did when he wanted to press a point. "You have chased after every damn shadow, every nibble, every look-alike. I let you go halfway across the country and back on this—twice. You've eaten up my budget, not to mention the assistance funds for those software people to run those photosuperimposition screens. I'm up to here with that damn skull kid. You're not spending your time correctly on your cases, and frankly that pisses me off."

"And frankly I'm tired of the shit cases I've been assigned—stolen bikes, kids drinking, wallet snatches—they're not even real crimes or ones that can be solved."

"Maybe if you did what you're told and dropped this thing, you wouldn't be getting shit cases. You aren't solving the ones you're supposed to anyway."

Gelford was right, and although he complained to his face, when Greg got home at night he fessed up. He'd go through the motions of investigating something, but he'd be only half there. "Joe Steiner doesn't make calls unless he's got something."

"And Joe Steiner isn't short of manpower," Gelford shot back.

"Two hours, T. J. That's all I'm asking. Two hours. If it's nothing, I'll bury it."

"Bullshit."

"It's not bullshit. Just two hours."

Gelford picked up the A.M. docket from a pile of papers. "Yeah, two hours of wild-goose chasing, while I'm looking at three domestics, an assault and battery, one victim in critical condition. A sniper's shooting pellets at motorists on Route 3, some asshole kids trashed the high school last night, and vacationers are pouring in by the thousands. You want some real crimes, I've got some for you."

Greg checked his watch. "Back by noon, I promise." He smiled, hoping to decharge the moment.

But Gelford did not smile back, nor did his manner soften. "This is *not* what we're paying you for."

"T. J., I've got a hunch there's a connection here."

"That's what you said the last time and twenty times before that. I've had it with your hunches up to here. Get ahold of yourself: The case is closed."

Greg took a deep breath to center himself. "Someone, somewhere, has lost a kid. Someone, somewhere, still misses him and has his picture hanging up. He's somebody's son."

"Yeah, but not yours."

Greg felt the sting of that. It was the mind-set of the barracks—that Greg's tenacity went beyond a professional determination, that it was borderline pathological. "Three years ago I made a promise to myself to find out who that kid was and what happened to him, and I intend to keep that promise."

"That's all nice and good, but nobody knows who the kid is, and not from the lack of trying," Gelford added. "You and two other detectives from the state hunted for the next of kin full-time for eight weeks. You canvassed the schools, day-care centers, pediatricians, and hospitals. Twenty thousand fliers from that reconstruction were distributed Capeside and off. We flooded the Internet, even got a fifteen-grand reward. You scoured all the databases, chased down leads from I don't know how many families looking for a son the same age. It's been three years, Greg, three years and nobody's called your hot line to claim him. What can I say? It's a fucking dead end."

He was right again. Given the department budget, they had pulled all the stops. And they had floated plenty of theories on why nobody had claimed the boy. He could have been abducted from out of state, far from the Cape and the publicity blitz; his parents could have died— maybe even with him—perhaps in a boating accident. His parents could be illegal immigrants, afraid to speak with police; or they could have even been the killers; or it could have been a cult murder. One possibility was as good as the next, and they pursued them all. But Greg refused to accept their finality or to let the child remain an unnamed, unclaimed victim of happenstance. Which was why he had taken the case on his own. Which was why after three years the kid was like family.

"I'd do this after-hours," Greg said, "but Steiner gets off work before I do. Please."

Gelford picked up the fax. "I don't know how to say this without saying it, but this obsession of yours has affected department morale. People are resenting how it's getting in the way of your real obligations, how you're not pulling your own weight. And so do I." He stopped for a moment. "Frankly, Greg, it's become something of a bad joke. They're saying stuff like how you should stop whacking your stick on this skull—and how you should get a wife."

Greg felt the blood rise in his face. He knew that he had distanced himself from the others, even dropping off the department softball team, and bowing out of picnics and fishing jaunts. He was even aware that other investigators were refusing to work on cases with him, including his onetime partner, Steve Powers. But the thought that he had become a department joke was mortifying. Suddenly he saw himself as a pathetic fool chasing his own tail.

Get a wife.

"This may be my hang-up, but I have not compromised my duties here."

"That's arguable," Gelford said. "But you've been at this for three years and you're batting a dead mouse." He handed back the fax.

Greg nodded but said nothing.

"I think you might want to take a look," Steiner had written.

Gelford studied Greg's face. "Noon, and not a minute over," Gelford said. "But if this does not pan out—as I expect it won't—you'll bury it for good. Otherwise . . . you know the rest." Gelford then picked up the phone to say that the conversation was over.

Greg folded the fax and put it in his shirt pocket.

"Similar markings."

"Thanks," Greg said and left, his mind humming to get over to the ME's office.

5

"A re you all right?" Martin asked.

"I'm fine," Rachel said.

"Well, you don't look it."

"Don't start."

"Don't start what? You look like you're about to go to your own funeral."

"I said I'm fine."

They were in the kitchen, and Rachel was making pancakes. She was still in her bathrobe, hunched over the stove, pressing chocolate chips into the frying batter. Dylan loved chocolate-chip pancakes, and she made them for him at least once a week. Martin was dressed and ready to go to work.

The bouquet of roses he had bought last night sat in a vase on the dining room table. They had never made it to the Blue Heron. Rachel said she wasn't up for it.

"You want pancakes?" she asked, her voice void of inflection. Her face was ashen and the flesh under her eyes was puffy. Her hair was disheveled and stuck back by a couple of hasty bobby pins. She looked as if she hadn't slept all night.

"I'll just have some orange juice," he said and poured a

glass. "I've got a breakfast meeting with Charlie O'Neill on the road."

She nodded woodenly. He hated it when she got in these moods. Upstairs Dylan could be heard singing while getting dressed. He liked show tunes, and at the moment he was wailing "Bess, You Is My Woman Now."

Martin studied Rachel while he drank his juice. She looked miserable, standing there hunched over like an old woman, her feet stuffed into a pair of old slippers, her face looking as if it had been shaped out of bread dough. "So, there's nothing you want to tell me?"

"I said *I'm fine*," she snapped.

"Then how come we haven't made love for over three weeks?"

Her body slumped in annoyance, but she didn't answer.

"How come you've been avoiding me like I'm the goddamn Ebola virus?"

Without looking up from the pan she said, "I haven't been avoiding you. And stop swearing, he'll hear you."

"You *have* been avoiding me. For weeks I've suggested we go out to dinner together or a movie or something nice and romantic, but you're too tired. You don't feel up to it. You've got a headache. You go to bed early. Except for bumping into me, I don't think you've physically touched me in weeks. Something's wrong, and I want to know what the hell it is."

Rachel continued staring into the pan, then slowly she turned her head toward him. She seemed just about to respond but then laid the spatula down and went to the bottom of the stairs and called up to Dylan that breakfast was ready.

When she returned, Martin said, "I don't know what the problem is, but you've been moping around here like you've got some goddamn—"

Suddenly she let out a scream, shaking her hand. She had burned the tip of her finger pressing chocolate chips into the batter.

Martin ran to her and put his arm around her shoulder. She was not just whimpering in discomfort. She was outright screaming, as if in outrage that the pan had done this to her. Then, she burst into tears.

Martin walked her to the sink and turned on the cold water and held her hand under it. With one arm around her shoulder, the other hand holding hers under the water, he could feel her shaking as she stood there, deep wracking sobs rising from a place that had nothing to do with burnt fingers.

"Mommy! What happened?" Dylan ran into the kitchen and instantly froze in place at the tableau of Martin holding Rachel's finger under the streaming water and Rachel crying, tears pouring freely from her eyes and her nose running.

"Mommy just burned her finger," Martin said. "She's going to be fine."

"Mommeee." Dylan ran over to her and hugged her about the middle and buried his face into her bathrobe, then he began to cry.

"It's burning!" Rachel shouted through her tears. "Turn it off."

On the stove smoke billowed up from the frying pan.

"It's burning," Dylan screamed. "Fire!"

I'm going to lose my fucking mind, Martin thought, as he shot to the stove, turned off the gas, and pulled the pan off the burner.

Suddenly the smoke alarm went off, filling the house with a hideous electronic wail.

While Dylan yelled, his hands to his ears, and Rachel stood by the sink crying, Martin pulled out a kitchen chair. *Yup! Any second now I'm gonna hear a snap like a celery stalk, and then I can join the chorus, screaming and blubbering. Yoweeeee!*

He punched off the alarm.

The pancakes looked like smoking hockey pucks. Martin felt the crazy urge to laugh, but pushed it down. Instead he tore a couple of sheets off the paper-towel rack and handed them to Rachel. While she dried her face, Dylan insisted that she hold her finger up so he could kiss the boo-boo.

Just another normal little breakfast scene in the happy Whitman household.

"I think you're going to make it," Martin said, looking at her finger, "thanks to ole Dr. Dylan here." He winked at his son. The tip of Rachel's index finger was a white crust of burnt skin. Martin tousled his son's hair. "You made her feel better already, right?"

Rachel nodded and caught her breath. She smiled thinly and gave her son a hug.

Seeing Rachel pull herself together again, Dylan rapidly repaired. "Am I going to be a doctor when I grow up?"

"I don't see why not," Martin said. "You've got the touch. Now maybe you should go upstairs and put the other shoe and sock on, okay, Doc?"

Dylan looked to Rachel. "Take two ass burns and call me in the morning," he said, and headed upstairs. It was something Martin said all the time.

Rachel nodded, then headed for the stove to clean the frying pan. Her body had slumped into itself again.

Martin came over to her and gave her a hug. She let him, but it was like hugging a dead person. "Are you going to be okay?"

"Yeah."

"Sure?"

She nodded.

"Are you going to tell me about it?"

She shook her head. "Nothing to tell," she whispered.

"I don't believe you. And *you* don't believe you." He kissed her on the forehead. "You never were a good liar."

Her eyes filled with tears again. "You're going to be late for your meeting. Say hello to Charlie."

He nodded. "I love you, woman, but I wish you'd let me in."

She hugged him weakly, and he left.

• • •

He was right: She never was a good liar.

Rachel watched Martin pull out of the driveway. She cleaned the pan and made another batch of pancakes. When she was done, she called Dylan down. And while he ate, she got dressed.

A little before nine o'clock she dropped Dylan off at DellKids and headed toward Rockville, which was nearly forty miles south of Hawthorne. They had thought of finding a local pediatrician, but Dr. Rose had attended Dylan since his infancy. And Rachel liked the man. More importantly, Dylan liked him. He was a warm and gracious man who never rushed through an examination.

To get to the highway, Rachel headed down Magnolia Drive, trying to ease her mind against the fugue playing inside her head.

Had the MRI results been normal, the doctor would have called himself and just said things looked fine. If there was a problem, he would surely have called himself—unless he didn't get the chance because of the emergency. Maybe he wanted to talk to her about some special learning programs for Dylan.

Yes, think Special Program, she told herself. *Special Program. Nice and normal. No problems. No tumors. No . . .*

It was her idea to have the scan in the first place, and Dr. Rose had agreed—a good precautionary measure since the procedure was easy and noninvasive.

Normal procedure. Normal precaution.

That was what she had told herself. Her cover story to herself.

As Rachel drove along, she felt the onslaught of an anxiety attack. She tried to concentrate on the scenery, tried to distract herself by taking in the arborway of maples and oaks and the seaside mansions that clutched the rocky coastline—mansions with their driveway entrances of granite pillars, some surmounted with large alabaster pineapples that forbade you to enter. The road opened up to a sea view and a scattering of shingled homes with deep and closely cropped lawns, sculpted hedges, and trellised gardens festooned with rose blossoms. In the distance, powerboats cut quicksilver plumes across the harbor under a brilliant blue sky.

It was all so perfect. All so good and pure. And now she was going to see if she had destroyed her son.

As she drove down Route 93 toward Rockville, her mind tripped back.

It had started rather casually—like the occasional cough that develops into pneumonia or the dull ache in the left arm that throbs its way to triple bypass surgery. The prelude was a casual note that came in the mail one day early last fall:

Dear Mrs. Whitman,
As you know, we have a parent/teacher's conference
in two weeks, but I'm wondering if we could meet
sooner—possibly next week. No big problem, but I'd
like to discuss Dylan's progress . . .

It was signed Karen Andrews, Dylan's teacher. They had enrolled him in a Montessori preschool in Plymouth because the place had one of the best reputations on the South Shore. It also had an admissions waiting list two years long. Not taking any chances and determined to get the very best for their son, Rachel and Martin had entered Dylan's name when he was eighteen months old. He was four when he started.

She could still recall how excited he was—how excited they all were. For weeks before opening day, they would lie down with him at bedtime and he would count the intervening days. When it finally arrived, Rachel had dressed him in blue plaid shorts, a white polo shirt, and new white and blue striped sneakers, of which he was very proud. With his hair, a shiny chestnut color, parted neatly on the side, and his big green eyes and sweet pink mouth, he looked positively gorgeous. Because of the occasion, Martin took the morning off so they could all go together. Rachel believed in rituals, and this occasion was tantamount to Dylan's first birthday or Christmas.

Before they headed off, Rachel had directed Martin and Dylan into the front yard where she shot a roll of color prints. Later she would select the best shots and put them in a special album of first-schoolday photos, documenting Dylan's progress from then to college.

The note arrived in mid-October—the sixteenth, to be exact. Ms. Andrews wanted to set up a conference with Rachel and Martin. They agreed on a day; but because Martin was unexpectedly out of town, Rachel met with the teacher herself.

Karen, a sincere and dedicated woman, began by saying that Dylan was an adorable and sweet child, a view shared by the entire staff. She also went on to say that he loved music and had a beautiful voice, and that he was popular with the other children. "He's very sociable and very caring of the other kids," she said. "He also has a great sense of humor, and gets the kids laughing."

Rachel nodded, thinking this was leading to a complaint that Dylan was too much the class clown, working up the other kids to rowdiness. It wouldn't take much to encourage him—just a couple of laughs to put him on a roll. But would clowning around be reason for a parental conference? "So what's the problem?"

"Well, his language."

"His language?" Maybe Dylan had picked up some swears from Martin.

"He seems to have some difficulty accessing and processing words. Each morning we go to the big wall calendar and put a Velcro star on that day. But first we recite the days of the week in unison. Dylan doesn't know them. He doesn't remember from day to day. He also doesn't know what year it is, even though it's written down in large letters and we do this every day."

"Is that so unusual at his age?" It was possible that he was just a little behind the other kids. Martin himself didn't learn to read until he was eight.

"No, but he also has problems with comprehending What? Where? When? questions. If I ask him 'What day is it?' he'll just repeat the question. Or if I ask 'Where are the crayons?' he'll just answer 'Crayons' or repeat the question. He doesn't seem to understand some basic language concepts. I mean, you must have observed these things at home."

She had but thought it was just his age. That he would grow out of the problem.

"The same in reading group," Ms. Andrews continued. "To make story time interactive, I read a few sentences then ask the children what they think about this or that or what do they expect will happen next. And we go right around the circle so each child gets a chance to respond and be rewarded for his or her input. But when it's Dylan's turn, he often won't recall what the story was about or what's been said about it."

Rachel began to feel an uneasiness grip her. "What do you think the problem is?"

"Well, it could be several things. It's possible he's experiencing some emotional difficulties at home."

"I can assure you that we're happily married," Rachel said defensively. "And if my husband and I have a problem, we make it a point not to discuss it in front of Dylan."

"I'm sure. But my point is that Dylan has some kind of LD problem."

"LD?"

"Learning disability."

"Learning disability?" She uttered the words as if testing a foreign expression.

"He seems to be developmentally delayed. One possibility is that he's dyslexic. Or he may have some form of ADD—attention deficit disorder. These problems are not uncommon. Twenty percent of all schoolchildren have some form of disability. But it's something that can be tested for and dealt with very effectively."

"You mean drugs? Ritalin or whatever?"

"That or other effective drugs. But I think you should consult your pediatrician and look for specialists to evaluate him. Maybe a neurophysician."

Rachel felt her insides clutch. *Learning disability. Dyslexia. Developmentally delayed. Attention deficit disorder. Ritalin.* In a matter of moments her son had graduated from class clown to a child suffering neurological dysfunctions.

While she sat there, Rachel's mind had scrambled for explanations—external realities that she could point to.

The environment. She had taken every precaution possible. Their first house had been built in 1935, and had tested positive for lead paint. So they had the place stripped of every square inch of old paint—which cost a fortune. Then they had all the asbestos insulation removed from the basement heating pipes and replaced with a nontoxic substitute. She had even tested the house for radon gas, finding it perfectly safe. Although Rockville water came from a local reservoir, Rachel took no chances and had spring water delivered to the house every two weeks.

Television. Even though she had restricted Dylan to maybe an hour or two a day—and exclusively to PBS children's shows—she would sometimes catch him watching it on the sly. God knows how all the rapid-fire cuts could mess up a child's brain development. Maybe Dylan had a special susceptibility to all the flash, compromising his powers of concentration. She knew Martin would resist because they already had fights over letting

Dylan watch sporting events and comedy shows. "It's quality time—what fathers and sons do," he had protested. "Sitting passively in front of a baseball game broken up by two hundred beer and car commercials isn't quality time," she had shot back. "If you want some quality time take him to Fenway Park or go in the backyard and play catch." Two hours after her meeting with Karen Andrews, Rachel had their cable TV service terminated in the family room. Martin grumbled for days.

Looking back, she realized how futile all that ramrod determination now seemed. Because the problem went back before that October morning, before Dylan's first day at preschool. Before his birth.

It went back to Halloween night of her junior year in college. She was at an all-night party at a friend's house, and everybody was doing acid. She had been dating a chemistry grad who made his own LSD in the school's lab. The stuff was easy to synthesize, and a lot cheaper than that sold on the street. But this one night he had introduced her to a variation—acid laced with another drug he had synthesized—the combo, he said, would make sex "cosmic." The street name was TNT. Like acid, the stuff was psychedelic, turning the bedroom walls into polychrome liquid crystal surfaces. But the real kick was sex: An orgiastic pulsation of light and sound where every physical sensation was amplified into starburst scintillations that climaxed in a supernova explosion.

As she pulled her car into the parking space behind Dr. Rose's office, the sick irony struck her: She was joining the ranks of other mothers and fathers of LD kids, fluent in the statistics, the lingo, and that antiseptic alphabet soup—ADD, ADHD, LD, FAS, WISC. IQ. MRI. LSD.

And the disorder had its source in her: TNT.

"You can take a seat, Mrs. Whitman. The doctor will be with you in a few minutes," said Liz, Dr. Rose's secretary, when Rachel entered the office.

Working to calm herself, she picked up a copy of *Parenting* magazine and thumbed through the pages, trying to focus her mind. It seemed every other story in the magazine was directed at her: "Raising an Eager Reader." "Baby Games that Teach." "Hyperactivity Hype?" "How to Help Your Kids Learn Better." "Great Expectations."

God, let him be okay. I beg you.

Liz opened the door. "The doctor will see you now."

Rachel followed her down the corridor to the doctor's office. "Sorry about the wait." Dr. Rose was a handsome man of about fifty with a simpatico face and large warm exotic eyes.

Rachel tried to read them as she shook his hand.

"Have a seat, please." When he sat back down behind his desk he picked up a folder from a pile of material. "Well, the results of the brain scan are back."

Tumor, whispered a voice in her head. *He's going to say Dylan has a brain tumor.*

The doctor got up and slipped the MRI scan on the light display board.

There were three separate black-and-white negative sheets with sixteen shots on each from different angles. It was shocking to see her little boy rendered as a specimen, stripped to his bones and teeth.

"As I explained the other day, brain scanners can't see individual cells, nor can they tell if brain cells have been rearranged or are missing. Only tissue samples or an autopsy can tell us that. But the images can tell us if there are anomalous structures or deformities—"

But Rachel cut him off. "Is he okay?"

"Well, there is an anomaly."

"An *anomaly*?"

With his pencil he pointed to an area on the left side of Dylan's brain. "Neurology is not my specialty, so I consulted with Dr. Gerald Cormier, a neurosurgeon at the Lahey Clinic, and according to his report there appears to be some developmental abnormality in the ventricular system over here." He pointed to a white area on the left. "It seems that Dylan has slightly dilated ventricles in this area which suggests some maldevelopment of the thalamus, which is deep in the brain in this area." He moved the pencil to the lower part of the brain scan. "This kind of malformation in this area is associated with the type of learning problems that Dylan has, I'm told."

Rachel's eyes flooded with tears. "My God, what does that mean?"

"I'm not really the one to say. But I did ask Dr. Cormier what the prognosis was for Dylan's cognitive development, and he said that, unfortunately, this kind of underdevelopment usually results in a reduction in learning abilities."

Rachel let out a groan.

"This really is not my area, but I've read that there's sometimes a compensatory phenomenon," he added. "When one side of the brain has deficient wiring, it's been found that the corresponding healthy region in the opposite hemisphere tends to develop more extensive patterns of connections than is normal. There's no way to tell from the scan, but it's entirely possible that the right side of Dylan's brain is developing excessive connections."

Rachel nodded, knowing that the doctor wanted to put Dylan's condition in the best possible light.

"If it's any consolation, both Einstein and the painter Rodin had deficient left-hemisphere language skills, yet they excelled in the right-brain skills as we all know."

His attempt to make her feel better produced the opposite effect, because she knew in her heart of hearts that Dylan was damaged, and to suggest he might grow up to be a mathematical or artistic prodigy was all the more painful for its improbability.

"How do you think it happened?"

The doctor handed her a box of tissues. "Well, there's no way of knowing for sure, but since there's no evidence of head trauma, my guess is that it either happened *in utero* or it's genetic. Given his medical history, we can pretty much rule out diseases. One possibility is prenatal exposure to environmental toxins which can affect brain development," he said. "You know, mercury, cadmium, arsenic, lead, or any kind of radiation. As far as you recall, were you ever exposed to any such chemicals while pregnant?"

"No."

"Chemotherapy?"

"No."

"Did Martin use any pesticides or insecticides to excess that you know of?"

"No."

"Or longtime exposure to carbon monoxide?"

The question jogged through her. "Do you mean did I try to kill myself?"

"That was not my question, but car exhaust is one form of the gas. Another is a faulty oil burner. Anything like that?"

Rachel shook her head. His questions were cutting closer to the quick. And she wondered if she were projecting the image of someone with a history of mental instability.

"Of course not," the doctor said, musing over the charts. "How about alcohol or drugs?"

She had sensed the question before it hit the air. "No. I drink very little, and I certainly didn't while carrying Dylan."

"Then my guess is that it's probably genetic since there's a lot of evidence linking heredity factors to neurophysiological disorders—schizophrenia, depression, stuttering, hyperactivity, alcoholism, and so forth But, once again, I'm not the man to ask. You really have to see a pediatric neurologist."

Silence filled the room as the doctor waited for her to respond. "Rachel, are you all right?"

She nodded ever so slightly, thinking how there was only one thing more devastating than discovering that your much-wanted child has a brain disorder: the thought that you may have caused that disorder. In a low voice, she said, "I took drugs when I was in college."

There! It was out.

Dr. Rose rocked back in his seat. "I see. And what did you take?"

"LSD laced with TNT," she said. "On and off for about two years."

"And you're wondering if that caused brain damage in your son."

She nodded.

"From what I know, there's no evidence that LSD is a mutagen—that it causes chromosomal damage that could affect unborn children. There were rumors aloft in the sixties, but none was ever found. But I don't know what this TNT is."

"It's also known as trimethoxy-4-methyl-triphetamine, TNT to street people." The name was etched in her brain.

Rachel tried to push back the tears as she reached into her handbag and pulled out a *Newsweek* article from three weeks ago. As was typical of newsmagazines its cutesy title belied the horrors: "Acid Kickback." As if they were reporting about heartburn. She handed the sheets to the doctor.

He adjusted his reading glasses. " 'New study shows evidence linking TNT-tainted LSD and genetic defects in users' offspring.' " Then he read the rest of the piece to himself as Rachel sat there slowly dying.

For years, she had rested easy in the knowledge that no evidence had been found that LSD was a mutagen. Then *Newsweek* and the wire services had picked up a recent study by a Yale research group that set off an alarm in Rachel's soul. The chief culprit was a family of synthetics chemically described as tryptamines, the ugliest of which was TNT, a substance hundreds of times more potent than mescaline. It was what Jake Gordon had synthesized and added to his acid back in school. According to the report, the stuff was genetically toxic, entering the reproductive cells of the female users and causing alterations in the ova, resulting in deformities in children. What startled Rachel was the figure: sixty-five percent of habitual female users of TNT-laced acid gave birth to children with cancers and birth defects. Two babies in the study were born without brains.

"Did you know for certain it was laced with TNT?"

"Yes."

If the doctor wondered why, he didn't ask. As all acid-heads knew, TNT-laced acid heightened sexual experience. For better orgasms, Rachel's son was now brain damaged.

"I've not seen the studies, so I can't tell you if what you took caused Dylan's problems. And ultimately it may not be possible to tell. But frankly, Rachel, I'm not sure just how useful it is to know that. You could end up consuming yourself with guilt."

She nodded. *I already am.*

"Have you discussed this with Martin?"

"Yes." She had not expected the question. Reflexively, she lied, knowing how much worse it would sound if she had kept it from him. Although Martin knew that she had taken drugs in college—something she had confessed years ago—he did not know about TNT. Maybe someday she'd tell him. But how do you admit to your husband that you may have ruined your only child?

"Well, I think the important thing is to decide on how best to help Dylan with his learning process—working with his school to get the best programs for him. I'll be happy to give you a referral to pediatric neurologists." He wrote some names on a notepad and handed them to her.

She thanked him and got up to leave, feeling sick to the core of her soul.

She took a long last look at the films against the light board, thinking that she would do anything to go back in time and undo what she had done.

Anything.

6

In the open, he was a monster. In the bush, he was invisible.

Billy liked that. He liked how he moved through the woods like a ripple. The alien in *Predator*. He liked how he could disappear by standing still. He liked how he could melt into scrub so that neither human nor beast could detect his presence. The excitement made him sweat all the more.

What he did not like was the heat.

He slipped out from the clutch of sapling oaks and crossed the clearing. The late afternoon sun sent thick shafts of light through the woods. He wished it were cloudy and twenty degrees cooler. He wished he were doing this someplace in the cool north and not these backwater woods of central Florida where the air felt like hot glue. He wished this were a simple *snick, snick, you're dead*.

The scent-free, 3-D hooded camo suit with the fake leaves sewn all over the surface was the stalker's dream. The ultimate in concealment, short of turning into a butterfly. But the material did not breathe. Inside the hood, his face was slick and his clothes were soaked with perspiration. That made him angry. That made him want to get this over with *snick snick*. But that wasn't the assignment.

Billy passed through the clearing to the shack by Little Wiggins Canal, as it was known to the locals, or Number

341 to the U.S. Geological Survey map. The structure was little more than a six-foot cube, banged together with old timbers and roofing sheets the kid's mother picked up somewhere. The floor was an ancient piece of linoleum over dirt, and the compressed-wood door and single window were crude. The interior consisted of a child's table and chair, some Matchbox cars, a butterfly guidebook, a Gators banner, and tacked-up pictures of the kid and his dog—rough gestures at clubhouse homeyness, Billy thought. The place was a second home to the kid, a hang-out for him and his dog, a place to play fort, games, hide-and-seek with other kids. A little tyke hideaway by the canal.

It was also the last place the little tyke would remember of his old life.

Through the brush, the battered blue and white Airstream trailer that the kid and his mother called home was barely visible from the canal, perched up on the bluff maybe a hundred feet from the shack. Because of the recent drought, the water was low so the mother had no reason to fear the kid getting swept downstream. Spring would be a different story altogether. She'd never let him come down here alone, especially since alligators mated in springtime. But it wasn't spring—and the canal wasn't raging and the fish weren't jumping and the cotton wasn't high.

So the boy came down. His name was Travis Valentine. Nice name, smart boy. The dog's name was Bo, short for Bodacious. Dumb name, dumb dog, but teeth down to here.

The dog came first. A black mongrel whose genealogy some Lab must have made a pass at. For Billy, the dog was an unnecessary complication—and half the reason for the getup. A third of the odors of human beings issued from the head—mouths, nostrils, eyes, facial skin. Another third from the hands. Thus, the face-plated hood and scent-lock surgical gloves. Without them Billy would have broadcast his presence the moment the dog stepped outside the trailer, setting off barking like a fire alarm. But Billy was a hunter. He knew better. Still, he didn't like to think what that dog could do to his ankle. He was a big muscular animal with a big bouldery head and powerful jaws that could crack through bone like that.

Billy heard the door of the trailer slap against the frame. "You got ten minutes, so be back when I ring. And keep away from the water, now." She'd summon him with a handbell.

The kid moved down the little path, the dog ranging widely, snorting after every critter scent, yarfing and whining to itself. Creatures of habit. Dinner over, and it was down by the riverside with old Bo. The same pattern Billy had observed over the past few nights.

It didn't take Bo long to pick up the rabbit. In a matter of seconds he found the half-buried carcass Billy had laid out earlier under a bush. And while the dog got lost in the bouquet of viscera, the little boy in the red shorts and white Kennedy Space Center T-shirt and sneakers came sauntering down the dirt lane to the shack. In his right hand was a long-handled net, a glass jar in his left. A butterfly hunt. The kid collected butterflies. And, as Billy had noted, the place was loaded with them.

In his mossy oakleaf Scent-Lok 3-D camo suit, Billy stood behind some trees just a few yards from the shack, his breath wheezing inside his mask and misting up the eye plate. He had used the outfit to hunt deer, but it was the first time on a kid.

While the boy was at some bush maybe twenty yards away, the scrub shifted behind the dog. The dog looked up, and before he could muster a growl, a muffled *snick* cut the air. And the dog's head blew open.

"Bo? Here, Bo?"

The boy had heard something and looked around. Just a half-note yelp. No more. He went to the shack and looked inside, thinking the animal had passed through the small swing flap. "Bo?"

Bo. That was the last syllable the boy uttered.

Billy slapped the chloroform-soaked towel against the kid's face from behind, raising the squirming body against his chest. He struggled with surprising vigor, whimpering into the towel, but the thick hand clamped the small face like an iron mask, forcing the pockets of his lungs to swell with the vapors. To prevent him from heeling his genitals, Billy pressed against the wall, locking his leg around the boy's shins.

The boy struggled and whimpered for maybe half a minute. Then it was over. A final twitch, and Travis Valentine's young-colt strength gave out. Billy lowered him to the floor as limp as a rag doll.

For a brief moment, Billy studied his prey. The kid was actually good-looking, with an oval face and short chin, small pug nose, and feathery brown eyebrows, a band of freckles across his nose, his shiny hair longer than was fashionable. His eyes were slitted open, and Billy could see the hazel irises. If he were a girl he'd be beautiful.

Enough of this, thought Billy. He had to get moving before the mother rang her bell. When the kid wouldn't come, she'd clang some more. And when he still didn't respond, she'd be down.

Billy unzipped a black body bag made of the same scent-free material as his suit, then took off the kid's shoes and laid him in it, then zipped it. He grabbed the butterfly net and went back down to the canal. The place was dead—not a sound except for the bugs and bats chittering in the darkening skies. He went back to the shack, and when he was certain that the woods were clear, he moved outside and with his gloved hands picked up the dog and scraps of brain matter and dumped it all and the rabbit into another bag. He sprayed the ground with coon urine from the aerosol can to deflect search-party dogs.

When he finished, he hauled the bags back into the woods maybe two hundred yards then turned west and headed to where yesterday he had dug the four-foot-deep hole, now covered over with brush. He laid down his bundles and uncovered the hole. It was deep enough and already limed. He dropped in the remains, filled the hole with dirt again, sprayed more coon urine, and then returned the brush.

But the exertion in the suit nearly made him faint. He trudged his way to the next clearing in the trees then crossed up and over the rise that would take him back to Little Wiggins Canal Road and to the cutoff in the woods where the van waited with the Igloo cooler full of ice and the six bottles of Coors Lite.

Billy thought about the beer then about the story in tomorrow's local papers: How little six-year-old Travis Valentine of Little Wiggins Canal Road and his dog Bo were missing, and how the authorities speculated that the boy had gotten lost in the woods. And in a few days people would begin to fear that the boy and his dog had been snatched by alligators because it was nesting season and males are very protective by nature. And then it would come out how some large bulls reaching upward of eleven feet had been spotted in canals not too far from here. Wildlife officers would comment that although gators generally fear humans, some local animals had lost their timidity because residents had been feeding them even though that was against the law, and that most gator attacks occurred around dusk. And a spokesman from the Florida Game and Fish Commission would say something about how the boy's death should not create a panic, that there had been only eleven confirmed deaths by alligator in the last twenty years, and that death by drowning and bee sting were more common. While that wouldn't be much comfort to Mrs. Valentine, the commission just wanted to put things in perspective. And the local sheriff's office would solemnly promise that his men would hunt and kill the animal, and that the Game Commission would dissect it to ensure it was the one that got the Valentine boy.

And the distraught mother would report how there had

been no screaming or barking or sounds of thrashing water. And how Travis would never disobey her and go near the water because he had more sense than that. He knew about gators, and even though they had almost never been spotted in the vicinity, she had schooled him right. Besides, he had Bo who would detect a gator if it were nearby.

But the authorities would express bafflement that even with a party of police, forest rangers, and a couple dozen backcountry volunteers with dogs, not a trace had been found of young Travis or his mutt—just a butterfly net and a solitary sneaker at the edge of the canal, leading them to rule out foul play, mountain lions, and bears, leaving them with the sad conclusion that both the dog and the boy had been snatched by alligators, the dog probably first—pulled right off the shore without a sound—then, when he went to help, another animal had burst from the depths and pulled in Travis, too.

No bloody clothes, no ravished bodies, nothing but a single sneaker and a butterfly net.

Like he had just up and disappeared *snick snick.*

7

To Greg's mind, the groomed piney acreage surrounding the medical examiner's office was an overstated apology for the interior grimness.

One of the three satellite offices of the Boston headquarters, the Pocasset unit occupied the dark concrete basement of Barnstable County Hospital, a former chronic care facility. Joe Steiner's office was off a labyrinthine hallway, which housed autopsy rooms, a morgue, and storage facilities filled with cadavers and body parts in plastic containers. Greg parked next to some white ME vans.

He hated the place, for it was where Lindsay had been brought that night two years ago. As he walked down the hall, he could still recall the soupy unreality of moving past these walls and doors to identify her body, knowing that she was dead, while at the same time a tiny part of his brain clung to a candle flicker of hope that it was another woman they had pulled out of the wreckage.

It had been a clear, cool starry April night—the kind that made you aware of infinity, and just how incidental human life is. He had been at home half-watching a ball game and trying to stay awake until Lindsay returned. She was late because one of the girls at Genevieve Bratton had tried to kill herself, and Lindsay was most of the crisis-management team. Over the years, she had seen girls whose young lives were full of horrors so awful that she had stopped talking about them. And many of those lives she had helped turn around. Her colleagues spoke glowingly of her compassion and skills in working with troubled kids. At a fundraising gala three years ago, she was commended for her work. A graduate who had come into the school at age fourteen—a suicidal victim of repeated sexual abuse, an alcoholic, and a drug addict with a rap sheet a yard long—personally thanked Lindsay for setting her on a path of recovery that had led to a college degree, a successful career, and a sense of self-esteem. Greg had tears of pride in his eyes as the audience gave Lindsay a standing ovation.

Greg moved down the corridor toward Joe Steiner's office, and he could still feel the horrid disbelief that clutched him as he walked into Room 55 two years ago to identify her body—how Joe had met him in the hall surrounded by troopers and other officers, including T. J. Gelford. How their faces appeared like a funeral frieze.

Today Joe Steiner was on his phone at his desk, the sports section of *The Boston Herald* spread open, and a cigarette burning in an ashtray beside an open bag of Cape Cod dark russet potato chips. An air conditioner in a high window groaned against the sultry ocean air. Through the plastic divider was the autopsy room, occupied mostly by a single white porcelain cadaver table under lights and a butcher's scale.

Reluctantly Greg's job brought him here a few times a year, and the place always looked the same. On the floor sat a stack of large white plastic formaldehyde containers labeled in Magic Marker—*heart, liver, uterus, lungs, brain*—each with a case number. Nearby was a cardboard carton of small screw-top specimen jars containing slices of different human organs. Also on the floor was a small white refrigerator, containing vials of blood and urine. The place was a human chop shop.

"Tonight's my last good night of sleep," Joe said when he got off the phone. "My daughter Sarah gets her driver's license tomorrow."

Joe was only half-joking. He had been a medical examiner for nearly twenty years, conducting more than a hundred autopsies annually. In his time, he had been host to every conceivable form of human death: by fire and water; in car, boat, and plane accidents; by their own hand and somebody else's. As he once said, he had seen it all. To him, the deceased's remains were no longer a human being but a scientific specimen containing information on it or in it—information that would assist the judicial system, public health office, police departments, and surviving families. But what still affected Joe—what still cut through that professional crust—was finding on his table a teenager who had wrapped himself or herself around a tree. "Such a waste," he once said with tears in his eyes.

"I wish they'd up the age to thirty-five."

"Or give them bumper cars for the first ten years," Greg said.

Joe smiled. He had sad blue eyes that reminded you of the unspeakable images they had absorbed in his two decades. "So, how you doing?"

Greg knew what he meant: Had he ridden down the grief? Had he gotten on with his life since Lindsay's death? Had he started dating other women?

During the first year after his wife's death, Greg's grief was ravenous, all-consuming. Early on, he wasn't certain he could survive—and several nights he had found himself gnawing on the barrel of his gun. He had lost the love of his life and his baby-to-be, and with them all purpose. Yet, knowing that Lindsay would want him to go on, he threw himself into his work, taking on extra cases, doing overtime. Still, there were days when he could barely function for missing her. It was like trying to breathe on one lung.

The thought of seeing other women during that first year was borderline heresy. In his mind, his marriage to Lindsay had been a rare alliance with a woman whom he respected as much as he had loved. It always amazed him that someone so extraordinary as she had settled for someone so unextraordinary as he. He felt truly privileged. So, in the second year when friends tried to fix him up, he knew he could not settle for just any woman. She had to be special. He dated casually a couple times and met some fine people. He even on occasion met a woman he had fantasized over. But he soon lost interest and gave up. Lindsay had spoiled other women for him.

Today, the pain of her loss was no less keen. It still throbbed at the core of him. He had just gotten harder around it. And instead of other women, he took up the Sagamore Boy case. It gave him uncompromising purpose.

"So, what do we have?"

"His name is Grady Vernon Dixon, age six, white male from Coldwater, Tennessee. He's been missing for fourteen months." From a file folder, Joe produced several color blowups of a human skull and a single long bone. As he had explained on the phone, the remains had been processed at the main office in Boston and the State Crime Lab in Sudbury. After twelve weeks, Gloucester and state police had exhausted all leads, as had investigators at the Tennessee end. All they had were the boy's abduction and an unattended death—no suspects, no evidence, no leads. Just two devastated parents. And a skull and leg bone.

Greg moved his chair forward and examined the photos.

"You can thank Patty Carney for the link," Joe said. "She's the forensic anthropologist at the Boston lab where they processed your Sagamore Boy. She made the connection just the other day and called me."

"Any idea how long it was in the water?"

"Hard to tell, but from the wear and tear from bouncing around the bottom, I'd say at least a year."

"So, it's possible he drowned."

"It's possible."

The skull, like the leg bone, was grayish-brown, not

bleached from the sun. Only a few of the teeth were missing, unlike the Sagamore Boy whose skull contained only the incisors and two half-grown back teeth.

"I think he was pretty deep, because there isn't the weight loss you'd get in warm water."

"How did they determine it's a male?"

"There was no soft tissue, but the leg bone had traces of marrow inside," Joe explained. "And with that, they could detect certain DNA markers which only occur on the Y chromosome—the male chromosome. The calibrations of the skull also point to a male. The same with his ethnicity. Different races have different skull-feature measurements. His age we determine by bone growth and plate fissures, but there's a larger window of error there—between five and seven years."

Steiner handed Greg some color photos of the remains lying on the boat deck among piles of scallops, fish, crabs, and seaweed. They looked so sadly out of place. "They were taken by the boat captain."

Greg turned to one of the several profile shots of the Dixon skull. "It's got the same holes."

"That's what I called you for."

There were two clusters each of ten small holes on the left side of the Dixon skull—one group between the eye socket and ear hole; the other above the left ear.

Joe opened his desk drawer and pulled out a folder with photos of the Sagamore Boy's skull. "When this came in three years ago, my guess was the holes were some marine-animal artifacts." From the same drawer he removed three large white quahog shells. "Also from Sagamore Beach," he said. He laid the shells under the desk light. Each of the shells had small-bore holes of roughly the same diameter. "These were made from calcium-loving worms called polychaetes. They bore holes that are almost perfectly round, about one to two millimeters in diameter."

"They look like the skull holes."

"And that's what threw me," Joe said. "Same size, but

they're not from polychaetes or any other aquatic organism I know of. These skull holes occurred premortem."

"How do you know that?"

"First, the animal holes are random and only partially clustered—maybe a dozen holes in an area then random spacing over a broader surface. Sometimes, as in this shell, you only get two or three on the whole surface, and some don't go all the way through. But the Sagamore skull and the Dixon boy each have a cluster of ten and twelve above the temple and another cluster of ten above the ear," he explained, moving from shell to photos. "And no other holes anywhere else on either skull, or the leg bone."

Greg studied the photos. Both hole clusters were located in exactly the same areas on the skulls. Too much for a coincidence.

"That's when I stopped guessing and put it under the scope." From the same folder he pulled out other enlargements.

"On the right is a polychaete bore, on the left a hole from the Dixon skull—both straight-on."

"They look the same."

"That's right." Then he laid out two more enlargements. He pointed to the photo on the right. "This is the cross section of a polychaete hole in skull bone. Notice the homogeneous field of small pockmarks." Joe then placed next to it another enlargement. "And this is one of the skull holes. See the difference?"

Greg studied the two for a moment. Laying his finger on the right photo, he said, "This one looks grooved."

"That's right. The polychaete worms leave smooth cavities. Those are cut marks from a drill."

"Jesus!" Instantly Greg conjured up Geoffrey Dahmer–style horrors.

"But it's not what you may think," Joe said. "From the angles and the smoothness of the bores, it looks like these were done with very high-speed cranio-blade drills under precision guidance."

"Meaning what?"

"Meaning nobody attacked the kid with a Black and Decker. He had some kind of medical procedure. There are no signs of the drill bit sliding on the skull or forced entry. Also, the cutting was fast and controlled—no microchipping or breakage like with a slower handheld instrument. This kid had some kind of sophisticated brain operation."

Greg looked at him blankly. "Like what?"

"If they were bigger and fewer holes, I'd say they were drainage shunts to relieve internal bleeding—say if he had sustained some kind of trauma such as a car accident." Joe let out a whimper as if reminding himself of his daughter. "With so many holes, my guess is some kind of biopsy."

"You mean if he had brain tumors."

"Or lesions, because something was either taken out of his brain . . . or put in."

"Like what?"

"Well, if he were an old man, he might have been treated for Parkinson's disease—except six-year-old kids don't get Parkinson's. Another possibility is he had several tumors. It's rare, but if that were the case, surgeons might have implanted radioactive seeds."

"Any way to test for that?"

"I asked Boston to do a radioactive scan. But, like I said, all soft tissue is unfortunately long gone—and no traces were detected in the bone."

Greg held up the profile enlargements of the two skulls. There were variations in placement, but the clusters appeared identical.

"Another thing," Joe added. "I checked around, and neurodrill holes are always refilled after such a procedure, either with some synthetic bone or even coral. From all microscopic indications, these were left empty."

"Maybe they came out in the water."

"Maybe. But I think there'd still be some signs of bone regeneration, which happens when there's a fracture or fissure. But I don't see any sign of the holes closing up."

"That could have been lost in the water too, no?"

"Sure, but still."

"If that were the case, it would mean that the kid died from the operation."

"Or shortly thereafter," Joe said.

Greg held up photos of the two skulls. "What's the likelihood of two kids treated for brain tumors being found dead in the waters off the Massachusetts coast?"

Joe nodded and lit up another cigarette. "You'd do better playing the lottery."

"And how the hell did they end up at the bottom of the ocean?"

"You're the cop."

"Do the parents know about the holes?"

"We notified the DA's office and the CO in Gloucester, who, by the way, has pretty much given up on the case. I guess they hit a dead end and deferred to Tennessee since it's where the kidnapping took place."

"And the remains?"

"Sent them back to the parents. We had no further use for them, and they were anxious for a burial. In fact, they threatened the DA with a court order."

"They could still be evidence."

"We've got plenty of photos and bone samples. And if something unexpected develops, they can always be exhumed." He coughed a couple times and stubbed out the second cigarette although it was still long. "From what I hear, they've hit a brick wall down there, too."

Greg picked up the card with the child's name on it. "Coldwater, Tennessee. Never been there."

"You and six billion other people."

"First time for everything."

Joe nodded at the Sagamore Boy shots. "Got anything here?"

"No, but we're trying to ID with photo superimposition."

"That's a good idea," Joe said. "I've seen the software and it's pretty sophisticated."

Greg was hoping to match the Sagamore skull to known missing persons registered in the National Missing Children Network. "As backup, we've submitted a reconstruction we got made by a forensic artist."

"*We* means *you*," Joe said.

Greg made a dismissive shrug. He picked up the folder with copies of the photos and ME's report on the Dixon boy and tucked it under his arm.

Joe nodded at the shot of the Sagamore Boy drawing. "You've really got a thing about this kid."

"He's some child who ended up a skull on a beach. I can't sleep with that."

"When the day is done, my friend, we're all skulls on a beach."

"Uh-huh, but before that happens, this one's going home, too."

8

Billy had done custody snatches before. But this was the first time he'd used the camo suit, and the first time any of the parents had included with the advance hypodermic needles full of sedatives and instructions on usage. That was fine by him, since it beat all the kicking and screaming. This was also the first time he'd been offered ten grand for a delivery—more than three times the usual fee. The old man must really want his kid back.

Billy didn't know who the guy was. In fact, rarely did he know his contact. Nor did he give a rat's ass. That's how these things got set up. A guy knows a guy who knows a guy who needs a job and has the cash. Billy's guess was that the old man had lost the custody case and had gone off with another woman and earned the dough to get his kid back—screw the mom. And if he had ten big ones to lay out, then the kid's probably better off where he's going, since the old lady lives in a goddamn bug-infested aluminum box in the woods.

About two miles out of Callahan, down service road 108 past the junction of 301, A1A, and U.S. 1 North, Billy spotted the red-white-and-blue Amoco sign.

He had no idea what the kid's father looked like or what his name was—Something Valentine. (Sounded like a Del-

bert McClinton song.) And all he'd been told was to bring
the kid to the blue shack in a lot about two-tenths of a mile
past the station on SR 108—which was where the transfer
would be made.

He also didn't know what the guy was driving. But the
guy knew what Billy was driving because they had supplied the van, dropping it off in a mall parking lot with the
key and an advance of three thousand dollars cash and
promise of the balance on delivery.

(It had crossed Billy's mind to take the money and run,
but he was told the guy was good people and true to his
word. And ten grand to bag a kid was a piece of cake. Besides, Billy had his professional code. Not good for business.)

He pulled slowly past the Amoco lot, which was one of
those gas station/minimart setups that were open twenty-
four hours and manned by a couple of kids. He drove on,
checking his rearview mirror. Nothing—just black road as
far back as he could see.

Around the bend, he saw the lot, and set back under
some trees a dark locked shack with a big sign reading
BOILED PEANUTS—SALTED AND CAJUN STYLE. They were
big in Central Florida with stands dotting the roadsides.
But Billy could never understand the attraction. They
looked like cat turds and tasted worse.

There were no other cars in the lot, so he backed in, facing the road, and turned off his headlights, keeping the motor running. He was early. He reached under his seat and
pulled out his Python. It was fully loaded. He always had it
on these jobs—standard operating procedure, whether he
knew his clients or not. It made him feel more comfortable
about driving off into the night with seven thousand dollars.

He kept the CD playing, but very softly so he could hear
the outside sounds. There were none but cicadas and frogs.

After ten minutes, he began to get nervous. He turned
off the CD.

After ten more minutes, he began to wonder if this was

the right place. He looked back at the kid, who had stirred, but didn't wake up. He wished the guy would arrive, because he didn't want to have to go back there and shoot up the kid again if he awoke. Let the old man take care of that. He had done his part.

Twelve minutes later, Billy was still waiting, the kid still asleep. The dashboard clock said 10:04. He was over half-an-hour late.

Just as Billy began to think he had the wrong place, a big black Mercedes pulled alongside. Startled, Billy gripped his gun, his heart thumping like a kettle drum in his chest.

The driver gave a little wave and got out. He was alone. He was about six feet and slender, dressed in dark pants and a pullover. His hands were empty and there was no gun in his pants or holster across his torso. But around his neck he wore a stethoscope.

"Sorry I'm late," said the man.

Billy nodded. Already he was feeling better, especially with the big M500. Billy imagined he was a wealthy millionaire who would take his kid off to a foreign country to beat an extradition rap. What didn't make sense was how he had ended up with a trailer-trash wife. Unless he had met her in a bar on some business trip down here and one drink led to the next and that led to some hotel bed where he knocked her up. Billy had glimpsed the mother during stakeout. She was a looker.

The man peered into the windows of the van. "You have Travis?"

"Yup."

"Good."

"You the father?"

"Uncle," the man said. "Can I see him?"

"First things first," Billy said. He got out of the van, holding the Python at arm's length.

"You don't need that," the man said. Then he turned around with his arms raised to show that he was carrying no weapons. But there was an envelope sticking out of his rear pocket. The man pulled it out and handed it to Billy.

Billy backed up a safe distance behind the van and with a penlight inspected the contents. Hundreds. A stack of hundred-dollar bills. He pulled a few randomly out of the pack and held them over his light to make sure they weren't counterfeit or photocopies. They weren't. When he was satisfied, he stuffed the envelope into his jacket and led the man to the rear of the Caravan.

They looked around and waited for a car to pass. Then Billy opened the rear door.

Travis was lying on a mattress with a blanket over him. He was still asleep from the shot two hours ago. Billy's instructions had been to avoid restraining the kid in any way— no cords or handcuffs. Just to put him to sleep. The stuff was good for a minimum of six hours—and they had supplied three backup needles. He was also told to drive under the speed limit and not to get caught, no matter what. There was no worry of that. Billy had been doing small heists for years and knew how to keep his ass off radar screens.

As Billy waited, the man pulled out a small penlight from his pocket and raised the kid's eyelids. With the stethoscope he listened to the kid's heart. Billy watched, thinking that the uncle was the family doctor, which explained the big German wheels. No doubt he was footing the bill for his po'boy country bubba.

When the guy was satisfied, he carefully lifted the kid out and hustled him to the Mercedes where he laid him across the rear seat, strapped him in, then covered him with a blanket. He thanked Billy and shook his hand. "This is going to make some people very happy. Thank you." With that he got in his car and left.

Billy watched the car turn east onto 108, which would take the guy back to A1A and onto U.S. 1 North—the big red taillights disappearing into the black.

Man, that was easy, he thought, and got into his van and pulled into the southbound lane. In his mirror, the road was an empty black as far as he could see. He would take the service road to the next junction, reconnecting him with A1A South.

About a mile down the road, no cars in either direction, Billy flicked on the overhead light and opened the envelope. "Oh, yeah!" he said, riffling through the wad of Benjies with his thumb. Seventy big ones. He flicked off the light and stuffed the envelope into his inside jacket pocket and turned up the CD—Delbert McClinton's *Nothing Personal.*

At about three miles down the road, Billy flicked on the light and once again inspected the money, his mind tripping over ways to spend it. First he'd get himself one of those fifty-inch TVs and a DVD player and a bunch of DV discs—*Predator, Terminator 2, The Score:* the good shit.

At about five miles down the road, Billy replaced McClinton with *When It All Goes South* by Alabama and began to sing along.

About six miles down the road, it crossed his mind that maybe he'd have a multidisc CD player installed so he wouldn't have to keep changing albums by hand.

About seven miles down the road, Billy's heart nearly stopped.

In his rearview mirror he noticed an unmarked cruiser with its dashboard cherry.

"SHIT!"

He had tried to keep under the speed limit. Maybe it was a busted taillight, but he pulled over, thinking that it could have been much worse had he gotten stopped an hour ago with a kid tied up in the back seat. Or maybe the van matched the description of a stolen vehicle.

"SHIT!"

He stuffed the package of money under the seat.

The cruiser pulled behind him, and in the mirrors Billy watched the lone cop get out of his car. He was out of uniform, which was unusual. Unmarked car okay, but with an unmarked officer? Probably off duty. Just Billy's luck. He could get three years in the slammer for driving a stolen vehicle. Then he'd have to explain the camo suit and bag covered with bloodstains from the dog.

"SHIT!"

He rolled the window down. "Hey!" he said, real friendly.

"Would you step out of your car, please, sir?" The officer was a guy about fifty, short and stocky.

"Pretty sure I was under the limit, Officer," Billy said, getting out.

The road was dark, and no other cars came by.

"Around this way," the officer said. He had black driving gloves on.

"Aren't you going to ask me for my license?" Billy said, reaching for his wallet.

"Not yet," the officer said, and led Billy around the front of the car which was nosed into thick brush under trees just off the shoulder of the road. The officer made him place his hands on the van's hood and spread his legs.

Shit! Billy thought.

The man patted him down. When he felt the inner pocket of his jacket, the man's hand went inside. Billy grabbed the man's arm to stop him when he heard *snick snick.*

Billy's hands went free. He looked over his shoulder and saw the long barrel of the man's pistol.

Just as he realized the extension was a silencer, Billy saw a flash of light go off in his face.

It was the last light he would ever see.

9

D addy, will you read to me?"
Wearing pajamas with big cartoon spaceships all over them, Dylan opened the door to Martin's office, a converted bedroom on the second floor.

Martin was at his laptop looking over the dossiers of recruits, most of them senior-level information technology experts. "Hey, you little monkey," he said with a glance.

"I'm not a monkey," Dylan protested.

"Just kidding," Martin said. "I'll be right with you." He finished what he was doing and followed Dylan to his room where he climbed into bed with a book called *Elmo the Christmas Cat*. It was part of a series of books about the adventures of an inimitable black-and-white cat.

"That's a Christmas story," Martin said, stretching himself beside his son. "Isn't it a little early?"

"I don't know."

"Well, it's only June, and Christmas is in December, which is six months from now."

"But I want *Elmo the Christmas Cat*."

Martin wasn't sure Dylan got what he meant. He had a little trouble with time abstractions. "Okay, but do you remember the months of the year?"

"Sunday, Monday, Tuesday, Threesday, Foursday, Fivesday . . ."

"Wednesday, Thursday, Friday," Martin corrected. "No, those are days of the week. I mean months of the year." Feeling a little frustrated, Martin pointed to the large kid's calendar on the wall. "You know, 'January, February, March . . .'" Martin began to sing.

They had been trying to get him to learn the days of the weeks and months of the year for a while. The odd thing was Dylan could memorize things if they were set to music, which was how he could sing the alphabet correctly and why he knew the lyrics of a couple of dozen show tunes. Yet he could not recite things straight. So they had made up little jingles for the days of the week and months of the year, but at the moment he was more interested in Elmo.

Martin opened up the book and began to read, wondering when the boy would be able to do this himself.

After a couple pages, Dylan noticed the small dark blood scab on Martin's cheek. "You cut yourself. How come?"

"Just from shaving."

Dylan touched it gently with his finger. "Does it hurt?"

"Nah."

"Want a kiss to make it feel better?"

"Sure."

"Maybe I'll be a doctor someday." Dylan kissed the scratch. Then he lay back on his bolster.

"Maybe." Martin read to him, thinking about his work. When he was finished, he turned out the light. "You know, hon, I'm not going to be home tomorrow night."

"How come?"

"Well, I've got to be in Boston tomorrow." He had a late conference in town and it made sense to stay over at a hotel.

"I hate Boston. You always go there."

"I promise I won't go back for a long time. But tomorrow you'll have to take care of Mom, okay?"

"Tomorrow we go to the zoo."

"You are?" Martin had forgotten that Rachel and Sheila MacPhearson were chaperoning Dells kids on a field trip to Franklin Park.

"Uh-huh. But you know what?"

"What?"

"Mom's sad."

"She is? Why do you say that?"

"Because I saw her crying."

Jesus, it was getting worse, he thought. When he came home a little after seven, she said that dinner was on the stove, then announced that she wanted to lie down because she had a headache. In fact, she had been lying down for nearly two hours now. The light was out in their bedroom and the door was closed, which meant that she was probably asleep.

"Well, I'll check in on her. I bet she was just tired."

"Dad, do you like me?"

"Of course I like you. I love you. Why do you ask that?"

Dylan shrugged. "Lucinda doesn't like me."

"Sure she does. And if she doesn't, something's definitely wrong with her."

"Something's definitely wrong with her," he repeated, and closed his eyes.

Martin had read someplace that it takes the average adult about eight minutes to fall asleep. Dylan was out in less than a minute, no doubt dreaming of some outsized cat in a Santa outfit coming down the chimney.

Martin got up and crossed the hall to their bedroom. The interior was dark, and Rachel was asleep on her side of the huge king-sized bed. Her sweatshirt was still on, but she had taken her slacks off and draped them over the footboard. The thought of her lying there in her panties produced a giddy sensation in his genitals.

He sat on the edge of the bed and she opened her eyes a slit.

"Are you in there?"

She nodded.

"How's the head?"

She nodded to say that it was okay.

"Well, I hate to wake you but it's nine o'clock. I thought you might want to change into your PJs."

She nodded, and closed her eyes again.

"You know what you could use? A few pages of *Elmo the Christmas Cat*."

She did not smile, or even open her eyes. She just shook her head ever so slightly.

"*Swann's Way* might be more your style."

Still nothing.

"I know," he said and stretched himself alongside of her and put his leg across hers. "How about Mighty Marty's Happy Beef Injection? Been known to cure PMS just like that." He gave her a little pelvic grind.

"Sorry," she whispered.

It was as if she had turned to wood. But in the scant light he could see tears pooling in her eyes. Martin pulled back. "Hey, girl, what's the problem?"

She shook her head slightly.

"Rachel, I've known you for nearly ten years. I know when something is eating away at you. And something is, and it's beginning to scare me. Really. I'm beginning to wonder if you have some awful disease you're not telling me about." Martin rubbed her shoulder. "Come on, Rache, what's going on?"

She took his hand and muttered something he couldn't get.

"What?" he said, and gently coaxed her face out of the pillow.

"I'm scared."

Martin felt a cold shock pass through him. *She has cancer.* "About *what*?" He snapped on the light.

"Dylan."

"What about Dylan?"

"His problems."

"What problems? What are you talking about?"

Suddenly she was sharply alert. "What do you mean, *what problems*?" she snapped. "His learning problems. His disabilities. His dyslexia. His . . . impairment."

Impairment. She had rummaged for the right word and came up with *impairment. Such a clinical term,* he thought. According to specialists Dylan had a language-processing problem. But that didn't make him *impaired.*

"Rachel, we've been through all this. He hasn't got polio, for God's sake. He's dyslexic, like millions of other kids in this country. We'll get learning specialists, whatever it takes."

"But they can't perform miracles."

"No, but they can help reverse the problem."

"It's not like having his feet straightened."

Martin wasn't sure what she meant. "It will take time. But we'll do the best we can and get beyond this. It's not the end of the world. Dyslexia can be dealt with."

"I'm thinking of taking him out of DellKids."

"How come? What happened?" They had waited a long time and pulled strings to get him into the program, applying months before they actually had moved to town. If it weren't for Sheila MacPhearson, they wouldn't have succeeded.

"It's more than dyslexia. He's just not in the same league as the other kids, and they're beginning to make fun of him."

"Make fun of him?" Rachel was like a mother bear. One of the kids must have mouthed off, Martin decided.

"Maybe if you spent a little more time with him you'd notice."

"What the hell does that mean?"

"It means that you're so damn absorbed with your work," she said. Then she added, "And so damn self-congratulatory."

He felt as if he'd been slapped. "Self-congratulatory?"

"You know what the hell I mean. Working in Cambridge in 'the brainiest mail zone on the planet.'" Her voice had shifted to a mocking singsong.

Why the hell was she throwing his words back in his face? Of course he loved being in Cambridge and out of that garret behind the Hanover Mall. He now had a five-room suite on the seventh floor of an office building near the corner of Massachusetts Avenue and Memorial Drive and a view of Boston that would make a hermit ache. In addition to the extra floor space and easier commute, he was thrilled to spend most of his day surrounded by MIT, and not just because it was his alma mater. With Harvard at one end and MIT at the other end, Mass Ave was like a giant filament blazing with the greatest concentration of mind power in the world. In those other buildings were people who prepared manned missions to Mars, spliced genes, designed robotic intelligence and nanomachines, and searched for quarks, quasars, and extraterrestrial life. Yes, 02141 glowed with the greatest cerebral wattage anywhere, and SageSearch sat at ground zero. Martin felt smarter just being here. "So, what's your point?"

"That you're never around long enough to realize your son's got serious language problems."

"But he's younger than the others, and young for his age," Martin protested. "Besides, wasn't the idea to put him in there where he can learn from other kids—something about a *mentoring theory*?"

"Maybe you should take a few hours off some afternoon and observe them. If that's mentoring, it's not working."

Martin saw that coming, but let it go. "Well, if you think it's not working, then maybe we should find another daycare place."

Rachel didn't respond. She seemed too preoccupied, too on the fringes. He watched her open her night table drawer, pull out the vial of sleeping tablets, and toss a couple into her mouth, washing them down with a glass of water.

"There are things we can do for him, tutors, special ed teachers," he said, trying to make her feel better. "Even special schools if need be. We can deal with it."

Still Rachel didn't respond. Instead she slipped her pajamas on and got back into bed. "I wish we were back in Rockville."

"Are you kidding? We're living in one of the best towns on the North Shore. You should be counting your blessings. Our blessings."

Without a word, she flicked off the light.

So that was it! he thought. *Christ!* He hated when she clammed up like this. "Guess it's good night." He hated another night going by without sex. It had been three weeks.

"G'night." Her voice was barely audible. Then he heard her mutter something else. In a few minutes the sleeping pills would kick in and she'd be out.

As Martin went to the bathroom, he realized what she had said: *I'm sorry.* But by the time he returned to ask what she meant, she was asleep.

For a long moment, he stood there watching her slip deeper into her Xanax oblivion. While her breathing became more peaceful, it occurred to him that no matter how much you think you know the person you love, even after ten years, there are always those damn little black holes in their makeup from where no light ever escapes. And yet, like the ubiquitous X-ray presence around collapsed stars that astronomers talk about, what Martin detected were the subtle signatures—those microsigns in Rachel's expression that told him she was holding something back. While she could control her wording and body language, she could not disguise that slightly askew cast of her eyes. It was there again tonight while they spoke. That look that said something was festering just beneath the skin of things.

10

Around eleven, the black Mercedes pulled into an abandoned lot about six miles west of Jacksonville.

Phillip was waiting for him. Oliver had ditched the dark blue Chevy that had doubled as an unmarked police car in the woods, then walked half a mile to the rendezvous site.

They drove another six miles to a dirt road that led to Lake Chino just below the Georgia border where they had left their DeHavilland Beaver floatplane in a black little cove.

Travis was still asleep under his blanket, and he would probably remain so for another couple hours. When he woke up, they would feed him because he probably hadn't eaten since breakfast. On the floor under the boy sat a large Igloo filled with sandwiches and drinks. They were still cool in spite of the hours the plane had baked in the sun.

Using a self-inflating raft, they floated him to the plane in the dark and loaded him into a seat in the rear, then strapped him in securely and covered him with a blanket. The night air was cool and the plane's heater was faulty.

Oliver, an experienced pilot, got behind the controls while Phillip took the passenger seat.

A little before midnight, in clear cloudless skies, the Beaver lifted off the black water, then banked to the right, heading northeast which would take them through Georgia, the Carolinas, Virginia, and, eventually, all the way up the coast to New England. It was not the kind of long haul Oliver liked to fly, especially at night. At a cruising speed of 110 knots, the flight would take about twelve hours with two stops for refueling. He had preselected small airports where you could roll up to a fuel pump and pay with a credit card like that Amoco station back there. And he had a fake credit card so he wouldn't be tracked. Because he was flying on visual, he did not have to maintain contact with regional operations as he would were this an instrument flight. Which meant no record or tracking of their plane.

When they leveled off to ninety-two hundred feet someplace over the southern Georgia interior, he looked over his shoulder. The kid was in a deep slumber, but breathing normally.

"He's got himself a good-looking kid here," he said to Phillip.

Phillip gave a cursory glance over his shoulder. "Yeah." He was more interested in the lights of the city in the distance.

"Too bad about the scratches on his face," Oliver said.

"Like we're going to have to take him back."

"Right."

Phillip checked his watch against the clock on the instrument panel. "Twelve hours. I'm getting tired of these long hauls," Phillip said.

"Take a third as long in a Lear."

"Except you can't land on water and do midnight drops. What did you fly in the service?"

"F-1011s. Quite a comedown, huh? Doing kiddie runs in a Beaver floatplane."

"But the pay is better."

"There's that."

"But you made good money as a PI," Phillip said, popping open a can of beer. "How come if you were such a crackerjack bringing in fugitives you stopped doing it?"

"Because it's against the law for a convicted felon to be a detective, private or otherwise."

"That's what's wrong with this country—they get everything backward. If you wanted to know how bad guys think, hire a crook, right?"

"And pay him good."

"I'll drink to that." Phillip looked over his shoulder at the boy. He was sound asleep. "We got another drop tomorrow night, but the forecast calls for a storm."

"Uh-uh," Oliver said. "No more repeats of the last time."

11

COLD CREEK, TENNESSEE

Vernon and Winifred Dixon lived in a single-level brick structure that could not have been more than thirty feet long and half as wide. If it had wheels, it could have been a trailer home made of brick.

The place sat at the edge of an endless woodland about twenty miles northwest of Chattanooga in an area of Cold Creek called Gad's Buck Knob, according to the map. Greg had no idea what the name meant; neither did Sergeant Andy Kemmer, the Tennessee State Police detective who had been assigned the Dixon case since the boy's disappearance sixteen months ago.

Kemmer, a tall, thin nervous-looking man about forty, met Greg at the Chattanooga Airport. He was dressed casually and driving a squad car, so there was no need for Greg to pick up a rental. Before they left the airport, Greg bought a bouquet of flowers.

On the phone, Greg had explained to Kemmer that he was here to investigate the similarities between the Dixon case and another he had been working on for three years. What Greg didn't mention was that he was here on his own money and time, which was why they were meeting on Saturday. As far as anybody at the Sagamore station knew, he was off fishing for the weekend.

Kemmer gave him a copy of the Dixon boy's complete

file, including the names, addresses, and depositions of everybody they had interviewed since the boy's disappearance as well as his medical and dental records. "Ten pounds of notes, and zero leads," Kemmer said.

The drive took over an hour, mostly through backcountry roads. On the way, Kemmer warned Greg that the Dixons weren't keen on the police. Apparently a few years back, Vernon Dixon had threatened a bank loan officer with physical harm because he couldn't make mortgage payments. When the sheriff's officer came by to investigate, Vernon met him with a rifle. He was arrested, put in jail for three days, and fined two hundred dollars for threatening an officer. "He's one of those people who just doesn't trust the law. Grady disappeared, and he refused to accept how we couldn't find him. Bitched and moaned we weren't doing enough, which was bullshit, man, since we had half the county looking for him, including dogs specially trained to sniff out cadavers. We musta covered twenty square miles of woods—and out there it's as thick as fur."

"Do you have kids?"

"Two." Then Kemmer considered the question. "Yeah, maybe when it's your own it's different. But, man, we hit stone. Not a flipping lead. But I'd be lying if I didn't say we felt exonerated when he turned up your way. But the old man's still pissing on us, so prepare yourself is all I gotta say."

As small as it was, the Dixon place was tidy and cheerful looking, belying the agony the inhabitants must have suffered. Against the red brick was crisp white trim, including a porch banister running the length of the place. Pots of red geraniums hung from support poles. The upkeep was no doubt an expression of the Dixons' hope against all odds. Greg wondered where people found such strength.

Kemmer pulled the car under a large shade tree. Sitting on a crushed gravel driveway was a battered gray station wagon. Attached to the side of the house was a propane tank. From a nearby willow hung a tire swing. A wading pool lay nearby. The water was bright green. What caught Greg's eye was the faded yellow ribbon tied around a tree at the edge of the drive.

Greg got out of the car and instantly he felt perspiration bead across his brow. The heat and humidity were border-line lethal.

Vernon Dixon came out to greet them. He was a heavy-set man, with thick hamlike arms, a balding head, and broad unfriendly red face. He was dressed in blue jeans, yellow work boots, and a black T-shirt. He nodded at Kemmer who nodded back and introduced Greg who handed Dixon a business card.

Dixon scowled at the card and the flowers in his hand.

"I'm very sorry about your son, Mr. Dixon."

He gave Greg a nod.

"What kind of a name is Zakarian?"

"Armenian."

Vernon grunted. "We don't get many of your kind down here."

"I guess not."

"Is that like Arabian?"

"No."

"Do you believe in God?"

"Is that important to know?"

"I asked you a question."

"Sometimes."

"*Sometimes?* What the hell kind of answer is that? You do or you don't."

"Mr. Dixon, are we really going to stand out here and argue my religious convictions?"

"I guess not. But I don't believe in the bastard anymore, because He let somebody take my kid." Then he tossed his head toward the house. "It's cooler inside." And he led the way.

The interior was cooler with the help of a small AC

humming in a rear window and a fan on the coffee table. They had entered a small living room with oversized chairs upholstered in green imitation leather. Mrs. Dixon was standing at the threshold to the kitchen wiping her hands on a towel. She was a solid-bodied woman with a drawn white face and short-cropped brown hair. She said hello to Kemmer and shook Greg's hand.

Greg handed her the bouquet of flowers. "I'm very sorry about your son."

She thanked him and went to get something to put them in.

"You boys want something to drink?" Dixon asked. "Beer? Lemonade? Dr Pepper? The lemonade's fresh. Winnie just made it."

Through the door Greg spotted an open container of frozen drink by the sink. "The lemonade will be fine, thank you."

"Ditto," Kemmer said. While Vernon went to get the drinks, Kemmer looked at Greg and rolled his eyes to say, *I told you so.*

Greg made a noncommittal smile and looked around. Most of the room was taken up by the couch and chairs. A faux fireplace mantel sat against the wall. On it sat several photographs of Grady. And one framed illustration of Jesus, his face raised into the light, his hands pressed in prayer.

Dixon returned with a tray with glasses and a pitcher of lemonade. "Do your people up there have any idea how Grady died, cuz the boys down here don't have a damn clue?" He said that without even a glance at Kemmer.

"Not really," Greg said. "But I'd like to ask you and your wife a few questions because we may have a similar case."

"We're goddamn questioned out. It's answer time."

Mrs. Dixon returned with the flowers in a glass vase and set it on the mantel next to the boy's photos. Her eyes were red and puffy. She had been crying in the kitchen. "They're lovely, thank you very much," she said.

Greg nodded.

From a pack of Newport Lights, she punched out a cigarette and returned to the kitchen where she turned on a burner from the gas stove, stuck the cigarette into the flame until it started burning, then sucked it to a blush. She then returned to the living room. She looked shaky. "Do you have children of your own, Sergeant Zakarian?"

"No, I don't."

"If you don't mind me asking, what kind of a name is Zakarian?"

This was becoming tiresome. "Armenian."

"That's Christian, right?"

"Yes," he said, hoping she wasn't going to begin another inquisition.

"Well, we had a proper Christian burial for our boy last week. Malcolm Childers, the reverend at Mount Ida's Baptist, gave a very special service for Grady. And after, his wife, Pammie Rae, held us a lunch. It was simply lovely. I swear half the county turned out." Her voice cracked, and she struggled to maintain composure. "There I go again, and I thought I was cried out."

"I'm sure it was."

"You know, just to give us closure."

"Closure!" Vernon grunted. "There's no such thing. Never's any closure when your kid's been murdered." He shook his head. "I just hope he didn't suffer, is all." His voice hitting gravel.

"Well, I feel better cuz he's home where he belongs."

"Only way I'll feel better is if I had five minutes in the room with the sumbitch who did this to him. Five minutes is all." As he said that, the muscles in his neck and arms tightened, and rage darkened his face. Greg could understand how Dixon had run afoul of the law.

Greg got up and went to the mantel to inspect the photographs. Several shots of the boy outside on the tire swing, at a birthday party, in the wading pool. "Handsome little guy."

"Here's the most recent one," Vernon said. "It was his first school picture. And his last." And he held up a T-shirt advertising missing children. On it was a picture of Grady along with his date of birth, height, weight, coloring, and an 800 number for the National Center for Missing and Exploited Children. The boy was smiling brightly. He was a sweet-looking kid with a bright chipped-tooth smile, and Greg tried to shake away the image of the specimen on Joe Steiner's desk.

"They posted his picture at airport kiosks, in public buildings, on the Internet, you name it. Mailed it all over the country, and even had a billboard on Highway 27 outta Chattanooga," Mrs. Dixon said.

"Lotta damn good that did," Vernon growled.

There were two rooms off the living room, and one of them was closed. On the door was a sticker with a cartoon bear. Greg walked over to it.

"We called him 'Lil Bear,' " Mrs. Dixon said. She got up. "You can take a look if you like. All the other officers did."

"He didn't come for that," Vernon said. "Fact is, I'm not sure what he came for."

"I would like to see his room, thank you," Greg said. He did not pick up on Vernon's bait. It wasn't the right time.

From a dish on the mantel, Mrs. Dixon removed a key and unlocked the door.

The room looked as if it hadn't been touched since the boy's disappearance. The air was close and scented with mothballs. There was a small bed with a stuffed bear lying at the foot. One wall was covered with banners and drawings signed by his classmates and teachers: "Come home soon" and "We Love You, Grady" and "We Miss You." Another wall had decals and pictures of cartoon bears, snapshots of the boy and a dog, a UT football banner, a poster-board drawing of the Dixon house with the tree swing, signed by Grady; another of Jesus in a pasture with children and sheep. On a small table sat a nearly complete truck fashioned intricately with Legos. A box of loose pieces lay by it in expectation.

"He liked to build things," Mrs. Dixon said. She opened a bureau drawer and pulled out some photos of Grady posed proudly with several different structures. "He'd sit in here for hours working away, his tape machine playing his stories." She nodded at a yellow plastic device and a stack of tapes. "He was a very neat boy, always picking up after himself at the end of the day. I almost never had to speak to him. Some kids are pretty messy, especially boys, but not him."

Against the rear wall was a small desk with a neat arrangement of books and a kid's Fisher-Price electronic keyboard toy.

"We were saving to get him a computer for Christmas." Mrs. Dixon sighed and began to close the door. "We had nothing to go on, but we always hoped he'd come back." Tears flooded her eyes. "I prayed every day he'd come home." Vernon put his arm around her.

Greg picked up Grady's baseball glove. On the strap that went over his left wrist Grady had printed his name with a black marker. As he stared at it, he wondered how these people could go on. They had so little and now they had lost everything that mattered. But he sensed that they *would* go on, and he drew from their strength.

They returned to the living room. "I want you to know that the investigation is ongoing in Massachusetts. We've not given up on Grady," Greg said. "And that's why I'd like to ask you a few questions, if I may, because we've found some similarities to another case."

Vernon Dixon didn't look pleased.

"'Spose it can't hurt," Mrs. Dixon said.

"Three years ago, we found the remains of another child—a boy about Grady's age—also in the waters of Massachusetts. We're trying to determine if there's a connection."

"I know what you're gonna ask," Vernon said, "and the answer is no. It's what I told him. We got no idea how he ended up in Massachusetts. We've never even been to Massachusetts. We ain't even got relatives or acquaintances in Massachusetts. 'Cept for you, I don't think I ever met anybody from Massachusetts."

Mrs. Dixon nodded in agreement.

"I understand that," Greg said. "But the other child we found had markings on the skull similar to Grady's." Greg could not get himself to use the word *holes*. "I'm wondering if you can tell me what kind of neurological procedure he had had."

Mrs. Dixon's face was a perfect blank. "I don't know what you're talking about, Officer. What markings?"

"The perforations, the holes." Greg raised his finger to the side of his head.

"What holes?"

He flashed a look at Kemmer for an explanation. Greg knew Joe Steiner had notified Gene Grzywna, the Gloucester case officer, about the holes, and he in turn had sent a report to Kemmer. Or he was supposed to have.

Kemmer made a faint shrug that said he didn't have a clue either. If there was a screwup, Greg didn't want to fan Dixon's contempt of police.

From his briefcase, Greg pulled out a computer schematic of a child's head, the holes in Grady's skull designated as black circles. Kemmer shook his head. He hadn't seen the drawing. Somebody in Gloucester had screwed up badly. This was not going to be easy. "Our medical examiner suspects that these are the results of some kind of neurological procedure. A brain operation."

"Brain operation? Good heavens, no," Winnie said. Suddenly the expression on her face turned dark with concern.

Maybe *operation* was the wrong term. "Did Grady ever have a biopsy for a lesion or tumor?"

Vern shook his head.

"Seizures? Blackouts . . . ?"

"Nothing like that. Hell, he never even had headaches."

"And we got all his medical records," Mrs. Dixon added.

"Is it possible to see them?"

Vernon looked hesitant, but Mrs. Dixon got up to get them. Vernon glowered at Greg. "Are you saying it might be some other child you found?"

"No, it's Grady, I'm afraid. We've got a positive ID on the DNA and dentals."

Was Joe Steiner wrong about the holes? That they were made by some marine organism?

Mrs. Dixon returned from the other room. "He was a very healthy boy." She was carrying a thin folder. "You can see for yourself." She handed it to Greg.

Inside were doctors' reports of vaccinations, checkups, paid bills, insurance statements, and receipts for medication. It all looked unremarkable. Twice, a few years back, the boy had been to the emergency room for a split knee and removal of a fishhook in his thumb. No paperwork from any neurologist or neurosurgeon's office.

Vernon looked at the schematic. "You're saying these holes were in Grady's skull?"

"Yes."

"So how in hell did they get there?"

"That's what I hoped you would tell me."

Vernon gave Greg a harsh look. "I just said he never had a brain operation."

"It's possible we're mistaken."

"Now there's a big surprise."

Deserved! Greg thought. "It could be some aquatic organism." And in the back of his mind he could hear Joe Steiner: *"The polychaete worms leave smooth cavities."*

Greg had worked with Joe Steiner for a dozen years and never found him wrong about anything. When he didn't know something, he'd say so. When he was uncertain, he'd go to people who weren't. He also said he had double-checked with his people at the Crime Lab.

Or these people were holding back—but why lie about your kid's biopsy?

Or the kid had the procedure after he was kidnapped. Christ! Nothing made sense.

"These holes were done with very high-speed cranio-blade drills with precision guidance."

Greg felt like a horse's ass.

"Guess that's not gonna help in your other case now, is it?" Vernon downed his lemonade.

"Maybe not," Greg said.

Kemmer checked his watch. Their stay was growing cold.

"Well, I feel for the parents," Mrs. Dixon said. "I know what they're going through. Grady could be a handful at times. There were days when I wondered if I'd given birth to the devil himself. He could be mighty stubborn." Her mouth quivered. "It's just that I'd give anything to see him walk through that door again."

She got up and went into Grady's room and returned with a small wooden box, fashioned after a pirate's chest. "These were some of his special things."

While Vernon looked anxious for Greg and Kemmer to leave, Mrs. Dixon suddenly seemed compelled to tell them about Grady. "Some of it's just his baby stuff," she said. Inside were a baby brush and comb set, a silver rattle, a crucifix, and a little envelope. From it Mrs. Dixon removed a reddish curl of hair. "It's from his first haircut. He had a head of ringlets, like a cherub." Her voice broke up.

"It's where they got the DNA stuff from," Vernon said.

"He was such a clever little boy," Mrs. Dixon continued, tears running down her cheeks. "He picked things up real fast. The teachers had him earmarked for the TAG program."

"TAG program?"

"Talented and gifted. They were going to start him in the second grade." She put the box down and removed a sheet from a file folder included with the medical report. "In fact, he was so bored in kindergarten that his teacher said we should have him special-tested. He got a ninety-ninth percentile straight across."

Greg looked at the score sheet. Listed in different boxes—Verbal, Analytical, Spatial, Logic, Sequencing, and so on—were numerical percentages. Each category was printed with a 99. At the bottom of the page was small print saying that the test was copyrighted by Nova Children's Center, Inc.

Greg handed Vernon back the folder. "I know it's in the file," Greg said, "but if you don't mind, I'm wondering when the last time was you saw Grady."

"On that swing outside," Mrs. Dixon answered. "Every day Tillie Haskell dropped him off from the school van in front. As usual, he came in and got his snack, then went outside to wait for Junie Janks to come by and play. Junie's the boy who lives down the road. You passed their place coming in. Junie is short for *junior*—his real name's Bernard, after his dad. About twenty minutes later, Junie shows up wondering where Grady is." Mrs. Dixon took a deep breath.

Vernon continued for her. "The county police said not to worry, he probably just wandered into the woods. But that was pure bulltiki, because the first thing you teach your kids down here is to respect these woods. The next house on the other side is seventeen miles. I've lived in these parts for forty-six years, and I could still get lost a thousand yards in. It all looks the same, and we got that through his head from the day he could walk. You don't go into the woods.

"Musta had two hundred people search for him—police, volunteer firemen, neighbors, and just about everybody at Mount Ida's. We looked for a week. But when he didn't show up by nightfall that first day, I knew we lost him. I knew somebody had taken him. I felt it in my bones. God only knows why."

12

Brendan was checking out the odd head scars in his bathroom mirror when it crossed his mind to kill his grandfather.

The notion just popped into his head without the slightest shock—like deciding to clip his toenails.

And it would be one-two-three easy. No fuss, no muss. No telltale fingerprints or DNA evidence to sweat. No decision about weapons or *modus operandi*. No having to bury bloody meat cleavers. No burning or cutting up the remains. No witnesses.

And no motive, unlike going back to the diner and putting a knife in Angie for publicly humiliating him. He had no motive—just curiosity. (Besides, what kid would kill his own grandfather—his last remaining relative?) And it would be the perfect murder: Just hold back on his pills and sit back and watch him gasp to death on his La-Z-Boy. That would be something. Might melt some snow.

"Hey, Brendan! Where the hell are you, boy?"

"Coming," he shouted. Richard wanted his refill. Grandpa Richard, although he never called him grandpa. Just Richard. Grandpa was a technicality of blood.

And no blood. No red hand.

His face would scrunch up in wincing pain as the realization swelled in his chest that he was going to die from arterial occlusion. Inarticulate sounds would rise from his throat, saliva stringing from his chin onto his shirt, his hands alternately flailing then clutching his breast, his feet kicking, his mouth shuddering, air squealing from a clenched larynx, trying to call for help, blubbering in disbelief that Brendan was sitting there transfixed in fascination just three feet away munching pretzel logs.

Maybe that would do it.

"Brendy?" he shouted from his chair downstairs in the TV room.

"In a minute!" Richard had called him that as long as he could remember, which wasn't much. It came from Brendy Bear, as in Brendy Bear Hugs because Brendan was always hugging and kissing people, Richard claimed. He didn't do that anymore. He hadn't touched his grandfather in years. He hadn't touched anybody in years. Nor did he understand the impulse. He had been misnamed.

Brendan really had nothing against Richard. In fact, he liked him the way a dog might like a devoted owner. He was a nice old man who treated him well, gave him money and, when he turned seventeen, his old Ford pickup which Richard had used for his plumbing business before retiring. Richard had taken him in when his parents died, raising him as best he could at his age. He was protective, kind, and generous with what little he had. There surely was no reason to kill him. It was purely academic. Brendan simply wondered what he'd feel—if anything. He wondered if he'd cry.

Richard had a bad heart. A couple years ago he had suffered a myocardial infarction and now suffered from ventricular tachycardia arrhythmia—rapid heartbeats. In his condition, Richard had maybe three years at best. His friends were dying off, one last week in fact—maybe his last. Brendan could tell that that bothered Richard.

"Old men know when an old man dies."

Yeats was right about that.

In the medicine cabinet sat a row of maybe a dozen little amber plastic pill containers. Richard Berryman.

I measure my life in Walgreen vials, he thought.

Lipitor, Enalapril, Demerol, metropolol, Pronestyl.

WARNING: This drug may impair the ability to drive or operate machinery.

WARNING: Do not use this medicine if you are pregnant, plan to become pregnant, or are breast-feeding.

WARNING: This medication may decrease your ability to be human.

Generic name: *Wintermind.* Take as directed.

One must have a mind of winter . . .
Not to think of any misery in the sound of the
wind . . .

Brendan closed the medicine cabinet and left the bathroom. At the bottom of the stairs the light of the television made the foyer pulse. Brendan walked down, the lines from Wallace Stevens's "The Snow Man" drowning out all the other clutter in his head.

He entered the parlor.

The old man was sprawled out in his La-Z-Boy, his wispy white hair barely covering the old pink dome, his T-shirt rumpled, his pajama bottoms half up his pathetic white sticks of legs, his bare feet knobbed on the footrest like claws. According to the old photos, he used to be a big, strapping guy.

Richard looked up, his eyes wet and yellow, like sad clams. Death would be a gift.

And, nothing himself, beholds
Nothing that is not there and the nothing that is.

Brendan knew he should feel something for Richard. Anything. He understood the finality of his grandfather's condition, that he could go any day now. He just wished he could feel something. Anger. Horror. Sadness. Love. He wished he could cry.

"I called it in three hours ago, so it should be ready." Richard held up a twenty-dollar bill. "And whyn't you pick up some mint chocolate chip while you're at it."

"I thought chocolate was bad for you."

"What the hell isn't? Here." He flapped his hand.

Let the lamp affix its beam.
The only emperor is the emperor of ice-cream.

Brendan gave his head a shake to snap away the poetry jamming his mind. It was a constant distraction. White rhyming noise in turbo. At the moment it was Wallace Stevens for some reason. In ten minutes it could be Elizabeth Barrett Browning. God! There wasn't enough room in his head. It was like a flash plague that would strike without warning—his only defense was to build mind quarantines to box them up.

"And get some hot fudge, while you're at it."

He could do it with the throw pillow from the couch. Or a quick shot to the throat, snap his trachea. Snap his limbs like carrot sticks.

Not even horror, like Trisha Costello dying the other night.

Can't even cry.

Brendan slowly crossed over to Richard and pressed his face so close to him he could smell his sourness.

The old man flinched. "What? What the hell you doing?"

"Do you kn-know anything about these scars?" He lowered his head and parted his hair.

"Jeez, I already told you I know nothing about them."

"Use your magnifying glass." Brendan handed it to him and bowed his head down again.

Richard peered through the glass at his scalp. "Just a few white spots. Where the hell you get them?"

"That's what I'm asking you."

"How would I know? Maybe your mother dropped you on your head. Probably explains things."

"How b-badly do you want me to get your pills?" Brendan tried to put on a mean face, but he didn't have anything inside to back it. Brendan never felt mean. He never felt much of anything. Just a flat-line awareness that something was missing.

"Here. Take these so you won't forget." Richard waved the empty vial. "What are you staring at me like that for?"

Brendan muttered under his breath.

"Aw jeez, Brendy, please no poetry, okay? I want to watch this show." Then he added, "I think I liked it better when you couldn't talk."

Brendan looked at Richard. "W-what's that?"

"I said would you please get me my pills."

"N-no, about how you liked it better w-w-when I couldn't talk."

Richard made a sigh of exasperation. "It was just a joke."

"Well, I missed it."

"It's just that you didn't start talking until you were four or five. I don't know. But God knows you've made up for it. So will you please get my pills or do I have to call 911?"

Brendan studied Richard for a few seconds then he picked the car key out of the candy bowl on the desk. Beside it sat a double frame with photographs of Brendan's parents. They had died in a car crash on the Mass Pike outside of Worcester when he was nine. They were returning to their Wellesley home from a Christmas party. It was a night of freezing rain. But it wasn't the ice that killed them. They were sideswiped by another vehicle on an empty stretch and driven into a concrete barrier. The impact was so great that they died instantly, said the reports. There were no witnesses to the accident, and the truck that hit them never stopped. But weeks later one whose paint matched that on his parents' car turned up some miles away. It had been stolen. The police had no suspects, and today it remained just another cold case of hit-and-run. That's when he was moved up here to live with Richard whose wife was still alive—Grandma Betty. She died ten months later. For the last seven years, it'd been he and Richard.

"I've got a question for you," Brendan said, before he left. "Did my parents drink any kind of almond liqueur . . . cordial? Amaretto?"

Richard shook his head. "Jeez, you ask the damnedest questions."

"W-when you visited them, what did they drink?"

Richard winced as if trying to squeeze up a memory. "I don't know. They weren't boozers, if that's what you mean. You mother liked white wine, and your dad was a beer man. Why?"

"Did they cook with almond extract—cookies, candies, ice cream—stuff like that?"

"Are you going to get me my pills? I'm not supposed to go more than four hours, and it's been six."

If Richard went into cardiac arrest and died, Brendan would become a ward of the state and turned over to some foster home or orphanage. That would not be good. "I'm going," he said. "What about you? Did you drink a-almond liqueurs or eat anything with a-almond extract?"

"You think I was some kind of boozer?"

"Did you?"

"Jesus Christ. What is it with you?" Richard looked confused and exasperated, maybe even a little frightened. "No. Scotch. I don't think I ever had any Almaretto or whatever. And I don't eat nuts because they get stuck in what teeth I got left. Okay? Now get me the damn pills before I croak."

Brendan put his backpack over his shoulder, feeling the weight of his field glasses inside. "I'll be back."

"Christ, and before dawn, please!" Brendan was halfway out the door when Richard called out: "Hey, Brendy, you're a good kid."

No, Brendan thought. *I'm a snowman.*

13

Every Thursday night, Cindy Porter would stop at Morton's Deli for some pastrami, sauerkraut, potato salad, kosher pickles, fresh sub rolls, and a copy of the *Cape Ann Weekly Gazette*. Then she'd head home and, weather permitting, she'd settle into the backyard hot tub with her boyfriend, Vinnie, and read the paper and pig out.

As a nurse, she knew better, given how the cholesterol, fat, and salt in one of her Mortons could probably send a hippopotamus into cardiac arrest. But the rest of the week, she did her tofu-wheat-germ-and-broccoli virtues. Besides, she had read about a study by some Harvard nutritionist who concluded that a steady diet of low fat and cholesterol statistically added at best two months to one's life. Her weekly Mortons were worth a measly eight weeks, especially since her parents were in their seventies and still going strong.

It was a pleasant evening, and, as usual, she changed into her bathing suit. Vinnie was visiting his mother in Connecticut and wouldn't be back until late. So she made herself a sandwich and settled into the tub with a cold Sam Adams and the *Gazette*. As the warm water gushed around her, she felt her muscles loosen in place. She took a bite of sandwich and washed it down with some beer.

The headlines were about the ongoing battle to build

low-income housing. She was against it, only because she knew that only ten percent of the actual complex would be for poor families, the rest for expensive country condo living that would amount to a bonanza for developers. And that meant more coastal acreage would be jammed with construction, and more traffic clogging town roads. She made note of the town hearing next week.

She turned the paper over. Catching her eye at the bottom of the page was the headline: "Human Remains off Gloucester Identified."

According to the story, a skull and a leg bone that had been pulled up by professional scallopers two months ago had been positively identified. She vaguely recalled reading about the discovery. Apparently the remains had been DNA-matched to a six-year-old boy from Tennessee.

Maybe he had been up this way on a summer vacation or a visit with relatives. The poor kid. There were boating accidents and disappearances every year, usually because people don't check the weather reports and then get caught in storms.

The story went on to say how forensics experts from the medical examiner's office in Boston originally were baffled by the mysterious holes in the boy's skull.

On an inside page, where the story continued, was a schematic drawing of the skull showing the odd cluster of holes—two sets on the left side of the forehead just behind the hairline, and above the ear.

Experts still aren't certain if the holes were made by marine organisms or had occurred before death.

The cause of death has not yet been determined. However, forensic scientists estimate that the remains could have been in the water for over a year, leading some to conclude that the child had drowned.

But according to Gloucester police who worked in conjunction with Tennessee authorities, the child's disappearance was being treated as a kidnapping and homicide.

The story went on to say that the remains had been returned to the parents for burial.

Cindy stared at the diagram.

That strange boy who came into the ER the other night had scars on his head just like these. The poetry kid. The savant.

Brendan something or other.

"Yes, they're drill marks," Joe Steiner insisted. "And you don't need to get a second opinion. While you were gone, I had Boston look at them. We got both stereoscopic and an electron microscopic analysis. No marine organism in the books made those holes. They also ruled out lasers, knives, ice picks, and every known kind of muzzle projectile—bullet, pellet, BB, buckshot, dart—you name it. They were drilled, Greg, and you can take that to the bank."

Greg was on the phone the morning after he had returned from Chattanooga. He would have called from the road yesterday, but Joe was out of the office yesterday, car-shopping with his daughter.

"How come the parents weren't notified about the holes?"

"Because somebody messed up, maybe at the Gloucester end, maybe Tennessee," Joe said. "It's possible it was simply overlooked, or somebody didn't think it was significant. Whatever, the Boston ME made it clear those perforations were the results of a neurological procedure. And that got into the report because I saw it."

"They didn't have a clue what I was talking about."

"If the kid had had an operation, the parents would have remembered. Nobody saw it as a cause of death. These things happen."

"Joe, you weren't down there," Greg said. "You didn't

see the expression on their faces when I told them that their kid's head had been drilled."

"I understand. That must have been a bitch. But when you calm down, you might want to give this woman a call."

"What woman?"

"Write this down: Cynthia Porter, R.N., at the Essex Medical Center."

"What's she got?"

"A kid with cluster-scars on his head identical to those of the Sagamore Boy and the Dixon kid," Joe said.

"What?"

"And he's alive."

14

Nicole was naked but for a tutu and doing peek-a-boo pirouettes while her boyfriend, the older guy from the diner, lay naked and panting on her bed in a state of red alert, his wanger armed and poised like a surface-to-air missile—when suddenly she glided to the window and dropped the blinds, cutting off Brendan's view.

Brendan lowered the binoculars. Whatever they were doing in there, only the fish in her aquarium could appreciate.

It was a little after midnight that same evening. For nearly half an hour he had watched her through her bathroom window just thirty feet from his perch, taking in every moment of her precoital ritual. She had stripped down to that pink-cream flesh then, with her back to him, she brushed her golden mane, after which, turning slightly toward him, she shaved herself at the sink, her arms raised like swan necks toward the ceiling so he got a full double-barrel shot of those pink-capped breasts, then raising her legs as if practicing a ballet move, running the razor in long strokes, turning this way and that, all the while oblivious to the raised blinds and Brendan in the tree right outside her window.

Even so close, he could not see his mark because she never faced him straight-on long enough—just a quick flash of the dark target area, then she slipped into the shower, which was one of those fancy all-glass-and-chrome enclosures that instantly misted up, rendering her a moving impressionism in pink. And when she was finished, he lost her to a towel.

Brendan slipped the field glasses into its case and slumped against the tree trunk. This was the third time he had staked her out. And another bust. *Next time.*

He didn't care about the boyfriend, who had climbed up the drainpipe onto the porch roof and into her bedroom. Brendan was only interested in Nicole.

Nicole DaFoe.

He liked to stretch the syllables like sugar nougat.

Ni-cole Da-Foe

DaFee DaFi DaFoe DaFum

I smell the blood of a Yummy Yum Yum

Nicole DaFoe.

Everybody knew her name because it was in the newspapers all the time about how she made the honor roll at Bloomfield—a precious little prep school for rich geeks—how she got this award and that, how she was at the top of her class two years in a row and won first place in the New England science fair, how she was nominated for a Mensa scholarship for her senior year and was going to some fancy genius camp this summer to study biology and astrophysics. But not how she danced naked for her boyfriends. And not what they all said: *Nicole DaFoe: the Ice Queen who fucked.*

Next time, he told himself. And up close and personal.

At this hour most of Hawthorne was asleep. Brendan had slipped out in his grandfather's truck and driven the fifteen miles to Nicole's house. From his perch high in an old European beech elm, he watched a blue-white crystalline moon rise above the line of trees and the fancy homes that made up her street. It blazed so brightly that the trees made shadow claws across the lawns.

But Brendan did not notice. He was now lost in the moon face—so much so that his body had gone rigid with concentration and his mind sat at the edge of a hypnotic trance. So lost that neither the electric chittering of insects nor the pass of an occasional car registered. So lost that the ancient shadows on the white surface appeared to move.·

He had nearly cleared his mind of the assaulting clutter—of verbal and visual noise that gushed out of his memory in phantasmagoric spurts—crazy flash images of meaningless things that would at times rise up in his mind like fuzzy stills, as if he were watching a slide show through gauze—other times they'd come in snippets of animated scenes, like a film of incoherent memory snatches spliced together by some lunatic editor—images of people's eyes, their faces blurred out—just eyes—and lights and shiny metal, television commercials, green beeping oscilloscope patterns.

And that Möbius strip of poetry.

He liked poetry, which stuck to his mind like frost—especially love poetry, not because he loved but because he couldn't. It was like some alien language he tried to decipher, his own Linear B.

Maybe it was because he had banged his head earlier that day, but his mind was particularly active—and from someplace he kept seeing flashes of a big smiling Happy Face cartoon.

It made no sense.

Nixon.

He almost had caught it earlier. *Nixon.*

Big blue oval face and a sharp almond odor he could not identify—an odor that was distinct and profoundly embedded in his memory.

Memory.

That was the problem: He had Kodachrome memory, ASA ten million, and one that didn't fade. Ever. He had been cursed with a mind that would not let him forget things. Although the Dellsies thought it cool having a waiter with total recall who could tell you the nutritional value of everything in the kitchen and remember what you ordered three weeks ago for lunch, his head was a junk-heap torture chamber. While other people's recollection was triggered by a song or a familiar face, Brendan's mind was an instant cascade of words and images, triggered by the slightest stimulus—like the first neutron in a chain re-action in a nuclear explosion. It was horrible, and it led him to avoid movies, music, and television. To keep him-self from total dysfunction or madness or suicide—and there were many days he contemplated braiding a noose—he had worked out elaborate strategies. Sometimes he would project the images onto an imaginary book page then turn the page to a blank sheet. Or he would write down words or phrases that just wouldn't go away—some-times pages worth, including diagrams and stick drawings of people and things—then burn them. When that didn't work, he would torch whole books.

Medication also helped. But when he turned sixteen, he had to quit school because he could not take the reading, not because he couldn't understand the material—*au con-traire*, the subjects were stupefyingly easy. It was that he couldn't clear his mind of what he read, and just to release the pressure, he would gush lines of memorized text—like verbal orgasms. Teachers complained. Classmates called him "freak." They called him "Johnny Mnemonic." They wanted him to do mind tricks like Dustin Hoffman in *Rain Man*—look at a shuffled pack of cards, then turn them over and recite the order, or spout off the telephone numbers of all the kids in class, or the amendments to the U.S. Consti-tution. Stupid razzle-dazzle memory stuff. It was easy, but no fun being a one-man carnie sideshow. So he stopped reading and quit school.

The other day he happened to walk by DellKids, and be-cause the door was ajar he overheard that little Whitman boy, Dylan, complain that he didn't remember something that he was supposed to. Brendan envied him that. He would kill to turn off his brain.

But some things remained buried, like his parents. They

had died when he was eight, yet he could only recall them in their last years—and nothing from his early childhood—as if there were a blockage. Also, there were things he wished he could selectively summon to the light—like that big smiling Happy Face that sat deep in his memory bank like the proverbial princess's pea sending little ripples of discomfort up the layers . . .

blue.

Big blue cartoon head and big bright round eyes and a big floppy nose. Bigger than life.

Brendan slapped himself in the face.

Don't be afraid . . .

Dance . . . Mister . . .

Almost. Big eyes. Funny nose. He felt it move closer.

He slapped himself again.

Mr. [SOMETHING] makes you happy.

And again.

He almost had it. Almost.

His face stung, but he slapped himself once more . . . and like some night predator, it nosed its way up out of a dense wormhole toward the light . . . inching upward ever so cautiously, so close . . . so close he could almost grasp it . . . Then suddenly without mercy it pulled back down into the gloom and was gone.

Brendan let out the breath that had bulbed in his chest and felt his body collapse on itself. He rested his head against the trunk and closed his eyes, feeling spent and chilled from perspiration.

So close, he could almost see it take form out of the gloom . . . and hear vague wordless voices . . . and almost make out a room and faces . . . hands and lights.

He banged the back of his head against the tree.

A bloody membrane away.

Brendan lit a cigarette and let his mind wander. He thought about how the tars in the smoke were filling the micropores of his lungs with dark goo that might someday spawn cells of carcinoma and how he didn't really give a damn. How nothing in his life mattered, including his life. How different he was from others. A freak who could recite the most exquisite love poetry ever written, yet who passed through life like a thing made of wood.

It was crazy, which was how he felt most of the time. Crazy.

Just before he climbed down, he let his eyes wander across the stars, connecting the dots until he had traced most of the constellations he knew, then reconnected the stars until they formed constellations of his own. The arrow of Sagittarius he stretched into a billion-mile hypodermic needle.

And Taurus he rounded out into a smiling blue face.

"Mista Nisha won't hurt you."

The words rose up in his head with such clarity Brendan gasped. Instantly he clamped down on them before they shot away.

He had them. HE HAD THEM.

"Mr. Nisha wants to be happy . . ."

". . . Don't be afraid . . ."

"Dance with Mr. Nisha," he said aloud. And he groaned with delight.

Thirty feet away, Michael Kaminsky also groaned with delight as he shed himself deep inside Nicole.

She felt the warm ooze fill the condom and kissed him. "Was that good?" she whispered.

"Ohhhhh, yeah."

"Would you give it an A?"

"A-plus," he panted. "Did you . . . you know, enjoy it, too?"

"Why do you ask?"

"Why? Well, because I'm never sure with you. You don't react much."

She didn't answer, but tapped him on the shoulder to get

up. The clock said 12:43. "You've got to go, and I've got to get up in four hours."

"But it's Saturday."

"I know, but my mean old history teacher wants my term paper by noon Monday."

"What a prick."

She slid her hand down his body and touched him. "I'll say." Then she got up and slipped on her nightgown.

Michael peeled himself off her bed and began to get dressed. "If they ever found out, I'd be hanged at dawn." He pulled up his shorts then sat at her desk and put on his socks.

"Well, that won't happen if you're real nice," she said, and put her arms around him. "Michael . . . ?" she said, glaring up into his eyes in her best pleading look.

His body slumped. "Come on, Nik, I can't do that."

"You have to, Michael. Just two-hundredths of a point."

He sighed. "You've got your A, but I can't do that to Amy, or any other student. I can't give her a grade lower than she deserves."

She squeezed his arms. "I want you to do this for me. Please." She kept her voice low so her parents wouldn't hear them.

"You know these Vietnamese kids. She killed herself on her paper. I'd have to make up stuff to justify a B. It was excellent. So was yours—"

"Then you're going to have to make up stuff, because this American kid won't settle for second place."

Michael got up and pulled on his pants. In the scant light from the fish tank, Michael looked around her room. Covering the walls were photos of Nicole as well as her various awards, plaques, citations, blue ribbons. Hanging over a chair was her Mensa T-shirt.

"It means that much to you."

"Yes."

She watched Michael move closer to inspect the photographs. There were a dozen of them. One caught his eye:

the group shot of the Bloomfield Biology Club on a field trip to Genzyme Corporation. Seven kids were posing in a lab with company biologists in white smocks. At one end was Nicole; at the other end was Amy Tran.

"Aren't you taking this a little hard? I mean, you've got a wall of awards. You'll probably get early admission to Harvard and be in med school in four years. What else do you want?"

Nobody remembers seconds.

Nicole moved up to him. "Maybe I am," she whispered. "But you have to do this for me. It means everything." She pressed herself against his groin.

"I don't think Mr. Laurent had this in mind," he said.

"Fuck Mr. Laurent." Her voice was void of inflection.

The Andrew Dale Laurent Fellowship was a prize that went to a member of the incoming senior class whose sheer determination and effort had "most demonstrated the greatest desire to succeed," as the write-up said. It was the most prestigious award at Bloomfield Prep, not because of the thousand-dollar prize, but because the benefactors stipulated that it went to the student with the mathematically highest grade-point average going into the senior year. It was the only award based purely on grades. And although the school did not publish class rank, everybody knew that the recipient was the eleventh-grade valedictorian. Number one.

"Numero uno," as her father said.

"Numero uno."

"Never settle for second best," Kingman DaFoe once told her years ago. And he had reminded her ever since: *"Who remembers vice presidents? Who remembers silver-medal Olympians? Who remembers Oscar nominees? You've got number-one stuff, Nicole, so go for it!"*

Daddy's words were like mantras. And ever since she had entered Bloomfield ten years ago, they were scored on her soul right down to the DNA level.

Nicole DaFoe had a grade point of 3.92, and Amy Tran had a 3.93. She knew this because she got Michael to check the transcripts. If Michael gave Amy a grade of B in his U.S. History course, she would drop to 3.91, leaving Nicole in first place. Which meant the Andrew Dale Laurent Fellowship was hers. And everybody would know.

"Michael, I'm asking you to do this for me."

"I'll think about it," he said, and headed for the window. She pulled him back. "Michael, promise me."

"Nicole, I think your obsession with grades is a problem."

"Say you'll do it."

"This is bad enough, but now you're asking me to compromise professional ethics and downgrade another kid so you can get an award."

"It's not just the award."

"That's what bothers me. See you Monday and get that paper in." He pulled his arm free and slipped out the window.

In a moment, he was climbing down the drainpipe as he had done before.

"Fuck your professional ethics," she whispered. "And fuck you, Mr. Kaminsky."

When he was out of sight, she looked back in the room—at the bookcase on the far wall. She walked to it and reached up to the second shelf and moved aside some books to reveal the small wireless video camera. She rewound it, pressed Play, and watched the whole scene from the moment Michael climbed through her window.

Then she looked at the photos on the wall. The shot of the Biology Club on a field trip. There was Amy Tran with the flat grinning face, the greasy black hair and chipped tooth, the stupid slitted eyes, the breathy simpering voice and ugly ching-chong accent that charmed the teachers who thought it wonderful how she took extra English courses and worked around the clock because she was a poor and underprivileged foreigner.

Nicole hissed to herself and gouged out Amy's eyes with a razor knife.

Nobody remembers seconds.

15

"Hey, look at the tiger," Dylan hooted.

On the far side of a small water hole was a long-legged cat pacing back and forth, his eyes fixed someplace in the far distance.

"That's not a tiger, it's a cheetah," declared Lucinda, pointing to the sign in front of Dylan.

A couple of the kids giggled at Dylan's mistake.

"C-H-E-E-T-A-H," Lucinda said. "Can't you read?"

"I can read," Dylan said weakly.

"No you can't," Lucinda said. "You can't read anything."

"Besides, tigers have stripes," said Lucinda's friend Courtney.

Lucinda shook her head at him in disgust. "You must be taking stupid pills."

Sheila and Rachel were maybe ten feet behind them, but Rachel heard the comment and instantly saw red. From the look on Dylan's face, he was clearly wounded. Rachel's body lurched, but she caught herself, exerting every fiber of self-control not to fly at Lucinda and smash her fat little self-satisfied face.

"Lucinda!" Sheila cried and grabbed her daughter by the arm. "I don't want to hear that kind of talk from you ever!"

she growled, wagging her finger in her face. "Do you understand me, young lady? Do you? DO YOU?"

Lucinda's face froze in shock at her mother's reaction.

"You do not talk to other people that way," Sheila continued. "I want you to apologize to Dylan right now." Sheila steered her toward him.

Rachel half-expected Lucinda to begin crying at the humiliation, but instead she turned her face to Dylan. "Sorreee," she sang out.

Dylan shrugged. "That's okay."

But Sheila wouldn't let go. She had taken Lucinda's arm and pulled her aside. "Say it like you mean it," she snapped.

"That's fine," Rachel said, wanting to stop her from dragging out the incident.

But Sheila persisted. "Say it *properly*."

"I'm sorry," Lucinda said in a flat voice.

Sheila started to insist her daughter affect a tone of remorse, when Rachel cut her off. "We accept your apology, right?" she asked Dylan.

"Sure," he muttered. He was beginning to squirm from the attention. He also wanted to get back to the others enjoying the cheetah. Then in all innocence he added: "I *am* stupid."

"No you're not," Rachel said. "You're *not* . . . Don't even use that word."

He and Lucinda moved to the group of kids.

"I'm really sorry about that," Sheila said. "Really. That was uncalled for."

Rachel nodded and looked away, wishing that Sheila would drop the subject. Her overreaction was making it worse—as if Lucinda had called a paraplegic a "crip." Because he was young, Dylan would repair. But on a subconscious level he must have absorbed something of the message. How many times must you be told you're a dummy before you internalize it?

The rest of the morning passed without other incidents.

Later, on the bus, Rachel could hear Lucinda challenge the other kids to an impromptu spelling bee, then an arithmetic contest—mostly who could add or subtract numbers in their heads. She was clearly the Dells power kid, always pontificating, always needing to show how clever she was, how much more she knew than the others. And even though most kids were too young to rank each other, Lucinda had already established the mind-set that Dylan was at the bottom of the hierarchy: the one to pick on—the class dope.

Throughout the ride, Rachel tried to keep up conversation with Sheila, but her mind was aswirl with emotion. By the time the bus arrived back at the Dells, she had put away the anger, resentment, and envy, leaving her with an overwhelming sense of sadness not unlike grief.

When she got home, Rachel found a voice message from Martin saying he would be getting home late that night and would have dinner in town. So she dropped Dylan off with her sitter who was free and headed to an afternoon exercise class at Kingsbury Club just outside of Hawthorne. It would feel good to throw herself into some mindless techno-music aerobics just to work off the stress.

The place, a large structure tastefully designed and nestled between an open field and conservation area, was a full-service fitness center with tennis courts, full-length pool, a workout gym with all the latest in exercise equipment. Shortly after she had joined, she convinced Sheila to do the same.

The parking lot was more than half-full at that time of day. When she did not spot Sheila's green Jaguar, she felt relieved. She didn't want to see her. She didn't want to talk to her.

Her aerobics class had about twenty women, some of whom she was friendly with. But she did not feel friendly this afternoon, so she skipped the two o'clock class and headed for the treadmills.

About fifteen minutes into her workout, Rachel spotted Sheila through the windows to the lobby. Before Rachel could duck out of view, Sheila waved at her. In a few minutes Sheila showed up wearing a black warm-up suit with white stripes.

"Mind if I join you?" she asked, getting on the adjacent machine.

"I'm only on for another ten minutes," Rachel said.

"That's fine. I'm here for a quick hit. I've got a place to show at three."

Rachel clicked up her speed a couple of tenths until she was at a full power walk. Meanwhile, Sheila got herself into a stiff gait. They kept that up silently for several minutes until Rachel dropped her speed to cool off and coast to a finish. Sheila did the same.

"Sorry about this morning," Sheila said, after catching her breath.

"No problem." Rachel got off the machine and mopped her face. She guzzled down some water from her bottle and started to head for the free weights, hoping Sheila would stay on her machine. But she got off, not having even worked up the slightest sweat. A quick hit that was hardly worth the effort.

They were in the main fitness room, a large chamber with nobody within earshot of them. So, on an impulse, Rachel announced, "I'm thinking of taking Dylan out of DellKids."

"God, I hope not because of what happened."

"No. It's not Lucinda's fault. We're going to look for a more appropriate place for him. There's a group in Bolton, and I hear the woman's got an opening."

Sheila nodded. "Have you spoken to Miss Jean?"

"No, but I will. And it's not her fault, either. She's been great with him. All of the DellKids staffers have." Rachel expected Sheila to go on to deny the obvious, to be a good friend and conjure up all sorts of rationalizations and consolations.

But instead she nodded. "Lots of kids have learning disabilities."

"I'm also thinking of finding a private school for him. I'm not sure Marsden Elementary has the best resources, especially with the budget cut. He's going to need a more nurturing place with better special ed teachers."

Sheila's mood shifted slightly. Her cheery interest had faded into more serious speculation. "There are many good special schools," Sheila said. "Chapman in Spring River is supposed to be excellent. There's also the Taylor-Blessington in Wilton. Of course, there are several boarding schools out of state, if you want to go that route," Sheila continued.

Suddenly Rachel wanted to end the conversation, and not just because the topic pained her. Something in Sheila's interest struck her as suspicious. Maybe it was just raw envy, but Rachel resented Sheila's solicitousness. She resented how Sheila could stand there smug in the certitude that her little brat had a lifetime ticket to ride while recommending for Dylan schools for intellectually handicapped kids. Besides, how the hell did she know so many special schools? "Can we change the topic, please?"

Sheila put her hand on Rachel's. For a long moment she locked eyes with Rachel until she began to feel uncomfortable. "It really bothers you," Sheila said, her face glowing with sincerity.

"What does?"

"His . . . disability."

Rachel was nonplussed by Sheila's obtuseness. *Of course it bothers me. How in hell could it not bother me?* "Sheila, why are you asking me this?"

"Because we're friends, because you're like me—the kind of mother who would do anything for your kid, right? Anything to make life better for them."

Rachel did not know how to respond. She could not tell

if Sheila was eliciting a genuine answer or just talking. "I'm sorry, but I don't know what you're getting at."

"Now you're getting edgy."

"Yes, I'm getting edgy. I appreciate your concern, but I just don't want to talk about it anymore. It's a private matter. You can understand that."

Sheila nodded. "What if I told you there may be something you could do for him?"

The intensity on Sheila's face held Rachel's attention. "Like what?"

"Something I heard about that you might want to look into, that's all."

"I'm listening."

"You once told me that Dylan was born pigeon-toed."

"What does that have to do with anything?"

"Well, you took corrective measures, right?"

"Yeah."

"Well . . . ?"

"Well *what*?"

"Well, you had the problem fixed, right?"

"So?"

Sheila leaned forward and lowered her voice to a conspiratorial whisper. "Well, I heard about a special procedure that's . . . *corrective*."

The word hovered between them like a dark bird. For a second Rachel felt as if the room had shifted. "But that was medical."

"I'm talking about one that, well . . . that *does* work."

"Works *how*?"

Sheila tapped the side of her head. "Improves a child's cognitive functions—you know, memory, language, logic . . . intelligence."

Intelligence. Rachel couldn't tell if Sheila was being vague on purpose or if she didn't know what she was talking about. "I'm listening."

"Well, they've got special procedures for children with learning disabilities and brain dysfunctions."

"Nobody said my son has a brain dysfunction."

"Of course not, but . . . Look, I'm no specialist. They can explain it better."

"Who's *they*?"

"The people in charge. Doctors."

Sheila was being irritatingly coy.

"Look, if we can get our kids' teeth and noses and boobs fixed, why not their IQs?"

Rachel looked at her in disbelief. "Sheila, how can they do that? And what's the name of the group? Who are they?"

Suddenly Sheila's face flushed as if she had gone too far. "Look, let me get you some names and numbers then you can go from there."

"But how come I haven't heard about them?"

"You're the new kid on the block. What can I say?"

For fifteen years Sheila had been working at New Century Realtors, the hottest franchise in the area. As office manager she was the undeclared mayor of Hawthorne. She knew everybody and their business. She was probably referring to one of those specialized instructional approaches that promised to raise your kid's test results by a couple points, like those SAT prep courses.

Sheila glanced at her watch. "Oops. Gotta run."

Before Rachel knew it, Sheila grabbed her water bottle and towel and gave Rachel an air kiss. "I'll check for you and get back. See you at the game Saturday. Thorndyke Field at ten." She meant the weekly soccer games for the town kids.

Rachel watched Sheila hustle across the room. She had a place to show across town in half an hour, surely not enough time to shower and change. In fact, she wasn't even sweaty. So why did she even bother to work out?

It was another fitful night for Rachel. She woke up several times in a cold sweat, her heart racing and mind tormented by the thought that she had traded her son's brain for good sex.

At one point she almost shook Martin awake and told him everything. But that would only have made things worse. No, this was her doing, and the punishment was hers to suffer alone. Besides, Martin would never forgive her. Never. And she could not blame him.

Sometime in the middle of the night, she decided she would call Dr. Stanley Chu in the morning. According to the *Newsweek* piece, he was the man who had headed up the research on TNT mutagenics. Maybe he could help. Maybe if he knew the nature of the damage he could figure out a treatment—some *corrective* measure, to use Sheila's word.

By the time she got out of bed the next morning, the man had become an obsession. She waited until Martin took Dylan to day care. Then about nine-thirty she called information and got the main number of Yale School of Medicine, which gave her the extension of Dr. Stanley Chu. Trembling as if there were a shaft of ice at the core of her body, she dialed. A woman answered. "Neurology."

"Yes, Dr. Stanley Chu, please."

"Who may I ask is calling?"

For some reason Rachel could not get herself to announce her name. "I—I'm calling about his study on birth defects."

"Yes."

"Well, I'd like to talk to him about it, please . . . to make an appointment if that's possible."

"I'm sorry but Dr. Chu is out of town today and won't be back until the end of the week. Is there something I can help you with?"

"No, I'd like to speak directly with him. I can come to his office when he's free."

"What is your name, please?"

Now she couldn't go back or she might be dismissed. "Rachel Whitman."

"Ms. Whitman, Dr. Chu is very busy. So if you could please give me some idea what your interest is—if you're a student, or a researcher, or a pharmaceutical rep . . ."

Before Rachel could think, she said, "I took LSD laced with TNT some years ago, and I'm concerned my child has been . . . affected."

"I see." There was a long pause. "He's free next Wednesday at one," she said, then gave directions to the office in New Haven.

When she hung up, Rachel's eye fell on the baby picture of Dylan on the fireplace mantel. He was sitting in the bathtub covered with big puffs of bubblebath and laughing happily. He looked gorgeous.

According to the report on Chu's study, two-thirds of the TNT women studied had given birth to children with birth defects, and half of those suffered damage to the brains.

Not my baby.
Please, dear God . . .

When Rachel got off the phone, there was a message from Sheila to meet her at the Dells. She had some "important information" for her. So she drove to the club and went in the side entrance, which took her through the lounge.

Because it was a little after ten, the room was empty. But as she passed through, she spotted Brendan LaMotte behind the large mahogany bar with a buffing cloth. But instead of polishing glasses, he appeared to be slouched low with his back to her. As she walked by, she caught him unawares, sniffing from an open bottle of liquor. Startled, he capped the bottle and pretended to be wiping it clean and lining it on the shelves.

Rachel did not want to make a scene, so she continued through the lounge with no more than a chirpy "hello" which was her cue that being underage, he would be fired if caught.

Sheila was waiting for her at a table. A waitress came over and took their orders and left.

"Here you go," Sheila said and pulled out one of her business cards. On the back she had written: "Nova Children's Center."

Also, a telephone number and address: "452 Franklin Avenue, Myrtle." That was a town between Hawthorne and Gloucester.

"So, what is the place?"

"A complete child-care center with therapists, child psychologists, pediatricians, development experts, neurologists, whatever. The whole shebang for kids."

"You mean a clinic?"

"Well, kind of. But it's *very* unique."

"I've never heard of them." But then again she had only lived in the area for six months. "So, what makes them so unique?"

Rachel lowered her voice. "Well, what I know is that they can help children with learning disorders and, you know, neurological problems, brain dysfunctions. Stuff like that. Some kind of *enhancement* procedures."

"Enhancement procedures?"

"Yeah, for kids with memory and information-processing problems. Whatever."

Sheila was being vague again, probably not to offend Rachel with the suggestion that Dylan had a neurological disorder. "You said something about corrective procedures."

"That's what I'm telling you. I've heard they can, you know . . . raise a kid's IQ—maybe even double it."

"Double it! That's not possible."

Sheila rolled her eyes in frustration. "Look, sweetie, I don't know the ins and outs, so I don't want to mislead and all. But they've got all kinds of programs, procedures, and stuff—I'm not sure of the details—but what I do know is that they're very exclusive, if you know what I mean. Like they don't take just anybody, and they're *très* expensive.

But you got their number, so why don't you just call them and make an appointment and bring in all your questions, okay?"

"How do you know so much about them?"

"Because this is a small town and I've lived here for twenty years is how come. Look, give them a call, they're supposed to be the best, and they're in your own backyard. If Dylan's got a problem, he can be fixed."

"Whom do I ask for?"

Sheila lowered her voice to a near whisper. "Lucius Malenko."

"Who?"

Sheila wrote the name on the card. "He's one of the directors. You're going to want to talk to him eventually, but first you'll have to bring Dylan in to be tested so they can see what his problems are. So, call and make an appointment. You can't lose."

Rachel thanked her and stared at the name. Lucius Malenko.

"If Dylan's got a problem, he can be fixed."

16

It was a little before noon when Greg showed up at the Essex Medical Center. He would have put it off until the evening, but Nurse Cynthia Porter and the others were working the ER day shift. Instead of reporting to Lieutenant Gelford where he was heading, Greg slipped out of the barracks and headed north.

He met Nurse Porter in a small conference room in the ER complex. With her was a radiologist, introduced as Dr. Adrian Budd, and a resident physician, Dr. Paul Doria. They were there at Nurse Porter's request.

Greg sat down opposite them and removed from his briefcase the photographs of the skulls, including the computer schematics with the holes marked. "There's a pattern of evidence that may shed light on what happened to these kids," he said, and he described the circumstances surrounding each of the remains.

While Greg spoke, Dr. Budd and Nurse Porter listened with interest. But Dr. Doria, a mutt-faced man with a goatee, nodded impatiently in time with his "Yeah, yeah, yeah." That annoyed Greg. When he finished, Doria glanced at his watch. "I wish we could help, but we can't."

"Why not?"

"Patient confidentiality," Doria said curtly. "We can't release the patient's name or discuss his condition." He made a move to get up.

Greg looked at Cindy. "On the telephone, you said you would be able to show me the X rays so we could make comparisons."

"I know, but then I checked with my supervisor, and we can't do that." She made a woeful expression. "I'm really sorry, Officer. I just found out, or I would have saved you the trip."

Greg looked at them, thinking of his two-hour drive and what Gelford would say if he found out that Greg had come up here and returned empty-handed.

Doria took a step from the table toward the door. "The only way we could release them is through a court order or a subpoena. Sorry."

Budd began to inch his chair back from the table also.

"Well, then, what can you tell me?"

"Just that the patient had scars on his head that looked similar to those in the newspaper," Nurse Porter said.

"Any idea where they came from?"

"No."

"Did you ask him?"

"Yes, but he didn't know."

"How could he not know?"

Her face clouded over since Greg wasn't going to let go. "Well, I don't know," she said reluctantly. "Unless it was some kind of procedure he had at a young age."

"Have you ever seen scars like those before?"

Porter glanced at the others. "Well, not really."

"They were very unusual," Budd added, and Doria shot him a hard look.

"Can you at least tell me how old he was?" Greg asked.

Cindy looked at Doria who made a half-nod to end the discussion. "Eighteen."

Greg conspicuously wrote down on his pad: "Male—eighteen."

"White?"

"Mmm."

"And what did he come into the ER for?"

"Excuse me, Officer," Doria cut in. "But we can't do this."

"Do what?"

"Try to get around protocol by playing twenty questions. I mean, if you had a crime and a court order, that would be different. But you don't, and we're not at liberty to discuss the case. Patients have their rights."

The others nodded.

"Then can you tell me what kind of medical procedure these holes might have come from?" He spread out the skull photos and moved them closer to them.

"I don't think we can continue," Doria announced, backing away.

"Why not?"

"Because you're indirectly asking us to disclose a patient's condition by having us diagnose these remains. And we can't do that."

"But you may help solve a crime."

"What's to say those holes had anything to do with a crime?" Doria asked.

"Because nobody knows what they were for. So I'm suspicious."

"Well, if you think there's a connection," Doria said, "then get a subpoena."

That was a legitimate option, but it could take days, even weeks. And that would alert Lieutenant Gelford, who would go ballistic to know Greg was still pursuing this. There was another option.

Greg stood up so he was eye to eye with Doria. "You worked on this patient, correct?"

"You know that."

"And you were aware that this eighteen-year-old had scars on his head that he himself was not aware of, correct?"

"So?"

Greg picked up the photocopy of the newspaper article on the mystery skull and held it to Doria's face. "This is child abuse as far as it can go—kidnapping and murder."

"What's your point, Officer?" Doria asked.

"My point is that in the state of Massachusetts, as doctors and nurses you are mandated reporters of child abuse. By penalty of law, it is incumbent upon you to report directly to the DSS any suspicions you have that a minor has been wrongfully injured. Failing to do so can result in your arrest and incarceration."

"But we had no such suspicions," Doria protested. "The kid had old scars."

"But you said the kid didn't know he had them."

Doria's face turned red. "Many adults walking the streets have scars from appendectomies, but they didn't get them from abuse as children."

"You've treated a patient with very unusual scars in his head similar to those of a murdered child. Did you notify the DSS?"

Doria looked at Dr. Budd who both looked at Nurse Porter. Sheepishly, Porter said, "Well, I called you."

"That's not what I asked you," Greg said. "Did you file a report with the DSS as mandated by law?"

"No."

"Wait a minute," Doria said. "Are you threatening us, Officer?"

"No, I'm offering you an option to jail."

"I don't believe this," Doria said.

"Believe it."

"So what are we supposed to do?" Nurse Porter asked. She looked scared.

"Show me the X rays."

"And if we don't?" Doria asked defiantly.

"Then I will file a complaint with the attorney general's office, and you'll be arrested."

Doria gave Greg a scathing look. "Give me a break."

"I am."

There was a moment of prickly silence. Then Dr. Budd said, "I have no problems with your seeing the films."

"Me, neither," Nurse Porter said.

Doria glowered at Greg like an angry schnauzer. "This is coercion, Officer, and you know it," he said. "You can see them, but I'm drawing the line on revealing the patient's name."

"Fair enough."

Doria left, and returned a few minutes later with a large envelope containing duplicates he had made without the patient's name or ID number on them. He handed them to the radiologist.

Budd pulled out the X rays and slid them onto the light board. He studied them for a moment, then with a pen he pointed to faint impressions on the top and side images. "These are the holes. There's a cluster of eight here above the left ear each about a millimeter and a half in diameter—and ten more above the eyebrow, just behind the hairline—here."

The holes appeared on the images as white dots on the left profile, and tiny transect lines in the top views. "Can you tell how they were made?"

"Since they're so sharply incised, my guess is a cranial drill," Budd said.

"As the result of some medical operation or procedure?"

"Yes."

The holes appeared to be clustered almost identically to those on the Sagamore and Dixon boys' skulls.

"The ones in front I noticed while working on him," said Cindy Porter. "But I didn't know about the others until I saw the films."

Budd continued. "What's even odder are the three holes just behind the temple about where the left ear begins." He tapped them out with the pen.

Not wanting to influence their interpretations, Greg held

back on Joe Steiner's speculations. "What do you make of them?"

"Well, I'm not really sure," said Budd.

"Have you ever seen clusters of holes like these before?"

"No," Budd said. "It's possible he'd been treated for multiple tumors."

"Except that the surgeon wouldn't have to make so many holes," Doria added.

Greg could see that he was warming up again. The threat of jail does that. "Why not?" Greg asked.

"Well, if you're going to drill so many holes—whatever the reason—it's a lot easier to pull back the skin first, then drill." He put his fingers to his forehead and rotated the flesh. "The scalp moves around easily. It makes more sense to do a line incision and push the skin back, then close the incision after boring."

"So you're saying that this is an unusual technique."

"Very," Doria said. "Why go to this length to make all these little incisions when it's easier to make a clean slice?"

"Unless he wanted to hide them," Cindy suggested.

"Why hide them?" Greg asked.

"Maybe the surgeon was trying to avoid leaving a long Frankenstein scar," said Budd.

"Couldn't he have made it behind the hairline?"

"Sure, but then the kid grows up and starts losing his hair, and there it is."

Greg turned to Nurse Porter. "You said he didn't know he had them."

"Yeah, he looked genuinely surprised when I pointed them out. In fact, he looked in the mirror like he was seeing them for the first time."

"Which makes sense, since they were flush to the scalp," Doria added. "Through the hair, he wouldn't be able to feel them with his fingers. And he'd never notice them unless he shaved his head."

"Why was he brought into the ER?"

"He slipped and banged his head against a glass door."

"And you took the X rays to see if he had a concussion."

"Yes," Nurse Porter said.

Greg jotted down what they were saying. "Does his medical file have any record of his having a brain operation?"

"No. In fact, the only entry for him is for a sprained ankle four years ago. He apparently slipped on ice. But that's it."

"You still haven't said what kind of brain operation this could be."

Doria took the question. "Because I'm not sure. Holes are made through the skull either to take something out of the brain or to put something in. If it was to remove something, then we're talking needle biopsies or the removal of tumors, lesions, or blood clots. But I have never heard of needing twenty-one holes for any of those procedures. Even if the patient had multiple tumors, I would think that the surgeon would have removed segments of the skull instead of making multiple holes over so large an area. And frankly, tumor masses that large would probably be fatal."

He was right about the size, since the holes covered an area constituting most of the side of the head.

"The other possibility is putting something into the brain. He could have had interstitial radiation therapy—the insertion of radioactive pellets into tumor tissue. What bothers me is that radiation therapy is local. It's not commonly used for widely spread or multiple tumors. Another thing, if he doesn't remember, he must have been very young. And multiple radiation implants in a child are almost never heard of, because a child's brain is very susceptible to radiation."

"So, what are you saying?" Greg asked them.

All three of them shook their heads. "I don't know what they did to him," Doria said.

17

From the inside of her closet, Brendan watched Nicole DaFoe undress.

It was Friday night, and she was home for the weekend again. As usual, her father had picked her up at school. Brendan knew the patterns of her movements. He had watched her ever since that day at the club swimming pool. She had been wearing a rather revealing white bikini of which her mother did not approve because when she arrived and found Nicole sunning herself in a lounge chair, she spoke sharply to Nicole who snapped back then grabbed her towel and huffed away. Nicole was something of an exhibitionist. And her mother was very proper.

But to Brendan's mind Mother DaFoe had no need to worry that her daughter was wanton, since she lacked the arousing fantasies and sexual urges of a true flasher. She had been genetically blessed with physical beauty and the instinct on how best to employ her baby-doll appeal for maximum gain. But she was like a polar cap—all light and no heat. Yet when she needed something, she could affect the turn-on, and the boys swarmed around her like heat-seeking missiles. And as long as the flesh was warm, they'd put up with anything, even a frozen core.

Ironically, it was the ice that drew Brendan.

When her parents drove off and Nicole went to the basement to do laundry, he slipped in through the back door and headed up to her bedroom, where he had waited for two hours until she had finished watching some medical video downstairs and came up.

But while crouched in her closet, he discovered a lockbox stashed behind some storage bins of clothes. The box was not an expensive thing, so it was easy to jimmy open with a penknife. With a pocket flash he inspected the contents.

At first glance it looked like a hodgepodge of things. But he went through them closely: two inexpensive men's watches; a curled-up leather belt; a Swiss Army knife; two smaller pocketknives; a leather Pierre Cardin wallet which still had some cash, two ID bracelets with different male names on them; a fancy pen; a Bloomfield football high school ring; and a man's gold wedding ring. They were all male effects. But, oddly, no photos or love notes or things that looked like gifts. On the contrary, they looked like collectibles. Probably from all the boys she had bedded. Things she had probably taken to commemorate her little conquests. Trophies.

When Nicole returned, she didn't go straight to bed. Instead, she stripped down to her panties and bra, then got down on the floor to do stretching exercises—probably one of her ballet routines. For nearly twenty minutes he watched her do sit-ups, push-ups, then an elaborate set of revealing stretches, at one point lying on her back and moving her hips up and down as if having sex with an invisible lover. Watching her like this, any other normal boy would have exploded on the spot. But Brendan just watched— feeling nothing. No, he was not gay. He was not anything.

Just dead.

When she finished, she pulled off her top and headed into the adjoining bathroom. He could not see her from his angle, but he heard the rush of water as she took a shower. He thought about taking a peek, but the glass door steamed up. Besides, she might catch him, which would be disastrous. So he remained in the closet peering through the black crack.

When she came out, she had one towel wrapped around her head, another around her body, so he could see nothing. She sat on her bed and removed the towel. Her breasts were like pink-tipped pears. He had never touched a girl and wondered what it would be like. Until Nicole, he had never seen one naked in the flesh.

She stood up and toweled her behind, then turned toward him and for a moment he saw her point-blank naked. But then she slipped into panties and a camisole top. A moment later she flicked off the light and got into bed.

He waited until he was certain she was asleep, then crept across the floor, guided by the glow light of her aquarium. The creak of the floorboards caused her to stir, but she did not wake up.

When he reached her bed he froze. Fortunately, she was sleeping on her right side. Fortunately, also, it was a warm night, so only a single blanket covered her.

He had to be swift. He reached into his pocket, and in a clean move he pulled back the covers and clicked on a penlight.

Nicole's eyes snapped open.

The next moment she yelped and jerked away. Before he knew it, she leapt off the bed and pulled a field hockey stick from wall mounts. Without a sound, she took a huge swipe at him.

He jumped back just in time. "*No,* please, d-d-don't," he cried. "I'm not going to h-h-hurt you. Really."

But she came at him and swung again. He reflexed again, but this time he stumbled backward over a stuffed animal and came down on his backside, his head slamming on the edge of the closet door. As he lay there, she came at him with the stick raised high.

"P-p-please, don't. My head."

"I know you. You're Brendan LaMotte," she gasped.

"Please don't h-h-hit me, okay? Just don't h-hit me."

Nicole backed up to her portable phone and picked it up. "You've been following me, you creep. At the club and the diner. You're stalking me."

"*No*. Please don't call the police. I b-beg you." He dabbed his sleeve on his forehead.

"Then tell me what the hell you are doing here or I'll call them."

"I will, I will, but please don't." He checked his hand. He was bleeding from the scalp. "Can I have a t-tissue?"

"No." She tossed the phone down and raised the stick like an executioner's sword. "Talk or I'll bash your brains in."

"You have a t-t-tattoo on your hip."

Instantly her face shifted, and her hands flinched. But she said nothing.

"I saw it once real fast when you were at the pool. You were wearing a t-two-piece white bikini, and you were on the lounge chair reading a copy of *Vogue,* with a picture of M-Meg Ryan on the cover—she was wearing red—so it must have been the May issue because June had Charlize Theron in white chiffon." He caught himself because his mind was beginning to flood with useless details that he could recite endlessly. He knew all the magazine covers because people left them at the pool all the time.

"How did you see it?"

"I c-c-can't swim, so I don't go up to the p-p-pool. Binoculars. I s-saw you through binoculars."

"You mean you broke into my bedroom to see my tattoo?"

He nodded. "Ummm."

"I don't believe this."

"It's important. Very important. Can I p-please get up? My head's bleeding." The second time in a week, he thought.

He started to pull himself up, when she whacked him in the leg. "What do you mean, it's important?"

Blood now trickled down the side of his head. He blotted it with his sleeve then reached into his pants pocket.

"Don't you dare," she said and raised the stick.

"No, don't." When she didn't strike, he said, "I just want to show you something. Please."

"How do I know you haven't got a weapon?"

"Because I d-don't." He slipped his hand into his pants pocket and pulled out a sheet of paper and unfolded it, revealing the blue cartoon. "It's Mr. Nisha," he said.

Nicole glanced at it, and for a second her face seemed to have turned into a plaster mask. As the image began to sink in, little expressions flickered across it like eddies of electricity. "Where did you get that?"

"You remember," he whispered.

She lowered the stick.

"Please, can I get up?"

She did not respond but took the drawing to the table beside her bed and turned on the lamp. While she studied the image, Brendan's eye fell on a photograph tacked to the wall—Nicole and a bunch of other kids on a field trip. The eyes of the Asian girl at the end had been poked out.

While Nicole continued to study the drawing, Brendan noticed a video camera sitting on the desk. Beside it was a cassette. Without thought, he picked it up, but she snatched it out of his hands and threw it into the desk drawer.

Then Nicole turned the light toward herself and pulled down one corner of her panties. On her left flank was the same serene blue elephant with the big floppy ears, fat snaky trunk, and fingered human hands. And on its head some kind of crown. It was nearly identical.

"W-w-where . . . ?"

"Hampton Beach," she said.

"B-but how did . . . ?"

"I wanted a tattoo, and when I saw an elephant sample, I knew that's what I wanted. But all he had was stupid pink elephants or that freaky demon-beast shit for bikers. I made him draw it on paper until he had it right."

"But why did you have it done?"

"Because I wanted a tattoo is why."

"But where did you get the image from?"

"Why's it so important to you?"

"Because I've been seeing this image for years in my brain. It's like a ghost of something, but I couldn't put it together. Until now. I th-think we're connected somehow through that image."

She did not respond.

"Does 'M-M-Mr. Nisha' mean anything to you?"

"Mr. who?"

"Nisha. M-Mr. Nisha. Or 'dance with Mr. Nisha'?"

Before she could respond, the sound of a car pulling into the driveway cut the air. "Shit! My parents! You gotta get out of here." He started for her closet, but she stopped him. "They saw my light on, so they'll be in. The window."

"We have to t-talk more."

"What for? I'm going back to school, then camp."

"But we have to."

"Go!"

Brendan was overweight and unathletic, so the prospect of climbing down was not appealing.

She pushed him toward the window and opened the screen just enough for him to climb out onto the porch roof. She pointed to the corner. "The drainpipe," she said, and shoved him through. "GO!"

He climbed out and steadied himself on the roof. He could hear the garage door close in the front of the house, leaving the night dark and still for his escape. From the roof, it was maybe a ten-foot drop to the ground, and little footholds attached to the corner column along the drainpipe made the descent easy. It was the path most taken.

As he eased his way down, he wondered about Nicole's other midnight visitors and wished that for one moment he could feel what they had come for. Just one little burst of spring fires. He would die for that.

18

The ride to Connecticut took about three and a half hours. After breakfast, Rachel bundled Dylan in the car and drove him to day care, leaving Miss Jean her cellphone number. Then she headed south on Route 95 to New Haven and the Yale University School of Medicine where she had a one o'clock appointment with Stanley Chu.

She listened to the radio to distract her mind. But she snapped it off after the news story about a controversial case of a mentally deficient man on death row in Texas. He could barely read and write and had flunked the seventh grade twice. He did menial work such as cutting grass. And last night, at thirty-three, after spending twelve years on death row for the rape and murder of a twenty-four-year-old woman, he had been executed.

She arrived at the medical school on time. A directory inside the main entrance led her to the Department of Neurology.

Dr. Stanley Chu, a slight man of about sixty with thinning hair and glasses, spoke with a faint accent. Rachel took a seat across from his desk. A folder containing Dylan's medical records sat open before him. She had overnighted the package last week.

Dr. Chu seemed a little put off by her visit and got right

to business. "I looked at your son's medical history, the test results, and the scans. As you know, there's some dysfunction of the left temporal lobe." From a folder he pulled out some of the films and slipped them onto the display board. "Dylan's brain is on the left, the one on the right is a child about the same age but with normal brain anatomy." He used a ballpoint pen to point out the shadowy shapes. "As you can see, the gyri of Dylan's brain—that is, the folds—are smaller and the sulci—the spaces in between—are larger. Usually, they are packed closer together as you can see in this normal scan.

"What this means," he continued, "is that the gyri of Dylan's brain are not developed normally, that he has experienced some cell loss here—maybe as much as twenty-five percent in this area."

"Oh, God," she whimpered.

"But I'm afraid the real problem is in the thalamus down here," he continued. "You can't see that as well from the scan because the structures are subtle. But there are some malformations of the thalamus, and we know this because one of the telltale marks of such malformation is the abnormal formation of the gyri up here."

"What's the thalamus do?"

"Well, the thalamus is a complicated area very deep in the brain," he explained. "It controls all parts of the brain affecting speech and motor functions, emotions, and sensory functions—so many aspects of our makeup. These kinds of structural deficiencies are commonly seen in individuals with language-processing problems such as Dylan's."

Rachel felt her soul slump. A silence filled the room as the doctor waited for her to respond.

Finally Rachel asked, "Is this consistent with the damage of the people you studied?"

"Do you mean did your use of TNT bring this on?"

"Yes."

The doctor took off his glasses and stared at her. "Mrs.

Whitman, why do you need to know this?" It was the same question that Dr. Rose had asked.

She shook her head, but said nothing for fear of breaking down.

"There's no way to know that. Some of the women who had taken TNT gave birth to perfectly normal children. All I can say is that it's statistically more probable that you suffered some reproductive cell damage which was passed on to your son."

"Is there anything that can be done?"

"Done?" He seemed unclear about the question. "Well, as I said there are medications that can help him focus better . . ."

"How about surgically?"

"To what end?"

"To reduce his problems," she said. "To increase his learning capabilities."

The doctor's eyebrows twitched slightly. "Not that I know of."

Rachel nodded. "I guess it was a dumb question, but I'm feeling very guilty and desperate."

"I understand, but I'm afraid, for all practical purposes, Dylan's brain has already wired itself as much as it is going to. As I said, there's a structural deformity that cannot be corrected because circuitry is missing. And it can't be manufactured. It's like wanting to regenerate an amputated finger. It can't be done."

Rachel looked at him and her eyes puddled. "So there's nothing that can be done? No new experimental procedures to help stimulate growth and regeneration of whatever . . . neurons?"

Dr. Chu shook his head. "Not that I know of." He then glanced at the wall clock.

"So he's going to be impaired for the rest of his life?"

He paused for a second, as if carefully measuring his words. "Without taking a functional MRI, all I can say is that the visible malformations are consistent with those found in individuals with language problems. This does not mean that special learning programs won't help his development—"

Her voice straining, Rachel cut him off: "I did this to him."

"Pardon me?"

"Because of me, he's going to go through the rest of his life mentally handicapped." The tears were flowing freely now, and she pressed a wad of tissues to her face.

"You don't know that."

"But I took the stuff. I did that to him."

"But nothing's conclusive. It's entirely possible that it's an hereditary expression or some other cause."

Rachel just shook her head.

"Mrs. Whitman, my suggestion is that you accept what has happened and go on from here. And, if I may, avoid the pitfall of so many of today's parents—namely the fixation on academic performance. Yes, it's understandable in our competitive culture, yet so much more goes into one's destiny in life, especially a child's emotional makeup and character. Unfortunately, too many people are stuck on a single notion of intelligence. In reality, intelligence is a multiplicity of human talents that go beyond basic verbal and mathematical performance. As someone once said, 'If the Aborigine drafted an IQ test, all of Western civilization would flunk it.' "

She nodded quietly, letting his words sink in.

He tapped the pile of papers that represented Dylan's test results. "IQ isn't the measure of a person. Believe me. I know many so-called geniuses who are failures as human beings."

"I realize that but, frankly, smarter people do better in life. You have to admit that."

Chu looked at her with a puzzled expression, perhaps wondering why they were having this conversation. "Mrs. Whitman, I admit that in some walks of life higher intellectual abilities may mean more opportunities. But a high

IQ is no guarantee of success, prestige, or especially, happiness in life."

She glanced around his office, at the photo of him and his wife and children posed in ski gear smiling gleefully with snow-capped peaks in the background. The Yale School of Medicine diploma on the wall. "You've done well." She wished she could retract the words the moment they hit the air.

"On paper, yes," Chu shot back. "But you don't know anything about my personal life or my psychological or emotional state. I could be miserable with my lot and contemplating suicide, though I'm neither."

"I'm sorry, please forgive me."

"Nothing to be sorry about. What you should do is spend less effort ranking your child and more trying to identify his natural gifts and competency. For all you know, Dylan may grow up to be an artist or musical genius, or someone gifted in social and interpersonal skills."

She nodded. "So you're saying that nothing can be done, I mean medically."

Dr. Chu looked at her quizzically, as if surprised that she had not processed his words. He took a breath and let it out slowly. "Your son's brain development is fixed. It cannot be structurally modified toward higher functionality. I'm sorry."

It was time to leave. She thanked the doctor and packed all of Dylan's medical records into her briefcase and left.

Outside the sky was overcast and it smelled like rain. Rachel walked to her car, feeling scooped out. In the distance lightning soundlessly flickered.

And her mind turned to Sheila MacPhearson as if she were some ministering angel.

19

It had been days since Travis Valentine had seen his mom, and he missed her. All he remembered was being down by the canal looking for butterflies, and then he woke up in this room with the TV cartoons going all the time and the animal paintings on the walls.

There was a tap at the door, then the turn of the lock, and a woman came in with a plate of cookies. She had said that her name was Vera. She also said she was a nurse and a friend of his mother's.

"Here you are," she said, putting the tray on the beanbag chair. "How you doin'?"

"When am I going home?" It was the same question he asked every time she delivered something.

"Soon," she said. "How do you like the books?"

On the floor there was a pile of picture books of butterflies. (Somebody must have told them about his hobby.) He already had three of them at home.

The woman picked one up and thumbed through it. "Very pretty. What's this one called?"

"A barred yellow swallowtail," he said, knowing she wasn't really interested.

"You're a smart little guy."

"Why did you bring me here?"

"Because you're special, that's why." Then she said, "I hear you have your own butterfly collection at home." She fanned through the book.

He said nothing. He did not like her face. It was pinchy and mean looking.

"Where's my mom?"

"She's home." Vera's mouth was small with thin lips that were very red. "And if you cooperate you can go home real soon."

Cooperate. That meant eat their food, swallow their medication, and take their tests. He didn't know what the tests were. But Vera had said that was the reason he was here: to take the tests. Then he could go home.

He looked at the cookies, but did not take one.

Vera got up. "Enjoy the cookies," she said and left using a key.

That was the only way out of the room—a key. And they didn't give him one.

He hated the room. There were no windows, the door had no handle and was always locked from the outside. The floor was padded with some plastic-covered foam. The furniture was also soft—beanbag chairs, air mattress on the floor, a plastic table, and a hanging plastic clothes organizer. There were five of everything—shirts, pants, pairs of socks. Five days' worth.

It was clearly a place for kids because of the stupid paintings on the wall and all the stuffed animals, the boxes of "nontoxic" Crayolas on the floor, and coloring books and paper. And there was nothing hard or sharp. No pencils or pens or metal or even wooden toys. Just soft puzzle pieces and rubber building blocks. And stuffed animals. Even the food was safe—sandwiches served on easily crumbled Styrofoam plates; and there were no forks or knives, not even the plastic kind. The only hard surface in the place besides the TV cover was the black plastic hemisphere on the ceiling.

Travis couldn't see the camera, but he knew there was

one inside because he had once asked his mom what those black bubbles were on the ceiling of the Target in Fenton on Florida Highway 75. Mom had said it's how the people in the back room make sure folks don't shoplift stuff.

There certainly was nothing worth stealing in here. But the folks in the back room were watching him—even when he went to the bathroom—which made him feel creepy. He hoped they went to sleep at night. That was another thing: The lights never went off, they just dimmed automatically at bedtime, which was when the TV went off.

In the corner was a toilet with a plastic blue curtain, but you could see through it. The TV was built into the wall and was covered with a hard Plexiglas front. It wasn't a real TV since all it showed were cartoons which he had seen dozens of times. And it was on whenever he was awake, so that the sound constantly filled the room. He couldn't hear the outside—no cars or planes. No sounds of other people.

He missed the canal. He missed the woods. He missed the sounds of birds. He missed his friends. But most of all, he missed Bo and his mom.

He didn't know where in the world he was, but he had a sense that he was far away. Really far.

He looked at the cookies which made him think of his mom and her cookies. And he began to cry. He didn't want to cry. He had done a lot of that for the last two days. Sleep, stare at the TV, and cry. But he couldn't help it.

So he lay on the mattress and cried a deep cry, hoping he would fall asleep and wake up at home.

20

The first thing Greg did on the morning after his visit to the Essex Medical Center was to multifax a memo to the medical examiner's offices throughout the state asking if anybody had seen any human remains with such a pattern of holes in the skulls as in the accompanying photos—holes that appeared to have been made by medical drills: "Any information may help in the investigation of two missing children, one of whom is a kidnap and possible murder victim." He left his name and number.

Nobody seemed to know what the holes were for, but every instinct in his being told him that there was some sort of plan—some sort of connection between the Essex case and the remains of the two kids.

When he was finished, his telephone rang. It was his supervisor, T. J. Gelford. He wanted him to come to his office. Something in the tone of Gelford's voice told him it was not a routine conference.

Greg went upstairs to the detective sergeant's office. Greg stiffened as he entered. Gelford was not alone. With him were Chief Norm Adler and the internal affairs officer, Rick Bolduk. They nodded when he came in, but nobody was smiling.

"Have a seat, Greg," Gelford said.

Greg felt his heart rate kick up.

"I'd like to know where you were yesterday afternoon."

Greg gauged their expressions as they waited for his answer. Their faces could have been hewn from Mount Rushmore. "I was on a case."

"Which case?"

Before he went off on a job for any length of time, he was supposed to report to his supervisor or at least leave word with the dispatcher, especially if the investigation took him out of town. But failure to report did not call for a tribunal. "I was on the North Shore."

"The North Shore? That's a hundred miles out of our jurisdiction. You were supposed to be working the high school break-in."

Some kids had broken through a rear window and trashed a room, maybe doing eight hundred dollars' worth of damage. It was not a Priority One crime. "That's not what this is all about."

"That's right," Gelford said and glanced at a piece of paper in front of him. "We got a call from a Dr. Paul Doria, an internist from the Essex Medical Center that you'd been up there mucking around about this skull case."

"I was investigating some leads."

"He said that you threatened him and two other ER staffers with arrest unless they showed you somebody's X rays. We contacted the other two, and they confirmed."

"Because they failed to report suspicions of child abuse."

"What suspicions of child abuse? The kid had some old scars in his head."

"That's right, and in the same places as the holes in the two skulls. I wanted to see if there's a connection."

"Is there?"

"I'm still working on it."

"No you're not, because you coerced three members of a medical staff to compromise a patient's right to privacy, and that's a violation of policy." He handed Greg a piece of paper.

Greg didn't have to read it to know it was a formal letter of reprimand.

"I sorry to say this, Greg, but you're being put on notice," Rick Bolduk said. "If you do anything else on this skull case, we will proceed with disciplinary action."

Greg stiffened. He knew what that meant. At best, they would take away his gold shield and bust him back to a foot officer chasing speeders. At worst, he could be suspended, maybe even terminated.

"Nobody wants to do this, Greg," Rick Bolduk added, "but you've stepped over the line and shown insubordination to your supervisor. Those are grounds for dismissal, but we're giving you a second chance. From this point on, you're off this case. Period."

Greg nodded.

"It's in the letter, but I'm putting you on night shift, seven to three," Norm Adler said.

Greg made a flat grin. "Great." Nothing happened on night shift in Sagamore except car accidents or drunks beating up their spouses. So what they'd give him to fill his time would be a bunch of petty larcenies and bum-check cases. His punishment was to further marginalize him. "Starting when?"

"Tomorrow."

Greg knew that it was useless to protest, only because they were right to do this. He had operated on hunches, none of which had panned out. And he wasn't doing his job in the town he was hired to protect.

"I apologize," he said, and got up to leave, taking the letter with him.

"Greg, I don't know how to say this without saying it, but maybe you should see a professional about this obsession you have for this skull case. I don't think it's healthy for you. I can give you some names."

He was saying that Greg was weird: that his pursuit of this case was pathological. That he could end up like Remington Bristow, the investigator in the Philadelphia medical examiner's office who spent thirty-six years doggedly investigating the 1957 "Boy in the Box" case, only to go to his grave without ever determining the identity of the murdered child found naked in a cardboard carton by the side of a country road—or his killer. That Greg should see a shrink.

Maybe they were right.

But it crossed Greg's mind that working nights freed up his days. He nodded his appreciation. "I'll be okay."

21

By eight-thirty on Saturday morning Thorndyke Field was a mob scene. The four adjacent soccer fields had been sectioned off with orange cones as eight teams all in different-colored uniforms practiced kicking maneuvers. Along the sidelines, parents and other spectators had gathered with orange wedges and coolers full of drinks.

The parking lot was nearly filled as Rachel and Martin arrived with Dylan. The boy looked positively adorable in his crisp white uniform and new blue soccer shoes and bright red sports bag over his shoulder, the contents of which consisted of three boxes of granola bars—enough for everybody on the team (his idea)—and his Curious George doll. At this age level the teams were designated only by their colors. This morning the Whites were playing the Reds.

As they approached their corner of the field, Rachel spotted Sheila. Lucinda was on the Reds. In Hawthorne, boys and girls competed on the same teams.

Dylan looked forward to these games, and he always arrived full of enthusiasm. This morning was no different. Dylan did not start, which was fine since there were so many kids on the team.

A few minutes into the game, somebody kicked the ball

point-blank into Lucinda's midsection, sending her to the sidelines whimpering. While Rachel took some shamed-faced satisfaction in that, Dylan went over to her and handed her his Curious George. It was clear from Lucinda's perfunctory dismissal of him that she did not comprehend the comforting gesture, or was just too grown-up to accept it. But Dylan's untainted compassion brought tears to Rachel's eyes. After a few seconds, Lucinda got up and joined her teammates, while Dylan returned to the sidelines.

After fifteen minutes or so, when the score was 3 to 2 in favor of the Reds, Dylan was sent onto the field.

Dylan was playing forward end. The kickoff went deep into the Reds' line. After some back and forth, the ball came to Dylan. He quickly positioned himself but kicked it the wrong way. A fast response from one of his teammates on defense sent it back toward the Reds. Dylan rushed into the fray and got the ball. Martin yelled and pointed toward the Reds' goalie, but again Dylan kicked it the opposite way.

Some of his teammates yelled at him, but Dylan ran after the ball and continued to run with it toward the Whites' goalie who tried to wave him back. But he was too lost in his footwork. And before anybody could stop him, Dylan toed the ball into the net.

The Reds jumped up and down and the Whites shouted protests.

The coach came out and put his hand on Dylan's shoulders and tried to explain to him that although he played the ball well, he had scored for the Reds. That he should run for the net with the Red goalie not the White goalie.

Dylan didn't seem to understand at first, but when he was taken out of the game, he began to cry. Out on the field, Lucinda was consulting with her coaches, looking like a World Cup champ discussing strategies. Meanwhile Dylan squatted behind the chalk line, crying in his hands. Rachel and Martin went over to console him. "There's nothing to cry about," Rachel said.

"I'm a dummy. Everybody says."

"No you're not. And don't say that."

Rachel looked at Martin. She could read his expression. Several times in the last few weeks Martin had practiced passing maneuvers with Dylan, trying to get him to understand which goal was theirs, but nothing seemed to have stuck. He simply didn't get the fundamentals of the game even though he had been playing for nearly two months. He was much better at T-ball, which started up next week. But Rachel still feared that he was developing an inferiority complex.

"Hey, Dylan," Lucinda sang out as she pranced by after the ball. "Thanks for the free goal."

Goddamn little bitch.

But Rachel said nothing. Across the field she spotted Sheila in a clutch of other parents rooting on the Reds. She had no idea that Rachel was fantasizing about Lucinda falling on her face. She knew it was awful of her, but at the moment she hated that little girl.

When the game was over, Sheila caught up to Rachel on the way to the parking lot and pulled her aside as Martin and Dylan went to their car.

"Did you give them a call?" Sheila asked, meaning the Nova Children's Center.

Rachel was still upset over the incident with Lucinda, but she did not let on. "Yes, and we have an appointment in two days."

She had spoken to a Dr. Denise Samson and explained the nature of Dylan's problems. The woman said to bring him in for an assessment. In addition to past test results, they needed a complete profile of his language skills, long-term/short-term memory, sequencing, abstractions/concrete tests, et cetera. They also wanted to schedule a functional MRI, which meant viewing his brain during cognitive testing.

Sheila seemed to beam at the news. "Great. You're not

going to regret it. They're miracle workers over there."
Then she checked her watch. "Oops, gotta go. Showing a
place on Magnolia Drive. Big buckaroos." She blew
Rachel a kiss, still grinning.

Rachel watched her hustle after Lucinda toward her car,
wondering why she was so elated over her appointment at
the Nova Children's Center. Much more than Rachel was.

As always when Dylan went to bed, Rachel or Martin
would read a book with him.

Tonight he had picked *Elmo, the Cat from Venus*. Of
course, Dylan technically could not read, but they called it
reading. He had simply memorized the story line with the
pictures and knew when to turn the pages. But it made him
happy.

Halfway through the book, Rachel felt her heart slump
as she thought of Dylan trying to entertain the Dell kids
with funny faces while they composed poetry on the computers.

She kissed his silky hair as he recited the pages, feeling
the warmth of his head beneath her lips. No matter how
hard he tried, he would forever feel stuck, humiliated, sur-
passed by other kids who would go on to bigger things.
And he would never grow to appreciate the higher aspects
of science, math, literature, or art. He would never know
the higher pleasures of discovery or creativity.

As she listened to him recite, all she could think was that
he would grow up feeling inferior—that his wonderful enthusiasm would turn in on itself as he learned what a lim-
ited space he occupied in the world.

After they finished reading, Rachel sat on the rocking
chair in his room and watched her son sleep, his Curious
George on the pillow beside him.

• • •

Sometime later, Rachel awoke.

She was in a hospital ward. For a moment, she was totally confused and frightened because she couldn't recall how she got here. Maybe she had had a stroke, that while putting Dylan to bed she'd been struck by an aneurysm, sending her into a blackout.

She was in a bed and hooked up to an IV and a vital-functions monitor that chirped as neon lines made spikes across the screens. They appeared normal. In fact, she felt normal. So what was she doing in a hospital?

As she stared around the room, odd features began to assume a pattern of familiarity: A small crib sat at the foot of the bed; flowers sprouted from vases on the tables; stuffed animals filled a visitor's chair. Hanging across the mirror was a CONGRATULATIONS streamer. And cards. Lots of cards on the food table to her right. Some with cartoons of naked bouncing babies. IT'S A BOY!!!

My God. She was in a maternity ward.

That couldn't be. She didn't recall being pregnant. Besides, that was medically impossible. She had had a hysterectomy two years ago. It made no sense.

Of course it made no sense, she told herself. This was all a dream. A flashback dream. And the sounds of someone approaching the room cut through the thick mist of sleep. And fear and confusion gave way to a sudden rush of joy.

"Here he is," announced the nurse.

Through the door came a nurse who looked vaguely familiar. But Rachel was too confused to rummage for an identity because the woman was holding a newborn baby. "Here he is," she sang out. And she gently placed the little bundle in Rachel's arms.

Rachel couldn't believe her eyes. It was Dylan, and a replay of the day he was born.

Tears of joy flooded her eyes. She was reliving the most beautiful moments of her life. The birth of her only child.

Her beautiful little boy. What a wonderful dream.

In that hazy margin between wakefulness and dream-sleep, she wished it wouldn't end. She wished the moment would telescope indefinitely. Because deep down in the lightless regions of her conscious mind she recalled a stalking fear born out of a report she had read somewhere. In the article a phrase had cut through all the technobabble like a seismic shock—the single solitary phrase: *chromosomal damage.*

Not my baby.

The moment passed as somebody put a hand on her shoulder. Through her tears she recognized Martin beside her in a chair. She hadn't noticed him before, but that was part of the Lewis Carroll absurdity of dreams.

"He's got your head."

"Yes," she said, not wanting to break the spell by questioning his odd wording. So she nodded as if Martin had said, *He's got your eyes.*

Dylan was wearing one of the little knitted caps they put on newborns. With the little point at the top he looked like a baby elf. But he was beginning to fuss. And though his face was still red and a little wrinkled, Rachel decided that the cap looked tight across his brow.

"It's okay, little man, it's okay. Mommy will remove this thing."

"I don't think it's a good idea," said the nurse. "It's a little cool in here."

"Oh, just for a moment. Besides, he's half-hidden."

The nurse rocked. "Well, I suppose."

Ever so delicately Rachel peeled back the little cap with her fingers. For a moment, Rachel froze.

Then from deep inside, a scream rose out of her as her mind tried to process what her eyes were taking in: The top of Dylan's skull was missing. And in its place was a gaping dark hole, edged with red raw tissue and a white layer of bone.

Rachel was still screaming as she stared into the gaping brain pan of her infant's head, wondering in a crazy side thought why no blood had stained the tiny white cap, and why Dylan was still alive, in fact, behaving like a perfectly healthy infant, staring at her wide-eyed, his little pink berry mouth sucking for her nipple, his hands making little pudgy fists—all in spite of the fact that the top of his head was missing.

Rachel's scream caught in her throat like a shard of glass. In the overhead light she spotted something inside his skull. It was his brain, but it was a tiny shrunken thing lying at the bottom.

"Boy, oh boy! He's sure got an appetite, haven't you, little guy?" the nurse chortled.

"Well, that's *something* he inherited from his old man," Martin said with a big happy grin.

Was it possible that they didn't notice? Rachel wondered. But how could that be under these harsh lights? Or maybe she was hallucinating?

While Dylan nursed happily at her breast, Rachel closed her eyes tightly, counted to three, then opened them again, hoping against hope that that hideous vision would go away. But it persisted. "Wh-what happened to his brain?" she cried.

"Oh, that." The nurse glanced over her glasses at Dylan. "Just your basic DBS."

"DBS?"

"Dope brain syndrome."

"WHAT?"

"Dope brain syndrome. *Dysgenic occi-parietal encephalation.* We see that from time to time. It's from mothers who did a lot of TNT when they were younger. Take enough of that stuff, and it discombobulates the chromosomes," she added while straightening out Rachel's sheet. "But, you know, except for the minibrain, you almost never see any funny physical stuff—flippers or webbed fingers or extra toes. Really, just the ole dope brain."

"Dope brain," Martin said simply, his voice without inflection. "He takes after you."

Then they both looked at Rachel and in unison said, "DOPE BRAIN DOPE BRAIN DOPE BRAIN—"

"Stop!" Rachel screamed. "Please stop."

"Nothing to get upset about," the nurse said, and poked her fingers into Dylan's skull and pulled out his brain as he continued to suckle. "Pardon my French, but you musta done a lot of shit, if you ask me, ma'am."

Paralyzed with horror, Rachel stared at the poor pathetic little thing in the palm of the nurse's hand. Like all the pictures of brains she had seen, it was yellow and split down the middle and wrinkled with convolutions. But so small. Like a peeled chestnut.

"See? It doesn't even bother him," the nurse said, and she dropped the thing back into Dylan's skull. "There you go, little guy."

Dylan burped and went back to the nipple.

"He's *awfully* cute, though," the nurse said, grinning expansively. "Aren't you, you little monkey."

"Don't call him that," Rachel protested.

Suddenly the nurse's face shifted as if the flesh were reforming across her skull. Her eyes narrowed shrewdly and suddenly she was Sheila MacPhearson. She pressed her face to Rachel's until it filled her vision. Her lips were big and rubbery and they muttered something.

"What did you say?" Rachel asked and woke herself up.

For a long spell, she looked around the room. The maternity ward had turned back into Dylan's room, still lit by the little night-light. The book they had been reading had slipped to the floor with a thud. Dylan stirred but did not wake.

A dream, she told herself as she sat in the dim light. *No, nightmare. A wretched, brutal nightmare that has left my mind tender and begging for forgetfulness.*

She closed her eyes for a minute, Sheila's voice still

humming in her head. She had said something that had gotten cut off.

Rachel got up to adjust Dylan's blanket when in the dim light all she saw staring up at her from the pillow was a dark little monkey head. She nearly fainted in the moment before she recognized Curious George. Suddenly she hated that thing with its insipid grin and stupid blank eyes.

She folded back the sheet to expose Dylan's face, and covered George with the blanket.

As she leaned over to kiss Dylan on his head, Sheila's voice cut through the haze.

"He can be fixed."

22

There were two things that Lilly Bellingham's mom told her that day: Don't go in the water just after eating; and when you do, don't go in above your waist.

Lilly wasn't that good a swimmer, so she understood the second Don't. But she had trouble with the first. "Why do I have to wait an hour after eating?"

"Because you'll get cramps."

"How can I get cramps?"

Lilly was only six, but she was very persistent. And smart. That's what all her teachers said. But there were times when Peggy was caught off guard. "Because," Peggy said, and took a swig of her diet Mountain Dew.

"But why *because*? I want to go in. I'm hot as hell."

Peggy shot her a hard look. "I don't like you using swear words, little missy, ya hear?"

"You use it all the time."

"That's different. Children aren't supposed to swear. Period."

"But *hell*'s not a swear word. Not like taking the Lord's name in vain, or the *f* and *s* words which Daddy uses all the time with Uncle Art."

"Well, he shouldn't. He knows better," Peggy said, knowing how feeble her response sounded, even to her daughter. "I don't want no daughter of mine using any of those words, including the *h* word. Period."

"So how come I can't go in the water?"

"Because you'll get cramps. You just ate and your tummy is full, that's why."

"Then how come I don't get cramps on land but will get them in the water? And how come I don't get cramps in the bathtub after eating?"

Damnation! Peggy thought. She was right. How come you didn't get cramps on land but were supposed to get them in the water? Lilly was looking at her for an answer, something that was supposed to make the sweetest sense and sit her little girl's fanny on her towel. But the best Peggy could come up with was, "Because that's what the doctor said." An even more feeble explanation and instantly Peggy knew Lilly wouldn't fall for it.

"What doctor? Not Dr. Miller. I never heard him say that. Not ever ever." And she stamped her foot in the sand. "And you know why? Because it doesn't make any sense. Standing in water can't give you cramps just like standing in air can't give you cramps after you eat. Besides, all those other kids just ate and they're in the water, and I don't hear any of them hollering about cramps."

Peggy sighed and glanced at all the kids goofing around in the shallows. Lilly was right: They had all just had lunch at a nearby picnic table and not a one of them was doubled over.

"So how come I can't?"

"All right, all right! Go in the damn water."

Lilly's face lit up.

"But if you get the slightest cramp, don't come whining to me, ya hear?"

"Mom, you said the *d* word." And she dashed down the sand and into the water.

"And not too far," Peggy shouted. "You hear?"

Lilly waved.

Peggy watched Lilly run in up to her waist then plop

down to wet her upper body. For a second she submerged herself then shot up because the water was cold. In her yellow bathing suit she looked like a canary. She had picked it out herself last week in Kmart. They were having a sale on kids' swimsuits, and it was marked down to $7.99. Lilly loved yellow. Half the T-shirts and other tops in her closet were yellow.

After a few minutes, Lilly wandered toward a group of kids about her age or a couple years older. They were tossing a Frisbee a few yards away. One kid overthrew and Lilly retrieved it. Although she didn't know the kids, it didn't take her long to make friends. In a matter of moments, she was tossing it with them, leaping in the air and splashing down to catch it. That was just like her—outgoing and sociable. Miss Chatty-Charm as Uncle Art had dubbed her. "She could sweet-talk the quills off a porcupine," he'd say. That was just the problem, Peggy thought. She was too friendly.

When she was satisfied that Lilly wasn't going to go in above her waist, Peggy stretched out on the blanket with her magazine. Every so often she'd look up to see how Lilly was doing and that she was keeping in the shallows.

But the warm sun made her drowsy, and after a while Peggy dozed off.

Several minutes later, she woke with a start. It was nearly three-thirty, and she had to get Lilly to her four-thirty interview with Smart Kids, a summer-school program for gifted children at the local high school. She was one of five selected from her elementary school. The announcement was in the newspaper and even on the Internet.

Peggy sat up. Lilly was standing in the water looking out over the lake. "Lilly," Peggy called.

But she didn't turn, too preoccupied with some ducks floating nearby.

"Lilly!"

Still no response. Now she was playing deaf just to drag out the day. But they had to get back.

Peggy got up and headed down to the water. "Hey, young lady!"

But she still did not turn around.

Now Peggy was getting angry. The initial chill of the water shocked her in place. She would never understand how kids could just bound down the sand and plunge into such freezing water. It must have something to do with their metabolism.

She was five feet from her daughter. "Hey, you!" As she said those words, a chill passed through Peggy.

The girl turned. It was not Lilly.

Similar yellow one-piece suit. Same sandy brown hair. Same length. Same body size, though she did seem a little taller, her legs a little longer—but Peggy had dismissed that for not having seen her daughter in a swimsuit since last summer.

"Oh, sorry."

The girl just shrugged, then waded to shore.

Peggy looked down the beach. No sign of Lilly. No other yellow suit.

She left the water, looking up and down the beach. Out of the corner of her eye, she noticed the girl in the yellow suit head toward the parking lot. As Peggy spun around trying to spot Lilly, it passed through her mind that the resemblance of the girl to her daughter from the rear was amazing. Before she bolted down the beach, Peggy caught the girl looking over her shoulder at her. For one instant, Peggy felt something pass between them. Something dark and jagged.

The next instant Peggy was jogging down the beach the other way, scanning the people on the blankets and in the water, and shouting out her daughter's name.

Oh, God!

In a matter of seconds she was running, her head snapping from side to side.

"Lilly. LILLY."

When Peggy ran out of beach, she shot to the lifeguard stand.

She could barely get the words out: "M-my daughter's missing."

23

Enhancement?" Martin said. "Sounds like some kind of religious experience."

As Rachel had expected, he was completely dismissive of the idea.

It was the next evening, and they were in the kitchen putting dishes in the dishwasher. They had just finished eating, and Dylan was upstairs taking a bath.

Still Rachel kept her voice low. She had related Sheila's claim about the Nova Children's Center. "She says they can improve a child's IQ by fifty percent or more."

His eyebrows shot up like a polygraph needle. "What? That's impossible!"

"I'm just telling you what she said."

Martin had an intelligent angular face—one that was capable of authority. He was not always right, but never uncertain. At the moment, his eyes narrowed cleverly, his mouth spread into a smirk, and his eyebrows arched the way they did when he was about to make a pronouncement. It was a look that annoyed her for its condescension. "Look, Rachel, you're born with two numbers: your Social Security number and your IQ. And neither can be changed."

"They also once declared the earth was flat."

"What's that supposed to mean?"

"Don't be so damn pigheaded." Frustration was tightening her chest.

"Unless these *enhancement* people have come up with some brand-new science, I don't buy it. You're born as smart as you'll ever be. Yeah, maybe you could add a couple points on a test, but intelligence is basically fixed."

"Keep your voice down," she said in a scraping whisper. She closed the French doors so their voices wouldn't carry upstairs. "I want to look into it."

"Fine, but keep in mind that Sheila loves to impress. She's always dropping names and telling secrets. She rents a place on Martha's Vineyard and leads you to believe she's drinking buddies with Diane Sawyer and Alan Dershowitz. Not to mention how much so-and-so paid for their house."

"So, what's your point?"

"My point is that Sheila MacPhearson embellishes the truth. She exaggerates. Remember what she said when she showed us this house? That it was the childhood home of a 'famous movie director.' Her exact words. For days I had thought Steven Spielberg grew up here. Then we find out it's some guy who did a music video for MTV."

"So you're saying that Sheila is lying?"

"I'm saying I don't believe they've got some procedure that can turn your average Jack and Jill into a Stephen Hawking or Marilyn Vos Savant."

"Well, I'm going to look into it."

"Suit yourself, but don't get your hopes up."

She hated his absolutist manner. It was something he used on his workers to bring them to their knees, but she resented when he brought it home. It was obnoxious and failed to intimidate her. She also hated the possibility that he was right. That out of desperation she was chasing white rabbits on some offhanded remark by good-hearted Sheila MacPhearson.

Martin must have read the turn of her mind because he instantly softened. "Honey, more than anybody else you should know how these things don't work. We tried every gimmick in the books and then some. It's all a myth: It can't be done—not in the first three years or the next or the next. That's all a pipe dream of die-hard liberals who want to believe they can make poor inner city kids intellectually equal to children of white affluent suburbanites: How to flatten the bell curve. But it doesn't work. The human brain is a Pentium chip made of meat: It's got all the circuit potential it's ever going to have."

There's a hole in our son's brain, a voice in her head whispered. *A gap. Missing circuitry. A deficiency in his left hemisphere. And I put it there for better sex.*

Every other minute of the day she had thought about telling him, of finally spewing the vomit from her soul; but she really didn't know if she could live with the consequence. She really didn't believe that Martin could ever forgive her. He was like that—he held grudges. And what greater grudge than that against the woman who had ruined his only child? Even if in time, she could work up the nerve to confess—fortified by the fact that at the time she was young, foolish, and unaware of the risks—the proper punishment would be to watch Dylan grow up impaired, her secret festering within her the rest of her life.

"I see no harm in looking into it."

Martin nodded. "By the way, did she say what the enhancement procedure actually is?"

"She didn't know."

"But she said it works wonders," he muttered sarcastically. "I'm just wondering: If they've got some kind of procedure to make you smarter, how come the world doesn't know about it? How come Peter Jennings and *The Boston Globe* haven't gotten the scoop on it? And how come there aren't IQ jack-up centers in every hospital and clinic in the country?"

Martin was no fool. If she protested too much, he would wonder at her desperation. "Martin, I really don't know," she said, trying to sound neutral. But she was struggling between anger at his patronizing manner and her own transparency. He was right: She knew nothing about the procedure or those behind it. She wasn't even sure where the place was located. "Forget it. Forget I ever brought it up," she said.

"But you did. And what bothers me is how come you're so wide-eyed about some foolish claim about boosting our son's intelligence?"

For a long moment she just stared blankly at him, not being able to summon an answer. She felt the press of tears but pushed them down. "Because I'm feeling desperate. Because it makes me sick to think what he's going to go through. Because . . . oh, nothing. Nothing!"

"Nothing," he repeated. "Well, the only enhancement we need around here is our love life."

Rachel slammed the dishwasher closed. She was not going to respond. He knew that she just didn't feel like having sex, that she was going through a down spell.

Suddenly the French doors flew open and Dylan walked in. He had his pajamas on, but the shirt was on backward and inside out, the label under his chin. In his hand was a big zoo picture book.

"Daddy, can you read me 'bout the aminals . . . I mean anminals . . . I mean anlimals?"

Rachel burst into tears and left the room.

24

If you keep this up, you're going to starve."

Vera glared at him. Travis didn't like Vera. She wasn't warm or kind like his mom, and she had hard flat eyes like a catfish.

Yesterday when he had stopped eating and talking, she called in Phillip to help. (Travis vaguely remembered him as the man who carried him out of the seaplane that first night.) They had wanted him to eat so he could be healthy for "the tests"—whatever those were. He wondered if they were like the ones he took in January for the SchoolSmart scholarship.

Phillip's was the only other face that Travis had laid eyes on here. And it was a scary face—a pale, tight, unsmiling stone with gray eyes that poked you when they stared. Vera had called him in to make Travis take his pills. He could still feel Phillip grip the lower half of his face in that big meaty hand and squeeze until Travis's mouth opened. Then Phillip tossed in the pills and squirted water down his throat with a plastic squeeze bottle and clamped his mouth shut so he had to swallow or choke.

While Vera circled him, Travis sat still in the beanbag chair looking blankly across the room at the TV. His eyes did not follow her, nor did he answer her.

He had stopped asking for his mother. He had stopped asking when he was going home. Most of the day, all he would do was stare at the television, losing himself in the mindless flickering of colors and squealy voices.

Beside him was a cardboard tray with a sandwich, a cup of carrots, pudding, and a carton of milk, now warm. There had been a Snickers bar, which he had pocketed. The rest he hadn't touched, and it had been sitting there for several hours.

Vera brought the tray over and handed him the sandwich wedge. It was peanut butter and grape jelly. She wagged it under his nose, but he turned his head away. She pressed it closer until it pressed onto his lips. He turned his head even farther away.

"I just talked to your mother on the telephone."

Travis's head twitched, and he glanced tentatively at the woman.

"She asked about you and said to tell you that you had to eat your food or she would be sad."

Slowly he looked at the woman.

She raised the sandwich to his mouth again. "She said that she missed you, so does Beauregard. But if you eat and get your strength back you can go home."

"You're lying."

Vera looked at him, shocked at the first words he had spoken in two days. "I'm not lying. I just got off the phone with her, I'm telling you. She called to see how you were doing on the tests. But if you don't eat, you can't take them which means you can't go home."

"His name isn't Beauregard."

She stared at him with those small dead catfish eyes. "Look, I made a mistake," she said. "So what's his name?"

"Bo Jangle."

"That's what I meant. I knew it was Bo something." She pressed the sandwich closer. "You going to take a little bite for Mom and Bo Jangle?"

That wasn't his name either, and he turned his face away without answering.

Yesterday he had cried. Vera had wanted him to take his pills again, but when he refused, she said that his mother would be upset. It was the first time they had mentioned his mother. He didn't want to cry, but he could not help it. And while he did so, the woman stood and watched him. She had lied to him then, too, he was certain. She didn't know his mother. Just like she hadn't just talked to her on the phone.

Vera got up and tossed the sandwich. "Well, you're going to have your test on an empty stomach, I guess." She went out and returned a few minutes later with Phillip who carried a tray with a cloth over it.

"Hey, Travis," he said, as if they were friends. "We just want to run a little test on you, okay? You're going to do this lying down, okay?"

Phillip led him to the bed and told him to sit at the edge. He handed him a piece of paper on a clipboard and a pencil. "I'd like you to write your name for me—first and last name."

Travis sat on his bed. He thought about not responding, but he recalled Phillip's hand on his jaw yesterday and wrote his name, thinking this was a dumb test.

"Good, now I want you to take the pencil with your left hand and do the same."

It was much harder with his left hand, but he struggled, making a real mess of it. When he was finished, he handed the clipboard back to Phillip, who looked pleased.

Then they made him lie on the bed. Vera then said, "I want you to count backward from twenty for me."

Travis did not respond.

"If you do, Phillip will take you outside. Promise."

He didn't believe them, but they would keep it up until he did. So he counted backward from twenty in a soft voice.

Vera then rubbed his neck with alcohol, a smell he knew from when his mother cleaned out a cut knee. She then rubbed some other stuff on the same spot. "This is to numb the skin so you won't feel anything. But you have to lie perfectly still, you got that?"

He nodded, but suddenly he felt scared by the way they were hanging over him, with Phillip tightly holding down his hands. "Close your eyes, kid," he said.

Travis hesitated for a few moments, then closed his eyes, but not all the way. Out of the crack he saw Vera stick a hypodermic needle in the right side of his neck and press it all the way. Instantly he jumped, but Phillip held him down.

His neck suddenly felt hot inside all the way up his head. But after a little while, he felt nothing.

"That wasn't so bad," Vera said. "Okay, keep your eyes open and count backward from twenty again."

He didn't know what they gave him, but he counted backward as she asked. Then they asked him to recite his address, his mother's and dog's name, and where he went to school. He did all of that. Then Vera held up a picture book with butterflies and asked him to identify the pictures. Then to read a few first lines of writing. He did that also. And when it wasn't loud enough, they made him do it again.

Phillip smiled. "You're doing good, kid."

"You have big yellow teeth," Travis heard himself say.

"Out of the mouths of babes," Vera snickered.

"More like out of a vial of truth serum," he said.

"Like my dog's," Travis continued.

"Fuck off, kid."

"And you've got a big mole on your face."

"Okay, Travis, you did good," Vera said. "Close your eyes for a few minutes and rest."

He closed his eyes and thought about his mother and home and Bo. Phillip did have teeth like his. And the mole looked like a bug had crawled out of his mouth.

Travis began to feel sleepy when he felt another needle jab on the left side of his neck. He let out a startled yelp, and the same hot pressure flowed up his neck and across his face, this time on the left side.

"Travis, again, I want you to count for me, backward from twenty."

Travis heard the woman's words but did not understand.

"Travis, count backward from twenty."

Still he did not understand.

"Travis, tell me your name," the man said.

Travis could not answer. He knew they were talking to him, he heard the words, but he did not know what the sounds meant. But he remembered that he once understood them. But not now. How strange.

The woman held up a book. "Travis, read me the title on the cover."

Travis did not understand.

Phillip picked up the small glass jar on the tray. "Amazing stuff, sodium amythal," he said. Then he looked at Travis, "You haven't got a clue, kid, but you just passed the Wada test. We first put the right half of your brain asleep to see what the other half would do. Then we put the other side of your brain to sleep to see what you'd do, which is nothing." He tapped the other side of his head. "You passed the first test, kid: You're a left-brainer." He looked at his watch. "And in about three more minutes, you'll be back to normal."

And they left.

25

The Nova Children's Center building was a handsome redbrick neo-Gothic structure with turrets and large windows that had been reencased. A converted old schoolhouse, it was set back from the road and surrounded by a sweeping lawn, in the middle of which sat a hundred-year-old beech tree ablaze with purple leaves. The place looked solid, established, and full of promise. Their eleven o'clock appointment was with a Dr. Denise Samson.

Rachel and Dylan drove around to the parking lot in the rear beside a playground and picnic area. The visitors' section was full of shiny upscale cars. This was not your typical learning clinic. And she had known several.

As they rounded the front, they heard children laughing and teachers talking. Through the windows, she could see young kids in chairs and adults working with them. In another room, children were at computer terminals.

"Is this my new school, Mom?"

How do you answer that? she thought. "It might be, if we like it."

She wasn't sure he understood, and he didn't pursue it, captivated by the playground apparatus.

In spite of its early twentieth-century vintage, the building's interior had been redone in bright modern, tasteful décor. A directory hung in the foyer. The only names she recognized were Denise Samson and Lucius Malenko. The receptionist said that Dr. Samson was expecting her and would be out in a moment. Meanwhile, Dylan headed for a small computer terminal with a video game, while Rachel sat and filled out a medical questionnaire asking the basics, including how she heard about the Nova Children's Center. She entered Sheila MacPhearson's name.

When she was finished, she picked up one of the glossy Nova brochures on the table. There were photos of the administration and staff, of students being instructed by specialists.

Inside was a note to parents:

If your child exhibits some of the following,

NOVA CHILDREN'S CENTER is a solution:
Poor reading comprehension • Slow reading • Spelling problems • Poor math skills • Low self-confidence and self-esteem • Poor handwriting, printing • Delayed language skills • Memory problems . . .

This list was a relentless description of Dylan. She read on:

What Can Be Done?

The **NOVA CHILDREN'S CENTER** *provides help for dyslexia and other learning challenges. We offer a variety of diagnostic testing to identify the problems . . .*

The brochure went on to describe how the center offered individualized learning programs for each child, all instruction given one-on-one. In bold was the statement: "Ninety percent of NCC students average one year or more improvement for every NCC semester." This was probably the *enhancement* that Sheila meant.

Rachel flipped through the pages. They recommended from two to five sessions a week lasting from twenty-four to thirty-six weeks per year. There was a multistep assessment procedure that was essential to define the problem areas. Another few pages were dedicated to testimonials of success by parents, teachers, and former students:

> *When Diana first arrived at Nova Children's Center, she could read words at her second-grade level, but she couldn't comprehend the content. She had difficulty connecting to language she read or language she heard. Words seemed to go in one ear and out the other. People thought she was not trying, and she had been labeled a "motivation" or "attention" problem.*

The report went on to explain the cause of Diana's problem with language comprehension. Then there was an explanation of how the Nova Children's Center approach improved language comprehension, reasoning, critical thinking, and language expression skills. At the end of that discussion, again in bold, was the claim that "most of the children at NCC gained one to three years in language comprehension in just four weeks on intensive treatment."

Rachel let that sink in. *He can be fixed.* Maybe that was what Sheila had meant.

A photo gallery of the staff was included at the end of the brochure. Nearly every one had a Ph.D. after their name.

The chief neurologist and one of the directors of the center was an avuncular-looking gray-haired man named Lucius Malenko. He had both a M.D. and Ph.D. after his name.

In the photo, Dr. Denise Samson was a handsome-looking woman about thirty-five to forty with pulled-back dark hair and heavy dark-framed glasses.

"Mrs. Whitman?"

Rachel looked up.

It was Dr. Samson herself. She was a tall, statuesque woman with auburn hair tied into a thick bun behind her head. She was even more attractive in person. "And this must be Dylan."

"Hi," Dylan said, glancing up from the computer. On the screen were funny little creature heads that you could eliminate by shooting blips of light from a spaceship. Dr. Samson showed Dylan how to do it then walked Rachel to a small conference room beyond a glass partition so that they could talk while viewing Dylan.

"As I said on the phone, this is a multidimensional assessment to help determine Dylan's various cognitive abilities—his information-processing strengths, problem-solving style, and problem areas. Since his problem areas seem to be language-based, we'll assess his oral language—phonics, word associations, sentence formulation, and the like. Then we'll do some visual/auditory diagnoses." She sounded as if she were reading.

Because the assessments were long and tiring for a child, they would be spread over two days. Tomorrow would also include functional MRI scans.

"After the assessments are in, we'll put together an individualized instructional program for him with one of our specialists."

Rachel listened as the woman continued. When she was finished, Rachel said, "I'm wondering if I might also speak to Dr. Malenko."

"Dr. Malenko?" Dr. Samson seemed surprised.

"I have some questions of a neurological nature that I'd like to ask him."

There was a pregnant pause. "I'm sure I can answer most of your questions, Mrs. Whitman."

"I have no doubt, but a friend recommended that I speak with him before we decide on a program. So I'd like to set up an appointment."

"I see. Then you can check with Marie out front."

Rachel could sense the woman's irritation, but at the moment she didn't care.

Rachel made the appointment for Thursday and gave

Dylan a kiss, telling him she was going to be right here in the waiting room. Dr. Samson then led him down the hall to the test rooms. He went willingly, looking back once to check that Rachel was still there.

Mommy's so sorry for what she did to you, my darling.

26

———————

That night Brendan woke himself up with a scream.

He looked around his bedroom. Everything was still. The green digital readout on his clock radio said 3:17.

He had had that dream again. The one with the blue elephants. They were circling him. Taunting him. Insane-looking creatures with wide grins and big floppy trunks and all the grabbing arms. Like the demon pachyderms in Disney's *Fantasia*, dancing maniacally around him, screaming at him to *be a good boy*, grabbing at him, poking him, pulling his hair while he cowered under bright white lights.

One of them came over to him and bent down. *How many marbles does Mr. Nisha have if I take away seven? Tell me. TELL ME!* When Brendan didn't answer, the creature pulled out a large sword and cut off his own head.

That's when Brendan woke up.

His shirt was damp with perspiration. His bed was a mess from kicking around.

Time to dance. Time to dance.

He went to the toilet and peed in the bowl.

Time to eat your soup.

He flushed the toilet. In the dim light from the street he looked in the mirror.

Count backward from twenty.

"I can't," he whispered.

Time to fix you up.

Which glass has more water?

The tall one.

Nope!

Time to fix you up. Time to fix you up.

Brendan lit a cigarette and went to the window. He looked across the front yard, the dark street, the field of scrub and landfill on the other side. A fat white moon had risen above the horizon and whitewashed the scene.

Ah, love, let us be true
To one another!

The Matthew Arnold lines jetted up from nowhere, as usual.

for the world which seems
To lie before us like a land of dreams,
So various, so beautiful, so new,
Hath really neither joy, nor love, nor light

He thought about Richard in wheezy sleep in the next room. He wondered how many nights the old man had. He wondered what would happen if he didn't wake up the next morning—if Brendan went in there and found him cold and blue. He wondered if he went in there and did something about it.

Would he be horrified? Would he cry?

He thought about Nicole. He wondered what nightmares she dreamed. He wondered if she cried.

Mr. Nisha wants you to be happy.

He raised his eyes and let the white light flood his mind.

A huge crystalline moon sat in the sky over Rachel and Martin like a piece of jewelry.

"There's something I want to tell you," she said.

"I hope it's how madly in love you are with me, and that you're finally over your PMS, which I thought was surely terminal."

He was making light of the moment, but she really couldn't blame him. They were sitting on the balcony of the Blue Heron overlooking Magnolia Harbor. The reflection of the moon made a rippling carpet all the way out to the horizon. Above was a cloudless black velvet vault dappled with stars. They had just eaten a sumptuous meal— Martin, the *frutti di mare*, and she, the Chilean sea bass—which they washed down with a bottle of Hermitage La Chappelle 1988.

"Martin, I think we should talk."

"Uh-oh. Is this the big thorn you've been sitting on for the last month?"

"It's a problem I have . . . we have."

Martin's face hardened. "Rachel, if you're going to tell me that you've found somebody else, I'm not sure I can take it."

"It's nothing like that."

"And you're not sick."

"No."

Martin nodded, as if to say that the high horribles had been eliminated. "Okay, hit me."

"It's Dylan."

"What about him?"

"He has brain damage, and it's because in college I took some dope, something called TNT, which some guy I know made in a chemistry lab. In any case, I read a report saying the stuff damaged female reproductive cells, resulting in chromosomal defects of their children. I had him tested, and the left hemisphere of Dylan's brain is underdeveloped, and it probably was caused by the TNT." Rachel was amazed at her glibness. That was totally unexpected.

She couldn't tell if it was the flickering light from the small glass kerosene lantern that sat between them, but

Martin's face seemed to shift several times as he struggled to process her words.

"You're telling me that my son has brain damage because you took a lot of bad dope?" His voice was a strange hissy whisper.

"Yes. His IQ is eighty-three, which is the low side of average." Again, she could not believe the smoothness of her confession—but, of course, she had rehearsed it so many times over the last several days that she had managed to strip the words down to their phonetic bones.

"Eighty-three. EIGHTY-THREE. My son is going to grow up dumb because you took some sex drug?"

"Martin, you're shouting."

"I don't care," he said. "I read about that TNT shit. It was for *sex* thrills. SEX THRILLS."

The people at other tables were glaring at them in astonishment.

"You goddamn idiot! You ruined my son. You ruined my only *child*."

"Martin, keep your voice down."

"No, I won't keep my voice down. That means he'll be handicapped forever, just because you wanted good orgasms."

The other diners were now muttering to each other and scowling at Rachel. Suddenly she recognized neighbors, acquaintances, and other members of the Dells. Even the minister from the Hawthorne Unitarian Church and her husband, the choirmaster. "How could you?" someone said. "Shame!" cried another. "Pigs like her shouldn't be allowed to have children."

"I didn't know," she said to Martin. Then to the others. "Really, I didn't know. I was young."

The entire balcony was glowering at her, their large rubbery mouths jabbering condemnations.

"You didn't know because you're *stupid*," Martin growled. "He was going to grow up to take over the business." Then he made that bitter mocking face she had come to hate. "Maybe he can head up the cleaning crew. President and CEO of latrines. The world's leading expert on SageSearch's urinal camphor. Can plunge a toilet and change the paper lickety-split." His eyes were huge and red and his teeth flashed as his mouth spit out the venom.

"I'm sorry. I'M SORRY. I'm SORRY . . ."

"Sorry? SORRY? You bet you're sorry," he said and picked up the kerosene lantern with the burning wick and smashed it on her head.

Even before the cutting pain registered, her head was engulfed in flames, burning hair dripping onto her dress and sizzling her eyes.

"SORREEEEEE!"

It was her own scream that woke her, and she bolted upright gasping to catch her breath.

It was Lindsay. Greg could not recollect the details of the dream, but he woke filled with the sense of her.

But as much as he tried, he could not recapture the scenario—just the afterglow of her presence, like the fast-fading image of a TV. He sat at the edge of the bed, wishing he could put the moment on rewind. He had had dreams of her in the past, lots of them—odd, disjointed scraps, floating images—sometimes of her alive and vibrant, sometimes of her on Joe Steiner's table. Once he had dreamt of her and their son—but not as a baby, but a little boy.

As he sat there thinking about the day, he felt the old sadness spread its way through his soul like root hairs. He knew if he let himself loosen a bit he'd dissolve into deep wracking sobs—the kind that had left him reamed out and barely functional. He had had enough of those and fought back the urge, telling himself that he didn't want to be one of those widowers who went through the rest of his life embracing his grief like a mistress.

A photo of Lindsay smiled at him from his bureau. It was taken in Jamaica on their honeymoon six years ago. She was dressed in white with a large red hibiscus behind her ear and smiling brightly at the camera in a tangerine setting sun. With her shiny black hair and large brown eyes and honey skin, she looked like a vision in amber. They had been crazy in love.

Greg got up.

It was nearly eleven, and the sun was pouring through the window. Although he had slept for nearly six hours, he felt fatigued. It had been four days since they put him on night shift, and he still could not get used to sleeping in the daytime. Most of the time he felt low and out of focus, as if he were suffering permanent jet lag. But it was worse when he was drinking. He had stopped fifteen months ago. He had been disciplined then, too, because he had showed up late for work and was nearly useless on the job. After a second verbal warning, he quit the booze cold turkey—a victory of which he was proud, telling himself that he had done it for Lindsay. The only strategy that worked. But there were nights when the craving made his body hum.

He pushed himself off the bed and headed into the kitchen and poured himself a glass of orange juice. He put on a pot of coffee, thinking how the caffeine would pick him up, maybe even shock the fur off his brain.

He wasn't sure how he'd spend the rest of the day. He knew he should check out some leads on the high school break-in, but he had done very little on the Sagamore Boy case over the last week beyond scanning the latest missing-children reports. No leads, as usual. The boy had been missing for over three years, and all that came in were bulletins of recent disappearances. The Dixon case had iced over also. He had nothing but faint hunches and colleagues who thought he was nuts.

The red light on his answering machine flashed.

It was probably Steve Powers calling to see if the kids he

interviewed the other night had given him anything on the school break-in. Unfortunately, the security cameras in the damaged area weren't functioning. All he had was names, some with prior records. He hit the button.

"Detective Zakarian, this is Adrian Budd, radiologist from Essex Medical. I'm not sure if this is significant, but after we talked the other day, it dawned on me why those holes kept bothering me. They just didn't seem random, nor did they look like all the needle-bore nuclear seedings of tumors I'd seen. Also, the number threw me. So I checked with some neurospecialists here at the center, and they confirmed my suspicions.

"Those skull holes—like the perforation scars of the patient you came about—form a neurotopographical pattern. They seem to trace out the surface area of the sulci folds of the cortex. And there are so many because the cortex folds in on itself, with deeper pockets of surface tissue—which is why cortex folds exist in the first place: to have a broad surface area. Otherwise we'd all be Coneheads.

"The long and the short of it is that the holes appear to trace the sulci of the cortical surface known as the Wernicke's Brain.

"I don't know what it means, but that's the area associated with memory and intelligence.

"I can't tell you the patient's name, and I'm not even supposed to divulge this, but the individual whose X ray you saw apparently has a remarkable memory. Nurse Porter thinks he may be a savant. Hope that helps."

And he clicked off.

27

A shiny red Porsche Carrera with New Hampshire plates sat in the slot reserved for L. Malenko. A sticker on the rear window read CASCO BAY YACHT CLUB. *The man is doing well*, thought Rachel as she headed inside the Nova Children's Center.

It was the following Thursday, and she was here for her eleven o'clock appointment. She had to wait only a few minutes before the receptionist led her down the hall to a corner office.

Lucius Malenko was not wearing a physician's smock as Rachel had expected, but casual whites—shoes, pants, and cotton pullover—all but for a lavender polo shirt whose collar stuck up around the back of his neck like a flower. He looked as if he'd dressed for a day of yachting or golf. Maybe the "casual Friday" trend was full-time here, a way of being less intimidating.

"Please, come in," he said pleasantly. He had a surprisingly small sharp hand, probably an asset in neurosurgery. The office was a bright open room with windows on two sides overlooking the greenery of the building's rear. "Where is Mr. Whitman?" he asked, peering down the hall.

"I'm sorry, but he couldn't make it."

"No?" Malenko closed the door. "I'm sure Dr. Samson

explained to you that we like to involve both parents where possible—right from the beginning." He spoke in an accent that sounded eastern European—perhaps Slavic or Russian.

Dr. Samson had explained that. "I'm sorry, but there was a last-minute conflict." That was the best she could do, hoping that the subject would be dropped. Rachel looked away, pretending to take in the office décor.

Malenko took his chair behind his desk, fixing her with his stare. "May I be so bold as to ask if Mr. Whitman knows you're here?"

"Well," she began, thinking how she didn't want to begin with a lie. She chuckled nervously. "Is it really that important?"

"Only because we'll be discussing matters that concern his son, too, no?" His manner was pleasant, although she was beginning to feel uncomfortable.

"Actually, he doesn't know. This is a kind of a reconnaissance mission. Maybe if things work out, I'll bring him next time."

He looked puzzled, but said nothing and affixed a pair of half-glasses to his nose and thumbed through a folder of Dylan's test results.

Adding to his immaculate appearance was his nearly pure white hair, which was combed back, emphasizing a broad aggressive forehead. In spite of the hair, he had dark, thick eyebrows and a smooth, boyish face that belied his age. He was a big man who might have been an athlete at one time. His eyes were heavy lidded and intensely watchful. But there was something disconcerting about his gaze—something she had vaguely registered the moment they had met. And only now did Rachel realize what it was: His eyes didn't match. One was reef-water blue, but the other looked black. On closer inspection Rachel noticed that one iris was all pupil, giving him a disorienting appearance—one eye icy cool, the other darkly alluring.

On the walls hung a few framed plaques—from the

American College of Neurological Medicine, the International Society of Skull Base Surgeons, the American Board of Neurosurgery. Also, a Kiwanis Club award for outstanding contribution. Clustered on the opposite walls were photos of him with groups of students from Bloomfield Prep and with people at black-tie functions. The only other form of decoration was a bronze sculpture of the Indian elephant-head god on the windowsill. It had four arms, and each hand held something different. Only one she could make out. It was an axe.

"His name is Ganesha," Malenko said, his face still in the folder. "He's the elephant-faced deity, sacred to Hindus the world over."

"It's rather charming," she said. The figure had a large potbelly spilling over his lower garment, and his eyes were large and his smile broad under his trunk.

"Yes. Indians revere him as a god of intellectual strength. Was your son named after Bob Dylan?"

"No, the poet Dylan Thomas."

"Ah, yes, the great Irish bard. 'Do not go gentle into that good night.' Wonderful stuff. Are you a literature person?"

"I like to read."

"A former textbook editor, of course."

Rachel wondered how he knew that, because she hadn't put that in the questionnaire. Perhaps it was in Dylan's medical records.

"Reading is the highest intellectual activity of the human experience," Malenko continued. "More sectors of the brain are active than in any other endeavor including mathematics or flying an airplane. It's the most totally interactive processing of information, even with children reading Mother Goose."

"I didn't know that."

"Well, now you do." He smiled and displayed a row of small but perfect white teeth in a sugar-pink mouth. "So, what can I do for you?"

The baldness of the question threw her. Dylan's records

and test results sat under his nose. "Well, you can see from his folder that he has serious learning disabilities."

Malenko removed his half-glasses. "Yes, he's functionally dyslexic, which means that the Wernicke's area and the angular gyri—those areas of the brain involved in deciphering words—are underactive. As Dr. Samson clearly explained, we have here some of the best LD people in the country who could construct a personalized curriculum for your son." He tapped his fingers impatiently as he spoke, as if to say, *Why are you wasting my time?*

"It's just that I wanted to explore other approaches."

"Other approaches?"

Clearly Sheila had not told him about her. She probably did not even know the man, just his reputation. "Well, you're a neurophysician, correct?"

"I also can be found baking cookies."

She smiled in relief that his manner had softened. "I'm just wondering if there was anything you could do medically to help him."

"Medically?"

"You know . . . some special procedures . . ."

"Everything we do is a special procedure. We tailor our programs to each child, according to his and her individual needs. I'm not sure what you're referring to."

"It's just that I heard you had some kind of enhancement procedures."

Malenko's eyebrows arched up. "*Enhancement* procedures?" He pronounced the word as if for the first time.

"To repair the damaged areas. Maybe something experimental—some electrical stimulation thing."

He looked at her for a long moment that reprimanded her in its silence. Then he glanced inside the folder again. "I see that you were recommended by Sheila MacPhearson, the real estate lady."

"Yes."

"And what exactly did she say, Mrs. Whitman?"

"Well, that you had some special procedures that can enhance children's cognitive abilities."

"Like cripples at Lourdes."

"Beg pardon?"

"We get some child to improve significantly on a math test or the SATs, and the word gets out that we're miracle workers." He chuckled to himself. "Mrs. Whitman, let me explain that we *do* perform miracles here, in a sense. We even improve a child's ability to take tests so that scores go up a few points. But that's incidental to our objective, which is to maximize a child's potential. I'm not sure what you are looking for, but this is not Prodigies R Us."

Rachel felt a little foolish. She had been caught in Sheila's exaggerated promise. Martin was right. "You've seen the MRI scans, correct?"

"Yes."

"Well, they're not normal. There's some kind of anomaly. I was just wondering if—you know—if anything could be done about that? I mean, with all the breakthroughs in medical science, aren't there any *corrective* measures that could be taken—some kind of neurostimulation procedure or something . . . ?" She trailed off, hearing Dr. Stanley Chu's response: *"It's like wanting to regenerate an amputated finger. It can't be done."*

Malenko stared at her intently as he considered her appeal, then he opened the folder and removed the MRI scans. "It seems to me, Mrs. Whitman, that you are confusing some magical medical fix with behavioral programs. I've looked these over, and I see no signs of hemorrhaging or lesions or tumors that might be impinging on your son's intellectual development or performance. If there were, then something possibly could be corrected by surgery or radiation."

"But the left hemisphere is smaller than the right."

"Mrs. Whitman, let me ask you why you had the MRI scan done."

Suddenly she felt as if she were entering a minefield. "Because I was worried that he had a tumor or some other problem."

"But what made you suspect a tumor or some other problem?"

"It was simply . . . I don't know . . . precautionary. His memory retention isn't normal."

"Had you consulted your pediatrician for possible psychiatric counseling or medications? Sometimes a child's memory problems are the results of environment issues or chemical imbalances."

"Yes, we went through all of that."

"And was it your pediatrician who referred you for the MRI?"

"Yes."

"And what was his evaluation?"

"That the ventricles in the left hemisphere of his brain were larger than normal, indicating some kind of underdevelopment in the thalamus."

"And what did the doctor recommend in terms of medical treatment?"

"He said nothing could be done."

"And you didn't believe him."

"I'm seeking a second opinion."

"Surely your pediatrician consulted neurologists for an evaluation."

"I wasn't satisfied."

Malenko listened intently, his bright eye training on her as if it were some kind of laser mind-scan. "Does your husband know about this?"

"No, he doesn't know, but why is that so important?"

Malenko leaned forward. "Mrs. Whitman, if we are going to work with Dylan, then we cannot have misunderstandings regarding the medical condition of a prospective student. If we are going to set for ourselves expectations and objectives, candidness is essential."

Rachel nodded.

"Good. Then am I correct in assuming that your husband does *not* know about the MRI scan or the dysmorphic abnormalities in your son's brain?"

She felt as if he had stripped her naked. "Yes."

"I see. Then may I ask what you are hiding?"

"Hiding?"

"Mrs. Whitman, you have an MRI done on your son's brain, you discover an anomalous formation, then two weeks later you come in here for consultation—and your husband knows nothing. I find that unusual, unless you are in the throes of separation or divorce. Are you?"

There was no equivocating with this man, Rachel thought. She struggled with the urge to tell him that it was none of his damn business, but she stopped herself. If she showed offense at his persistence, he might dismiss her. "No, we're not."

Malenko looked at her with a bemused expression. Then he picked up the film scans and clipped them to the display board on the wall. "This disparity between the hemispheres of Dylan's brain could be the result of many different causes, including infant trauma." He glanced down at her.

Christ! Now he's wondering if I had battered my own baby.

"It could also be chemical, genetic, oxygen starvation *in utero* . . . a number of possibilities. Sometimes these structural deformities can occur as the result of chromosomal damage, usually from the mother's side."

For a prickly moment his eyes gauged Rachel's face.

chromosomal damage
from the mother's side

He suspects, she told herself. *He is a neurologist so he surely knows about the Chu study and recognizes the TNT signature damage.*

"Did you smoke or take any unusual medications while carrying your son?"

"No."

"Any medical emergencies during pregnancy—emergency room visits? Hospitalization? Any intravenal medications?"

All this was on the questionnaire. He was testing her. "No."

"Another possibility is alcohol. Did you drink while carrying your son?"

"No."

Malenko handed her a box of Kleenex without comment.

Rachel wiped her eyes, feeling that any moment she would break down.

"MRI scans can only give us gross anatomical pictures, not minor neurocomponents. But the left temporal horn is dilated. Given your son's test results, my guess is that the cortical regions have been short-circuited to the hippocampus, which is involved with recurrent memories and might explain his linguistic deficiencies."

There was no reason to dissemble with this man. "I took some bad drugs in college. Something called TNT. The chemical name is trimethoxy-4-methyl-triphetamine."

Malenko's eyes flared. " 'TNT for dynamite sex. Get off with a bang.' "

The old catch phrases for the stuff.

"And I suppose your husband doesn't know that either—which is why you're here."

Rachel knew that under ordinary circumstances she would have dismissed Malenko's unctuously manipulative manner and got up and left. But she suddenly felt a preternatural numbness from all the grief and guilt that had wracked her soul for the last weeks and just didn't care about his obtuseness. Perhaps it was just the relief of getting it all out—like lancing a boil. "I've mentally crippled my son," she said softly. "I just don't want him to suffer. I don't want him to go through life feeling inadequate and inferior."

"And that is why you've not told him."

She nodded.

"Probably a good reason." Malenko moved back to his desk chair and sat down. "I'd like to meet your husband."

"I don't want him to know."

"Telling him is your business, not mine, Mrs. Whitman. But I think we all should meet again to weigh the options."

Weigh the options?

She looked up. "Are you saying there's something that can be done?"

"I'm saying simply that we should meet again." He glanced at his watch then closed Dylan's folder and dropped it on a pile of others with a conclusive snap. "What kind of work is your husband in?" The discussion was over.

If he had some experimental procedure in mind, he wasn't talking. Yet Rachel felt a flicker of promise. "Recruitment. Martin's in the recruitment business."

"Ah, you mean a head hunter."

"Yes, for the high-tech industry."

Malenko nodded in approval. "So he matches up eggheads with egghead companies."

"Something like that."

"Very good. Is it his own business?"

"Yes."

"And business is good, no doubt?"

She nodded. She felt emotionally drained. "Mmmm."

Malenko smiled, probably because it suggested that they could afford their pricey services. Then he picked up Dylan's folder. "I will look these over more closely," he said. "Let me suggest we meet next week, and with your husband. About the MRI, I will explain that you came in here on referral from a local friend, and we had a scan done as a matter of protocol."

He was saying that she could lie, and he'd swear to it. "Thank you."

"You can make an appointment with Marie. Good day."

Rachel left the building, torn between renewed hope and

the overpowering desire to drive home and fall into a long dreamless sleep.

Through the window, Lucius Malenko watched Mrs. Rachel Whitman cross the parking lot to her car, a gold Nissan Maxima. Not a Jaguar or BMW, but also not a Ford Escort. He watched her pull out to the road that would lead back to her perfect little seaview home on the perfect little hill surrounded by perfectly nurtured horticulture.

He had seen her likes by the dozens over the years: yuppies, suburbies, and middle-aged country-club parents of different ethnicities and races—all driven by guilt and vanity and all devotees of the new American religion of self-improvement. From birth and even before, they were obsessed with rearing the supertot. They put toy computers in their children's cribs. They sent them to bed with Mozart and bilingual CDs. They muscled their way into the best preschools. Infertile couples advertised for egg donors in the *Yale Daily News*. Others doled out thousand of dollars for the sperm of Nobel laureates. Some had even consulted geneticists, hoping that they could locate a "smart" gene to be stimulated. There is none, of course, nor any known cluster or combination, but that didn't prevent people from spending small fortunes. It was all so amazing and amusing.

"Nobody wants to be normal anymore," he said aloud.

As Mrs. Rachel Whitman drove away, a new silver BMW 530 two-door pulled into the slot just vacated by her. It was Mrs. Vanessa Watts, coming in to consult about her Julian's behavior problems. Years ago, she had come in just like this Rachel Whitman, gnarled with despair that her youngster was distracted all the time, unfocused, a slow learner, and that he had scored in the fortieth percentile on his math aptitude and fifty-five on the verbal. She was likewise desperate to know what could be done to boost his ranks, otherwise he would never get into Cornell where his father had gone or even into Littleton State where, after some unpleasantness regarding a paper on Jonathan Swift, she eventually earned a doctorate in English literature. And that just could not be—not her Julian. No way. It was unacceptable, and they would do *anything,* pay *anything* to make him a brighter bulb.

He watched Vanessa Watts cross the lot to the front entrance as she had on several occasions to come up and complain that they had succeeded too well—that her Julian was too absorbed in his studies, in his projects, that he had become antisocial: that his filament was all too brilliant.

Never satisfied, these bastards. Especially this one— Professor Loose Cannon. And now she was here with her ultimatum. Fortunately, he had one of his own.

He picked up the phone and dialed Sheila MacPhearson.

28

Brendan found Nicole in her ballet class in a building off Bloomfield Prep's central quad. She was with seven other girls and an instructor in a dance room with mirrors and bars.

Through the glass door, Nicole was dressed in white tights. Her shoulders were bare, giving her long-neck Modigliani proportions. She looked like a swan. They were going through motions called out by a woman instructor dressed in a jogging outfit.

Because it was the last day of classes, the place was empty, so Brendan watched without being discovered. Nicole was perched with one leg up on the bar in line with the other girls. In the reflecting mirror, they looked like twin rows of exotic roosting birds, their faces in a numbed tensity. Suddenly the instructor said something, and they went into leg-flashing exercises. Nicole was second in line at the mirror, her long legs kicking out with elegant precision as if spring-loaded. From a CD player flowed the sweet violin strains of *Swan Lake*. The instructor shouted something, and on cue Nicole broke into her solo, going through complex leaps and pirouettes across the room. Brendan was amazed to see how totally involved she was in the movement, and so precise and athletic. Her teeth were clenched, muscles bunched up for each vault, her shoulders and face aspic'd with sweat, those muscular semaphore legs moving with effortless grace as she flashed around the room. She was a diva in the making.

When the instructor turned off the music and announced class was over, Brendan left the building and waited for her behind some trees in the quadrangle.

Several minutes later, he saw her with two boys coming down the walk toward him. She had changed and was heading for the cafeteria.

"What are you doing here?" Nicole said when he stepped out from behind a tree.

"I have to t-talk to you."

"How did you find me?"

"That's n-n-not important." He pretended the two boys weren't there. "Look, we h-have to talk." According to her schedule she had a forty-minute lunch break before her next class.

"I have a conference with one of my teachers. I can't." She made no effort to introduce Brendan to the others, and he was grateful.

"It's very important," Brendan insisted. He had not foreseen a conference lunch. Or maybe she was just making that up.

She looked at her watch. "I've gotta go. Call me later."

He had promised Richard to take him for his doctor's appointment in two hours. "I can't. We have t-t-to talk now. Just two minutes."

"Hey, man, she said she's got a conference," the taller boy said, trying to puff up. He was a smooth-faced kid who looked like the poster boy for Junior Brooks Brothers. He was dressed in beige chinos and a stiff blue oxford shirt. The other Nicole drone, a black kid with wireless glasses, had on the same chinos but a white golf shirt. "What part of *no* don't you understand?"

"Now there's an original expression," Brendan said. "D-d-did you read that in *A Hundred Best Comebacks*?"

The kid looked baffled, but before he could respond, Nicole said, "Forget it, I know him."

"You sure?" asked the taller boy, eyeing Brendan as if he were toxic waste.

"Yeah, I'll be fine."

"Good luck," the black kid said to her, probably referring to her conference. Then he glanced at Brendan's baggy jeans and black T-shirt with the multicolored tie-dyed starburst on the front. "Nice threads," he sneered.

"Up your J. Crew b-bunghole." As soon as the words were out he felt a surprising flicker of pleasure.

"Cut the shit, both of you," Nicole said.

As the boys moved away, one of them said, "Speaking of the devil."

Coming down the path was an older man in a sport coat and tie and carrying a briefcase.

Nicole's face went to autolight: "Hi, Mr. Kaminsky." She beamed at him as he approached. "I'll be right there."

The man scowled at Nicole. "You know where I'll be." He did not look pleased. As he walked away, he glanced at Brendan, and recognition seemed to flit across his face, but he continued down the path toward the next building.

It was the bushy-haired guy in the diner. And the one she had shacked up with that same night.

"I'll catch you later," she said to the other boys, dismissing them. As they walked away, she looked at Brendan blankly.

"Your teacher," he said, barely able to hide his dismay.

"So?"

"Nothing." But he could tell that she remembered Brendan seeing them holding hands at Angie's. She had no idea, of course, what he had seen through her window.

"Okay, make it fast."

"I had a dream the other night. It was c-c-crazy, but I was in a hospital bed."

She looked at him incredulously. "So?"

"I had never been in a hospital before, at least I d-don't remember."

Nicole checked her watch. "You've got twenty seconds."

"M-Mr. Nisha was there. He said I had to be a good boy and take my medicine. It was crazy, and I don't know what or who he was—just that image floating and 'Mr. Nisha wants you to be happy' stuff. I don't understand. Also, there were other kids there, too."

Nicole continued to stare at him blankly. "I've got an A hanging on this conference, and if I'm late, he gets pissed and takes off, and I'm screwed out of a four-oh. I'm not going to lose that because you had some stupid dream." She started away.

"Okay, but just one question," he pleaded, chasing after her.

"Later," she snapped. "At the club party."

Dells was sponsoring a Scholar's Night Saturday for caddy scholarship winners and the publication of Vanessa Watts's book. Brendan was scheduled to serve hors d'oeuvres.

Brendan moved in front of her. "Please, j-just one question."

"What?" Her otherwise remote, expressionless face suddenly tightened like a fist.

"Did you ever go to a hospital?"

"No."

"Nicole, think!" he said, running after her.

"I said no."

"Never?"

"NO."

"You sure?"

Suddenly she stopped. "Get out of my *way*." Her voice hit a nail.

He caught her arm. "Can I look at the top of your head, please?" He moved his hands to part the hair on her crown.

"Get out of here." And she whacked his hand.

"Do you have any scars on your head?"

She did not answer him and ran down the path to the cafeteria. Before entering, she stopped in her tracks. With an almost robotic movement, she turned and looked back at him for a long moment. Then she ran into the building.

Brendan followed her. The cafeteria entrance was toward the rear. He stuck his head in. Because most upperclassmen had left for the summer, the place was only partly filled with students.

In the rear of the room he spotted Nicole and Mr. Kaminsky at a table by themselves. They were not eating, but talking heatedly. After a few minutes, Nicole slipped him a package. He looked in and slipped out the contents, inspected it then put it back in the envelope, dumped it into his briefcase, and left.

She followed him with her eyes until they landed on Brendan just a moment before he slipped out of view.

Instantly, he disappeared out a side door, leaving her wondering if he had noticed that she had given Kaminsky a videocassette.

29

Travis could tell time, of course. But he had no idea what hour of day it was or what day of the week—or how many days he had been in this room. Everything was a big bright blur. But he figured it was two days since the needle test, because his neck didn't hurt anymore—yesterday it was like bee stings.

Today was another test day, but no needle this time, Vera said. He also knew that if he didn't cooperate, they'd send him back to his room and turn off the lights for hours. That was the one punishment he couldn't take. Total blackness in that locked room. The first time they did that he screamed and cried until he thought he would die. In fact, he knew he would rather die than go through that again.

Vera came in with Phillip. Although Travis could walk, they put him in a wheelchair and snapped a harness on him like a seat belt so he couldn't get up.

For the first time they brought him outside the room.

He was in a long dimly lit corridor with pipes overhead. On either side of the corridor were windows with shades drawn down from the outside. The only sounds were from television sets. There must have been a set in each room all playing the same stuff because the sound followed him as they pushed him down the hall.

At the end of the corridor, they turned left into a room full of shiny metal equipment and computer terminals. They wheeled him to a table near a computer with some electronic equipment attached to it.

"Don't be afraid, this isn't going to hurt," Vera said. "We're just going to look at pictures of your brain."

Travis's heart pounded. He didn't like this. He didn't like the looks of those machines and another man sitting in the dark rear of the room at another computer terminal.

Phillip pulled up a chair in front of him. "Listen, kid, this is going to be a piece of cake. You're not going to feel anything, it's not going to hurt. Just answer a few questions and do a few puzzles. That's it. It'll be fun, okay?"

Travis nodded.

"It's just a simple test. Vera's going to ask you some questions, and you're going to give the answers. Got that? So, be a good boy." Phillip stared at him hard, and Travis heard: *Or else I'm going to take you back to your room and turn off the lights.*

Vera came over and put gobs of jelly stuff on his head and rubbed it into his scalp through his hair. It didn't smell bad, but it felt yucky. She told him it would wash right out. Phillip then fitted onto his head a tight black rubbery cap. It had lots of red wires attached like snakes. Those Phillip connected to the machine and the computer. He pulled the cap tightly over Travis's eyebrows and fastened it across his chin so that only his face was exposed. Then he taped some wires on Travis's cheeks and the space above his eyebrows.

Travis sat still at the table, listening to the faint hum of the machine.

When they were set, Phillip joined the other man at the computer in the back, and Vera sat at the machine. "Just relax and answer the questions," she began. "Some of the questions will be easy, some will be hard. But the important thing is that you try the best you can. Okay? Because the better you do, the sooner you go home."

Travis looked at her blankly.

As if reading his mind, she said, "Yeah, for real. You do real good on these and you can go back to your mom."

He didn't know whether to believe her or not, but he didn't want to take the chance. "Okay."

She set the small clock down beside her and opened the booklet she had. "How many states in the United States?"

"Fifty."

"Good."

"How many days in two weeks?"

"Fourteen."

"Name me six types of trees."

"Um . . . Pine, oak, birch, beech, magnolia, orange."

Vera nodded and scratched in her book.

She asked several easy questions like that, then said they were going to switch to different kinds of questions. "While training for a marathon, Jack ran fifty-two miles in four days, how many miles per day did he average in this period?"

"Thirteen."

"Excellent."

After a few more like that, the questions got harder. "Now I'm going to say some letters, and you repeat them after me. *T-R-S-M*."

"*T-R-S-M*."

"Good."

"Do the same with these: *P-G-I-C-R-W*."

"*P-G-I-C-R-W*."

"*M-F-Y-U-W-R-S-D-A*."

"*M-F-Y-U-W-R-S-D-A*."

Vera nodded. "Good," she said. "Now give me the letters in the backwards: *Y-L-X-F-R-W*."

"*W-R-F-X-L-Y*."

"Do the same with these: *X-D-E-W-Q-A-F*."

"*F-A-Q-W-E-D-X*."

Vera whispered, "Jesus!"

Then she did the same, adding one more letter each time, until he repeated a ten-letter series backward. He could tell he got them right because Vera's face lit up as she marked down the score and checked the computer monitor.

"Okay, now I'm going to read you a sentence, and I want you to repeat it exactly as I read it. Okay? Good: *'Janet, who lives on Brown Street, got for her birthday a dollhouse with green shutters and a red roof.' "*

" *'Janet, who lives on Brown Street, got for her birthday a dollhouse with green shutters and a red roof.' "*

This went on for almost an hour until he was tired and wanted to rest.

When the testing was over, Vera said, "You're a very bright little guy."

"Can I go home now?"

"Soon," Vera said. She disconnected all the wires on his cap, removed it, and wiped his head with a towel. His scalp was sweaty from the cap and sticky with the jelly. "For the time being, we're going to take you outside."

"But you said I could go home."

She didn't answer, just nodded Phillip over.

They pushed him out of the test room and down the corridor to a staircase at the end where Phillip and the other man lifted the wheelchair and carried him up to the top. Vera then pushed him through a series of rooms to an outside deck.

The shock of the bright sky made him wince. It felt good to be in the warm open air. There were tall pine trees all around. In the distance he could see a lake sparkling in the sunlight. It must have been late morning.

But what caught his attention was the sound of children. To the far right he spotted a small playground with climbing structures and a slide with kids on it. Nearby a woman watched them.

Two of the children had white bandages on their heads.

One of them was on the grass dancing with someone.

At first he thought it was another kid dressed up in some

kind of costume. But when the girl spun around, Travis realized that she was attached to a life-sized doll—that the thing's feet and hands were strapped to the girl's shoes and hands, and that she was laughing and chanting something, although the words weren't right.

It took Travis a moment to make out the doll, but when the kid turned into a shaft of sunlight he could see that it was a big blue stuffed elephant with a wide grin and human hands. The same stupid creature they had painted on the walls of his room. And in the puppet-show video they played.

And in a singsongy voice, the woman chanted: "Dance with Mr. Nisha. Dance with Mr. Nisha. Dance with Mr. Nisha."

30

Greg met Joe Steiner at the Quarterdeck, a popular bar and restaurant in Falmouth center. Sitting with Joe was another man introduced as Lou Fournier, a neurologist from Cape Cod Medical Center.

"I think Lou might be able to give you a little more insight about your skull cases," Joe had said. Greg didn't have to be at work until seven, so they met at five-thirty. Joe knew Greg had been put on night shifts. He also was beginning to suspect that Greg might be on to something odd, although he didn't know what. And that suspicion was why they were meeting.

Fournier was a man in his sixties with a round broad expressive face that made you think of Jonathan Winters. According to Joe, he had been chief neurologist in a hospital in Trenton, New Jersey, but had gone into semiretirement on the Cape. Joe had shown Fournier the photos of both sets of remains and the diagrams of the anonymous Essex Medical Center patient.

They ordered some beers. "I don't know what I have," Greg said. "It might all be a grand coincidence."

"What does your instinct tell you?" Fournier asked.

"That the odds are against coincidence, that there's some pattern, some connection."

"I'm not sure, either," Fournier said. "But I'd say your instinct is right on." He laid the two skull photos side by side with the drawing of the Essex patient. "On the Sagamore Boy, you've got twenty-two holes all on the left side of the skull. On the Dixon boy, you've got nineteen holes on the left side of the skull. On this kid from the Essex Medical Center, his X rays show eighteen holes on the left side. I think Dr. Budd is correct: The areas seem to map out interconnected circuits of the cerebral cortex that's associated with intelligence and memory."

Using his finger to illustrate, he continued. "This area here is the frontal lobe, or prefrontal cortex, and is important for planning behavior, attention, and memory. This other cluster is over the parietal lobe and is part of the 'association cortex,' known as Wernicke's area."

"Wernicke's area?"

"Yes, the area of the brain associated with language and the complex functions of understanding. People with damage to this area suffer aphasia—they lose their ability to comprehend the meaning of words and can't produce meaningful sentences."

"What about these other holes?" Greg asked, pointing to seven around the ear area.

"That's even more interesting," Fournier said. "These cover what's called Broca's area, which is associated with the analysis of syntax and speech production. If someone experiences damage in the Broca's area, they lose their ability to speak."

"So you're saying the holes cover the entire language center of the brain."

"Yes, but it's important to note that these same areas make important connections with many other areas of the brain involved with thinking abilities, conceptual skills, and memory."

Greg nodded and sipped his beer.

"What do you know about this Essex patient?" Fournier asked Greg.

"Almost nothing—a male teenager from someplace on the North Shore, but that's it."

"Then you don't know his handedness—whether he's a righty or lefty."

"No."

"How about the Dixon boy?" He picked up the Dixon photo.

Greg thought for a moment. Grady's first baseball glove. "Right-handed."

Fournier nodded. "You're sure?"

"Yeah. But why is that important?"

"I'm not sure, but more than ninety-five percent of right-handed males have language localization in the left hemisphere. Left-handers are bilateral, that is, they have language centers on both the right and left sides of the brain."

"But the kid never had any kind of brain operation, his parents said. And I saw his medical records, and his pediatrician confirms."

"I understand, but these holes are not random, so somebody did something to him. And these others."

"Like what?"

Fournier took a sip of his beer. "These holes I'd say were made by stereotaxic drilling. It's an alternative to removing large sections of the skull to reach target areas of the brain—a pinpoint-drilling procedure to remove lesions, abscesses, or tumorous tissue. Or to implant electrodes or radioactive seeds for killing tumors.

"The sheer number suggests mass intercranial lesions or multiple tumors—except the likelihood of survival for young kids is nil. Even with the most precise 3-D imaging, a surgeon can get lost trying to determine where a tumor ends and normal brain tissue begins. And in these areas, that means damage to important neurocircuitry, which could result in serious physical and emotional problems. So I'd rule out any orthodox neurological operation.

"The other possibility is radioactive seeding. But that's

not likely, either." Fournier picked up the schematic of the Essex patient again. "This is what throws me the most. If this kid underwent extensive stereotaxic surgery, he's either a walking miracle or he's walking brain-dead."

"The nurse said that he looked perfectly healthy and that he has a remarkable memory," Greg said.

"Then something else is going on."

"Like what?"

Fournier shook his head. "Some kind of exotic experiment, but nothing I've seen before," Fournier said. Then he added, "But if these two kids are dead, and this one is walking around, you might want to look him up, because he's making medical history."

31

Fine gray drizzle was falling the morning that Martin and Rachel met with Dr. Malenko. The air was unseasonably cool, making the day feel more like a morning in October than late June.

The appointment was set for noon. However, they did not meet at Nova Children's Center. Instead they were directed to Malenko's private office in Cobbsville, a small town just over the New Hampshire border, about a half hour drive from Hawthorne.

Martin was quiet on the drive over, commenting perfunctorily on the rain and scenery. If he was nervous, it did not show. If he was incredulous, he didn't let on. He had lapsed into a mode of slightly irritated neutrality—irritated because he had to cancel a meeting in Boston with an important client.

Rachel disregarded Martin's mood, too lost in her own vacillations between hopefulness and nagging anxiety. She had told Martin that she had consulted with Malenko last week, but didn't go into details. All she said was that the doctor had agreed to meet with them both. About what she didn't know.

Number 724 Cabot Street turned out to be a small nondescript ranchlike house with pale green aluminum siding and black shutters behind a hedge of mulberry. Except for the cherry-red Porsche with the gold Bernardi dealer's decal in the driveway, Rachel would have thought they had the wrong place. No M.D.'s shingle hung outside, no name above the bell.

Malenko heard them pull up, because he opened the front door to greet them. He shook Martin's hand. "Please come in."

A small reception area had been carved out of a front parlor on the left, but no receptionist. In fact, from what Rachel could tell, no one else was in the house.

Malenko led them into a rear office furnished in leather and dark muted reds, greens, and gold. Bookcases lined two walls, full of medical tomes and technical journals. On a table beside some plants sat another elephant-god statue in tarnished brass.

"You *are* your son's father," Malenko said. "The resemblance is striking." A school photograph of Dylan was included in the folder.

"Poor kid," Martin joked.

"On the contrary," Malenko said, and took his seat behind the desk.

The resemblance *was* uncanny, something everybody picked up on. It was as if Dylan were a miniclone of Martin, Rachel thought, his own Mini-Me—as if she had passed nothing on to her son but a damaged brain.

"Well, now," Malenko began, glancing into the folder before him. "When you came in here last week, Mrs. Whitman, you expressed interest in the center finding a program that would best be suited for Dylan."

Rachel nodded, not knowing where this was going, but feeling her anxiety mount.

"As you know, we had him assessed with an expectation of designing a program tailored to his talents and needs. Because of his language-processing problems and memory lapses, we conducted a body of tests, both neurological and behavioral, including an EKG and MRI scan."

Rachel felt her heart gulp as he pulled out a large envelope with MRI scans. She didn't know if she could sit through another gruesome profile of her son's disabilities.

"The results show that there are region-specific language problems that are associated with the regional-specific deficits in Dylan's brain, not unlike those we see in patients with dyslexia. As you well know, Dylan has a tendency to overregularize verbs—saying *I singed, I goed, I knowed.* He also has problems with the use of other morphemes such as possessives and verb agreements. Instead of *the cat's paw,* he'll say *the cat paw.* Or *she talk* instead of *she talks.*"

Rachel took a deep breath and swallowed it before it came out a groan.

"He also has problems with certain reasoning aspects associated with language—the use of the passive voice, subjunctives, and *if* clauses. He was asked the classic test in the field: Who did the biting when he heard the statement *'The lion was bitten by the tiger.'* His answer was the lion. He was not able to understand the causality. He heard *'The lion bit the tiger.'"*

Rachel put her hand to her brow as Malenko went to the light board and pointed out the anatomical disparities in Dylan's brain for Martin. Her heart raced, and she bit down, trying to keep herself from spinning out of control.

"Jesus!" Martin said, as he listened. "The left looks smaller by a quarter."

"Yes, at least," said Malenko.

"But why?" Martin asked.

Rachel stiffened. If Malenko even faintly intimated that she had brought this on with drugs, she knew that she would explode.

"There are several possibilities," Malenko began, "though none we can exactly determine. My best guess is that it's a genetic aberration. Who knows? But that's not the important thing. It's what we can do for Dylan."

Rachel caught Malenko's eye as he sat down again. He must have detected the insane heat in her eyes because he addressed Martin. "Your son will have to have a comprehensive individualized instruction program geared to improving his word recognition and comprehension, grammar, reading, and critical-thinking skills."

"How long a program are you talking about?"

"Typically, from seventy-five to a hundred hours of instruction, and up to four hours of instruction per week. But given Dylan's assessment, I'd say he would need instruction on a daily basis for a hundred to two hundred hours. Maybe more."

"God! It's that bad?"

Malenko leaned back in his chair and for a brief moment studied Martin's reaction. "Mr. Whitman, I'm sure you're aware that no test can exactly measure a person's intellectual ability, including standard IQ tests. I mean, how can a test assign a number to creativity or artistic skills or leadership, curiosity, musical talent or physical prowess or social skills, emotional well-being, and so on? It's impossible. However, the composite IQ score measures verbal and logical thinking, which is the best overall predictor we have of educational achievement and success.

"Your son's intelligence quotient falls in a range of seventy-nine to eighty-four which is the low side of the national average. He needs special attention."

"So it's not just some attention-deficit thing that can be treated with medication?"

"I'm afraid not."

"Jesus," Martin said. "Maybe it was some lead paint he was exposed to. Or mercury or some other crap. I don't get it. We've got lawyers and engineers on both sides of the family. How the hell . . ." And he tapered off.

"How it happened isn't the issue, Mr. Whitman. There are people with less intellectual talent than Dylan who are happy and productive members of our society."

"Yeah? Name me one."

Rachel shot a look at Martin.

Martin turned to her. "What?"

"Stop it!"

"Stop what? He's handicapped and I can't accept that. Okay?"

Rachel knew it was totally irrational, but all the outrage, despair, and vexation that was racking her soul converged like rays in a magnifying glass on Martin's face. And at the moment she hated him. He was condemning their son to a life on the margins.

Malenko cut in. "I can't name names just like that. But you know what I mean—sports people, entertainers, actors, musicians, singers—people in the various trades, business people who surely would qualify."

Martin made a cynical grunt.

"Mr. Whitman, your son is a charming and handsome little boy with a lovely voice, I understand. Who knows, he may grow up to be the next Luciano Pavarotti or Frank Sinatra."

"Hmm," Martin said, feeling Rachel's eyes burning him.

To break the tension, Malenko said to Martin, "Let me ask you a question. You know something about the different programs we have, and you know your son's potentials and limitations. Given all that, what exactly are your expectations for Dylan?"

"My expectations? I don't follow you."

"What would you like for Dylan?"

"I would like him to have more of a head start on life."

"And you, Mrs. Whitman? Do you feel the same way?"

Rachel took another deep breath to steady herself. "I'm not sure I understand the question." She could hear the deadness in her voice.

"That you would like for Dylan to have more of a head start on life?"

Still not certain she understood him, she said, "I suppose." Tears began to fill her eyes. She felt as if she were dying inside. All she wanted to do was to go home.

"Good, because that's what we intend to give him—the chance to live up to his abilities."

"That's not what I mean," Martin said.

"Then what do you mean, sir?"

"Even if we sign him up for the best tutoring—"

"Instruction," Malenko insisted, cutting him off. "Not tutorial. There's a big difference."

"Okay, instruction. Even with the best people you have, he's got an eighty IQ. That wouldn't be an issue if this were the eighteenth or nineteenth century. You didn't have to be very bright to make it. But it's the twenty-first century, and the brightest people occupy the highest-powered professions. Simple as that. The best instruction you can come up with won't raise his capabilities."

"No, but we may get him to work at his best. What more can you ask for? Your son is not retarded or autistic."

"No, but he's the low side of average. Just how far can that take him? It's like asking him to run a race with a club foot."

There was a humming pause for a few seconds. Rachel began to cry.

"Well, what exactly do you want of him?" she heard Malenko ask.

"I want him to be smarter."

"But, surely, being smart isn't the only measure of people."

"No, but it will get you places."

Rachel cried into her handkerchief while Martin's and Malenko's voices blurred like white noise. They seemed not to notice.

"Like his mom and dad."

"What's that supposed to mean?"

"I'm just wondering whom you are here for, Mr. Whitman: Dylan or yourself. I seem to be hearing less about what we can do for Dylan and more about reducing your dissatisfaction with your child."

"I beg your pardon, Doctor, but I love my child very much." Martin's face was flushed.

"Your love is not in question, Mr. Whitman. But what I'm hearing is that you don't have the child you wish you had—a child who would grow to share your intellectual, cultural, and aesthetic interests. A child who will be your equal someday, not an inferior."

Martin's eye twitched, and Rachel half-expected him to flash back at Malenko. But something in Malenko's manner extinguished whatever impulse Martin felt. "I'm here for Dylan," he said flatly. "I just wish he could have the opportunities other kids have."

"What other kids?"

"Other kids in his school and play groups," Martin said. "You know what I mean. Kids who aren't intellectually handicapped. You're saying that our son has a serious brain deficiency that's crippled his verbal skills. We live in a heavily writing-dependent society, which means that he'll be targeted as somebody who's dumb."

Rachel got up.

"What's the matter?" Martin asked.

"I'm leaving. You can stay, but I'm going." She started toward the door.

Malenko rose to his feet. "Please, please. Let's all calm down."

"I am calm," she said, barely able to disguise her emotions. She began to open the door when Malenko came over to her and took her arm.

"Please, sit down. I'll call Marie to bring in some coffee."

"I don't want coffee," Rachel said. "I want to go."

Something in Malenko's expression gave her pause. "I think there's more to discuss. Please." And he beckoned for her to return to her seat.

Martin was on his feet looking at them both wide-eyed.

Rachel felt herself consent. But with tears rolling down

her cheeks, and her voice trembling, she said, "I don't want to hear any more about how my son is intellectually handicapped. Okay? Or how he's not going to make it in life." She glared at Martin.

"Yeah, sure," Martin said feebly.

She took a deep breath, and in as steady a voice as she could muster, she announced, "I want to discuss an instructional program for him. Period."

Malenko nodded, and led her back to her seat.

An uncanny silence fell on the room, as he seemed to turn something over in his head. He then picked up the phone and called the secretary to bring in three coffees.

They sat in an uneasy silence as the coffee was delivered.

Rachel sipped from her cup and stared blankly at the floor. All the swirling eddies of emotions had receded to the rear of her mind leaving her at the moment feeling dead. She could register Martin's presence beside her and Malenko's behind his desk. But it was as if she were occupying that quasi-conscious state in dreams.

But the spell suddenly broke when Malenko clinked down his cup. "Mrs. Whitman, when you first came in here last week, you asked about special medical procedures to enhance your son's IQ. At that time, I had said that there were no accepted strategies to accomplish that."

Rachel looked up.

"I had assumed you were interested in standard medical practices, which to my knowledge do not exist. I had not assumed that you were interested in alternate procedures, thus, I mentioned none."

Rachel felt her heart jog. The room seemed to shift its coordinates. "Alternative procedures?"

"Yes. There's an experimental treatment that's been known to have significant effects in lab animals. It appears to work by stimulating areas in the cortex and hypothalamus that affect memory and cognitive performance."

"Lab animals?"

"Yes, maze tests with mice and more sophisticated problem-solving tasks for higher animals including monkeys. And the results are rather remarkable."

"Has it been tried on people?" Rachel asked.

"Yes, and with remarkable results, but I must caution you that this is a purely experimental procedure akin to what's used in the treatment of certain cerebral dysfunctions, including Parkinson's disease. I'm talking about measures that are drastic and unconventional. Is this something you'd be interested in?"

"You mean a brain operation?"

"Yes, an invasive procedure."

Rachel wanted him to continue, but Martin cut him off. "And what are the results?"

"They're not always predictable, but the neuronal pathways in those areas associated with intelligence show marked blood flow and heightened electrical activity, including abnormally developed areas."

"Meaning what exactly?"

"Meaning enhanced performance in language and analytical skills."

Sheila's face flashed across Rachel's mind—that look of burning import. Suddenly the line between hope and the emotional muck of grief, anger, and guilt had shifted.

"That's incredible," Martin said.

"But, once again, this is not orthodox methodology," Malenko cautioned. "It's an experimental alternative."

"And it's been done on people? Children?" Rachel asked.

"Yes."

Rachel's mind was spinning in disbelief. "Is it safe?"

"Like any operation, it has its risks, but it's categorically safe."

Malenko's manner was purposely guarded. Rachel was about to ask him to elaborate when Martin cut her off again. "What exactly is the science—some kind of genetic therapy?"

"Before I continue, I must tell you that what we are discussing is strictly confidential. What we say in this room will not go beyond these walls. Do I make myself clear?" He looked from Martin to Rachel.

"Yeah, sure," Martin said.

Rachel nodded, feeling a bit dazed at the new possibilities. It suddenly occurred to her that their previous discussion had been a test—and that they had passed.

"Good," Malenko said. "The procedure involves the introduction of certain agents that stimulate neuronic connections and open new pathways."

"You mean like stem cells?" Martin asked.

"Something like that. The target areas of the brain are infused with a cocktail of various substances including growth factors. Intelligence is a multifaceted phenomenon consisting of different potentials—mathematics, linguistic, logic, spatial, and so on—and each specialty has a field locus in the brain. Dylan's musical talent has an associative field of activity in his cortex. However, there are underdeveloped areas where the field potential is low and where lateral support cannot be assumed by other specialized areas."

He opened a desk drawer and removed a diagram of a human brain.

"I'm not saying it will work, but it might be possible to stimulate cell development in those language-deficient areas so that they'll connect up to those specialty areas to make for more integrated brain dynamics." He used a pen to demonstrate on the scans. "Essentially, it might be possible to compensate for the developmental deficiencies *in utero*."

"That's incredible," Martin said.

"You said *invasive*. You mean an operation?" Rachel asked. "Cutting open our son's head?"

"Actually, it's done by stereotaxic surgery—drilling tiny holes then implanting stimulants by use of needles."

Rachel let out an involuntary groan, and Malenko picked up on it. "Sorry to say that this can't be done intravenally. But stereotaxic procedures are performed all the time, and it is very precise, of course, and monitored in three-dimension by CAT scans."

"And where do the stem cells come from?" Rachel asked.

"There are donor banks."

"Who would be doing the procedure?" Rachel asked.

"We have a surgical team."

"And your role is what?"

He smiled thinly. "I'll be in charge."

"So you've done these procedures before?" Martin asked.

"Yes."

The guardedness in his manner was almost palpable. Rachel could sense that they were treading on territory that had vaguely been charted—some forbidden zone behind the chrome and green Italian marble veneer. "What about the risks?"

"Risks are inherent in any operation, but with this procedure they are very small. At worst, there would be only a minimal regeneration of neuronal networks, with modest improvement in performance. But that possibility is far exceeded by the benefits."

"Such as?" Martin asked, his eyes wide with supplication. He was suddenly enthralled by the possibilities.

"Your son's IQ will be higher."

"It will?" Martin's voice skipped an octave. He could not disguise his excitement. "How much higher?"

Malenko smiled. "How much would you like?"

"You mean we have a choice?"

Malenko chuckled. "Enhancement can't be fine-tuned to an exact number, of course." He then unlocked a drawer from a file cabinet behind him and removed a folder from which he removed some charts. The first was a lopsided bell curve showing the IQ distribution of high school seniors and the colleges they attended. On the fat right end of the curve where the scores went from eighty-five to one hundred and five, the schools listed were community colleges and Southern state schools. But at the long thin tapered end were the A-list institutions—Stanford, Cal Tech, MIT, WPI, and the top Ivy Leagues.

"Dylan's IQ is currently about eighty-two. Let's say, for instance, that it was enhanced by fifteen points, he would just get by in the typical high school. Another fifteen points would mean he'd perform well in high school and just passably at a mid-level college. Another fifteen points would mean he'd do well at the better colleges. Another fifteen points—an IQ about one hundred forty—would mean he'd do a sterling job at the better colleges. Another fifteen points and he would have an incandescent mind capable of doing superior work at the very best institutions."

"Incandescent mind." The phrase hummed in Rachel's consciousness.

"Wow," whispered Martin.

Malenko seemed bemused at their sudden display of interest. Or maybe it was the kind of sneaky pleasure one gets from sharing secrets.

The second chart showed a correlation of IQ scores with various occupations—physicians, mathematicians, scientists, accountants, lawyers, business executives, teachers, bus drivers, and so on.

"As you said, there was a time when people of high intelligence were scattered across a range of employment. But over the last two decades, that population has squeezed into a handful of high-powered professions. No longer do you find the brilliant shoemaker or ditchdigger. Instead, they're running laboratories, law firms, the world's most important corporations, and"—he gave a little smile— "egghead-recruitment companies. So the benefits can promise years of success for Dylan.

"But they go beyond professional. The statistical correlation of high intelligence with financial and intellectual achievements is an obvious gain. Not so obvious are the *intangible* benefits of high intelligence, such as maturity, superior adjustments to life, general health, and happiness—all of which I assume you desire for your Dylan."

He raised another chart—an actuarial graph of life expectancy measured against IQ. "One of the ancillary benefits of high intelligence is lifestyle, including diet, personal health care, and basic survival. In other words, as you can see, smarter people are happier, healthier, and live longer lives." He ran his finger up the curve showing the higher survival rates for those at the upper end of the IQ scale.

While Rachel listened half in awe, it became clear that this was not just a glib explanation of some experimental neurophysiological procedure, but a sales pitch. That Malenko had had these charts prepared, and that he had been through this spiel with other parents who had sat in these same chairs, twisting with anxiety and hope that they could make life better for their children.

Malenko is selling IQs.

"I should add that individuals at the lower end of the spectrum are, statistically speaking, people with more serious psychological problems and emotional disorders. Nor should it surprise you that the majority of people on welfare and in prisons in the United States have an average IQ of eighty-seven."

That comment jabbed Rachel like an ice pick. "Those are blind statistics," she said. "And I resent the implication."

"Of course, of course, they're blind statistics," Malenko said. "And in no way am I suggesting that Dylan would otherwise grow up to be a criminal or on welfare. I'm just telling you what studies have found."

He slipped the charts back into the drawer and locked the cabinet. "So?" he said, waiting for a response.

"So, you're saying that you can do this—that you can increase Dylan's intelligence?" Martin asked.

Malenko smiled. "That's what I've been telling you."

"That's incredible." Martin's face looked like a polished Macintosh.

"What about the side effects?" Rachel asked again.

"*Side effects* might be the wrong term, madam," Malenko began. "Intelligence is holistic. It's intricately bound up with a person's ego, his self-projection, his personality, and character—and all his or her assorted talents. So, the person that Dylan will become would most likely not be the same person he would be were he not enhanced. Depending on the emotional complexity of a person, much of the difference would have to do with confidence and self-esteem.

"Studies have shown that intelligent people are more centered, more self-assured, more self-confident, and less timid than those who are intellectually challenged." He turned to Martin. "You see it all the time in your profession—that special poise, presence, and strength not found in people possessed of lower intellectual skills."

"But you're talking about changing who Dylan will be," Rachel said. "I don't want him to be intellectually enhanced if his personality changes . . ."

he kissed my boo-boo

". . . or he loses his love for singing or baseball." Although he could not read music, he had a voice like wind chimes. It was a talent that distinguished him and brought him pleasure.

"Mrs. Whitman, forgive the analogy, but he would be like the child who had been stricken with polio. Without the vaccine, he'd grow up wearing leg braces or confined to a wheelchair. Now consider that same child who at age seven was given his legs back and all that went with that.

Which child do you suppose would have the happier, longer, better life?"

He did not expect an answer, nor did they offer one. But Rachel was vexed by the man's pronouncements.

"Before we go any further," he said. "I must know if this is something you would consider for Dylan. Mrs. Whitman?"

Rachel felt confused and overwhelmed. "I don't know where to begin." It was as if Malenko were no longer a physician but some kind of self-proclaimed Fairy Godfather. "You're talking about surgically manipulating my son's native intelligence. That's not something I can make a snap decision about. There are too many questions and unknowns."

"Of course, nor am I asking for a snap decision. I'm simply asking if you are interested in pursuing the matter. If not, then we can go back to our original plan for an instructional program."

"Well, *I'm* interested," Martin announced. He looked at Rachel beckoningly. "I mean, isn't this what we wanted?" He was almost giddy.

Rachel was not sure what they had wanted. "I think I need time for all of this to sink in."

"Of course, but I should caution you that the time for best results for the procedure is when the child is between three and six years of age. Any older and enhancement diminishes in effectiveness. And Dylan is six years and two months."

"You mean there's a deadline?"

"The earlier the better. As a child approaches puberty, everything changes. Yes, nerve cells are still generated— even in adults. But the massive wiring of the brain takes place early. More importantly," he added, moving his finger across his head, "the long axonal connections from one section of the brain to another are most important in terms of cognitive functions, and they're laid down and fine-tuned well before puberty. At six, your son's brain is still experiencing large-scale cognitive development. But it's already begun to diminish."

"I understand," Martin said. He was beaming.

Malenko's face seemed to harden. "There's something else that you'll need to factor into your decision: I ask that you maintain total confidentiality even if you decide against this. And I'll be honest with you: Enhancement is not standard clinical procedure for the treatment of LD children. It's an alternative, but it's not FDA-approved."

"May I ask why not?"

"Because, although the procedure is medically safe and sound, it would be something of a social taboo. It's not *politically correct*. And unless they wanted full-scale riots on their hands, no government administrators would support the procedure. And until they do, we play hide-and-seek."

The unexpected element of secrecy made Rachel even more uneasy and confused. On top of all the disquieting medical unknowns, she now had to be concerned with social and ethical issues. Malenko was right: If word got out about a medical procedure that enhanced the intelligence of children, the social implications would be astounding. Every parent who could afford it would have his or her LD kid fixed. In the long run, that would throw off the balance of society, the intellectual diversity. Not to mention the class problems—the haves versus the have-nots. Enhanced versus the enhanced-nots. Not to mention how every liberal left of Joseph Goebbels would raise a stink about *eugenics* and *social engineering*. And rightfully so. But at the moment, social questions weren't most pressing. "But you say the procedure is medically safe?"

"Absolutely, and one hundred percent effective."

"Meaning what?"

"Meaning every enhanced child is now a genius."

Martin looked at Rachel in wordless amazement. "And how many is that?" she asked.

"Several." His expression was unreadable.

Trade secret, she thought.

"But what about the ugly stuff," Martin asked. "Cost?"

Malenko made a bemused smile. "A lot, but nothing we should discuss now. First things first, and that's letting this all sink in." He stood up and came around the desk. The meeting was over.

"What I'd like you to do is go home and think about this. Think if this is something you want to go through with, because you'll be making a lifetime decision for your son, probably the most important in his life and yours. It's a decision that transcends the merely medical. If you're uncomfortable with the philosophical or social implications, then this is not for you. If you feel this runs counter to some ethical position you maintain, then this is not for you. But if you take the less global view—that this is your son and that your son has but one life to live—then you may accept the tenet that *intelligence is its own reward.*"

Rachel and Martin rose.

Malenko walked them out of the office to the front door. "Once again, I must caution you about confidentiality. Security is supremely important. Be it understood that this will not work if people talk. You are not allowed to discuss this with others. You are not allowed to seek others' opinions. You are not allowed to put anything in writing. There will be no enhancement if I suspect that you will breach confidentiality. Is that understood?"

"Yeah, sure," Martin said weakly.

Rachel nodded.

"Good. If we agree that this is the best thing for Dylan, then you'll be asked to sign a nondisclosure agreement, the details to be explained later. Then we'll discuss the ugly stuff." He shook their hands. "Now go home and think about all this, and we'll talk next week."

Throughout the interview, Rachel had seen in Malenko a man of intimidating self-assurance and intelligence, a man whose polished rhetoric and keen instinct had nearly stripped her of defenses, had maneuvered her and Martin nearly to admit that they were here because of their dissatisfaction with their own son. And while part of her hated how she had bought into the presumption that intelligence was it own reward, this was the first time in their hour-long discussion that she sensed an abstract menace behind the porcelain smile.

Malenko opened the front door. "By the way, is Dylan right-handed or left?"

"Right," Martin said.

"Good," Malenko said, but did not elaborate.

"Doctor, I want you to know that before I can make a decision," Rachel said, "I would have to meet some enhanced children."

"You already have."

Then like a half-glimpsed premonition she heard Malenko say: "Lucinda MacPhearson."

32

B ut she's brilliant?"

"She is now," Sheila said. "They raised her score by seventy-something points."

They were at the Dells, in the café just outside the day care center having a muffin and café au lait.

"It'll be two years in December. We took her in over the Christmas break from preschool, and when she returned her hair had grown back and nobody even knew. Then over the next months, she began to show signs of improvement—talking better, understanding better. In a year she was reading and reasoning and thinking. God, it was like somebody cranked up the rheostat."

"That's incredible."

"You're telling me? And they can do the same for Dylan. I mean, it's a miracle. She was this hairless little monkey, and now she's . . . Lucinda."

"Hairless little monkey." Was that how she regarded Dylan?

"If you don't mind my asking, what was the nature of her problem?"

"What do you mean?"

"Brain deformities or anomalies or whatever?"

"No."

"Some kind of accident or trauma?"

"Not really."

"Well, what made you bring her?"

Sheila looked at her incredulously. "She was slow."

"Wait a minute. You're mean these enhancement procedures aren't just for kids with neurophysical defects?"

Sheila's face darkened. "Well, a few are."

"You're saying that most are kids with no physical abnormalities—lesions, tumors, malformations—or whatever? They're just . . . slow?"

Ever since Sheila had hinted at enhancement, Rachel had assumed it was a medical procedure to correct some anatomical defect of the brain. Now she was hearing something else: a secret practice for raising the intelligence of kids who tested low and whose parents had financial resources. In Martin's words "an IQ jack-up" for the privileged. Rachel was about to articulate those thoughts, when Sheila's eyes suddenly filled up and her mouth began to quiver.

"I didn't want to tell you at first," she whimpered, "but I could see how you were agonizing over his problems. I knew exactly what you were going through, watching your child struggle with things other kids get automatically. Lucinda couldn't follow the simplest directions. She didn't understand the simplest concepts. It would kill me to watch her try to put together her little puzzles—baby puzzles—cutouts with the pictures under them. She couldn't do them," Sheila said, wiping her eyes. "It ate me up to see how frustrated she'd get and end up throwing pieces across the room. So I knew completely what you were going through. But I really couldn't say anything."

Rachel nodded, feeling a vague uneasiness in Sheila's tearful response.

"So, I'm telling you it's like a miracle what they did for her, and they can do the same for Dylan."

"Except I'm not sure I can grapple with manipulating his intelligence. Or even what that means. I thought you were telling me about a procedure to medically correct brain abnormalities."

"I am, and it means making him smarter, simple as that."

But it isn't as simple as that, thought Rachel.

"Look, no two brains are alike—like people's faces. Slow brains are different from smart brains, is what they told me. So, it's like a *brain lift.*" Sheila wiped her eyes and chuckled at her own analogy.

"What do you know about the operation?"

"Just that they make little incisions and implant some kind of neurostimulation like what they do for epilepsy and Parkinson's disease—stem-cell stuff. I don't know the details, but what I do know is that after a year or more, the kid's a little whip. Like day and night.

"At three, Lucinda couldn't distinguish red from green even though she wasn't even color-blind—the next year, she was reading at third-grade level. The year after that she was doing fifth-grade math. What can I say? A miracle. She was like a sponge—and still is. Everything she's taught she learns like that and *remembers*. And what's more, she's a regular Miss Confidence. Sometimes it's Miss Obnoxious, but she's got self-esteem up to here. What can I say?"

As she listened to Sheila, Rachel had a mental flash of Lucinda sitting poker-straight at her computer screen, her dual golden ponytails rising from the top of her head like bullwhips, her fingers on the keyboard like a concert pianist, her little pink mouth flapping directions on how best to navigate the search engines. Miss Confidence.

Miss Obnoxious.

Then Rachel saw that fat pink chipmunk face fill with noxious glee.

"That's not a tiger, it's a cheetah."

"You must be taking stupid pills."

"Hey, Dylan, thanks for the free goal!"

Children could be astonishingly cruel, but Lucinda was

a soulless little bitch. "And she's okay?" Rachel said. "No personality problems, behavioral issues, side effects, headaches?"

"Uh-uh. It's been great. She's already talking about being a doctor when she grows up."

Rachel nodded, studying Sheila's responses. "And where is it done?"

"They have some off-site location. But they'll fill you in."

"And you have no regrets?"

"Regrets? Unh-uh. No way."

Sheila shook her head a little too much and could not hold on to Rachel's stare.

"Nor did Harry," Sheila added.

From what Rachel knew, her late husband was something of an intellect, a great reader and a man who became a chief engineer at Raytheon. He had died a year ago, so she couldn't get his input. That was unfortunate because Rachel could sense something forced in Sheila's manner—overwrought confidence.

"Does Lucinda know she's been enhanced?"

"God, no! And there's no reason. In fact, the doctor says that it's best they don't know. Besides, she was sedated the whole time and remembers absolutely nothing."

"How long did it take?"

"The operation? A few hours, I guess. They kept her a couple days in recovery, which she slept through, and when she came home she didn't have a clue. Not even a headache. And when the hair grew back, she stopped asking about the boo-boos."

"Amazing," Rachel said. And yet, all she could think of were the countless and dark unknowns. "What about the fact that it's not legal?"

Sheila rolled her eyes. "Legal-schmegal. Forty years ago abortions weren't legal, but that didn't stop people from getting them. It's just that enhancement isn't very *PC*, if you know what I mean." She made a dismissive gesture with her hand. "Stuff like that gets out, it could cause class warfare." She chuckled nervously at her own glibness.

"But that's a legitimate ethical concern," Rachel said. "It's just one more advantage the rich have over the poor." And that bothered her. If this was the miracle it appeared to be, then it opened a Pandora's box of social woes, not the least of which was the fact that it ran counter to everything democracy stood for and to Rachel's fundamental beliefs in social justice and equality. A secret privileged thing that was tantamount to intellectual apartheid.

"First, enhancement does work. And second, you're looking at it the wrong way, hon. This is for your son. For his future. That's where your priorities are. You're talking about making life better for him, right? Right. Which means if you can afford it, you have a moral obligation to do it. It's for your one-and-only kid, and that's what counts, period! In a sense, it's good for society too, because—who knows?—Dylan may grow up to be a great scientist or doctor. He may even be president someday. Or better still, another Bill Gates."

"And what about this Dr. Malenko? What do you know about him?"

"Talk about brilliant! The man's a world-class neuroscientist—a pillar of the community, a member of every civic group. He's on the board of Mass General Hospital and the Lahey Clinic. A member of the Brain Surgeon's Society or whatever. What can I say: He's the cream of the crop, is all."

Rachel listened and nodded, and took a sip of her coffee. Outside two greenskeepers were leaning against the pickup truck and laughing over some joke. One of them, a man in his fifties, probably had done manual labor most of his life and lived with his wife and kids in one of the humbler towns in the area, or maybe New Hampshire. He couldn't be earning more than thirty thousand a year. She wondered about his life. She wondered if he was happy being who he was.

"Another thing is the fee. When we asked, he just said it was expensive."

Sheila's eyebrows arched. "It *is* expensive. But you're making an investment like nothing else in life. You're buying genius for your son. His enhancement could mean the difference between a so-so life and a great one.

"Think about that and about how much you'll save in pain, missed opportunities, humiliation, and the rejection your child would suffer—not to mention costs for tutors, therapists, special schools—including Nova Children's Center—SAT prep courses, et cetera. Or imagine the emotional payback when your kid wins a science fair, or writes the class skit, or is editor of the school newspaper, makes the honor roll, the National Honor Society. Or he graduates at the top of his class at Harvard only to start working at seventy-five thousand dollars a year at the tender age of twenty-two, or younger since he'll probably skip grades. How do you put a price tag on all that? You can't. Honey, if you can afford it, then you owe it to him. *You owe it to him.*"

Inside the playroom, Miss Jean was wrapping up the hour. Lucinda made a wave through the one-way window at Sheila. She couldn't see her, of course, but she knew she was there. She knew it was a one-way window. Behind her Dylan watched in puzzlement as she waved at a mirror.

They got up to leave. "Do you know other enhanced kids?"

"There aren't many in the area, but I know a couple."

"Anyone I know?"

Sheila suddenly seemed torn. "Well, you may know *of* them."

"Such as?"

"Look, I'm not supposed to tell," Sheila whispered. "I mean, everything is *très* confidential, especially the identity of the children, if you know what I mean."

"Sheila, if we're going to consider this, I want to meet other children and talk to the parents."

Rachel could see her struggling but Sheila was not someone who could sit on a secret.

"Julian Watts," she whispered.

"You mean Vanessa's son, the boy who wrote a book on mazes?"

"Uh-huh. He's like *megasmart* and talented. I don't know his case history, but his mother, Vanessa, is this superstar scholar and the father, Brad, he's an architect. And Julian was born . . . *challenged*."

"We got an invitation to her book party at the club." A fancy invitation had arrived the other day for a double-header Scholarship Banquet next Saturday night celebrating both caddy scholarship winners and Vanessa Watts's publication of her new book on George Orwell. Rachel had met Vanessa in passing at the club, although she didn't know her. Nor her son. "How do we go about meeting them?"

Sheila leaned forward into her conspiratorial huddle again. "Let me first explain that these kids don't know they're enhanced, know what I mean? It's just not a good thing if they think they were *made* special. I mean their ego, and stuff. So you can't really talk to them about, you know, before and after."

"How could they not know they had a brain operation?"

"I'm telling you they don't. They've got this amnesia drug the doctors use—something called 'ketamine' or 'katamine.' Whatever, it's used for trauma cases, and whatnot, but it works like magic. They just don't remember anything including how they were once, you know . . . different."

"What about follow-up visits? Dr. Malenko said he checks up on their progress."

"They only need to be seen two or three times until things level off, which is about a year or so," Sheila said. "But it's the same thing. They go in, he gives them the ketamine/katamine stuff. They get checked up and are sent on their way, and they don't remember a thing. It's incredible."

"So these kids don't even know about other enhanced kids."

"Not a clue."

Through the window Rachel could see Dylan put on his backpack. "I'd like to talk with the Wattses and meet Julian."

"I'll have to check, but I'm sure it can be arranged."

As they walked outside to meet the kids, Sheila stopped. "I think you're making the right decision for him."

"But we haven't made a decision yet."

"Well, I mean you're thinking about something that will make all the difference. I mean, I know, believe me. It's like she got over multiple sclerosis or blindness or something."

They walked into the sunlight. It was bright and warm, and the grass and leaves on the trees seemed to glow. Other mothers were waiting in the shade of the huge elm chatting among themselves.

"You know," Sheila said as they walked outside, "there was this poll I read about the other day. You know, one of those factoid things you see on CNN? Well, they did a national survey of a few thousand people. They asked a simple question: 'If there was one thing that you could change about yourself what would it be?' The choices were to be better looking, younger, taller, nicer, less selfish, more outgoing et cetera. Even wealthier. You know what over eighty percent of the respondents said they wished?"

"What?"

"They said they wished they were *smarter*."

Sheila walked away to greet Lucinda who stood like a statue waiting. Behind her Dylan burst out of the door with the others. "Hi, honey," Rachel said as she stooped to catch Dylan. He gave her a big hug.

"Mom, you know what?"

"What?"

"I know all the days of the week."

"You do?"

"Uh-huh."

"Monday, Tuesday, Wegsday, Fursday, Somesday."

In the distance, Lucinda walked toward the green Jaguar holding Sheila's hand in her left and a laptop in her right.

33

"D-d-did they love each other?"

"Of course they loved each other," Richard growled. "What the hell kind of a question is that? They were crazy about each other."

"I was j-just wondering."

"You must remember them."

"Kind of."

"And if they were alive today, they'd want your ass back in school."

They had been through this countless times since he quit last year, and Richard looked for every opportunity to nag him about it.

Brendan continued driving without comment, hoping that Richard would just run out of steam. They were coming back from Richard's men's club where he'd spend the afternoons playing cards with some of the other Barton old-timers.

"Why don't you go back in the fall, for cryin' out loud?" he asked. "You're not going to get anywhere waiting tables. You're too damn smart for that. I don't want to see you waste your life."

"I d-d-don't like school."

"You didn't give it a try. I almost never saw you crack open a book, except all that poetry stuff."

Brendan didn't respond.

"You finish school, go to college, and get yourself a degree like all the other kids. Your parents did. Jeez, if they were still alive they'd kill me for letting you quit. You should do it for their sake, for cryin' out loud."

"M-maybe." Brendan's mother had been a defense lawyer and his father was a librarian. And, as Richard often reminded him, they were "education-minded" people.

"Otherwise, you're gonna end up like me, working with your hands and killing yourself for every buck you make." He held up his hands, now knobbed and bent with arthritis.

"But you liked being a plumber."

Richard humpfed. "Yeah, I did. But tell that to my joints and lower lumbar." He rolled his head the way he did when the arthritis in his neck flared up. Richard once said that he had lived most of his life without pain—it had been saved for the end.

Brendan turned down Main Street of Barton. To the right was Angie's Diner. For a second, he felt his head throb. "Was she pretty?"

"Who?"

"My m-mother."

"How could you not remember? She was beautiful." There was a catch in his voice. Richard was Brendan's mother's father. "She looked like her mother."

Brendan gave him a side-glance. Richard was crying. He had not seen Richard cry since his wife, Betty, died some years ago. He envied Richard, because Brendan could not recall ever crying. Maybe it was the medication his doctor had him on. Or maybe he was just dead. "I remember her," he said.

"You should with your memory, for cryin' out loud."

But the truth was that Brendan only recalled his parents during the last few years of their lives. Before that—before he was seven—he drew a near blank, including nothing of his earlier years; yet he could recite most of what he had read or seen and could recall great sweeps of recent experiences in uncannily vivid details. It was as if his life before age seven didn't exist.

"I w-w-wish I'd known them better."

Richard nodded and wiped his eyes.

I wish I could cry like you, Brendan thought. *If I took your medicine away and let you die, would I cry like that? Would I?*

(God! Do I have to think murder to feel human?)

They rode in silence for a few minutes. Then Brendan asked, "When you were in the war, did you ever kill anyone?"

Richard gave him his wincing scowl. "Why the hell you want to know that?"

"I'm just w-w-wondering." Richard once told him he had spent weeks in Okinawa.

"Yeah, I killed some people. Why, you thinking of killing somebody?"

"I'm just w-w-wondering how it made you feel afterward."

"They were Japs, and it was war. It was what I was supposed to do."

"Later on, after the war, did it b-b-bother you when you thought about it? That they were human beings you'd killed?"

"No, because I didn't think about it. Just as they didn't think of all my twenty-year-old buddies they killed as *human beings.*" Richard's voice cracked again. "Jeez, can we change the subject?"

The thrum of the wheels filled the silence. Then Brendan asked, "Were you scared of dying?"

"Of course I was scared. We all were. What do you think? We were kids, for cryin' out loud. We had our whole lives ahead of us."

"What about now?"

Richard humpfed. "I'm seventy-nine, Brendy. That's a

lot of mileage. I'm ready to get off the bus, but I'm not scared. Not at all. Why you asking?"

"Just curious."

Richard humpfed. "But there's a few things I want to see get done before I go. Like seeing you getting your ass back in school and going to college. Don't give me that look. You're a talented kid—I just don't want to see you waste your life. That's the promise I made to your mom, and that's what I want to take to my grave with me."

Brendan's eye fell on the Christopher medal on the dashboard. "D-do you believe in God?"

"What are you doing, writing my obituary or something?"

"J-j-just curious."

"Yeah, I believe in God." Richard winced and rolled his head again. Then he chuckled. "But I'm not sure He believes in me."

Brendan turned down their street, thinking that he might actually miss Richard.

Richard wiped his nose on his handkerchief as they approached the house. "You know, there are a couple boxes of their stuff downstairs in the cellar you might want to go through," Richard said. "A lot of old papers and things. Maybe even some old photographs. I don't know what's in there. Your grandmother had packed them away, but you might want to look. It'll be good for you."

Brendan pulled the truck into the driveway and helped Richard into the house. While the old man settled in his La-Z Boy with the newspaper, Brendan went down to the cellar.

The place was a mess. Beside the workbench was an old lawnmower engine on a mount which Brendan had taken apart to rewire. He liked working with machines. Just for the challenge of it, he would disassemble clocks or old motors until he had a heap of parts, then reassemble them from memory. He never missed.

He moved to the very back of the cellar and opened the small storage room which sat under a window through which, in years past, a chute would be lowered to fill the area with coal. Now it was stacked with boxes and old storage chests.

On top lay Richard's shotgun in its imitation-leather sheath. They had used it for skeet shooting when Brendan was younger. He zipped it open and studied the weapon. It was a Remington classic twelve-gauge pump action piece with contoured vent rib barrels and twin bead sights. It had been fashioned of polished blue steel and American walnut. The wood had lost most of its gloss and the barrel badly needed polishing. But it was still a handsome weapon. As he felt the heft, scenes of skeet and trap shooting with Richard flickered though Brendan's mind. And the nights when he contemplated blowing his own head off.

He put the gun away and went through the boxes.

Many contained baby effects—clothes, shoes, a set of Beatrix Potter baby dishes and cups. There were also some of Brendan's early school- and artwork. The drawings were very primitive, stick-figured people and houses barely recognizable. The schoolwork was also unimpressive. He recalled none of it.

After several minutes, he located a carton with papers and photographs. His mother apparently was something of a photographer because she had put together albums chronicling Brendan from his earliest days as an infant up to five years of age. The photographs mostly in color, a few black-and-whites, were arranged chronologically and dated. Brendan spent nearly an hour going through them page by page.

Although he recognized himself and his parents from other photographs upstairs, it was like looking at somebody else's history. None of the locales, toddler clothes, toys, or even images of his parents seemed to connect to him—none triggered a cascade of recollection. Nor a nostalgic glugging of his throat.

Behind the other storage boxes was a metal strongbox—the only metal container and the only one that was sealed with a lock. The box was heavy and not just from the metal. He had no idea where the key was, of course; but that was no problem since the lock was cheap hardware-store fare. He got some wires and a jackknife from the workbench and popped it open in a matter of moments.

The contents were mostly papers in folders and manila envelopes. There were various medical reports and letters.

One particular folder caught his attention. Inside was a generic medical form for Children's Hospital Office of Neurology. It had been filled out just after his ninth birthday but for some reason never submitted. The front listed Brendan's name, address, date of birth, et cetera. On the reverse side was a long checklist of various ailments including several lines at the bottom asking simply for "Other." The form had been filled out and signed at the bottom by his mother. Brendan stared at the list. She had checked off several boxes including *Headaches, Sleep disorders, Depression, Nightmares,* and *Mood swings*. In the margin she had written in: "hears voices" and "verbal outbursts—Tourette syndrome?"

In the spaces at the bottom she had penned "Tried to kill himself."

He remembered that vividly. He had seen a show on television where some guy committed suicide by sitting in his car in an enclosed garage with the engine running. He had tried that and recalled getting his father's car keys, going out to the car, closing the door with the remote control attached to the sun visor, turning it on, then sitting and waiting. He even recalled getting sleepy. The next thing he remembered was waking up in the emergency room at Newton Wellesley Hospital.

After that they had upped his meds. He remembered because it was around Thanksgiving. Then a few weeks later, his parents were killed. Then he moved in with his grandparents and they found him a pediatrician who just continued the meds. Soon Brendan began to better mask his problems, internalizing them, developing strategies to keep the demons in low profile.

He continued through the papers.

What caught his attention immediately was a large accordion folder. On the tab, somebody had written BRENDAN. There was a date from when he was five years old. He unfastened the string close and opened it.

Inside was another large envelope containing several black sheets. He removed one and raised it to the light. And for a long moment he looked at the images.

They were X rays of his brain.

34

"You told her about Julian Watts?"

"They want to meet another child and the parents. They won't consider it otherwise."

"That's not the point, Sheila," Lucius Malenko said. "You were not to say anything until you cleared it with me first."

"But she insisted."

"You were not sanctioned to reveal names. Do you understand?"

"I'm sorry, Doctor," she pleaded, "but, you know, he's a real showcase genius, he's perfect. And she knows Vanessa."

"You do not make the decisions, is that clear?" The scalpel-edge of his words cut into her brain.

"Yes, I'm really sorry," Sheila whimpered into the phone. For several seconds all she could hear was the sound of an open line. While she waited for his response, her insides tightened.

"They'll have to observe him at school to keep things anonymous," he said.

"Of course. No other way."

"You'll have to arrange that."

"I can do that, no problem," Sheila said, feeling her organs settle in place again.

"No private interviews with him."

"No, of course not. I promise."

"I'll handle the parents," Malenko said. "In the meantime, you will say nothing, you will do nothing. Is that understood?"

"Yes, absolutely."

Sheila was in her office in the loft on the third floor of her house. Being so high up, she had a commanding view of their backyard. In a few days, the area would be decorated for Lucinda's birthday party. Sheila had invited ten girls from school, from DellKids, and the neighborhood. At the moment, Lucinda was downstairs playing with her birthday kitten. Sheila could hear her talking to it over the songs on her CD player.

Two days ago, Sheila had given Lucinda the kitten so that she could get used to it before all the kids showed up for the party. It was Lucinda's first pet—a beautiful little orange and white longhaired twelve-week-old thing with big round blue eyes. Sheila had gotten it from the Salem Animal Shelter. Lucinda had taken to it immediately. Sheila's mind tripped back:

"She's so pretty, Mommy," she had said. "But aren't cats sneaky?"

"No, they're not sneaky, hon."

The kitten sat curled in a basket with a cushion in it, which was how Sheila had presented it to Lucinda.

"What shall we call her?"

"Whatever you like. I'm sure you can think of a clever name."

Lucinda knelt down beside the basket, and the kitten seemed to cower slightly. It was clearly shy of people. "It has big white paws," she said. "How about Mittens?"

The kitten looked up at them and made a faint mewing.

"That's a nice name," Sheila said.

Lucinda's eyes raked Sheila's face. Then her expression hardened. "You don't like the name!"

"Yes I do, honey. Mittens is an adorable name. Just like in the nursery rhyme."

"No, you don't like it. I can tell from your expression."

There was no pretending with Lucinda. She had developed a frustratingly keen instinct for catching her. "I love it," Sheila insisted. But in truth, she had expected a more imaginative, more creative name from her—and not some trite kiddy moniker from her books. But how do you say that to Lucinda?

"No you don't," she said in a scathing voice. "You think it's a dumb name. You do, you do."

"No I don't. Mittens is a lovely name."

"You're a dirty rotten liar."

Although Sheila should have been used to her daughter's occasional lapses, she was always taken aback. "Don't talk to me that way, young lady."

"Then don't lie to me, *old lady*. You hate the name. Admit it! ADMIT IT!"

Lucinda's icy blue stare stuck Sheila like a paralyzing needle. "I *don't* hate the name."

"You do. You do," she screamed. "I hate you. I hate you. I hope you get cancer and die." Lucinda then snatched up the kitten from the basket and stormed out of the room. "Stupid bitch!"

As Lucinda headed for her room, Sheila heard Lucinda cry out, "Ouch! Don't do that, you dummy!" Before Lucinda banged her door closed, the kitten let out a long sharp cry.

Was it worth it? a voice deep in Sheila's mind whispered.

"Perhaps you can arrange a school tour," Malenko said, snapping her back to the moment.

"Yes, of course. I know one of the admissions officers." It would have to be soon since school was nearly out.

"Good."

There was another pause on the phone, which tugged at Sheila. She had sold hundreds of homes over the years. She had haggled over prices, P&S agreements, split hairs, gone back and forth with buyers and sellers. She was used to talking turkey about price. But with Lucius Malenko, she always felt as if her will were extinguished. "And if they agree . . . you know, go all the way, then . . ."

"You'll get your finder's fee, Sheila."

"That's great, thanks." Sheila felt a cool rush of relief. He had promised her five percent commission. Five percent didn't sound like much, but it would help. Harry had been a top electrical engineer, but clueless when it came to financial planning, leaving her only a pittance in death benefits. Given the considerable debt they had gotten into with Lucinda's enhancement and the weakening real estate market, Sheila was in dire financial straits. So when she had approached Dr. Malenko about Rachel Whitman, he had agreed that if things worked, she would get a commission—a finder's fee. She only wished there were something in writing. But this was not that kind of contract.

While they continued to talk, Sheila heard something from down below. A kind of muffled whirring sound. It was hard to determine because Lucinda's CD player was blasting a sound track from *101 Dalmatians*. Like all large old houses, this had several different sounds—the hotwater heater, refrigerator, the dishwasher, the washing machine and drier, the water rushing in the pipes, the air-conditioning system—so she wasn't able to determine what she was hearing under the music.

"By the way," Sheila said, "I think the husband, Martin, is very interested."

"So it seems," Malenko said.

The blender, Sheila thought. Lucinda was using the blender. She liked to make milk shakes with ice cream, milk, and fruit, and Sheila had bought a quart of strawberries yesterday for that purpose. And although Lucinda was only seven, Sheila had shown her how to use the device safely. Besides, the blades could only be activated with the top fastened.

"I will contact Vanessa and get back to you," Malenko said. "Then we'll talk about a visit. The sooner the better."

"Yes, of course," Sheila said.

"And, once again, you will say nothing until you hear from me."

"Absolutely."

Malenko hung up, and Sheila put the phone down, her heart still racing. She had blabbed and felt stupid, and Malenko all but said that. If he wanted to, he could cut her off immediately.

From below, the music was now resonating throughout the house. She didn't know if the kitchen windows were open, but Sheila's first concern was not the neighbors but Lucinda's ears. She could permanently damage her hearing.

Sheila opened the door of her office and headed down. "Lucinda," she called out. "Is everything okay?"

But the music drowned her out.

"Lucinda?" Sheila rounded the second-floor landing. When she reached the stairs, the music suddenly stopped dead, and a gaping silence filled the house, the only sound being Sheila's shoes as she came down the stairs.

Before she got to the bottom, she heard Lucinda cry out from the kitchen: "Mommy, Mommy."

Sheila's heart nearly stopped. "What is it?" she cried, as she hustled down the hall to the kitchen.

"Mittens ran away."

"What?"

"I went outside and couldn't find her," Lucinda said, grabbing her mother's hand and pulling her to the back door.

"How did she get out?"

As she opened it, Sheila noticed her hand. There were thin scratches just above the wrist.

"Your hand is bleeding. What happened?"

Through gulping sobs Lucinda said, "I was unloading the dishwasher to get Mittens' dish when I scratched it on a stupid fork. Then her face hardened. "It's your fault. You know you're not supposed to put the forks tines-up but tines-down. You know that, MOMMY."

"I'm sorry, honey," Sheila mumbled.

"I had the back door closed, but when Joe the mailman threw in the mail, he left it open and she got out." Her face crumbled. "He's a stupid old man, Mommy. I hate him." And she ran outside.

Sheila followed her, a low-grade humming filling her head. Before she stepped outside, she looked back in the kitchen. She was right: On the counter sat half a bowl of strawberries, and the blender containing the bright red drink. The smell of strawberries laced the air. Everything looked normal—except for the empty cat basket.

"Here, Mittens. Here, Mittens," Lucinda cried, running across the backyard and making kissing sounds. "Come home, please. Mittens, come home."

Sheila felt oddly distracted as she watched her daughter go through the motions of finding her kitten. "Did you see which way she ran?"

"Yes, this way. I think she was chasing after a bird."

"Well, I'm sure she'll come home."

Lucinda dragged Sheila into the woods, and they looked and called for the kitten. But after several minutes, Lucinda tired of the search and headed back to the backyard and flopped down on her swing. She stuck her lower lip out. "She's never going to come home."

Sheila squatted down beside her. She had splashed some berry juice on her T-shirt. "Yes she will," Sheila said. "She's probably out there under a bush watching us right now. She'll be back."

But something told her that was not so.

Lucinda looked up at Sheila, her eyes like marbles and

her face set the way it got when she was reading Sheila's manner. Suddenly she broke into a smile and spread her arms. "I love you, Mommy."

Sheila embraced her. "I love you, too."

Lucinda then got up and took her mother's hand and headed back to the house. "You know, I miss her already," she said, and licked the back of her other hand. "She was such a nice kitty."

"But she may still come back."

"I know, but if she doesn't can we get another one?"

"Sure."

"And without claws?"

35

───◆───

Julian's just finishing up at school, but I think I can get us a visit." Sheila once sold a house to the Bloomfield Prep admissions officer. "This way, you can see him in action."

It was Friday afternoon, and Rachel had picked up Sheila for a three o'clock meeting with Vanessa Watts who lived up the coast a few miles. As they drove along, Rachel kept asking herself why she was doing this when her instincts told her it made no sense, that there were too many unknowns. But she had promised herself to remain open-minded.

The Wattses' house sat atop a rolling green lawn that looked like a green broadloom carpet. It was a white clapboard-sided Colonial of understated elegance, surrounded by mature foliage that made the place look as if it had naturally grown out of the ground decades ago. Even the row of pine trees along the drive looked just the right size and had been planted in just the right place. Along the front was a low dry stone wall and tidy beds of flowers and decorative grasses. The place bespoke a world that was perfect and good.

Vanessa greeted them at the door. In her forties, she was a tall woman with short golden hair, no makeup and a mobile toothy mouth. She was dressed in chinos, a green golf shirt with the collar up, and white running shoes. She looked very Cambridgey. According to Sheila, she was a professor of English at Middlesex University, and her book on George Orwell was apparently getting considerable attention.

She led them into the living room, a large cheerful space furnished in white—stuffed chairs, sofa, and wall-to-wall carpeting. The carpeting made Rachel conscious of her shoes. It was hard to believe people lived in the house, especially two teenagers. The only colors breaking up the antiseptic effect were two paintings and a shiny black baby grand in one corner. On the key guard of the piano was a Franz Liszt music sheet.

"Who plays?" Rachel asked, trying to make conversation.

"Right now only Julian. Lisa, my daughter, is a violinist, Brad doesn't play, and what I do doesn't sound like music."

"He must be very talented," Rachel said. "Liszt is very difficult."

"He's getting better," Vanessa said.

Rachel sensed a note of studied coyness in her response. The kid was probably a musical prodigy. Because Dylan loved to sing and was good at it, Rachel had arranged for him to take piano lessons last year. Unfortunately, he lasted only four sessions. His music teacher called in desperation one day for Rachel to pick him up. It just wasn't working—Dylan was out of control. As much as she had worked to get him to focus on finger exercises, he would not cooperate. And the more she tried, the more frustrated he became. When he finally went into a full-fledged temper tantrum pounding the keys with his fist, Mrs. Crawford called Rachel, and that was it for piano. "Some younger children have problems with drills. But they grow out of it. Maybe next year." Then as an afterthought she added, "But he's an adorable little guy, though. Sings beautifully."

"An adorable little guy, though": slow, but adorable.

"Here he is," Sheila said, sounding like a proud aunt. She handed Rachel a framed photograph of Julian.

Wearing scholarly looking rimless glasses and dressed in a blue and white school baseball uniform, a bright gold *B* on his hat, the thin-faced boy was smiling widely and holding up his index finger. Probably, Rachel thought, to let the world know he was an alpha child—one of the chosen elite who would become a permanent resident on honor rolls, who would score 1600 on his SATs, who would get early admission to Princeton, who would grow up to be Zeus.

"Would you like some coffee or tea?" Vanessa asked.

Rachel could feel her face flush for entertaining such petty jealousy. She hadn't even met Julian and already she resented the kid. "Coffee would be fine, thank you."

"Me, too," Sheila said.

Over the fireplace hung a large photograph of the family—Vanessa and Brad in the background, Julian and his sister, Lisa, a high school junior. They were a handsome family poised on the bow of a windjammer pulling into some tropical harbor. Another photograph showed Julian with his Bloomfield Prep soccer team.

Sheila moved to the corner and punched her cell phone to call her office. "Shoot! The battery's dead."

Vanessa nodded to the other side of the house. "You can use the one in Brad's studio. He's at the office, of course. You know where it is."

"Thanks," Sheila said, and left the room.

When they were alone, Rachel asked Vanessa, "What does your husband do?"

"He's a commercial architect."

"Very nice."

"Except I see him once a month. He works long hours and travels a lot. What about you and your husband?"

"At the moment, I'm just bringing up my son. I used to be a college textbook editor. But I gave that up when Dylan was born," Rachel said. "My husband has a small recruitment company."

Vanessa nodded. "How do you like Hawthorne?"

"So far we're enjoying it." Rachel tried to force an expression to fit her words.

"Yeah, it has a lot going for it, if you're the right kind of people." She kept her voice low so Sheila wouldn't hear. "I know you're supposed to be true to your town and all, but it's become claustrophobic—which, I guess, is the nature of small towns: Everybody knows everybody else's business." Vanessa looked as if she didn't want to elaborate for the newcomer. "Let's just say the place has its pressure points. We're thinking of moving."

"You are?"

"Mmmm, to a place where we won't have—" She cut off and put her finger to her mouth as Sheila returned. "Get through okay?"

"Yeah, and I wish I hadn't. The P and S fell through on the Rotella place. We were supposed to have an exclusive, and some *unnamed party* bid eighty thousand over the asking price." Sheila shrugged. "That's the name of the game in this business." She flopped into her chair. "You win some, you lose some. But it's one hell of a way to end the week."

Sheila's expression said that the commission loss was going to hurt. Vanessa went to the kitchen and returned with a tray of coffee and cookies. "So, you're interested in the enhancement procedure for your son."

"I'm thinking about it."

Vanessa nodded and straightened out a picture on the wall. "What's his name—your son?"

"Dylan."

"Well, it worked wonders with ours, the way it has for Lucinda." She said that as if she were talking about a new acne cream.

"Absolutely," Sheila added.

"How exactly?"

"Well . . . I guess for the lack of a better expression, he's a hell of a lot *smarter*. He picks things up much faster. He's quicker in his response to ideas. His memory is greater. And he's focussed. Oh, boy! Is he ever! When he sets his mind to doing something, he's . . . well, like a magnifying glass." She appeared to catch herself.

"And how was he before the procedure?"

"It's been some years, of course, but, frankly, Julian could best be described by what he *couldn't* do. It's like night and day. Don't get me wrong. I mean, he was a happy little boy, but he was miles behind the other kids. I could show you some of his early testing and teachers' reports. They were pitiful. I mean, he couldn't *read*, he couldn't *add*, he got totally confused by the simplest *directions*. His teachers said that he was not working to his capacity. But the sad thing is that he *was*."

As Rachel listened, she thought she heard something forced in the woman's explanation—as if she were trying to convince herself instead of Rachel.

Vanessa fell silent for a moment. Suddenly she flicked her head, and made a bright smile. "Last term he got all As. What can I say? What they did was nothing short of a miracle. Really!" Again she shifted. "So, what's he like, your son . . . Darren?"

"Dylan." Rachel didn't like making public statements about his problems. "He's a sweet little boy—active, friendly, considerate."

As she spoke, Vanessa looked at her with a flat expression as if to say: *They all are, so get to the important stuff.*

"He has some language-processing problems." And she elaborated a bit.

"Sounds familiar," Vanessa said when Rachel was finished. "We tried everything: one-on-one tutoring, special classes, and, of course, all the hot meds. But you can't blame their brains, nor can you fill them up with Ritalin. Yes, they can get special support, blah blah blah, but the bottom line is that they're handicapped, and will always be. Sure, some of them can be happy and have quote-unquote productive lives. But let's face it, just how productive can you be if your IQ is seventy-five? What I'm saying is, if it's important to you to have a smart kid, then this might be for you."

"Looking back, are you happy you had it done?" Rachel asked. "Any regrets?"

Vanessa made a fast glance at Sheila who took the cue. "The alternative was bringing up a backward child. What can I say?"

"I know I sound rather hardheaded," Vanessa continued, "but before the procedure—when he was six—he still could barely recognize letters or numbers. And his memory was hopeless: He couldn't remember basic family facts, like our street address, his own birthday, or his father's first name. It was very distressing."

Rachel nodded as her mind slipped into a disturbing recollection from last week. Dylan had just finished watching a video of *Pinocchio*—a movie he had seen half a dozen times. When she asked him to retell the story for her, he could barely recall the names of the characters—Jiminy Cricket was "the green boy," and Figaro was "the cat"—or simple words like *whale*. Nor could he put key plot events in proper sequence. After a few moments, he simply gave up in frustration.

"Now he's getting terrific grades and winning science fairs," Vanessa continued. "He's a different person."

"Have you noticed any personality or behavior changes?"

"Of course!" Vanessa declared. "You don't become a genius overnight and not undergo personality changes. Tasks that used to intimidate he now takes to like a fish to water—or maybe *shark* is closer. I can't tell you how confident he is—and driven to excel. And he loves school, we're happy to say—believe me! The same with Lucinda, right?"

"Absolutely," Sheila shot back without missing a beat.

"She can be a Miss Smarty Pants at times, but that's more of a maturity problem."

Their enthusiasm bordered on salesmanship, Rachel thought. "About the procedure: It's an operation of some sort, I understand."

"Well, I'm sure as Sheila told you we can't go into those details, not until you move to the next stage. It's silly, but those are the conditions. We don't make the rules, but you can understand—revolutionary procedures need to be guarded."

"Sure, but we're talking about an invasive procedure of the brain, so you can understand my concern."

"Of course."

"What I'm wondering about are the side effects—pain, impairment of functions, personality change, anything like that."

"He had a minor headache for a couple days but that was it, and no impairment of functions. Except for his cognitive abilities, he's a typical fourteen-year-old boy who plays video games and does boy things." She looked to Sheila. "Right?"

"Absolutely."

"If you don't mind, I'd like to meet Julian someday."

"I have no problem with that, but he's still at school," Vanessa said. "But, you know, you can tell a lot about a kid from his room. Would you like a look?"

"Sure."

Rachel got up and walked over to the wall of photographs. "Are you interested in photography?"

"I do a little."

A large framed black-and-white shot showed a ragged mountain range backlit by the sun sending shafts of light through heavy clouds with a deep foreground of thousands of brilliant wildflowers. "This really is a great photograph. The composition and lighting are amazing. In fact, it looks like an Ansel Adams."

"It is. Well, actually, the original is. That's a painting."

"A painting! It can't be."

Vanessa turned the picture around and unfolded a book photo that was stuck behind the canvas. "This is a copy of the original Adams." The photo was an exact miniature of the painting. "He copied it from this."

"Who?"

"Julian."

"But how did he do it? I can't see any brush marks."

Vanessa made a dry chuckle. "With a *lot* of patience." Vanessa didn't elaborate.

Rachel couldn't separate herself from the picture. She moved from side to side to study it from different angles, barely able to detect surface texture. It was so indistinguishable from the photograph that she wondered if the boy had done it with some fancy computer-art software— scanning the photo then printing up an enlarged version. "That's remarkable." Einstein, Van Cliburn, and Maxfield Parrish rolled into one. "Was Julian artistic before?"

"Not really. He had my tin ear and did mostly stick drawings. He really blossomed after enhancement."

She led them upstairs to a large landing off which were the master bedroom, a bathroom, and two other rooms. One door had flower decals and a porcelain plaque saying LISA. Across the other door was a yellow and black sign: DO NOT ENTER—TRESPASSERS WILL BE EXECUTED.

"I must warn you, he's something of a neatness freak. If you pick something up, *please* put it back where you found it." She opened the door.

The immediate impression was how much stuff there was. The second impression was its preternatural orderliness. One whole wall had floor-to-ceiling shelves of books—all upright and lined up by size. Another wall was full of space posters—all the same size, all squared with optical precision—one, a shot of the earth, rising over the lunar horizon; another of the *Atlantis* shuttle. Against the far wall was a huge wall unit containing a television and electronic sound equipment. Beside it was a draftsman's work board with pens, razor knives, and other tools—all lined up neatly. There was a single bed tightly made with three decorative pillows arranged so precisely that the points lined up. The place looked as if a fussy old woman rather than a fourteen-year-old boy occupied it.

But that was just more sour grapes, Rachel chided herself. Dylan's room was in a state of perpetual disaster—clothes and toys all over the place. Any straightening out was Rachel's doing, because he could not catch on to a system of order. Once she had rationalized that the chaos was the result of his being a late starter or immaturity or maybe a male thing—that he had an overactive guy-sloppiness gland. Now she suspected it reflected some haywire brain circuitry.

"If for nothing else, this was worth the fee," Vanessa said.

Rachel wanted to ask about that, but the subject was off-limits. She smiled, but thought that the excessive neatness was creepy.

Beside the bed sat a large desk with a computer with an oversized monitor and printer—probably used for his cyberart. The screen saver was a continuously changing maze with red balls trying to make their way through the shifting network. It looked like graphics designed to drive the observer mad.

Above the computer hung a framed document announcing that Julian Watts, age eleven, had won first prize in his age group in a regional science fair. The title of his project: "How Different Types of Music Affect the Ability of Mice to Run Mazes."

On a corner table sat a large flat surface with a maze. Near it was a cage with some mice. "Very impressive," Rachel said.

"You wouldn't think so at three in the morning," Vanessa said. "He played everything from *Aïda* to Zambian tribal chants. Around the clock."

"And what did he determine?"

"That mice ran better with the longhairs than with rap. I'm not exactly sure how that affects the rest of the universe, but he had a good time."

On the bulletin board were Museum of Science membership announcements and a list of upcoming museum shows and movies. Also, some snapshots of Julian's class at Bloomfield Prep. The room contained all the adolescent accouterments of a kid who was going places. Nerd perfect. The kind of room Martin would love for Dylan.

As Rachel passed through the door, her eye caught on a curious little cartoon figure the boy had drawn and tacked over the light switch. Among all the high-tech paraphernalia it was the sole reminder that Julian was still a boy and not a grad student in astrophysics. It seemed so out of place: a happy-faced blue Dumbo.

"I'm not sure what—" But a loud crash from below cut Vanessa off.

They moved out to the landing. More pounding, then around the bottom of the staircase stormed a teenage girl. She looked very upset.

"Lisa!" Vanessa said. "What happened?"

Lisa looked up at her mother, unrestrained by the presence of the other women. "I told you it wasn't right!" She slammed down her backpack, and stomped her way up the stairs. She wagged a paper at her mother. "I told you to let me do my own work."

Vanessa looked mortified by Lisa's outburst. "Maybe we can talk about this later."

When the girl reached the top, she stopped nose-to-nose with Vanessa. Rachel noticed that the tips of Lisa's fingers were all red where the nails had been chewed to the quick.

"Thanks to you, she gave me a fucking Incomplete!" she screamed in her mother's face. "Now I have to redo it, and the best I can get is a C."

Vanessa's cheeks were burning dark red, as if she'd just been slapped. "Lisa, we can work this out, okay?"

" 'The words are too big, the syntax is too sophisticated,

the prose is too polished,'" Lisa singsonged in a voice mocking her teacher. "It wasn't me," she screamed. "And I'm not Julian. You get it?" She slammed the flat of her hand onto her door. "SHIT! Now I'll never get into AP English." Lisa burst into tears and pushed her way to her room.

"Lisa . . . ?" Vanessa pleaded after her.

"Go fuck yourself!" Lisa cried and slammed the door.

The noise was like a gun blast. A moment later, they could hear more swearing and sobbing.

Vanessa looked at Rachel and Sheila and made a tortured smile. "Now, where were we?"

36

I hate the whole damn charade," Rachel said, as they pulled into the parking lot of Bloomfield Prep.

"Well, it's the only way we're going to meet him. He heads for camp next week," Martin said.

Located an hour and a half west of Boston, it was a school for wealthy whiz kids. "Pretending we're prospective parents is just so unfair to Dylan."

"Maybe for the time being."

She looked at him. He did not appear to be joking.

At ten-fifteen sharp, they met Sheila in the parking lot near the white Colonial that served as the admissions office. Because it was the last week of classes, regular tours were no longer given. However, Sheila knew the admissions officer, Harley Elia, so they could visit different classes including Julian's, posing as parents seriously considering the school as an option for Dylan.

It was a beautiful place, its brick and stone buildings nestled in fourteen acres of green hills, thick with maples, oaks, and pine that lined paths through ample grassy fields reserved for sports and play. According to Sheila, Bloomfield, which went from fourth through twelfth grade, was on a par with Exeter and Andover Academy.

Lining the walls of the foyer in the admissions office were

numerous group photographs of smiling students, some in
their team outfits, some at play in the fields, some in gradua-
tion robes. Over the fireplace hung an oil painting of the
founders, Stratton and Mary Bloomfield. They had started
the place in a backyard barn in 1916 "to keep the minds of
children alive and open, to instill a love of learning, to pro-
vide a life of fullness and rich possibility, to secure freedom
of body and spirit." Like the school, the inscription was in-
spiring, but it held little promise for Dylan.

While waiting in the reception area for Ms. Elia, Rachel
nearly told Martin that she wanted to leave. The place was
a sanctum for gifted children, and pretending that Dylan
was—or would be—a candidate for admission was self-
flagellation. A tour would only heighten her resentment of
other kids and sharpen the sting of what she had denied
Dylan. But she held back. Martin's interest was picking up
by the minute. He was particularly taken by the catalog's
boast that fifteen percent of the last graduating class went
on to MIT. Most of the rest went on to Harvard, Yale,
Princeton, and the other *incandescent* institutions.

After a few minutes, Ms. Elia emerged from her office.
She was an attractive and smartly dressed woman in her
forties with bright blond hair and a cheerful face. She embraced Sheila then led Rachel and Martin into her office
where she took down information about Dylan. For a
painful fifteen minutes, Rachel held forth about how sweet
and sociable a child Dylan was and his love for music as
the woman avidly took notes. Martin just nodded. She said
nothing about his language deficiencies.

When that was over, the woman took them on a tour,
outlining the school's history and accomplishments.
Rachel said very little, but Martin engaged Ms. Elia with
questions about the science curricula and computer labs.
After maybe half an hour, they entered a modern redwood
structure with a sign saying GRAYSON BIGGS ART STUDIO.
Sheila nudged Rachel that they were heading for Julian
Watts's class. According to Sheila, he was one of only two

enhanced children in the school. She would not reveal the name of the other.

"It's one of the more popular places," Ms. Elia said. "Kids come here after classes and work on their projects."

Scattered around the large bright room were about a dozen children. Some were painting; others were in the corner at potter's wheels. Others still were working with wood carving tools. Two teachers were moving about quietly commenting on the kids' progress.

The walls were covered with student work—big splotchy impressionistic paintings, simulated rock posters, odd multimedia canvasses thick with paint, fabric, glitter and other materials. Most were colorful, and a few showed some talent and inspiration.

One drawing caught Rachel's eye—a sepia reproduction of the campus chapel, a small stone Gothic structure. Even the intricate carvings and details on the stained-glass windows were captured. If it were not stretched on a canvas, Rachel would have sworn it was an enlarged photograph. The signature at the bottom was printed in tiny block letters: JULIAN WATTS.

While Ms. Elia chatted with Ms. Fuller, the art teacher, Sheila nudged Rachel and nodded at a bespectacled boy in a blue shirt hunched over a stretched canvas at his table. Rachel walked quietly past some children who broadstroked gobs of paint across their canvasses, moving their brushes like young orchestra conductors in training.

By contrast, Julian sat rigidly, wearing headphones and hunched over a canvas. From a distance, he looked as if he were suffering from tremors, but up close his left hand moved with delicate robotic precision. Rachel had to repress a gasp of amazement. The boy was painting with an architect's pen. In fact, there were several of different sizes neatly lined up. Awestruck, she and Martin watch him dab away in microscopic detail, occasionally switching instruments. He did not seem to notice their presence.

"The assignment was a self-portrait in any medium or

style," the teacher said. "The only directive was to capture something of their personality."

Pinned to his easel was a black-and-white photo of Julian that appeared to have been done by himself at arm's length. He was dressed in a black T-shirt and staring at the camera through his rimless glasses. The intensity on his face was startling—as if he were possessed. Although he had traced the oval of his face with a pencil, in the center of the canvas were two intense eyes so realistically rendered that the canvas appeared to be studying Rachel.

The teacher tapped Julian. The boy looked up and turned off his headphones. The teacher introduced them.

"We didn't mean to disturb you, but that's incredible," Rachel said.

The boy muttered a "Thanks." He had an edgy shyness, and it was clear he wanted to go back to his canvas.

"How long did it take you to do that?" Martin asked.

The boy reached into his mouth and removed plastic teeth guards. "About three hours."

Rachel felt a small electric shock pass through her. Julian's teeth were nearly stubs. Her first thought was that he had had some kind of accident. But they were so evenly ground down—top and bottom—and flattened off as if filed.

Rachel tried to hide her shock and continue as if she hadn't noticed. "I've never seen anything like it before, except the French pointillists."

"Yeah," Martin said. "In fact, I thought you were touching up a photograph."

Rachel wanted to engage him more, but the teacher said he had to get back to work. Julian put the guards back in his mouth, slipped on the headphones, and went back to the canvas.

"He's something else," the teacher said. "He's got a really unique talent." Then she lowered her voice so the other kids couldn't hear. "He's also one of our most gifted students." And she saucered her eyes for emphasis. "Straight As."

"Does he always paint with a pen?" Martin asked.

"Yes. It started a couple years ago when we did a unit on pointillism, and that's now the only medium he works in. We tried to get him to move into brushes and pastels, but he prefers points. You know these dedicated artists."

During a moment's silence, Rachel realized that it wasn't music Julian was listening to but spoken audio. Except that the voice didn't sound human. She looked at the tape recorder—an unusual-looking unit that was set on fast-forward.

"What is that?" she mouthed to the teacher.

"Spanish. I think it's *Don Quixote*."

"But . . ."

The teacher nodded knowingly. "Yeah, he's trained himself to understand it on double speed. Last year he learned Italian that way." Then she just shook her head in dismay. "What can I say? He's something else."

"My God," Rachel whispered. The fixity of his expression as he jabbed away while absorbing the high-speed prattle sent a shock through her. He looked like some alien creature in the semblance of a boy receiving coded messages from afar.

As they started away, Rachel looked back. Julian's mouth was moving. At first she thought he was chewing gum until she realized he was tapping his teeth guards in sequence to his hand movement. Then she realized that he wasn't keeping pace—he was counting.

They visited two more classes and ended up in a psychology lab. All along, Ms. Elia went on about the school and the programs and how ninety percent of the graduating class goes to college, half to the Ivy Leagues. "Four of our graduates are freshmen at Harvard this year."

"How nice."

Rachel was anxious to leave. The tour was only an hour long, but it seemed to last all morning because Martin kept asking questions. Sheila was just along for the ride and said very little.

The psychology lab was a large open room with many windows and rows of workbenches all equipped with computers, scales, and dispensers, electronic devices with lots of wires connecting equipment. Along one wall were cages of large white rats with electrodes connected to their heads. The sophisticated setup looked more like a university research center than a lab for high schoolers.

As Ms. Elia led the three of them into the lab, the kids looked up casually, apparently used to prospective parents' tours. The teacher—a pleasant man, about thirty, dressed in chinos and a blue work shirt—explained the psychology program and what the students were doing. "It's a term project on operant psychology techniques—a classic conditioned-response study in learning behavior," he said.

Rachel could not have cared less, but Martin was fascinated, of course.

"At the beginning of the term, each student was given a rat, and over the weeks, they shaped the animals' responses by rewarding them with small electrical stimulation to their brains. First they learned to press a lever, then a second lever, then a third, until they learned to tap a particular sequence of what the students decide upon—ABCD, BCAD, CBAD, or whatever."

"So it's cumulative?" Martin asked.

"Yes, and increasingly complex, which is why it's taken an entire semester to get to this point. This is their wrap-up day. Their reports are due next week."

Rachel was ready to scream. But Martin asked, "What does the electricity do?"

"It gives them a two-volt hit to the pleasure centers of their brains." The teacher pointed to a plastic device beside the computer about the size of a tissue box. "That's the stimulation chamber which is connected to the animal and the computer, which regulates the parameters—voltage, pulse width, frequency, et cetera. And that's a printout of the responses." He pointed to a scroll-paper ink-needle printer.

At various benches, quiet buzzers and lights were going off in the cages as students hooked up their rats and were recording their responses as they tapped the levers.

"Did you have any problems with the animal rights people?" Martin asked.

"I'll say, but that's the good thing about Bloomfield. The headmaster agreed to institute an animal care-and-use committee to be in compliance with state regulations. That took some string-pulling, but we eventually got approval as long as the instructor does the implant surgery and supervises the experiments. But the kids put together all the equipment and run the experiments. It's been great."

"You can understand that the kids become very attached to their animals," Ms. Elia said. Nearly every cage had name stickers—Brad, Snowdrop, Vinnie B, Snagglepuss, Bianca, Mousse, Dr. Dawson, Rumplemints, and so on.

"I bet," Martin said.

"By the way, we have another student from Hawthorne." Ms. Elia nodded to a tall pretty blonde who was putting her rat into the test cage. Because of her height and bearing, she projected considerable presence. "Nicole DaFoe."

Rachel didn't recognize the name.

At the next bench, an Asian girl was fixing something on her printout machine before she set up her rat. Rachel heard her say she was out of paper, and the teacher said to check the supply closet in another room. The girl fidgeted with the machine then left.

"Amy Tran. She's one of our best," the teacher whispered to Rachel. Then he said, "You folks have got to see this." And he led them into the adjoining room.

As Rachel began to follow, she happened to look back. Something about the tall blond girl held Rachel's attention—the body language and a heightened awareness. Rachel pulled behind a partition as the others left, and through a slot, she watched. The girl looked around until she was certain the visitors had left, then while the other students busied themselves at their stations, she slipped to the nearby computer and ran her fingers across the keyboard. She then went back to her own station and flicked the start switch on her animal's cage to run the program. The animal tapped a series of buttons until the cage light went on and the animal reared up in pleasure from the stimulation.

A few moments later, the Asian girl returned with the scroll paper, fixed it into her machine, then got her rat whose name was Sigmund. She removed him from his box, gave him a few affectionate strokes with her finger, then put him into the test chamber. She wrote something down on her clipboard, said something that amused the blonde on the next bench, then flicked the external switch.

Picking up the cue, Sigmund moved to the levers and began to tap through a very elaborate sequence. When it apparently finished, a cage light went on to signal the reward. The animal sniffed the air a few times then reared up with pleasure.

Suddenly the animal stiffened and let out a high piercing scream then shot straight up into the air as if launched. There was a terrible sizzling sound, as Sigmund fell onto the cage floor, his body violently twitching and smoke rising from his head.

Amy cried out in horror.

Other kids ran over to her. And a moment later, the teacher reappeared. "What happened?"

The girl was crying. "He's dead! He's dead."

The teacher looked at the rat lying on its side, a pungent odor of cooked flesh filling the air. He went to her computer and tapped some keys. "Jesus, Amy, you had the voltage set for twenty instead of two."

"No, I set it for *two*," Amy gasped in protest through her tears. "I know I did. I know it."

"Well, it says twenty." He stepped aside to show her. He looked very upset. "Why didn't you double-check as you were supposed to?"

"I did." Then too distraught to continue, the girl broke down.

Nicole put her hand on Amy's shoulder. "It's okay," she said. "We all make mistakes." And she shot Rachel a look that sent a shard of ice through her heart.

"I think she sabotaged her experiment."

"Based on what?"

"I'm telling you, I saw her do something at the Asian girl's keyboard."

"They were sharing computers," he declared. "She probably turned on her own software. What's the big deal?"

There it was: his absolutist certitude, and that damning tone that said Rachel didn't know what she was talking about—that her woman's intuition was off again. "Martin, it's how she looked—like she was doing something sneaky," she said, feeling her own certainty slip. "Two minutes later, the rat dies."

"Coincidence," he said. "Besides, why would she do that?"

"I don't know—maybe she had it in for her. Maybe she's a bitch."

"And maybe the Chinese kid just screwed up."

"The teacher said she's first in the class—which means she's not the type to make simple errors. And she's Vietnamese."

Martin shrugged. "Whatever. Even whiz kids make mistakes. What can I say?" Then he added, "If you were so sure, then why didn't you say something?"

"Because . . . Christ, forget it."

He smiled. "Like I said in the first place, you were mistaken."

It was that evening, and Rachel was putting her pajamas on. Martin had put Dylan to bed and was on their bed with the current issue of the MIT alumni magazine. He yawned. "Whatever, that teacher's ass is grass with the animal-rights people. So is little Suzy Wong's."

Rachel went into the bathroom to brush her teeth, and scrub away her irritation at Martin. She could still feel the freezing look in that Nicole's eyes.

When she stepped out, Martin said, "You must admit the little bastards are impressive. I mean, the rat-fry aside, they're fucking smart. And that Julian is something else with the pointillism stuff. Jesus, the kid's like a human Xerox machine."

"I wish we could have talked to him," she said. "He seemed so obsessed. How do we know that's not the result of the enhancement?"

"Malenko said there's no effect on the personality, just cognitive powers. Ms. Elia said he's nearly a straight-A student."

"Well, I've got a few dozen more questions I want answered."

"Yeah, like *how much*. I'm almost afraid to ask."

"We'll know soon enough." They had their next appointment with Malenko tomorrow morning at his Cobbsville office.

Martin turned off the light and pulled Rachel to him. "It's been so long, I'm not sure if I remember how it's done."

She was not in the mood, but said, "I'm sure it will come back to you."

But halfway into their lovemaking, the telephone rang. "Leave it," Martin said.

She would have, but she was expecting a call from her mother. She had left a message earlier to see how she was feeling.

Rachel flicked on the light and grabbed the phone. It was her brother Jack. Their mother, Bethany, was going into the hospital in two days for open-heart surgery. She had felt weak for the last few weeks. But when she went in for a checkup the other day because of shortness of breath, the doctor discovered a slight heart murmur. They did an echocardiogram only to discover that she had been born with two aortic valve flaps not the usual three. Because it was a hitherto undetected congenital aberration, Bethany would need a replacement—a routine operation, with expectations of a full recovery since her heart was strong. But it meant that Rachel would fly to Phoenix. The operation was scheduled for four P.M. Monday.

Martin could tell from listening what the call was about. "I want to be with her," Rachel said when she hung up.

Martin nodded. "Of course."

She would book herself on a Saturday flight. She climbed back into bed, feeling as if this were some kind of omen.

Martin sidled up to her and began stroking her thigh again. "You haven't lost it, have you?"

"You and Dylan will be all right without me, won't you?"

"Why shouldn't we be?"

"I don't know," she said and turned out the lights.

37

One million dollars?"

"Half to be paid in cash before the procedure, the other half in two months."

"You've got to be kidding," Martin said.

"Did you think genius comes cheap?"

It was Thursday, and they were back at Malenko's Cobbsville office.

"It's just that, well, frankly, that's much more than we had expected, or can afford."

Malenko's eyebrows shot up. "Those are two different issues, the first more complicated and interesting than the second. I have taken the liberty of doing some research into your financial status, and I must say that you are doing fairly well. You own a house worth one point six million dollars in the current market, and your total business assets amount to six million dollars, which, by the way, is three million less than what you told the bank it was worth when you filed for a business loan last year."

"Where did you get that from?" Martin said. "You have no right . . . That's very private information."

"So is what you are asking me to do for your child, Mr. Whitman."

A silence fell on the room.

Malenko rolled back in his chair and peered over his glasses at them. "And because it is so private, there is another aspect to the fee—a guarantee that privacy is maintained at a premium—a security insurance, if you will. Should you decide to go through with enhancement, you will be asked to place another five hundred thousand dollars in an escrow account, half of which will be returned to you in three years, the balance in another three years, interest paid in full."

"*What?*"

"If in that time I discover that either of you has breached the nondisclosure terms, you will lose that five hundred thousand dollars and the fee. If, however, in three years I am certain that you have not talked and that you can be trusted, I will return to you half with interest and in six years the balance should you continue to maintain confidentiality."

"That's . . . that's . . ."

"*Ridiculous* may be the word you're trying to avoid. Even so, these conditions keep lips sealed, yes?" Then Malenko clasped his hands together and leaned toward them over his desk as if sharing a good joke. "Listen to me. You came to me with the single desire to do something about your child's intelligence. You were offered extensive programs to address his needs with the best LD staff in North America. But you were clearly more interested in a medical procedure with immediate results. You wanted Dylan to have the kinds of advantages brighter kids enjoyed. You didn't want him to run the race with a clubfoot to use your phrase. You wanted a smarter son.

"That left one option: *enhancement*—a procedure that is not sanctioned by the FDA or the medical establishment, and one that will raise the backs of ethicists, social workers, the clergy, politicians, and a lot of others. It is also a procedure that could cause a backlash against orthodox science. If we do this, you will be asking me to put my medical license on the line. That I do not do lightly. Nor at a cut rate."

"I hear you," said Martin.

Malenko's manner softened. "Look, you come from a privileged life where people don't hurt each other, where people are trustworthy. But I come from a place where people hurt each other all the time, where the system was more important than the individual. Where betrayal was rewarded. So I've been imprinted with a cynicism about human nature that just won't go away. Sad, but I cannot be certain that people won't blab. Thus, the high price tag."

Martin nodded.

Rachel felt numb. They didn't have that kind of money.

"Once again, I remind you what this is all about: Your son's future is in the balance. If you go through with this, Dylan will grow up with a brilliant mind that will profoundly enhance his life, his success as a thinker, his health, his happiness, and his function as a human being. It may also affect his children and his children's children because, for no other reason, he will value the life of the mind. He will not be the boy you are now raising. If you are not comfortable with that, forget it. If you don't like the financial conditions, forget it. If you're not at ease with the sociological, philosophical, bioethical matters or whatever, don't do it. If you are not comfortable with me, if you fear that I might take your money and run, then don't do it!

"However, you will have to trust that I won't take your money and run. As a matter of fact, I like where I am. But if you are nagged by doubts, just say no." Malenko stood up. They were being dismissed. "Go home and think it over."

Suddenly everything took on a whole different perspective to Rachel. What started out as some variation of the Hippocratic code had turned into a simple business deal, and little else. The red Porsche, the elegant walnut-burl desk, the sailboat, the summer home on the Maine coast. The man was living the good life but not from tutoring children.

Malenko checked his watch. "Any questions?"

"No," Martin said.

"Yes," Rachel said. "If we were to agree to this, what about follow-up treatments for him? Monitoring his progress. What if something goes wrong?"

"You come to me," he declared. "This is my procedure, and I am the only one who can help him and the only one who is able to monitor his progress."

Malenko came around his desk. "Let me assure you that I am not going to abandon you like some old-time back-alley abortionist who plies his trade then drops off the planet. We are in this together for your son's betterment. Enhancement does not end with the operation. Dylan will come in for regularly scheduled examinations like any other patient. Because of the special nature of the procedure, there are very special postoperative treatments to be certain all is going well."

"And if it's not?"

"I have done enough of these to be ready for any contingencies." He extended his hand. "Believe me."

Rachel took it, thinking that she wanted to believe him with all her heart.

"I understand your concerns, and you probably will think of many more questions. So call me early next week, and we can talk more about this."

"I'll be out of town next week," Rachel said. "My mother is going to the hospital."

"Well, when you get back. The sooner, the better. There are considerable preparations to be made. I'm also leaving the country in three weeks."

"Where exactly do you perform the procedure?"

"At an offsite facility."

He wasn't going to specify.

"A regular medical facility, fully equipped and staffed?"

"Yes, of course. In fact," he said, opening one of his desk drawers, "here's what it looks like."

He handed her three color blowups of an operating room. It looked like the standard ORs she had seen—operating tables, lights, electronic equipment, and what appeared to be brain-scan monitors. "These are for stereotaxic viewing of the procedure."

"Meaning what?"

"Meaning we can view the interior structure of his brain in three-dimension on monitors while we are performing the operation. The real-time coordinate imaging guides us with the probes. It's standard operating procedure in neurosurgery in the best of institutions including Mass General."

Rachel nodded. She didn't know anything about the equipment, but the photographs were impressive. In one, Malenko wore scrubs. No other people were in any of them, of course. She handed them back. "What about the rest of the staff?"

"For obvious reasons, I cannot tell you who they are," he said. "But working with me will be the best there is, I assure you."

"Practicing neurosurgeons?"

"Practicing neurosurgeons, anesthesiologists, scrub nurses, circulation nurses—the full complement."

Rachel nodded, questions jamming her mind. "The other day you mentioned the cocktail of ingredients that you'd be using," Rachel began, unable to actually say the words *injecting into my son's brain*.

"Yes. I won't bore you with details, but the whole field of implantation is very intricate and complicated. But we use a mixture of certain chemical stimulants, protein growth factors, and dissociated tissue cells which will on their own genetic program create new axonal structures where deficient."

Rachel nodded with guarded satisfaction. "We will be able to visit him, of course?"

"After the procedure is completed." He opened the door. "Call me when you get back. Should you decide this is for you, then we'll answer the rest of your questions."

"Say we did this," Martin said. "Just how long would it be before we see results?"

"In about three to six months you will begin to see improvement in his cognitive behavior. Because the process is progressive, it should continue for another six to nine months until it plateaus."

"Which means in about a year and a half he will . . ." Martin trailed off.

"He will have an IQ of one hundred forty or more," Malenko said.

"Oh, wow," Martin said. His eyes filled up.

It was nearly noon, and Malenko led them out.

As they stepped into the hall, Rachel happened to notice another folder on the reception desk, apparently that of another patient. Rachel couldn't help but glance at the name printed in black Magic Marker on the outside. BERNARDI.

Even as they walked back to their car behind the Porsche, Rachel did not connect the name. Her mind was too scattered with thoughts about Dylan, enhancement, and her mother to notice. And now there was a damn time constraint to consider. If they were going to put him through this, it had to be done soon.

That was absurd. How does one make a snap decision about subjecting one's child to a secret brain operation to raise his intelligence and alter him and his life forever?

When the Whitmans left, Malenko went downstairs into the basement where he had set up a gym with weights, treadmill, StairMaster, and a speed bag.

He had never done competition boxing for obvious reasons, though he would have loved to. He knew as a young man he had had it in him to be a fine boxer—the strength, the timing, the aggression, and the deep-seated need to pound another's face. But that wouldn't be, so he worked out on the inflated black leather bladder, taking pleasure in the satisfyingly hypnotic rhythm and imagined enemies.

He changed into his sweats and pulled on the gloves while standing in front of a wall mirror. Maybe it was something the Whitman woman had said. Maybe it was what stared back at him in the mirror—that dead outsized pupil of his left eye. The heat of rage had grown cold over the years, but he could still hear those little bully bastards cawing in their stupid peasant dialect. In a flick, the bag was their faces, and he pounded it to a rhythmic blur while his mind slipped back.

Kiev, the Ukraine. It was the day after his eleventh birthday, and he was in Martyr's Park playground near the Cathedral of St. Sophia trying out his new kite. The bully-boys from the church school were kicking a soccer ball on the nearby field. Young Lucius was like catnip to them.

It began, as usual, with taunts—this time, the bright pink and yellow stripes of his kite—*girl* colors, *homosexual* colors. Then they moved to his short stature. Then to his nose—"eagle beak" they had called him. Then inevitably to his mother's Jewishness. In a matter of moments, word exchanges became blows, and young Lucius Malenko found himself on the ground being punched and kicked. Like the rest of the peasant rabble of the village, these boys harbored a contempt for Jews not because Jews had different rituals or an arcane tongue or because their Sabbath was on Saturday, or even because they were "Christ-killers." It was because the Malenkos were smart and successful—the source of the unstated resentment that the boys' parents had passed on to them. And because the locals were poor and stupid.

In one stunning moment, while Oleg Samoilovych and Ivan Vorsk held him down to make a target of his head, Nestor Kravchuk, a fat oaf whose father worked at a foundry, kicked the soccer ball full blast into his face. The blow was so powerful that for several days Lucius could not see out of his left eye. When the vision returned, the blood sac had sunk to the anterior chamber; and given the poor medical care in Kiev, nobody noticed the minor deformation of the pupil. But over the years, the condition gave way to traumatic glaucoma that eventually impaired his vision. Eye surgery years later restored it enough for him to finish medical school and conduct his research. He had even managed to establish his stateside practice that prospered magnificently. But then the darkness began to close in, and he was forced to abandon a lucrative practice for part-time consulting.

The ring of Malenko's pager stopped him.

He mopped the perspiration from his head and called in for the voice message. Sheila MacPhearson had received the video: All was set for Saturday night.

That was good news. It would be a real surprise party. Too bad he would miss it.

"Where are we going to get that kind of money?" Rachel asked on the way home.

"Do you have any idea what your mother's open-heart surgery will cost? About two hundred thousand when all is said and done. Maybe more."

"But insurance will pay for most of that."

"And thank God," Martin said. "The point is the operation will probably keep her going for another ten years. Enhancement will benefit Dylan for a lifetime. And it's not like we don't have the resources. We could sell some stocks and cash in mutual funds."

Rachel looked at him while he drove. "You're serious."

"Yeah, I'm serious." And he went on about what an investment it would be—how smart people accomplished more in a lifetime than less brainy ones, which is why so many prodigies become millionaire CEOs by the time they turn thirty.

"There are still too many things I'm uncomfortable with."

"Like what?"

"Like sending my son off to have a brain operation and not knowing where the hell he is. I want to be outside the operating room. I want to be there when they wheel him to recovery. What if something happens?"

"But they've been doing this for a dozen years. Look at their success stories."

"But something can still go wrong. He could end up brain-dead." The very thought sent a bolt of electricity through her.

"That's not going to happen."

"We don't know that. Another thing, why all the secrecy if it's so successful? Why an undisclosed location?"

"He explained that. It's a revolutionary thing, and he can't get FDA approval because of all the social stuff. Like he said, think of it as abortion before *Roe* versus *Wade*."

"Yeah, butchers in back alleys."

"Aren't you being a little dramatic?"

"Because I don't like it. We also don't know anything about Malenko. He could be some kind of a quack."

Martin laughed. "Quacks don't have a wall full of degrees and plaques. The guy's a leading neurosurgeon and child development expert. Besides, look at Lucinda. She was turned into a prodigy. So was Julian Watts. So were dozens of other kids."

"Yeah, and Lucinda's a bossy little bitch and Julian's a human sewing machine who's ground his teeth to nothing."

"That's got nothing to do with enhancement. Lucinda will grow out of that, and Julian might be a little compulsive, nothing that a little Ritalin won't solve. The point is, two slow kids got turned into geniuses, and that's what I want for my son."

He had an answer for everything. And maybe he was right. Maybe deep down she wanted to be convinced. In her mind, she saw the planar cuts of the distorted ventricles of her son's brain.

Acid kickback.

"What if there's something about the procedure that's

just not right? Something not medically right. I don't know . . . We don't even know how he does it."

"Why should he give away trade secrets?"

Rachel stared out the window as they drove down their street. "Maybe I'm just paranoid," she said. "It's just that I can't blithely send him off to have his brain cut open. Besides, he could have a perfectly happy life the way he is."

"He's operating on less than three-quarters of normal capacity."

"Rachel, we live in a meritocracy where an eighty IQ is a formula for losing."

That was just like Martin: He thought in numbers. They were the fundamental condition of his existence—how he gauged business and people. An IQ was just another way to keep score—like rank in class, sales quotas, revenue figures, stock options, salary.

"That's not true," Rachel said, her eyes filling up.

"You know what I mean. Of course, there are happy people with below-average intelligence. But they spend their days stocking shelves at Kmart, making eighteen thousand dollars a year and living in tiny apartments watching reruns of *Forrest Gump*. Frankly, I don't want that for my son—and we have an opportunity to do something about that—and the money."

"But a fancy job isn't the end-all of life."

"No, but it's one hell of an advantage."

And in her mind Rachel heard Martin's familiar refrain: *"Life is hard, but it's harder when you're stupid."*

"Think of his self-esteem," he continued. "You know what it's like when you meet someone with a mental handicap. You instantly dismiss him: He's not good enough to take seriously, to do business with, to be my friend. You smile in his face and thank God he's not you—or yours. It's sad and cruel, but it's reality. And I don't want that for my son—even if it costs me a million dollars."

As they pulled into their driveway, Rachel suddenly realized that she was trembling. Her eyes fixed on Dylan's soccer ball that lay on the grass beside his sandbox. While her pursuit of Sheila's lead had never been whimsical, Rachel had deep down not considered enhancement a real possibility. It was just something in the speculation mode—an option to consider. But nothing was definite, and no irrevocable action was in place. Even their visit to Malenko Rachel had thought of as reconnaissance—a fact-finding mission. Now, in the matter of an hour, Martin was talking about cashing in investments to buy their son a new brain.

She looked at Martin. "You've got this all figured out."

"Rachel," Martin said, softening his voice, "before we ever heard about Lucius Malenko, we had resigned ourselves to raising a mentally challenged child. Whatever went wrong with the genetic dice, he came out impaired. Now we have a second chance—a privilege open to only a handful of kids. The implications are mind-boggling. So are the possibilities for him. A second chance to begin his life near the top." His eyes were wet from tears. "Don't you want to do this for him? Don't you?"

In a voice barely audible, she said, "I don't know."

38

Sheila stood by the kitchen window making hot chocolate for Lucinda's party.

Two days had passed, and the kitten was still missing. She had searched the backyard woods several times since that first day, without luck.

After the initial shock, Lucinda did not seem to suffer the loss—which Sheila attributed to budding maturity. She had just resigned herself to such mishaps and went on with her little life. Oddly enough, she didn't bring up a replacement kitten again. And neither did Sheila.

Outside the huge magnolia tree had lost its blossoms, giving way to a profusion of waxy green leaves. Across the branches, Sheila had draped colored streamers, big shiny cardboard Japanese lanterns, and bright animal piñatas—which complemented her marigolds and roses—all in full bloom. Because of mature growth, their backyard was cut off from views of the neighbors, making the yard a magical sylvan grotto—so safe and secret. Lucinda's own little green world. *Storybook perfect*.

There used to be a secret passageway connecting their yard to the Sarris family next door, but some unpleasantness had estranged their children. There were two of them, snippy little brats who snitched on Lucinda.

"Lucinda said I'm a dummy."

"Lucinda made me eat a bug."

"Lucinda put a frog in the micro."

Eventually the Sarrises—or Soarasses, as Lucinda called them—

(such a devilish wit, too)

—closed off the passage, erecting a fence and some high bushes, essentially shielding them off as if Lucinda were some kind of poisoned child.

The bastards.

Thankfully, they moved away. They were just a bunch of dumb second-generation Greeks anyway.

The backyard scene made Sheila's heart gulp for the beauty. It was like one of those Hallmark cards: Lucinda in her new pink dress under the magnolia and holding her own party and chattering away at her guests. Today wasn't officially her birthday. That was last week, but only three kids of the ten invited could come. A few had colds—

some kind of bug going around

—another was visiting her sick grandmother in New York. Somebody had forgotten that it was ballet recital rehearsal. Another couldn't get over because her asthma was kicking up again. One had an unscheduled riding lesson. Blah blah blah.

Their excuses annoyed Sheila nearly to the point of complaining to the mothers. But if the kids were sick, they were sick. And to call them liars would only make things worse the next time. The only ones who showed were Franny Alemany, Annette Bonaiuto, and MaryLou Sundilson—three cute little girls from school, but not girls she was particularly friendly with. Then again, what children make close friends at seven?

Because it had rained, they moved inside—which was a shame, since Sheila had decked out the backyard. The magician she had hired ended up doing tricks for Lucinda and the three others who sat there like waxed fruit. Half an hour of cake and ice cream, half an hour of magic, and it was all over. The girls had to go—other commitments. Sheila could have screamed.

But deep down she knew the reasons behind the bullshit excuses. The other kids were threatened by Lucinda: She was "bossy" and their mothers thought her "managerial." The long and short was that Lucinda was head and shoulders above them—smarter, quicker, and more confident. So the mothers kept their boring little dolts away.

But Lucinda didn't mind. She had her other friends. And Rachel Whitman had sent over a gorgeous doll. It came with a little card, saying her name was Tabitha from Jackson Hole, Wyoming, and she loved animals. She was made of a durable plastic compound and was fully poseable with jointed elbows and knees and two outfits, one a red pullover under a jean jacket and beige chinos, and the other which Rachel had ordered specially—the same pink dress Lucinda was wearing today. It must have cost Rachel a small fortune.

More amazing was the doll's resemblance to Lucinda. Besides the pink dress and thick blond hair, the face looked like hers as a baby—the little pug nose, the huge crystalline blue eyes, the chipmunk cheeks, the cleft in the chin, and the roundness of the forehead. It was uncanny. As if Rachel had had it specially made from a baby photo.

(She would have to send her a special thank-you note. To Dylan too, since it was technically from him, even though he didn't have a clue, the poor kid.)

Luckily, today was warm and sunny. Garden-party perfect. And that's exactly what Miss Lucinda was doing: having a private little rain-check celebration of her own—and perfectly content, thank you. That was the thing about being so advanced: You gained strength from your disappointments and went on with your life—a surprise benefit of enhancement. Lucinda was totally resourceful. Totally comfortable in her own head.

The whistle of the teapot snapped Sheila back into the moment.

She poured the hot water into the porcelain pot from Lucinda's own tea set and then added the cocoa and stirred. She then dumped the extra hot water down the drain.

A faint foul odor rose up.

Sheila let the cold water run for several seconds. But it was still there—a sharp little curlicue of rot rising out of the hole. She ran the hot water for maybe a full minute. That only made it worse. She reached under the sink and turned on the disposal with the water running. There was that rattle sound as if something were stuck inside, something that wouldn't break up. Then the disposal shut itself off. It would be several minutes before it could be reset. Sometimes Lucinda accidentally let the plastic cap of an orange-juice carton slip down or a spoon.

For a protracted moment, Sheila looked down at the opening with the black rubber splashguard. Although she had warned Lucinda never ever to do this, Sheila pushed her hand through. Her fingers touched the smooth rounded blades. Blades that under power could grind meat and bones to pulp.

She felt something that had not been completely ground to pulp—something hard and rounded by the blades and snagged in a mat of wet fibers. What felt like the stringy cellulose stuff that made up celery stalks and banana skins—or maybe lemon peels that just hadn't gone through. And the hard thing was probably a piece of plastic spoon—like what Lucinda was using outside for the ice cream. Of course, Lucinda knew hard objects didn't go down the drain. But as brilliant as she was, she was still only seven—just barely. Still played with dolls. In fact, she was out there talking up a blue streak with Tabitha and the others.

Sheila slowly pulled her hand out of the garbage disposal drain.

In her fingers was a piece of curved white bone in a wet tangle of fibrous brownish muck and long thick strings of orange hairs. The thing stank of decay.

Sheila stared at it without shock. She did not scream, she

only gagged reflexively. Then she dumped the awful finds into paper towels and flushed them down the toilet. She washed her hands and looked in the mirror. She barely recognized her own face.

Dr. Malenko said it had nothing to do with it. That it only affected her intelligence. That her makeup otherwise was as it would have been.

He promised. No change. Just smarter.

She shook away the thoughts and headed back into the kitchen. In a vague trancelike state, she stirred a little more milk into the porcelain server. The set was Sheila's birthday gift—an eight-piece collection in porcelain and hand-painted with birds and flowers. It had cost her over four hundred dollars—expensive, but exquisite. Besides, Malenko would be paying her the finder's fee soon. Fifty thousand dollars.

She placed the pot of chocolate on the tray along with the chocolate-chip cookies she had baked earlier. For a brief spell, Sheila paused at the rear door to take in the scene of her daughter sitting outside.

Harry would have said you're in a state of denial, she thought. *That our daughter is a little monster.*

Lucinda was sitting at her table with her back to the house under the magnolia.

Not so! And Harry was dead.

Her guests looked on as Lucinda regaled them nonstop. Sheila couldn't hear Lucinda's words because her portable CD player was blaring music. Her Disney album—"A Very Merry Unbirthday to You" from *Alice in Wonderland.*

She's brilliant. IQ 150. Superior intelligence range.

Incandescent mind.

Sheila took a deep breath and stepped outside with the tray of cookies and hot chocolate.

The air was clear and keen. She crossed the brick walk onto the spread of lawn that connected their splendid little greenworld to the vast, manicured carpet of yardgrass that rolled from neighborhood to neighborhood all the way across the vast green continent.

The closer she got, the clearer Lucinda's voice. She was fully animated, demonstrating something with her hands. Meanwhile, the music was bubbling out of the player like champagne.

An absolutely magical scene, Sheila thought.

The table had been set for eight, seven places occupied by stuffed animals. Lucinda's favorite sat to her right: a big old Dumbo they had bought last year at Disney World—a doll that had jumped out at her the moment she laid eyes on it. Sheila still recalled how Lucinda had frozen in place—unmoved by all the Mickeys, Minnies, and other stuffed cartoon characters—as if seeing an apparition.

Sheila moved within a few feet of her daughter's back. She looked like a peony in her pink dress. The music continued playing, and Lucinda was chattering away to her guests, giving instructions.

For a moment Sheila thought she would drop the tray. But some instant reflex caught her, stunning her in place.

Sitting on the table in front of her was Rachel's Miss Tabitha doll in pink. Sheila's first thought was that her daughter had fashioned a punk hairdo for Tabitha. But then it came horridly clear.

With a pair of scissors, Lucinda had cut all the hair off the doll down to its rubbery skull, and with Sheila's new chrome wine-bottle opener, she had methodically corkscrewed holes into its skull through which she had stuck colored cocktail toothpicks.

"Lucinda . . . Wha-wha . . . ?"

Lucinda turned. Her face was an implacable blank. "Oh, how splendid. Mommy brought the chocolate and the cookies. Miss Tabitha is going to be delighted. Aren't you, Tabitha?"

Then, before Sheila could say something, Lucinda's

voice became some squeaky alien thing: *"Yes, I am because it's my birthday, too."*

"Lucinda . . . why did you . . . ?" Then something around the doll's neck stopped her cold. "What's that black thing?"

"Oh, it's Tabitha's boa," Lucinda proclaimed. "It's just like yours, Mommy."

Sheila reached for it, but her hand froze. It was the kitten's tail. She could see the white bone cut at the end. Lucinda had colored the fur black with her markers, though the orange still showed at the roots.

"I made it, but it doesn't fit right," Lucinda said, and she took the thing in her hand and bent it into a circle—the cracking sounds sending barbs of horror through Sheila. "That's better," Lucinda said, fitting it in place.

Sheila tried to catch her breath, but before she did, Lucinda shot her a look of wide-eyed pride. "I'm going to be a doctor when I grow up. So is Miss Tabitha. Aren't you, Tabitha?"

"Yes, I am," Tabitha replied. *"I'm going to be an anesthesiologist. What kind of doctor do you want to be?"*

"Lucinda, what—" Sheila began.

But Lucinda cut her off. "Mother, *please* don't interrupt." Then she turned to Tabitha again. "I want to be a surgeon, because I would like to see the insides of people's bodies, especially their heads." Lucinda pushed another pick into Tabitha's crown. "Did you know that the average adult brain weighs approximately three pounds and an elephant's brain weighs thirteen pounds?"

"I didn't know that. How much does my brain weigh?"

"You're just a newborn, so yours weighs less than a pound, but it's going to grow very, very fast." And she stuck in another pick just above the eyebrow.

"That tickles," Tabitha squealed. *"But it's okay because I'm going to be a smart little girl just like you."*

"And make tons of money, right, Mommy? *RIGHT?"*

39

Lucius Malenko slid open the glass doors on the balcony and let the cool Atlantic breeze flush over him.

From his perch on the granite cliffs a few miles below Portsmouth, the glittering blue filled his vision. In the gauzy distance, sailing vessels made their way toward the harbor past the small humps of Big Frog and Little Frog Islands. It was a million-dollar view. Or, more exactly, four million, bought and paid for by the upper end of the bell curve.

Malenko took in a cool deep breath of assurance that he had it all—a home by the sea, a remote country estate in the woods, and a fifteenth-century villa in Tuscany where in three weeks he would relax for a month. He had nearly every mode of transportation. On the walls behind him hung original seascape oils by Marshall Johnson, Thomas Birch, and Winslow Homer. Atop pedestals and on shelves sat various objets d'art from his foreign travels. Lighting up the computer monitor in the adjacent room were his investments showing cumulative capital valuations of over forty million dollars. What he called his "Smart Money portfolio"—pun intended.

His was the good life, to use the hoary old American expression—a life that was far beyond the meager earnings of a consulting senior neurologist working two days a week at Nova—and a life that was light-years beyond where he had come from in the Ukraine.

As he stood on the balcony sipping his morning coffee, with the sultry ocean air combing through his hair and the warm sun on his face, he recalled the dark and twisted road that had led him here from the dismal, concrete-poured flats of the Kiev State Research Center of Neurosurgery.

It was the early 1970s, and he had headed up a project with the long-range goal of alleviating the effects of certain human neurological afflictions. The radically new approach involved the transplantation of healthy animal brain tissue into like regions in other animals with various neurological defects. The theory was that primitive rat or monkey brain cells could "reseed" those areas of nerve degeneration and take their cues from existing brain matter to mature into the needed cell types. This way, human neurological diseases—including multiple sclerosis, strokes, or multi-infarct dementia—might eventually be treated by neurotransplantation.

But in the early stages of his research, Malenko made a series of astounding side discoveries. He had located areas of the cortex and hippocampus that affect memory and cognitive performance and which energize other brain systems. When he treated those areas in a control group of newborn mice with a dopamine-protein mix that promoted neuron connections, he discovered that their long-term memory was superior to that of untreated mice. Not only did they run their mazes faster, but also they could speed through complicated new structures as if radar-guided.

An even greater surprise came when he injected a cocktail of growth factors and neural tissue from one maze-whiz mouse into that of an untreated cousin. The injected cells did not produce a glob of cells in one place in the brain. Instead, they migrated to underdeveloped areas of the brain. Remarkably, the recipient mice ended up solving complicated maze problems, shooting through the structures instead of blindly poking their way. He repeated his experiment several times using different control groups until he was absolutely certain of his results: The enhanced neurological circuitry had been passed from harvest to host animals. He had transplanted high-intelligence animal brain matter into the skulls of dim-witted cousins and produced a smarter mouse.

Over the ensuing months, he all but abandoned the Parkinson's project and moved his experimentation to rhesus monkeys with the similarly amazing results. Once the word got out that his lab had boosted animal intelligence, the Soviet government stepped in to raise the sights.

As always, the interest was purely political. For years, the government had been concerned over the "brain drain" of homegrown scientists to other countries as well as the precipitous drop-off in the number of young people interested in science and mathematics. While blaming the "techno-lag" on the corrupting influence of Western culture, it was clear that the Soviet Union was losing its competitive edge in the world. And for the Defense Ministry, technical inferiority would surely accelerate the decline of the republic's world status and internal solidarity. That could not be. So, in desperation to salvage the country's intellectual viability, the Malenko Procedure was given top secret priority. People would be made smarter.

The project had first struck him as foolishly naïve—another scheme of a few old-fart Cold War–niks who measured scientific progress in terms of how to beat the Americans. Two decades earlier, like-minded KGB idiots squandered millions of rubles to finance research in ESP with the dream of creating telepathic superspies. There was no limit to their creative fantasies.

But as the social theoreticians worked on him, pounding him with the bleak statistics on Soviet society, scales seemed to melt from Lucius Malenko's eyes: Stupid people were toxic to the Soviet system. They were responsible for three-quarters of the crime, poverty, drug and alcohol abuse, homelessness, higher teenage pregnancies, and diseases. And they produced children destined to create more of the same *ad infinitum*. Intelligence was the panacea. And he possibly possessed the magic elixir.

Of course, the step from rhesus macaques to the top of the Great Chain of Being was forbidding. The first problem was the lack of human neural cells. At the time, there had been some success in grafting brain tissue from aborted fetuses into adults with Parkinson's disease. Although there was no shortage of aborted embryos, there were fundamental unknowns such as which regions of the fetal brain to extract from. With pea-sized mouse brains, the challenge was minimal. But human intelligence was a matter of memory and the retrieval of that memory, and those connections ranged globally throughout the brain. He tried extracts from numerous loci, but after four agonizing years of experimentation, he concluded that fetal grafts lacked environmental adaptability and, thus, were ineffective in enhancing human intelligence. Three years later, that failure led him to the needed breakthrough.

Unfortunately, the Soviet Union was in the throes of collapse. So Malenko found himself playing "beat the clock" with perhaps the most extraordinary discovery in the medical world—if not in all of science: a project on par with the splitting of the uranium atom, the discovery of the DNA molecule, and the first moon landing. There he was, a modern-day Paracelsus, converting base materials to gold—only to watch his lab close down.

But all was not lost. A year later, in 1987, he was granted a work visa to the U.S., whose government, hampered by the tenets of democracy, would not approve of his project— at least not publicly. Secretly recruited by a clandestine cell of the National Security Agency, he was eventually given full-citizen status. In exchange, Dr. Lucius Malenko labored to perfect human enhancement—a project that lasted two years until the agency closed him down, claiming the risk factor was too high. Three subjects had died.

In the intervening years, he worked his way up from research assistant in neurology at the Commonwealth Medical Center in Boston to chief surgeon until his eye failed him.

Ironically, he had discovered the keys to the kingdom, unlocking one of nature's great black boxes—human intelligence—and, except for a handful of people in the world, nobody had a clue, including his colleagues at Nova Children's Center. He was simply mild-mannered Dr. M. who came in twice a week to consult with his patients.

What they did not know was that he had moved his kingdom underground, which was fine since Lucius Malenko was beyond the need for recognition. Years of clandestine Soviet research had conditioned his ego to darkness. Besides, nothing about enhancement was fit for public consumption. So he did his public persona thing, while on the side he quietly played Shiva.

The telephone rang, bringing him back to the moment. It was Vera asking about the Whitman case.

"We're still working on that, but it's moving in the right direction."

"Good. By the way, this last one is on yellow."

As usual, Vera was being discreet in her word choice. What she meant was that little Lilly Bellingham was being readied for preop. "I'll be up tomorrow," he said. "There are a few things that need to be attended to on this end first."

"Of course," she said. "And I assume the package arrived."

"Yes, it has."

"I'm sorry I'll miss all the fun."

"Likewise, but I'm sure we'll hear about it."

40

Brendan felt ridiculous in the tuxedo and white shirt that was required of the wait staff on party nights—like some exotic partridge. He moved through the crowd with trays of fancy dips and canapés.

Nicole DaFoe was there with her parents, looking void of affect as usual. She was wearing an ice-white dress with white high heels. It was the first time Brendan had seen her dressed up.

"Would you like some hors d'oeuvres, Ms. DaFoe?" he whispered. "We have m-m-mushroom caps stuffed with dog vomit and road pizza on a stick. The yellow dip is p-pus, and the brown sauce is—"

"You're not funny," Nicole said under her breath. She took a mushroom cap and popped it into her mouth. "Too bad you're not in school, or you'd have gotten one of these scholarships. You're poor."

Brendan's mind flooded with comebacks, but he did not respond. She started away. "Congratulations, by the way," he said.

She snapped her head toward him. "What for?"

She was playing coy. It was in the local newspaper. "I guess you got your A in history."

"Pardon me?"

"You won the Andrew Dale Laurent Fellowship Award. F-first in your class. A perfect four-oh. You aced out Amy Tran." Amy got honorable mention in the story, which ran with pictures including one with Nicole shaking hands with her history teacher, Michael Kaminsky. Amy's photo was separate, and he recognized her as the girl in the field-trip photo on Nicole's wall. The one with the holes in her eyes.

Nicole studied Brendan's face as if trying to gauge his attitude. Then she said simply, "Thanks." She started away, then stopped. "What time do you get off?"

"Eleven. Why?"

"Come to my place. I want to show you something. My parents are going to friends' house after this. I'll let you in the back way."

Brendan could not read her expression. "What's up?"

"Just be there."

Yes, mein Führer, a voice inside said. "Okay."

"I'm out of here. By the way, who's that woman in the green?"

Vanessa Watts was standing with several people, including a woman with a long green dress with her back to them.

"She visited the school the other day."

"Are you sure?"

"Yes, I'm sure. Don't move." She slipped behind him. "I don't want her to see me."

"Her n-n-name is Rachel Whitman. She's new. Moved here about seven months ago. Her husband's the guy in the olive d-double-breasted Armani. He owns an egghead recruitment company called SageSearches. It's the same suit on the cover of last month's *GQ* with Keanu Reeves. It's in the m-men's lounge—"

"I don't care about his suit," she snapped. "They were on a parents' tour. She must have a kid who wants to be a Bloomie."

"They have a six-year-old son, Dylan, but he's not Bloomie material. A nice little kid, but he's kind of l-l-limited."

"Do they have other kids?"

"None listed on her m-membership application. Just Dylan—signed up for day care and tennis lessons. Has a good swing. Also sings like an English choirboy."

"Then how come they were on tour?"

Brendan shrugged. "Maybe the old B-B-Bloomies are becoming more liberal with their standards. A kind of n-noblesse oblige, like the Dellsies with the poor-boy scholarships."

"Tell me another."

"Nice perfume, by the way."

"It's my mother's. It's called Joy."

"Ah." And the magazine ads lit up his mind. "Jean Patou. The world's most expensive fragrance. By the way, do you know how many flowers go into one two-ounce bottle of *eau de parfum*?"

"No, and I don't care," Nicole said.

"Six hundred and seventy-five."

"Where do you get all this useless information from?"

Before he could answer, somebody called for him—some guy in a grotesque maroon houndstooth sport coat and baby-blue gabardine pants was waving him over for some food. "Have to g-go."

"Even if Dylan qualifies, I don't think they'll send him. There was an accident in psych lab." She did not explain but flashed him a cool, sly look and headed for the rear exit, while Brendan headed for the houndsteeth.

Rachel watched Brendan LaMotte wend his way through the guests. He was quite dashing in the tuxedo. And, for once, his hair looked washed and neatly bound behind his head. She was tempted to go over and compliment him, but he'd probably discorporate. Or worse, tell her all the ingredients of his canapés.

Rachel was grateful for the party, because it took her mind off the enhancement option, which had left her ill-at-ease. Holding Martin's hand, she moved through the crowd. There must have been a hundred people in the grand ballroom, some parents and friends of the scholarship winners, others, associates of Vanessa Watts. Also a few media people, including reporters from local TV stations. At the center of the room was a large table with an ice fountain sculpted as a swan, behind which waiters served champagne and other drinks. Nearby were tables of fancy hors d'oeuvres. In one corner sat a table artfully stacked with copies of Vanessa's book, plus life-sized displays of the cover. Also behind the podium were blowups of each of the scholarship winners, all Dells caddies. The evening was a double-header billed as Dells' Scholars Celebration.

At the far end of the room sat a huge television monitor for a video presentation for later. Sheila was by the equipment chatting with some club staffers. When she saw Rachel she fluttered a wave.

Vanessa, who stood nearly six feet tall, was in a clutch of people chatting away. She was dressed in a striking black sheath with boat neck and capped sleeves that accentuated her long tanned arms and chest. A simple strand of pearls hugged her neck. Her golden hair had been elegantly styled with an upward flare adding to her stature. On her feet was a pair of pointy-toed black slides. She looked less like a professor of English and more like a fashion model. Rachel pulled Martin to join her.

"Congratulations," Rachel said with genuine admiration. Vanessa was a brilliant and accomplished woman, and now the pride of Middlesex University. She had taken several years off to raise Julian, and in her spare time she worked on her book, *Dark Visionary: A Literary Biography of George Orwell,* which was on its way to becoming an academic and commercial success, a rare accomplishment.

Vanessa thanked Rachel and introduced them to her agent and editor. Before they moved on, Rachel mentioned how they had met Julian at Bloomfield and how impressed they were.

Vanessa nodded. "Are you still thinking of . . . your own son?" she asked in a low voice.

"Yes, very much," Martin said.

Vanessa looked at Rachel for a response.

"I still have a lot of questions."

Vanessa pulled her aside. "I'll call you tomorrow," she whispered. "We have to talk." The intensity on her face was almost startling.

"Sure," Rachel said. "Is there a problem?"

Then somebody pulled Vanessa away to meet another guest. "I'll call," she said, leaving Rachel wondering at the urgency.

After nearly an hour of cocktails, a representative from the club announced that the program was to begin. There were ten scholarship recipients—nonmember caddies from area high schools—each of whom would receive a four-year fifteen-thousand-dollar scholarship to the college of his or her choice. The announcer read off their names and called them to the podium for an envelope and a framed plaque—nine boys and one girl who would be matriculating in the fall, most of them at A-list institutions.

Rachel watched the recipients receive their accolades, smile for the cameras, and return to the hugs and kisses of proud parents. As she scanned the crowd, her eyes landed on Sheila who was studying Rachel from across the room. Sheila smiled and held her gaze, nodding knowingly. If she could have read Rachel's mind, she would have registered cross-currents of emotions—yes, pained awareness that Dylan would never receive such a plaque and envy that she would never feel the elation of their parents.

Until two weeks ago she would have accepted such a fate. *So what? Scholarship isn't the measure of us.*

But that had all changed now. And it wasn't just the TNT story and the ragged guilt. It was Lucius Malenko. She wished she had never heard of him and his damned enhancement. She wished she had never said anything to Sheila, because all that had done was corrupt her evaluation of her own child and others. She could not go about her daily chores without thinking of people in terms of their IQs—from bank tellers to people stocking shelves at the supermarket. Who was to say that they weren't happy, productive individuals? Who was to say that a fancy college degree and a fancy job were all there was to living a successful life? And it left her feeling ashamed of herself.

Worse, her exposure to all the little geniuses threatened her appreciation of Dylan. Now when he rummaged for a word or came up with the wrong expression, she felt an irritating impatience, hearing a snippy little voice inside saying: *Lucinda or Julian wouldn't do that.* It was awful. She was beginning to resent her own child.

From across the room Sheila flashed her a thumbs-up sign.

"He can be fixed."

(You bought this. Damaged goods. It's yours to return.)

Rachel broke the contact and glanced at Martin. But he was grinning and returning Sheila the hand sign.

When the applause died, the host turned to the second part of the program. He made some brief congratulatory remarks about Professor Watts, the segue being a celebration of new scholars to a professional who was a model for the younger generation to emulate. He then introduced Vanessa's editor who commented briefly on how impressed he was with the manuscript and how he knew instantly that it was an important work which would be appreciated by an audience beyond academia.

The host returned to the microphone. Before introducing Vanessa, he announced a special surprise congratulation. When the lights dimmed, the huge TV monitor was turned on. To instant applause, the screen lit up with the face of the governor of the commonwealth, who congratulated Vanessa on a fine book. Following the applause, the picture shifted to the department chairman and the president of Middlesex who also added their congratulations and best wishes. Then a group shot of her colleagues in the department all saying "Congratulations" in unison and waving and blowing kisses.

Across the room Rachel could see Vanessa beaming and thanking people.

A scrambled void filled the monitor with snow as if the tape had been roughly edited. The screen went black for a moment, and somebody said "Is that it?" when the monitor again lit up, this time on the face of a serious-looking man about forty with a VanDyke beard. Nobody seemed to recognize him. And Rachel glanced at Vanessa who looked frozen in place.

"My name is Joshua Blake, and I was a graduate student of Vanessa Watts fifteen years ago at Middlesex University. At the time I was pursuing my doctorate in English, and Professor Watts was my advisor. My thesis, which was completed in 1988 and published in monograph form two years later, was entitled *In Defense of the Defensible: An Intertextual Study of the Dystopian Politics of George Orwell*.

"Some weeks ago, a reviewer for *The Modern Novel Quarterly* sent me an advance copy of Professor Watts's book to inform me that she had plagiarized my dissertation."

A murmur rose up from the crowd. Rachel looked over to Vanessa who appeared stunned.

"At first I was incredulous, since I remember Professor Watts as a brilliant and honorable scholar. Yet, after reviewing her book, I can only conclude with shock and great disappointment that she had engaged herself in massive and deliberate theft of my research, my conclusions, and my words. In fact, there are pages of identical or parallel passages, including whole paragraphs lifted word for word."

Across the room, Vanessa slumped into herself. Amazingly she did not protest but stood glaring at the screen in strange resignation. A stunned hush fell on the crowd, which stood transfixed at the split screen with pages from

Blake's dissertation juxtaposed with those from Vanessa Watts's book.

"Aside from a few feeble attempts at rewording, large passages are nearly identical, as you can see," Blake continued. "I don't know what your motives were, Professor Watts. Perhaps you had just assumed that because I was a lowly grad student you could help yourself to my material while I disappeared into the world and my dissertation molded away in the basement of Middlesex Library. What amazes and saddens me even more is that nowhere in your book am I acknowledged—not a single word of attribution. It pains me, but I accuse you of gross theft of intellectual property, and a violation of trust."

Vanessa put her hand over her eyes, while her husband tried to comfort her. Meanwhile, the tape continued. "I have informed my attorneys to file suit against—"

"Turn the goddamn thing off," Brad Watts shouted. "Turn it off!"

The picture went dead.

While the crowd looked on in disbelief, Vanessa pulled herself free of her husband and walked out of the room without a word. Brad began to follow, but she waved him back and left.

"My God," whispered Rachel to Martin. "That poor woman."

Vanessa rode around for nearly two hours hoping to find her center again. She had no place to go, nor did she want to drive home and face her family. Although Lisa was sleeping over at a girlfriend's house and Julian would be doing his silent-troll routine (he couldn't care less about her), Brad would want a full explanation.

In one stunning moment, she had been totally and permanently destroyed. And tomorrow, to forestall litigation, her publisher would publicly express embarrassment and apologize for the gross act of plagiarism and announce that it was halting distribution of her book, and that all fifty thousand copies would be taken off the market and destroyed—and that the twenty thousand scheduled for release in the UK and Europe next month would also be junked. The press would crackle with scathing indictments, contempt, and ridicule from colleagues and associates at Middlesex and other institutions around the country. Some would speculate on reasons—arrogance, entitlement, and academic pressure. Others would offer up the "death wish" theory, since this was such a careless, wholesale case of plagiarism.

The president would apologize while expressing concern for the kind of example this set for students and faculty alike, declaring something to the effect: "Originality like free expression is sacred in the academic world. This is an utter abuse of our trust as well as an affront to the academy and an example of intellectual corrosion."

For the next several days, her telephone would ring off the hook with reporters scrambling for a statement—for the scoop on her ruination. There would be an inquiry at the university; and in a few weeks she'd be relieved from her teaching post. Meanwhile, her publisher would demand reimbursement of the $70,000 advance and present a bill for another few hundred thousand dollars to cover the cost of the worldwide withdrawal and destruction of her books.

By this time next week, she, like her book, would be pulped.

As she drove around in the thick of the night, the reality of it all had hit her, rising up from that warm protected recess of her mind where she had packed it away for all these years. Joshua Blake was right: She was a plagiarist. She had stolen his work. And in the world of academic publications, that was the highest crime—tantamount to murder and suicide.

murder and suicide

She had taken his material not because it was so much better than hers, but because she was desperate to get the book into production and out in time for the 2003 George Orwell centennial. Adding to the pressure was her publisher's insistence that the book had high sales potential—a promise, which realized, could reduce the enormous debt incurred by Julian's enhancement and pricey education.

She had done it for him, she told herself. For Julian. She'd been on an unpaid leave of absence, racing to meet deadlines so he could nurture his genius. For her son. A mother's sacrifice.

As for the actual plagiarism, she was certain she could have come up with Blake's very insights. He had not made any conclusions of which she was incapable. In fact, she had felt entitled to them—more so for being his former advisor. And, yes, she had assumed he had disappeared and would never know.

Denial: the curse of the species.

And she had done it before. At Littleton College in New York where she had plagiarized a paper on Jonathan Swift in a graduate eighteenth-century course. At the time she was a doctoral student and a TA, and under tremendous pressure to excel at both. But she was young and foolish and for twenty dollars bought a paper on Jonathan Swift from one of those term-paper houses. Unfortunately, the same paper had been turned in the year before to the same professor. She had done stuff like that in undergraduate school, but this time she was given a term's suspension—a permanent note on her transcript.

We are what we ever were, she thought. *We never change.*

murder and suicide

Vanessa's insides were wracked with agony, but she did not go directly home. Instead she drove in the dark talking into her portable tape recorder, the one she kept in her car and used while working on her book. Her remarks were brief and pointed. When she was through, she drove to the home of the Whitmans and dropped off the recorder with tape in the glove compartment of Rachel's Maxima. Luckily the car was unlocked.

She then drove home.

Brad had left the downstairs lights on, but the rest of the interior was dark. All but Julian's room.

Shit.

She didn't want to see him. She didn't want to see anybody. All she wanted to do was go into a deep sleep and not come out of it. Thankfully, Brad had probably given up waiting and gone to bed.

She looked up at Julian's bedroom.

What the hell is he doing up at this hour? Christ, it's nearly two.

She pulled the car into the garage. Julian's skis were hanging up along the back wall. New parabolics that had cost over seven hundred dollars. They had been used once, on their winter vacation in Vail last year. He had no interest in skiing, and the entire week he spent inside the condo doing his pictures—stippling away like some crazed gnome. He had gotten soft and flabby, and given up everything physical. At school he was known as "Dots."

She unlocked the door and pushed her way inside. Except for the hum of the refrigerator, the place was dead quiet. The only relief from the dark was the light strip under Julian's door at the top of the stairs.

Vanessa climbed the stairs, feeling old and weary. On the landing she looked into the master bedroom. Brad was asleep. She then stopped just outside of Julian's door and listened. Nothing. No CD, no television, no sound of some mindless video game. He had probably fallen asleep on his bed. Good. She'd just flick off his light and let him sleep out the night.

She tapped quietly. Although he slept little, he would occasionally pass out from sheer exhaustion. She tapped again, and still nothing. Gently she turned the knob and pushed open the door.

Julian was not in bed but at his workbench.

The halogen lamp glowed brilliantly over the tilt board. His back was to her and his head was hunched below his shoulders. For a moment she thought that he had fallen asleep in place, because he did not move as she entered. But as she moved closer, she noticed his left hand.

"You're still up." She tried to sound pleasant, but the effort was strained. The public humiliation had its source in him; and at the moment it took every fiber of her being to feign civility.

Her eye fell on a photo of her and Julian at his music summer camp last year in the Berkshires. He had just finished his recital to a standing ovation. They were posed at the piano, she with her arm around his shoulder and smiling proudly, he standing limp and glowering at the camera with one of his pained grimaces. That photo was so much them, she thought: her needy pride, and his refusal to give. Such a pathetic symbiosis. To think what she had sacrificed to get him in that picture—the money and years, the leave of absence—just to be available to guide him, to drive him to his music and art lessons, getting him into one of the best prep schools in the country. And what does she get back at the height of his achievement? A fucking scowl. He had perfected the art of rejection. *The ungrateful little prick.*

Looking at him frozen in that old-man hunch, she could feel her blood pressure rise. To think what he had put her through to raise him up from the quagmire of mediocrity. To think how she was ruined because of him. King Lear was right: *"How sharper than a serpent's tooth it is / To have a thankless child!"*

"Julian, I'm talking to you."

Still nothing.

She took a deep breath. The only thing keeping her from exploding was a voice in her head: *He's your son. He's your own flesh and blood. Love him for what he is.*

But another cut in: *Would this still have been my Julian?*
The question was unanswerable.

"It's rather late," she said, straining to keep her voice
neutral.

But Julian still did not respond—not even a stir. That
was strange. Ordinarily he would tell her to leave his room.
For whatever reasons, he never allowed her to see what he
was working on. Even with a vacation school project, he'd
lock himself in here, then wrap it up and take it back to
school, never once allowing her a peek. That's the way he
was: self-absorbed and totally ungiving.

Only once did he let Vanessa see a work-in-progress. It
was a year and a half ago when out of the blue he called her
upstairs into his room.

"Well?" he had said in a flat voice, letting her look over
his shoulder. Vanessa remembered her surprise at the subject matter: a bowl of fruit on a table by a curtained window. His subject matter back then—and still—had been
fantasy superheroes with massive bodies of rippling mus-
culature, swords, gee-whiz weaponry, and disturbing bug-
eyed alien heads, all done in garish color. While Vanessa
had spurned the subject matter, technically his work was
extraordinary, given that it had been done completely in
pinpoint dots. So a simple bowl of fruit was a delightful
departure. Maybe at last he was moving into his postimpressionist phase, she had thought.

"It's beautiful," she had said, tempering her praise so as
not to take it away from him. "Is it a class project?"

He flashed her a hurt, truculent look. "Why do you say
that?"

"Well, I don't know, it's just different from what you
usually do. That's all."

"You mean, the usual *crap.*"

"I didn't say that."

"It's your birthday present," he said in a dead voice.

"Oh, Julian, how sweet of you." She was taken aback and felt tears rise. "How considerate."

"You don't like it."

"What do you mean? I love it. I love it. I'm telling you, it's beautiful. Really. And I'm flattered, I'm touched." And she was. This was the first time in years that he had even remembered her birthday, let alone given her something that he'd created. Last year she had to remind him, and he went out and bought her a key chain.

"Well, I don't like it," he said. "It's stupid."

"No it's not."

"It's stupid!" And with that he slashed the drawing with his razor knife.

"What are you doing?" she had cried, trying to stop him. But he slashed and slashed the paper until it was hopelessly shredded.

Then without a word he pushed himself from the bench and went downstairs, leaving Vanessa standing over the torn-up picture, crying to herself.

"Do you know what time it is?" She moved deeper into the room. "Two-fifteen."

Still nothing. Not even a turn of the head to acknowledge her presence. He was pulling his silent treatment on her again. She didn't need this shit. She didn't need his sour, precious fucking rejection routine. Not after what she had been through.

"Julian, I'm speaking to you." She crossed the room.

He was wearing that awful black shirt with the hideous Roaring Skulls picture on the front and their disturbing slogan on the back: LIFE SUCKS scribed in ghetto scrawl, as she called it. God! When the hell was he finally going to grow into his own talent? Here he was an accomplished musician who could play Shostakovich and Lizst, and he went around in heavy-metal shirts emblazoned with unseasoned nihilism. (Thank God Bloomfield had a dress code.) Moreover, his artistic talent was such that he could get into the finest art schools in the nation, and he wasted his hours on testosterone brutes. "It's time you went to bed."

He still did not respond, and she felt herself heat up.

You bastard.

"Lights out."

She marched up to him. Still he did not turn or say anything, but continued stippling away. She glanced at the easel.

At first, she thought it was another of his fantasy characters. But as her eyes adjusted to the figure on the sheet, she felt a shock of recognition. It was a self-portrait, except that Julian's face looked like that of a snake or lizard. The thing's head had the same general shape as his own, just as the mouth and eyes were clearly Julian's. But the features were all somehow stretched into a distinctly reptilian impression. The face was elongated, and there were scales covering its head and body. But it was Julian for sure. It was grotesque, but like all of his works it was precisely crafted.

What struck her was the color—reddish-brown, not black, his usual color.

He took out his mouth guards and laid them on a dish. "It's a self-portrait," he said. "Like it? I mean it's not *Sunday Afternoon on the Island of Grande Jatte* or anything, but it has a nice likeness, don't you think, Mother?"

He had said *Mother* as if he'd spit something up. She was forming a response, when Julian slid back.

Vanessa let out a gasp. Julian's right hand was a bight red mess of pinpricks from his knuckles up to his elbow. He was stippling the portrait with his own blood.

"What are you doing?" she screamed.

"Ms. Fuller says that I should work in different mediums." And he took his point and jabbed it into the back of his wrist.

"Stop that!"

But he continued stabbing himself with the point so that

beads of blood rose up. He then dipped in the pen tip and began tapping away on the picture.

"I said to stop that!"

But he continued.

"STOP THIS MINUTE!"

Slowly Julian turned his face up toward hers. And in a scraping whisper he said, "I can't."

A bright shock froze Vanessa in place.

"Because of what you did to me, Mother."

"What? What do you mean what I did to you?"

"What you let them do to my head."

"I don't know what you're talking about."

"My head, Mother. They did something to my head. My brain."

"I don't know what you're talking about or why the hell you're doing that to yourself. But I want you to stop. Do you understand me, Julian? It's goddamn sick, and you're going to give yourself blood poisoning." It crossed her mind to tell him not to drip on the wall-to-wall carpet she had spent a fortune on.

Julian laid down the pen and raised his bloody hands to his head and parted a section of hair above his hairline. Then he stuck his head under the lamp. "Look. Look at the scars, Mother."

Vanessa felt as if she were suddenly treading on barbed wire. "What about them?"

"Where did they come from?"

"You know perfectly well. I told you that you fell off your stepstool in the bathroom and hit your head on the radiator when you were two."

"These are little spots, not a regular scar," he said. "You're lying, because I remember. Besides, how could I fall from a six-inch stool and land on the top of my head?" His eyes fixed her.

"You don't remember anything."

"I remember going to a hospital and having some kind

of operation. I remember being bandaged up and seeing things. And taking tests and stuff. And other kids." Then his voice became a bizarre falsetto: " *'Mr. Nisha wants you to be happy. Just relax and watch the video. For Mr. Nisha.'* "

"I don't know what the hell you're talking about. You took tests to see if there was any brain damage. And, thank goodness, there wasn't," she added, feigning motherly relief.

"But there was, and it wasn't because I hit my head. It's because you had me fixed."

"Julian, I'm in no mood for your crap, okay? This conversation is over."

As she started to leave, Julian shot to his feet. Because he was still small for his age, Vanessa towered over him by a foot.

"What if I did that to your head, huh? What if I operated on your head to make you smarter? Huh?"

"What are you talking about?"

"I remember being tested. Aptitude tests—intelligence tests. Three years straight of tests. I'm still taking them. And why? Well, I put it all together. I wasn't supposed to remember, but I did. How would you like it if I did that to you?"

She did not respond.

"I asked you a question, Vanessa?" he said, in perfect mimicry of her. "I'm *speaking* to you. Answer me. Count back from twenty, Vanessa!"

She turned. He was standing there with one of his pens in his hand, the point aimed at her. "Don't you threaten me, you little—" But she stopped short.

"What? Say it. 'Little creep,' right? Is that the expression you're searching for, huh? *LITTLE CREEP*. That's what they all say. 'Julian the little creep.' Why should you be any different?" He took a step toward her. "How would you like it if I operated on your head because I didn't like how your brain worked? Huh? How would you like it if I cut you up to make you smarter? HOW WOULD YOU

LIKE IT IF I MADE YOU A FUCKING LITTLE CREEP?"

"I don't know what you're talking about," she said, her voice like acid. "And don't you speak to me that way. Not after what I've put myself through for you."

"You know what I'm talking about. You had me fixed because I wasn't good enough for you and your fancy friends at the club and university. You wanted a little superstar to parade around. Well, you got him, Vanessa! You got yourself your little genius, and his teeth are all ground down, and he's taking five different medications because he's a little GENIUS."

As he screamed at her, his tongue flashed against the row of yellow stumps in bright red gums and spittle shot from his mouth. His face filled with blood and his eyes bulged like hens' eggs. He looked positively grotesque. "How would you like a little brain surgery, Mother? Then you'd know what a miserable hell it is to be me—what it's like to be possessed. What it's like to hate you the way I do."

As he approached, his face filled her vision. "HOW WOULD YOU LIKE THAT, MOTHER?"

As if to the snap of her own mind, Vanessa felt herself lurch forward.

"You little bastard!" she heard herself scream. "Because of you I'm ruined. They did this to me. They set me up. Because of you. Yes, because you're such a fucking monster. BECAUSE OF YOU!"

Her hand shot to the jar of tools and pulled up a long sharp metal ice-picklike thing. The next instant, she buried it in the crown of Julian's head.

Instantly blood geysered out of the boy's skull as he let out a faint cry.

For a telescoped moment, she watched in numbed horror as Julian jerked about and rose in place on his toes as if trying to follow his own blood, his eyes widening in utter dismay, his mouth slack-jawed and moving wordlessly like a marionette's trying to form a question. An involuntary pocket of air bubbled out of his throat as blood streamed down his face and onto his shirt. Then just as he seemed about to gain stature, his mouth spread into a hideous grin, and he collapsed backward onto his tilt board, the long instrument still stuck in place. Because of the internal pressure, blood shot out across the self-portrait picture, bedewing the paper in a postimpressionist spray.

Panting uncontrollably, Vanessa tried to comprehend what her hand had done. She did not cry out nor did she touch her son. She just stood there gasping for air and watched him die.

When she heard the deep-throated gurgle, she turned. Without deliberation, she removed a razor knife from the scattered implements.

They did this to me, she told herself.

She didn't know how they knew about Blake's paper, but she knew they had set her up tonight, contacted the prick and arranged for that video. It was their doing. Because she had wanted her son back. Because she had insisted they undo what they'd done to him. Because she threatened to blow the whistle when they refused to even try, filling him full of useless chemicals that made him even worse.

"When dealing with the human mind, there's no way to predict collateral effects."

Such bullshit. Collateral effects! He was a freak. She had threatened to take him elsewhere, so they brought her down in public. On her night of nights.

She moved to Julian's bed and sat against the bolster. She glanced once across the room at her son dead on his tilt board, his blood streaming onto the carpet.

For a second, the image of him nursing at her breast flitted across her mind. She let out a long pathetic groan.

Then she slashed her wrists.

For the next several minutes, with her knees clutched to her chest, and her wrists bleeding into a pillow, she whimpered softly and rocked herself to death.

41

Brendan had been in the kitchen cleaning up when the video exposure of Vanessa Watts was going on. He had only learned about it from another waiter on his way out.

Around eleven-thirty, he parked the pickup down the street from the DaFoe house so it wouldn't be noticed. The only car in the garage was a Lexus SUV. It was green, the color of money, which Nicole's parents had in abundance.

Unlike the simple little six-room Cape that he shared with his grandfather, Nicole's home was a big white Colonial with a sweeping lawn, fancy shrubbery, and that European beech elm where he had spent several nights watching her undress, and one having sex with her history teacher.

Nicole let him in the back door. She had changed into green jeans and a yellow top. She looked like a daffodil. She was holding a glass of orange juice.

"You stink," she said as if announcing the sky was black.

"From the g-g-garlic in the crab cakes' dip. Carlos always adds too m-much. I'll w-w-wash up."

"And work on that stutter while you're at it." She led him upstairs to her bathroom.

He said nothing, inured to her bluntness. On one level, it fascinated him that she was so lacking in social cues. He at least had some residual instinct. She waited by the door as he washed up. "You missed quite a scene." He told her about the plagiarism charge. "That's not going to go over big with the administration at Middlesex U."

Nicole shrugged. "I didn't like her anyway. And her son's a dweeb."

Brendan opened his backpack. "By the way, c-close your eyes."

"You've got a surprise for me?"

"Not that kind of surprise—I mean g-g-giftwise. Just keep your eyes closed, and inhale and tell me w-what comes to mind."

"Is this some kind of joke?"

"No."

She closed her eyes and faced him, and he placed the bottle under her nose. "Okay, inhale and tell me if the odor reminds you of anything."

She sniffed and snapped her head back. "Smells like . . ." She opened her eyes and snatched at the small glass container. "Extract of almond." She glared at him.

"Well? Does it remind you of anything?"

"No."

"But you didn't even try."

"I smelled it," she snapped.

"No associations, no recollections, no images come to mind?"

"No."

"Think hard." And he held it to her nose again.

She pushed it away. "I said *no*. It reminds me of nothing."

He stared at her for a moment then screwed the cap back on and stuffed it in his pocket. "How about Mr. Nisha?"

"I told you I never heard of Mr. Nisha."

"Okay, forget it." Something about her reaction bothered him. She was too quick to reject it. "I just get some really weird vibes from the odor. So what's up?"

"Your turn. Close your eyes."

"What?" Hesitantly he closed his eyes, then heard her leave the room.

"Keep them closed," she said from the other room. A few moments later he heard her return.

"Okay, open them."

Brendan opened his eyes. Nicole was stark naked.

"W-w-w-what are you *doing*?"

Her eyes were small, no dilation in her pupils. No affect in her manner. No warmth in her response. "See if you can figure it out."

All he could think was: *Why is she doing this?* But it came out: "W-w-w-w- . . . ?"

"Why do you think?"

Brendan suddenly wished he were home, that he had not agreed to come over. That this was not turning out well. "I d-d-dunno."

"Is that the best you can do?"

He scanned her body. "You're very p-p-pretty," he said, hoping that she'd put her clothes back on.

"P-p-pretty?"

"Okay, b-beautiful."

"So," she said, spreading her legs slightly and leaning on a hip. "Is Mr. LaMotte still a virgin?"

She was a thousand Internet images—a thousand pixel pixies. *She wants something,* he told himself. *Nicole is hell-bent to succeed in life, so she wants something.*

"Well?"

It was not a question he wanted to answer. Nor did she wait for one, no doubt assuming he was. She undid his belt and unzipped his fly. He stood there as if he had been shot with a stun gun. He wanted to stop her, and he wanted her to continue—not because he was getting aroused, but because he wasn't.

She slipped her hand into his pants and rubbed his genitals. He could feel himself stir slightly, but he did not sprout an erection. In fact, the only erections he ever had resulted from unconscious friction with his bedding, but never from sexual musings, or sex magazines or Web porn sites. Naked women, men, children: nothing. Nada. His mojo wasn't working. He couldn't even properly masturbate if he wanted to; and the only orgasms were those in his sleep, unattended by raucous adolescent dreams—pure and simple biology: the press of backed-up sperm.

Not getting any reaction, Nicole pressed herself against his groin. He drew back because it hurt. "W-w-why are you doing this? I didn't c-come here for this."

"Because I f-f-felt like it." She made a mirthless laugh. "I remember how you looked at me the other night in my room."

That was a phony response—one reserved for the legions of normal heterosexual males whose hopeful glances told them she was "hot." That was not his look. He did not have the hunger. Nor could he imagine that she liked him. They weren't friends, nor had she ever shown him any interest except to make fun of his stuttering. In fact, whenever she addressed him he felt as if he were being razor-gashed. Besides, being the looker she was, Nicole should be pursuing the alpha studs—those cool, smart jocky dudes everybody else looked up to. He was surely not one of those. Yes, he was smart and tall, but two hundred and sixty pounds of baby fat surmounted by a long shiny black ponytail, braces, facial blemishes, and enough tics to make the Top Ten Geek List. Nicole did not give herself away for nothing. No, it wasn't how he had looked at her in the bedroom. It was what he had seen in there.

Suddenly she took his hand and put it on her crotch.

My God! He thought. *The Mound of Venus. The Delta of Desire. Ad glorium pudendum.* And his mind flooded with lines from a dozen erotic poems.

It was the first time he had ever touched female genitalia, but he felt nothing inside—not a bloody damn flicker. He could have been fondling her kneecap.

She planted her mouth on his and pushed her tongue

through his teeth, moving in deliberate cadence with the grinding motion against his hand.

"Orange juice," he said. "You t-taste of orange juice."

"Because I just had a glass, asshole."

acetaldehyde
alpha terpineol
ethyl decanoate

"Did you know that orange juice contains over two hundred different chemical compounds?"

pentane diethal ether
myrcene

"No, and please don't tell me," she said, grinding her pubis against him.

valencene
methylene chloride
limonene
3-ethanoxy 1-propanol

He wished he had not mentioned the orange juice, because his mind was now ticking off a slew of hydrocarbons, alcohols, aldehydes, and esters.

2-methyl propanic acid
methal octanoate

He squeezed down to force the runoff into a rear-brain compartment, which he sealed off and bolted. Then he strained to get back to the moment. But that was the real problem, because although he could recite the most obscure facts, he did not know how to react to Nicole. He knew he was supposed to "feel" things, to enjoy a flood of emotions, but he could not react accordingly.

ethyl butyrate
4-vinyl guaiacol

And, yet, he was fascinated by her performance. While she came on as sexually precocious, her moves seemed studied. Her lips, which were full and fleshy, opened and closed around his like a suckerfish in the throes of some mating ritual. Part of him liked the bizarre, almost nursing, sensation—something she had cultivated in her considerable experience. However, he was not sure he liked her tongue swabbing out his mouth. He could faintly detect the orange juice behind other tastes.

As he feared, his mind filled with biology-class videos of microbes teeming in human saliva. Then he became fixed on the disgusting white bacterial gunk that collects on the back of human tongues from the lack of oxygen and makes for sulfur-foul breath.

Then he saw her as one of those colored anatomy-book drawings of the digestive system—her insides a pack of shiny red organs and alimentary tubes leading from her mouth down through twenty feet of twisty yellow intestines partly full of feces.

He squeezed down on those images, pressed them into a small box, and stomped it with his heel. And for a blessed moment, the assault was over.

As Nicole moved against his hand and closed her eyes to groaning sounds, Brendan could not help but think that he was engaged in one of the highest fantasies of the male breed: fondling the sex of a gorgeous, compliant sixteen-year-old. He knew he should feel special, even privileged—for some men would kill for the opportunity. And while he watched Nicole writhe, he could not help but wonder at human sexuality—how in the zoological kingdom we were the only species that copulated face-to-face: An evolutionary marvel whose anatomy had evolved for the look of love—face-to-face, man to woman: passion *by design*.

And he had none.

"Do you like that?"

No, he thought. "Mmmm," he mumbled.

"How 'bout this?" And she then slipped to her knees and lowered his shorts.

God, this too?

His penis stuck out from his pubic hairs like an over-grown slug. It was mortifying. Here was Nicole DaFoe, the

teenage equivalent to the Whore of Babylon, his own mo-
mentary Lolita on her knees performing the supreme male
fantasy, and he couldn't even summon a glandular twitch.

God, if you can hear me, PLEASE!

Nicole tried everything, rubbing her breasts against him,
twiddling him, even kissing him. Still nothing, though he
was straining with all he had to engorge himself with blood.
But nothing. It was awful. Where were the *fires of spring*?
The *eternal fever*? Andrew Marvell's "rough strife"?

She did everything possible—humming, moaning and
groaning. It was horrible—the ultimate curse, but for old
men, like Richard, not a healthy adolescent who should be
pulsing with magma heat.

As he pushed with all he had to stiffen himself, fighting
the damning humiliation, a side-pocket awareness struck
him: Not how experienced Nicole was, but how rote her
movement. As he watched her head move below him, she
appeared to him as a mechanical doll running through a
naughty little program, not aroused, just studied. Robotic.
Even her kissing lacked genuine heat. She didn't even
breathe heavily.

He was about to push her head away, when in the light
his eyes caught something in her hair. He put his hands on
her head pretending to caress her. As he spread her hair, he
could see a cluster of small white nubbinlike scars barely
visible about an inch behind her forehead hairline and running across the side of her head.

Suddenly Nicole froze. "What are you doing?" Instantly
she was upright.

"Y-you've got the same scars I have."

Nicole's face shifted as if trying to land on the right expression. "What?"

He lowered his head and parted his hair where the nurse
had shaved. "See?" he said, showing her in the mirror.
Then he moved his hand to show her what he'd seen under
her hair, but she pulled away. "Let me show you."

"Get out," she said. He could not tell if the blaze in her eyes meant that she was angry with him for the aborted sex, or scared.

"Let me show you. Th-they're little white dots."

"From chicken pox."

"Chicken pox? No," he insisted. "Ch-chicken pox scars would be r-r-random. These are bunched together. And they're in the same place as mine."

Nicole's face hardened. "I told you I had chicken pox. I remember it was all over my face and head."

Brendan shook his head. "Not chicken pox."

"Then what are they?"

"Somebody did something to our heads when we were kids."

"Shut up. Scars are long lines not little white dots."

"I don't know how, but somebody did something—to both of us. I have images and d-dreams of hospital rooms, of w-w-white lights and monitors, of people with surgical masks. And you've got the same scars and that t-t-tattoo I keep seeing. Elephants with hands grabbing at me."

She started away. "That's your problem."

He caught her arm. "N-no. It's too much of a coincidence. I'm t-telling you we're c-connected somehow. Maybe we were out of hand, and they did some kind of lobotomy or s-something on us."

Nicole's eyes got very small, like ball bearings. "You're nuts. You're also a faggot."

"No I'm not."

"You're a goddamn faggot, and that's what this is all about." It was the first time he heard a tinge of emotion in her voice. But he wasn't sure if it was anger or fear.

"No." *I'm nothing,* a voice in his head whispered.

"Between the desire
And the spasm . . .
Falls the Shadow"

"That's not it." He pulled his pants back up and zipped his fly.

"You're gay, and you're giving me all this other shit."

"No, I'm not gay."

I am a hollow man.

"Then you're a chickenshit virgin. The big love-poetry guy can't get it up for a first-class BJ."

It wasn't her bluntness that surprised him, but the edge in her words.

As she started away again, he said, "What about you? Is it worth it?"

Her head snapped around for an explanation. "What's that supposed to mean?"

"I know why you're doing this, because I saw you with your teacher. This is your way of b-b-buying my silence."

Nicole opened her mouth to protest, but caught herself.

"If the word got out you were having an affair with your teacher, you'd lose your grade, and the award, and he'd be out of a job. That's what this is all about. Not because you like me, or even sex."

Expressions flitted across her face like the things that scurried under a rock in damp soil. In a low menacing voice, she said, "Don't you dare say anything." When he didn't respond, she said, *"Ever!"* And she gave his genitals a hard squeeze.

The wincing pain nearly took his breath away. She wrapped a towel around herself. "You d-d-d-don't even en-joy it."

"Enjoy what?"

"S-sex."

"What do you know?"

"I th-think you don't. I th-think you don't enjoy this. I th-think sex is just how you g-g-get what you want. How you end up number one."

"I'm where I'm at because I've got a brain and know how to use it."

"But you don't feel anything."

"Get out of here."

"You weren't even breathing hard. You weren't even excited."

"Because you don't turn me on. Because you're a fat ugly shit."

"M-m-maybe so, but I think you're a f-f-fake. I think you're like me—impotent. Dead. That you j-j-just go through the motions like a robot, pretending, experimenting with other people's emotions because you've got none of your own."

"I have emotions," she said. But her voice was void of protest. Dead.

She started to leave, but he took her arm. "Nicole, somebody messed with our heads. I don't know who or why, but we're different. I've got a brain that won't let me forget anything. I can quote you a hundred poems from start to finish but I can't feel them, Nicole. I CAN'T FEEL THEM! I can't feel anything. Like I'm emotionally dead. Like I'm another species." He fought down the urge to confess how he actually contemplated killing Richard just to see if he'd feel remorse.

"That's your problem."

"You know exactly what I'm talking about." He slid back the mirrored panel on the side wall and pulled out a bag full of prescription vials—all serotonin-reuptake inhibiting (SRI) drugs : Luvox, Zoloft, Paxil, Prozac, Anafranil—drugs for depression, obsessive-compulsive disorders, seizures, for "bad thoughts"—all with her name on them, all old friends to Brendan. "It's why we're taking all this crap: We're damaged goods, Nicole. We're freaks. We're *freaks*."

She swiped the bag from his hand and tossed it on the shelf. "Get out of here!" Her eyes clouded over but not with tears, because she was incapable of them—something else.

He stepped out onto the landing at the top of the stairs. "They did something to our heads and left us dead inside."

She did not respond—as if someone had pulled her plug out of the wall.

He stepped back from her, and for a long moment before he started down the stairs, she glared wordlessly at him through unmoving orbs of ice.

"One must have a mind of winter to behold the nothing that is not there and the nothing that is . . ."

42

Middlesex University English professor Vanessa Rizzo Watts and her son Julian, fourteen, were found dead in their Hawthorne home in what police say appears to be a murder-suicide initiated by Professor Watts . . ."

Lucius Malenko muted the radio as he rolled down the window to pay the toll. It was the middle of the next morning, and he was at the New Hampshire border on northbound I-95. In seconds, he had the Porsche purring at eighty-five in the fast lane again. He unmuted the radio as a country club official claimed that the Blake excerpt was not part of the original sent by the university. "My only guess is that somebody swapped videos with the intention of embarrassing Professor Watts. We don't know who or why, but we're looking into it."

"You do that," Malenko said and changed stations.

The world was abuzz with the story—headline news in *The Boston Globe* and *The Boston Herald,* the radio-news lead. Throughout the day experts on criminology and psychology would try to make sense of "the terrible family tragedy" that had hit affluent Hawthorne where such things just don't happen. Fuzzy-haired pundits would speculate about the severe competition to publish within institutions of higher learning; others would hold forth on the evils of the patriarchal academic establishment whose excessive pressure on women invariably led to such disasters. Others still would wonder why so bright and talented a woman as Professor Watts would need to plagiarize.

Malenko had expected a resolution, but not a double death—convenient as it was. The intention was to send her a definitive statement that her actions must desist immediately. He knew that the woman was fragile, at the edge with misgivings about her son. Clearly the public humiliation had pushed her over—more than he had hoped for. And it took the proverbial two birds with one stone.

Eighteen months ago, she had complained that Julian was not right, that he could not free himself of his obsessions—how he would slice his food into neat little cubes before eating them; how he had to do things just so, according to his little odd rituals; how he counted everything—cars on the street, birds, houses, telephone poles, dots. The worst of his obsessions was his pointillist paintings. She complained that he'd work hours on end, sometimes skipping sleep. That he wore his teeth to stumps.

Malenko could not be certain that such obsessions were the consequence of enhancement. In spite of his suspicions, he claimed that Julian's OC behavior was genetic.

Yes, they had had their failures—mostly from the early vintage of clients, before Malenko had perfected multiple stereotaxic insertions. Although they had been rendered brilliant, some developed unfortunate behavior problems. Three years ago, the son of an airline executive committed suicide, apparently having developed temporal lobe epilepsy. Another, a female, died of an embolism. Another still was convicted of murdering his parents, claiming that beetles were eating his brain.

But those were sad exceptions. Most enhanced children developed into highly intelligent and socially adjusted people—the *summum bonum* of the species. In his office, Malenko had a private photo album of "his children" who were scattered across the continent and beyond. Only a few lived in the area, and they were doing well. One was still at Bloomfield—Nicole DaFoe, whose high cerebral wattage was matched by genuine beauty. She wanted to be a physician when she grew up, possibly even a neurosurgeon. There was also young Lucinda MacPhearson—another prodigy, skilled in computers.

Because the brain is a black box of wonders, something went wrong with Julian Watts—perhaps some collateral damage from probes into the right frontal lobe. Nonetheless, the symptoms were treatable with medication, and Malenko had prescribed a variety. But the boy had refused, complaining that they just dulled his senses and diffused his focus. Then his mother threatened to take him to other neurophysicians to see what could be done. Although enhancement was too subtle to detect by any scans, he feared she would tell all. That could not be, and Malenko had reminded her of their contractual agreement, her escrow bond, and her willingness to accept any risks to enhance her son. *"I don't care about that!"* she had declared. *"I want my son back!"* That was when they sent the anonymous package to Professor Joshua Blake containing side-by-side photocopies of his book and hers.

Experience had taught him the hard way to protect his security against bigmouthed parents. Some years ago, after a difficult couple made noise about going to the authorities because their little darling was acting oddly, Malenko resorted to Oliver's "wet work" skills. They were eliminated in a car accident one icy Christmas Eve. From that moment on, there were no more mistakes.

Now in screening candidates, they investigated strengths—ideological and financial—as well as useful weaknesses—legal, financial, marital, psychological, even medical—as backup insurance against sudden impulses to blow the whistle. Dirty little secrets—fathers who liked young girls or who had some business indiscretions; mothers who cheated or who had problems with drugs or alcohol. Whatever would dampen impulses to blab.

The background check on Vanessa Rizzo Watts had revealed that as a graduate student she had been suspended for plagiarism. Because she had been a popular TA, the episode made the student newspaper, a copy of which was attainable from the archives of the *L.U. News* by Malenko's private investigator Oliver Vines, a doggedly persistent agent. Although Ms. Rizzo had been reinstated, that episode told the story of a bright but driven woman who needed to prove herself, who needed to excel, perhaps to overcome deep-seated suspicions that she was not as clever as she appeared on paper. And human nature being what it is, Malenko had a hunch that she would revert to her old habits in pursuit of recognition and easy success.

When her book was published, they parsed the entire text for key words and phrases. Then using a Boolean search engine, they scanned the Web for database matches to key word strings including the name George Orwell. In a process of elimination, one solitary record had multiple hits—the Web site of Mr. Joshua Blake who had included with his curriculum vitae a link to his doctoral thesis for perusal by interested scholars. It did not take long to realize that Vanessa Watts had lifted whole chunks from Mr. Blake.

As the Porsche hummed its way up the coast, Malenko's mind turned to the Whitmans. With the same degree of scrutiny they had investigated the husband's financial dealings with Cape Ann Banking and Trust where he had filed a fallacious claim about the worth of SageSearch on his bank loan application. The other useful piece of information was that Whitman knew nothing about the wife's TNT past or her guilt. To his mind, their son's disabilities came up in the genetic dice roll. But not a clue how Mom had loaded them. All of which meant that he had some goods on each of the Whitmans.

• • •

A little before one, Malenko turned onto Exit 7, which would take him to smaller routes that would eventually branch off to an ancient logging road that led to the compound.

Camp Tarabec was nestled in the woods at the edge of Lake Tarabec, a large and private body of water with its own woodland island about a half-mile offshore. The place was Maine-idyllic, with neat log cabins, a central meeting ground, flagpole, playing fields, climbing apparatus, and a little beach which was barricaded a hundred yards offshore to keep swimmers and canoeists from wandering into deep water.

Only seven years old, the camp was operated by a private organization founded and directed by Lucius Malenko. Although it was advertised as a summer camp for "special" kids, to those few in the know it was a "genius camp"—where gifted children went for in-depth, hands-on learning in disciplines from astronomy to zoology.

It was a little after two when Malenko arrived, so it was "free time," which meant that the kids were engaged in outdoor activities—canoeing, swimming, tennis or baseball, archery, et cetera. After that it was snacks and back inside to the computer labs or science projects. Because the children here were gifted, the counselors sometimes had to pry them away from their terminals or labs to go out and be physical. Malenko parked the Porsche and went into the main office.

A boy about sixteen behind the reception desk smiled as Malenko entered. "Hey, Dr. M."

"Hello, Tommy. How's the boy today?"

"Pretty good. How's the Red Menace? Still doing zero to sixty in five point eight?"

"Only when the police aren't looking. And it's five point two."

"But who counts?" Tommy said and laughed.

He had been coming to the camp for the last three summers, ever since his parents had him enhanced. They had been dissatisfied with his poor analytical skills, particularly with math and logic. At their wit's end, they came all the way from Chicago to the Nova Children's Center where they met Dr. Malenko. When all else failed, they put up an expensive summer home as collateral. Now Tommy was a sophomore math major at Cornell. He was also a computer wizard who taught compu lab here. It was he who had done the Boolean search that linked Vanessa Watts to Joshua Blake. Her own little Big Brother.

He stepped into the main office behind the reception desk and said hello to Karl who managed the camp. He handed Malenko some mail. "Oliver's waiting for you."

Malenko took his material and stepped back outside. On the baseball field across the way, two teams in red and black T-shirts were at play. At one end of the first-baseline bench, some second-stringers were at a laptop, probably working out the odds for a hit based on the batter's record and pitcher's ERA.

Some kids in the tennis court across the dirt road saw him and waved. "Hi, Dr. M.," one of the boys in white shouted. "How about a game?" The girl across the court waved at him.

Malenko smiled and waved back. "Maybe some other time."

The boy's name was Fabiano. He was the son of the Brazilian ambassador to the United States. Eight years ago he had an IQ of 75 and was a boarder at a school in New York City for the learning disabled. Today at sixteen, he was entering his sophomore year at Columbia with interests in astrophysics. And the young girl was interested in international law. As with all the Tarabec children, they would be getting the intensive exposure and training that would propel them toward their goals. Next week, for instance, they would be guests of astronomers at the observatory at the U. of Maine where they had use of the large reflector telescope.

Malenko got back into the Porsche. Some of the kids hooted him on to peel out. That would not set a very good example, he thought, but he trounced the accelerator and lurched forward in a cloud of dirt. In the rearview mirror, the kids waved and cheered.

Malenko pulled down a small dirt road to the water and into an old boathouse that also served as his garage. He parked, took his bags, and headed down to the dock.

As Karl had said, Oliver was waiting in the boat, a long white twin-engine outboard. He took Malenko's bags and started the engines. "You made good time." Oliver removed the ropes.

"Traffic was light." Malenko took the passenger seat behind the windshield. Oliver maneuvered the boat through the little channel and around the floats that forged the barricade to the open water. In a few seconds, the big Mercury engines were cutting a wake to the island.

Oliver Vines was a carryover from their NSA days—a onetime operative who had assisted Malenko in the enhancement project, which back then was known as "Project Headlight"—a dumb name, but that was governmental skulduggery for you. Once that was terminated, Oliver and Malenko went their separate ways until ten years ago when Malenko set up his private practice. What made Oliver particularly valuable were his connections—from former government ops to private investigators to small-time crooks. He also had a total lack of compunction about performing matters that made others squeamish. Like excessive exposure to radium, governments did that to people. But it also meant that he left no trails—such as that snatcher he had hired in Florida.

Oliver had two passions—money and flying, the former he shared with his wife Vera, a former nurse's aide who watched over the children. Of late, he had done considerable flying—little midnight excursions.

As they rounded the eastern flank of the island, the blue and white DeHavilland Beaver came into view at its berth on the small dock just offshore from the compound. If the weather held, Oliver would make another run in the plane later that evening. And because he would mostly be over water, he needed a clear sky to fly.

Oliver pulled the boat up to the dock then took one of Malenko's shoulder bags as they climbed the dirt lane to the main building, a large brown structure that had once been a fishing and hunting lodge.

Before he entered, Malenko waved to Vera who was in the backyard playground with some of the children. Oliver led him inside where they were met by Phillip who poured Malenko a cup of coffee he had just made. In spite of the fact they were brothers, Phillip looked nothing like Karl back at the camp. Phillip Moy, a former private investigator who had run afoul of the law, had been recruited by Oliver. Phillip was proficient at running background checks on people. He was also handy with machinery and computers, which made him very useful keeping things in operating condition. On occasion he worked with the kids or accompanied Oliver in the dirty work.

"How's Miss Amber doing?" Malenko asked, sipping his coffee.

"A little dopey," Phillip said.

"Of course."

As with all the patients, she had been administered an IV containing a mild tranquilizer that diminished anxiety over being away from home. They had also given her cyclohexylamine, also known as Ketamine, an anesthetic that produced amnesia, effectively blotting out all recall of the enhancement procedure. It was a remarkable drug, almost one hundred percent effective.

While Oliver took the bags upstairs to the bedroom,

Malenko followed Phillip down the main hallway to the door in the rear storage room off the kitchen. He unlocked it and the next door at the opposite end, and they descended the stairs to the cellar.

They proceeded into the long bright tunnel that ran nearly a hundred feet under the backyard woods. At the far end was the operating room. Along the tunnel walls were windows spaced a dozen feet apart—one for each dormer. A dormer for each patient. The glass on the windows was thick and one-way visible, a reflecting surface on the obverse side giving the impression of a simple wall mirror, framed to complete the illusion. Because they were underground, the air was cooler and less humid than above. It was also filtered against dust and microbes.

Malenko stopped at the first room and pulled up the blinds on the one-way glass.

Inside was a little girl of six dressed in blue shorts and a white and blue pullover. He tapped the door lightly then let himself in with a master key.

Amber Bernardi. She was a plain child with large dark eyes and black hair. She was also the daughter and only child of Leo and Yolanda Bernardi, owners of Bernardi Automotive Enterprises which had Volkswagen and Porsche dealerships all over New England. Three days ago, they had dropped her off to be enhanced. There was the usual separation crisis: The child cried and fussed until they sedated her after her parents left. Then she was driven here for preop procedures.

To fill her time and minimize distress, they had provided her with television, videos, toys, games, and books. Vera or Phillip would occasionally drop in to chat or take her to the playground. Because of the sedatives, she was quite manageable.

"So, how is Miss Amber today?"

"Fine," she said, drawing out the syllable.

She was sitting on a chair looking at a book while holding one of the stuffed dancing dolls. Years ago they had ordered a couple dozen of them from overseas because they proved to be a hit with the children. It seemed an appropriate choice, since it was a nearly life-sized version of Ganesha, the elephant god of India.

According to Hindu legend, Ganesha was born as a normal child to Shiva and the goddess Parvathi. But Shiva liked to roam the world. After his son was conceived, he went on a journey and did not return for several years. Because Ganesha had never seen his father, he did not recognize him while guarding his mother's house. Since his mother was taking a bath, Ganesha demanded that Shiva go away. Angered that the young stranger told him to leave his own house, Shiva chopped off Ganesha's head and went inside. Realizing that Shiva had killed his own son, Parvathi wailed in grief and demanded that Shiva bring Ganesha back to life. When he confessed that the boy's head was severed, Parvathi instructed him to take the head off the first living thing he saw and attach it to Ganesha's body so he could live again. It so happened that an elephant walked by. Instantly, Shiva beheaded the animal and attached its head to his son. Today Ganesha is revered as the god of wisdom.

It was the symbolism that had originally attracted Malenko to the creature. The kids referred to him as Mr. Nisha.

Amber flipped through the book looking at the pictures because, of course, she could not read. "When am I going home?"

"In three days." Malenko held up his fingers. "How's that?"

"But I wanna go home now," she said, her voice thin and distant.

"Well, not for another three days."

"How come?" she whined.

"Because."

Because, he thought, *you're a stupid little girl and your parents have dropped a million dollars so you won't grow* *up to be a stupid woman who will get herself knocked up by some equally stupid boy and end up wasting away your family's fortune because you were incapable of a decent education and couldn't get a decent job and would spend your life producing stupid babies, at least one of whom would go to prison to the tune of $40,000 per year. That's how come.*

"Would you like some milk and cookies?" he asked sweetly.

"Nah. I have some," she said, and pointed to a paper cup and plate on the floor. She looked at him with flat vacant eyes. "I want some Saltines. I want some Salteeeens." She began to blubber.

"We'll get you some in a minute," he said and got up. He gave her a lasting look. In twelve months, she would be completely transformed—almost another species. After all these years, it still awed him what he could accomplish here. They were right: He was a miracle worker. Perhaps Shiva. Or maybe Jesus, raising the dead. Or Jesus' father, creating new life.

As he closed the door on Amber, Malenko's mind tripped back to when the miracles began.

It was 1985, and Lucius had been summoned to the headquarters of the Kiev State Police where two KGB agents led him to a one-way glass wall that looked into an interrogation room within which sat two men in prison clothes smoking cigarettes. The older agent, a Vladimir Kovalyov, explained, "The one on the right is a former researcher from the Steklov Physics Institute of the Academy of Sciences. He was caught selling secrets. The other man shoveled sand in a cement factory in Zhytomyr. He killed a policeman in an antigovernment rally."

Six days later, the two men were lying side by side on tables in a makeshift operating room the government had set up in the basement of Malenko's lab. The physicist's name was Boris Patsiorkovski. He was forty-four and the father of one. The stupid man's name was Alexei Nedogoda. He was twenty-nine and the father of two. They were enemies of the state, Malenko told himself, and he sawed off the tops of their heads.

A hundred and twelve political prisoners later, Malenko had perfected surgical methodologies and had experimented with unilateral and bilateral implantation, using different harvest sites, different implants, different proportions, different postoperative drug therapies, and so forth. With each operation he learned something new about transplantation and the brain's capacity to respond.

But the hope that tissue grafted from high-IQ brains into duller ones to produce smarter people was dashed. No enhanced cognitive powers were detected in the recipients. Thirty-three subjects had died, most of the rest had been rendered brain-damaged. After four years the project was terminated.

The magnitude of that sacrifice had bothered the young Malenko early on. Here he was a physician attempting to bestow benefits on human life, not eliminate them. But the reality was that each of the prisoners had been scheduled for execution; so, in effect, they were making heroic self-sacrifices for the state. And after his fifth or sixth transplant, he was too absorbed in his quest to be bothered by higher moral issues. His concern was enhancement not ethics.

Within the last two years of his tenure in the Ukraine, and while the Communist system was beginning its death rattle, Lucius Malenko made his ultimate breakthrough—and one which would carry him to this day.

The reasoning was exquisite in its simplicity. As had been empirically evident, the transplantation of *embryonic* tissue had failed to establish specific nerve pathways because they were too new to take cues from the existing host brain to produce cells and connections in those areas associated with intelligence. Likewise, *mature* brain matter was too old to reseed target sites. That left the inevitable option.

"This one's a goddamn little tiger." Phillip turned his head to show the scratches on his cheek and neck.

"Occupational hazard," Malenko said. "How's she adjusting?"

Across the hall, Oliver pulled up the blinds on the one-way glass to another dormer. "As good as can be expected."

Her name was Lilly Bellingham, and she was sitting on the bed staring at a piped-in video of *Roger Rabbit*. She was wearing Farmer John bib blue jeans over a yellow T-shirt, and her long yellow hair was held back in a ponytail. Because of the sedatives, she was docile. On the table beside her sat a tray of macaroni and cheese, salad, milk, and chocolate cake—all untouched.

As Malenko watched her, he thought how at seven Lilly was still at the optimum age. In spite of popular claims, the turbo production of brain-nerve cells did not decrease after the third year of life, creating a permanently hardwired organ. On the contrary, the gene that stimulates axonal growth—that increases communication throughout the brain—is active up to age eleven. After that, the ability to make gross anatomical changes diminishes—which is why a prepubescent child can still learn a foreign language without an accent while his parents can't, though they might learn fancier vocabulary. Because children of higher intelligence possess brains of greater neuroplasticity, they have a greater capacity to learn, better memory storage, and better access to those memories.

At this very moment, behind those big green eyes, little Lilly Bellingham's cortex was busily wiring itself for increased neurotropic functions, making of itself a faster, smarter CPU while her hippocampus, like the hard drive of that computer, was organizing that memory for easy access—and all the while taking in the foolish antics of Roger Rabbit.

"She's not eaten," Malenko said.

Phillip shook his head and showed him the clipboard schedule of meds, feedings, and her vital signs. Malenko studied the charts then slipped the board into the tray by the window. "If she doesn't by this evening, we'll have to go with the drip."

Phillip nodded. "She wants her daddy. When he shows, she'll eat."

She had been picked up last week at a swimming hole in upstate New York. Phillip and Oliver had done well. They had snatched her from a beach using as decoy one of the other children from the camp, effectively fooling the mother long enough to make the switch.

Were she to grow to maturity, Lilly would be brilliant. But she was dirt-poor. And in spite of good Samaritans and all those financial-aid programs, chances were that dear sweet Lilly would end up filled with drugs and booze and living on welfare, festering at the bottom of the social compost heap, raising trailer-park brutes. What good was genius when tethered to the bed, the bassinet, and the kitchen stove?

Besides, she was also worth a million dollars.

Malenko took the clipboard. Lilly Bellingham. Age seven. From Henley, New York. Forty-eight inches tall. Forty-three pounds. And she had an IQ of 168.

And tomorrow, little Amber Bernardi.

Malenko bid a silent *night-night* to little Lilly and moved down the corridor to the window at the end.

Travis Valentine. He was asleep on his bed, a book on butterflies lay open beside him. The TV monitor flickered mindlessly.

According to the tests and functional scans, he had very high language proficiency—ninety-ninth percentile, in fact. Left-brain incandescence. He would probably grow up to be a first-rate writer or lawyer.

And if the parents decided not to keep him a dim bulb, so might young Dylan Whitman.

43

Because he was now on night shift, Greg didn't get to bed until around seven A.M. So he was in a deep sleep when the phone rang at nine-thirty that Wednesday morning.

A female identifying herself as Patty Carney from the medical examiner's office in Boston said she had read his bulletin from last Thursday. Greg was still too furry with sleep to register the name. The forensic pathologist.

"We had a homicide victim two days ago. You probably read about it. A kid from Hawthorne, killed by his mother who then killed herself?"

"Yeah, sure." The story was all over the media.

"Well, we did an autopsy on the kid, and when we removed his brain we found that he had the same skull perforation clusters as in your bulletin. Thirteen along the left side of his head from the frontal cortex above the eyebrow to over the ear. But there's a difference from the others. He had eight other holes on the right side of his head, too. And they were clearly done in a medical neurological procedure, probably when he was very young, from the healing signs. But I can't tell you what for."

"What's his name?"

"Julian Watts. The obit's in today's paper. The funeral's

tomorrow." She gave him some of the details. "I sent you a scan of the photo taken from the inside of his skullcap. I don't know what they're from, but I thought you'd be interested."

Greg was suddenly very awake, and his heart was pounding. He thanked the woman, saying that he would get right to his computer for the scan.

"Oh, yeah. One more thing," Patty said before hanging up. "His brain was over one point six kilograms."

"Is that significant?"

"Well, the normal fourteen-year-old male's brain weighs one point four kilos. His brain was nearly half a pound heavier."

"How do you explain that?"

"I can't."

44

Brendan sat by himself at the rear of the Hawthorne Unitarian Church trying not to lose his mind.

He recognized several people from the Dells and the surrounding towns, getting lost in naming each of them and their family members, addresses, the kinds of cars they drove, golfing handicaps, and other biographical junk. That was the danger of large crowds, and the reasons why he hated function nights at the club. To stem the data tide, he tried boxing himself into a single distraction, such as the organ music—except he found himself visualizing the score until the inside of his skull was a running video of endless musical staves and prancing notes. If he took any more medication, he'd go to sleep. What he needed was something in the moment to focus on and cut out all the noise.

He couldn't flip through the hymnal because he'd only get stuck in lyrics which would play in his head the rest of the day. He tried to think of Vanessa and Julian Watts lying in their coffins, but he began to imagine their state of necropsy, how their bodies had been drained of blood—what was left of it after the police had found them—and replaced with embalming fluids, and how in a few days they would begin to turn dark, and shrivel, and the fluids would begin to leak from their orifices.

He then ran through the capitals of the world, as stupe-fyingly boring as that was, then moved to the most popu-lous cities including their populations according to the latest *World Book of Facts*.

What snapped him back was Nicole.

She had entered the rear of the church with her parents. Before they could move to a pew, he put his backpack on his seat and got up. "I have to see you," he said, pulling her aside.

She gave him her blue-ice look. "Leave me alone."

"Look, it's v-v-very important."

She started after her parents without response.

"Please."

When her mother looked back, Nicole flashed her face to him. "Later," she said through her teeth. Then she moved down the aisle.

Brendan returned to his pew and watched her move to the front of the church to join her parents. She was dressed in a simple dark blue sundress with white trim and dark blue pumps—an ensemble that projected a nautical motif, as if she were some kind of naval recruit. As he watched her settle, his mind slipped to that tattoo she wore.

While he worked on that for the hundredth time, he spotted Rachel Whitman walking in with her husband. Nicole had said that they had been on a parent tour of Bloomfield, which didn't make sense.

A few minutes later Sheila MacPhearson came down the aisle with her daughter, Lucinda, who was carrying a Palm Pilot. They took seats beside the Whitmans. The women were friends—Rachel Whitman of 224 Morningside Drive and Sheila MacPhearson of 22 Willow Lane.

Mrs. MacPhearson's husband, Harry, had lost all his money in a dot-com venture, then died of heart failure a year ago. According to rumors circulating at the club, he had left his wife with considerable debt, which might ex-plain why she was always hustling off to show a property.

Lucinda fascinated him. She was clever, cunning, and

very authoritarian with other children. He once caught her
sticking a pin into the head of the rabbit in play school. She
also knew how to turn on the charm, winning over Miss
Jean and other Dellsies. Her mother, she wore like an en-
gagement ring.

The two caskets lay side by side at the altar.

Rachel sat between Martin and Sheila MacPhearson.
They had left Dylan with a sitter for the morning. However, Sheila had brought Lucinda, who was pressed beside
her and working on a small computer—probably calculat-
ing the flaws in the unified field theory, she thought sickly.
Rachel felt the urge to grab the damn thing out of her
hands. She also was irritated that Sheila let her click and
poke away at the keys while people filed in solemnly.

Rachel was sick at the sight of the two caskets with the
twin wreaths of white roses. Such a tragic waste. Last week
the world appeared to be Vanessa's oyster. Then, in a matter
of hours it was all over. Apparently the public humiliation
had driven her to the brink. But why take Julian with her?
How could she kill her own son? And a son she had been so
proud of. Something clearly had snapped—and now there
was a dead mother and son. Nothing was as it seemed.

Nobody could explain where the incriminating videotape came from or how it had gotten switched for the original. Apparently no fingerprints were found on the cassette.
A Hawthorne policeman had come by to ask if Rachel
knew of any enemies of Professor Watts since it was clear
that somebody had been out to get the woman. Rachel
knew of none. In fact, she barely knew Vanessa. He also
asked if she knew any possible motives for her killing of
her son. Rachel had no idea.

The newspapers had carried an interview with Joshua
Blake who said he had been alerted to the plagiarism
anonymously while on sabbatical in Western Samoa. He
said that he had been encouraged to make the videotape to

discourage Professor Watts from going ahead with the publication. He explained that he had just set up his own video camera, taped the interview, then overnighted the cassette to an anonymous post office box in Boston. He had also sent a copy to Vanessa's publisher by airmail, which explained why her editor at the party was unaware of the plagiarism. He added that he had no idea who was behind the exposé.

Sheila was sniffling into her handkerchief and checking her watch as the service began. When Rachel could see that she was not going to stop Lucinda from playing with her Palm Pilot, she leaned across to her and in a dead flat voice said, "You can put that away now."

Lucinda looked up at her with chilling menace. Before another word was exchanged, Sheila snapped the thing out of her daughter's hand and stuffed it in her purse.

While her parents were huddled by the gravesite, Brendan nodded to Nicole to come over. When she disregarded him, he started toward her—and that got the expected reaction. She came over not out of interest but because she did not want her parents and all their friends to think that golden-girl Nicole DaFoe was pals with the local weirdo—which is how everybody saw him: a creep to shield their children from, a schizoid basket case who talked to himself and suffered poetry seizures; the idiot savant who could recite the script of any movie he had seen. The kid nobody wanted their kids hanging with. Brendan LaMotte, goblin of Cape Ann.

"Make it fast. I'm going back to camp." She followed him to a spot behind a large gaudy obelisk that blocked the view of the others.

From his backpack he pulled out a folder, saying how he had found it buried in his cellar. "I-it's a WISC standard intelligence test taken when I was five." He pointed to some numbers. "My IQ was seventy-seven." Then he showed her another test taken two years later. "Same test, but intelligence quotient one hundred thirty-nine. That's practically double. My verbal went from forty-three percentile to ninety-nine."

Something slithered across her face. "I have to go."

"N-no, there's more."

He then pulled out a photocopy of two canceled bank checks for three hundred thousand dollars each, made out to cash and signed by Brendan's father, Eugene LaMotte. The dates were two weeks apart and about six months before the date of the second WISC test.

Nicole put her dark glasses on and started away.

"Wait. I also found MRI scans of my b-b-brain," he said. "They operated on me. They did s-something to make me smarter."

In the distance, her mother was waving her over. "Be right there," she called.

She walked away, but Brendan caught up to her. "Nicole, listen to me. They did the same thing to you."

She looked at him, her face appearing as rigid and white as the nearby headstone.

"Here, look." In his hand he was holding a slip of paper—a piece of personalized stationery with the address and name of her father, Kingman DaFoe. Written in pen on it was a telephone number with an old exchange.

And the name Lucius Malenko.

Greg sat through the double funeral service at the Hawthorne Unitarian Church. He had removed his weapon and badge from his belt and he tried not to look conspicuous as he made mental notes of family members and close friends. He also tried not to think of what T. J. Gelford would say if he knew Greg was here. But that wouldn't happen.

At the cemetery, he receded into the background and

watched through dark glasses. It was a tasteful and dignified event, where a woman minister gave a moving eulogy before the matching bronze caskets poised above their plots. A large hushed crowd of mourners surrounded them, and a niece read a poem she had written. Greg spoke to no one.

From the newspaper obits, he got the names of the immediate survivors—Bradley Watts, the husband, and Lisa, the daughter. Watts was a tall patrician-looking man in his fifties with streaks of white around his ears, and a tanned angular face. His daughter was a pretty sandy-haired girl with a white full face and red eyes. The girl was not doing well and kept breaking down, so that Watts kept his arm around her throughout the ceremony.

When the service was over, people laid flowers on the coffins and paid their final condolences.

Greg pulled closer. At one point he overheard somebody agreeing with Brad that getting away was the best thing. He thought he heard someone mention Oregon.

Because of the awful circumstances of their deaths, there was no postfuneral dinner. That was unfortunate, because he wanted to speak to Bradley Watts in a more appropriate venue. The gravesite was definitely not the place, but he and his daughter could be departing for Oregon tomorrow, maybe even that night.

As Watts and his daughter started away from the grave toward the limousine, Greg pulled him aside. He expressed his sympathies and introduced himself. The daughter, whose eyes were still wet, stood there limply.

Watts thanked him and looked at the card. "Zakarian, good Albanian name."

Greg didn't bother to correct him. "I apologize for the intrusion, but I'm wondering if we could set up a time to ask you a few questions."

"What about? I've already spoken to the police."

"I realize that, but there are some things I'd like to ask about Julian that may shed light on other cases I'm investigating. Maybe we can meet tomorrow or the next day, at your convenience?"

"I'm taking my daughter to camp tomorrow, and I'm going to the West Coast and won't be back for a few weeks." He again glanced at Greg's card. "Sagamore?"

"I can explain," Greg said. The daughter looked distraught. So, to show her some interest, he asked, "Where are you going to camp?"

"Allegro Music Camp outside Toronto." She seemed to perk up a little.

"You must be quite a musician. What do you play?"

"Violin," she said. Then she added, "Julian was supposed to go to the Nova Children's Center camp at Lake Tarabec, but . . ." She trailed off into a choke.

"I'm very sorry," Greg said. "From what I read, he was a very bright young man."

Watts gave her a comforting squeeze. "Maybe when I return," he said.

"I'd rather we talk before you left," Greg said.

Mr. Watts sighed and told his daughter to get in the limo, that he'd be right there. The girl slumped away to the waiting car.

"Officer Zakarian, I'm taking my daughter home where we'll try to relax as best as the medication will allow. At nine o'clock tomorrow morning we are out of here. So if you have any questions I'll take them now."

This was not how Greg wanted it—standing just feet away from his wife's and son's caskets.

"And, please, be brief and to the point."

Greg nodded. "According to the autopsy report on Julian, clusters of scars were found on his skull. You're no doubt aware of them."

Watts's eye twitched ever so slightly. But he did not respond.

"You do know what I'm talking about?"

Watts's expression seemed to stiffen. "I'm listening."

"Can you tell me how they got there?"

"Why are you asking me this, Officer?"

Briefly Greg mentioned the two other cases. He would have preferred to do this in the man's house or office, but he pulled out the schematic of the skull with holes.

The man glanced at the drawing then looked at Greg. "Julian was treated for epilepsy as a child. He had a severe case."

"So you're saying he had some medical procedure."

"Yes," Watts said. He gave Greg a saucer-eyed look that seemed to blot out any suspicions that what he said was not the absolute truth.

"Was Julian right-handed or left-handed?"

Watts hesitated for a second, no doubt wondering about the odd question. "Left."

"Can you tell me the name of his doctor?"

"Daaad?" It was his daughter calling him from the limousine.

"Good day, Officer," Watts said, and he walked away to the car and got in.

Epilepsy.

Greg looked around. The place was emptying out. People were walking to their cars, and cars were moving in a slow caravan toward the exit. Nearby he spotted a big kid with a black ponytail showing something to an attractive tall blonde behind a monument.

Greg watched the limo pull out of its spot by the edge of the grass. Lisa was sitting at a rear window. He gave a little wave and watched the car pull down the lane.

Nova Children's Center. The words spread through his mind like a crack.

45

The Whitman home was located in an upper-middle-class neighborhood of Hawthorne where stately Colonials and Tudors reminded Greg that he was an outsider.

On Friday afternoon around two, he pulled in front of a handsome brick garrison with a slate roof, two stately chimneys, and black shutters with white trim. A gold Maxima was parked in the driveway. Because it was next to an open lot, he could spot an elaborate wooden play structure in the backyard. He had a mental flash of the Dixon place with its redbrick box, front yard of scrub and dirt, the tire swing. It was this place, but a couple decimal points to the left.

A bed of daylilies and groundcover neatly lined the flagstone walk to the front door. He rang it and a woman who looked to be in her thirties answered. She was very attractive with shoulder-length shiny black hair, and jagged bangs, and large amber eyes. He had seen her and her husband yesterday at the Wattses' funeral.

"Mrs. Whitman?"

"Yes."

"My name is Greg Zakarian. I'm a detective from the Sagamore Police Department." He handed the woman his card. She looked instantly concerned. "I'd like to ask you a few questions about the Vanessa and Julian Watts case."

"But I've already spoken to the police."

"I understand, but there are some elements in the case that may have bearing on another case." Understandably she looked puzzled but let him inside.

He followed her through the living room, attractively decorated in bright colors and oriental rugs. On the coffee table sat copies of *The New Yorker* and *The Quarterly Review of Wine.*

She led him to a screened-in porch that was furnished in white wicker and floral cushions. Large pots of red geraniums sat on the floor. Some children's books were piled neatly on a chair. From the porch he could see that the backyard climbing structure was an elaborate redwood system with ropes, hang rails, and a large yellow sliding tube. Not your basic tire swing. A little boy sat digging in a nearby sandbox.

Mrs. Whitman offered him some coffee or a soft drink, but Greg declined. She glanced at his card as she sat down. *"Eench bess ess?"* she said.

"Shad lav em," he replied in Armenian to say he was fine. "I'm impressed. You're the first person in two weeks who hasn't take me for a space alien."

The woman smiled. "My roommate in college was Armenian—Sue Ekizian. Lovely people and wonderful food. I still on occasion go to Watertown for the rolled grape leaves, the lamejuns and pastries."

"Eastern Bakery has wonderful paklevah."

"Yes, and my son just loves that," she said, smiling. And she glanced toward the little boy.

"Handsome boy. What's his name?"

"Dylan."

"Am I hearing things, or is he really singing 'There is Nothing Like a Dame'?"

Rachel laughed. "Yes. His father has a collection of Broadway shows. I'm afraid the lyrics aren't very liberated."

"Gee, why would you think that?"

She laughed as the boy reached the finale, which he belted out with amazing gusto and dramatics:

There ain't a thing that's wrong with any man here
That can't be cured by puttin' him near
A girly, womanly, female, feminine dame!

Greg quietly applauded. "Bravo, bravo," he called out to the boy.

Dylan, who was wearing huge sunglasses and a crooked Red Sox cap, looked toward the porch, then, grinning widely, he rose to his feet and took a dramatic bow, still standing in the sandbox. Then he went back to his digging.

"A spirited little guy."

"Thanks . . . and a born ham," said Mrs. Whitman, beaming.

His instinct was to look away, to get to business, but he couldn't help staring at her. The feathery black eyebrows, the jagged spikes of hair on her brow, the warm spark of light in her eyes, the high cheekbones, the fullness of her mouth. She was very attractive.

"How old is he?"

"He just turned six. Do you have children, Officer?"

"No. My wife died before we could have kids." As soon as his words hit air, Greg wished he could have edited them out. A simple *no* would have done it. In fact, he did not know why he had said that. Widowerhood was not how he identified himself to others. He almost never mentioned losing Lindsay if for nothing else than to avoid the mood slump and obligatory condolences. But for some reason, he wanted this woman to know.

"I'm very sorry to hear that."

"Thank you."

The mood lightened when outside, Dylan had switched to *The Sound of Music* and his rendition of "My Favorite Things." As he listened, it struck Greg just how good a singer the little boy was. Not only did he have a beautiful voice, but he also had a fine ear. With remarkable accuracy he had captured Julie Andrews's delivery, right down to the British dialect and inflection. In fact, Greg couldn't help but comment on the boy's talent.

Mrs. Whitman got up to refill her coffee and Greg agreed to a cup of black. When she returned they chatted some more about Dylan and his interest in Little League. His first game of the season was this coming Saturday.

While Mrs. Whitman described how excited the boy was in anticipation, Greg listened with admiration. She was engaging, her manner was open and warm. And regarding her son, she was manifestly devoted and adoring. When the boy passed through the porch for a cookie she could not help but pull him to her and plant kisses on his sandy red cheeks.

As he watched her, he wondered what it would be like to kiss her. He quickly snapped off the thought.

"My name is Greg," he said to Dylan and put out his hand. Dylan slapped him five. "Do you like ca-ter-pil-lars?"

The boy's enunciation was measured, and he flashed a glance at his mother who smiled and nodded approval. Maybe he had just learned the word. "Caterpillars?" Greg said. "I love caterpillars."

The boy smiled and handed Greg a jar with some leaves and a bright orange caterpillar inside. "That's good. You can have her and watch her grow wings."

"Thanks. That's very nice of you. But what do I feed her?"

"Leaves and butter." With that, Dylan went into the house for his cookies.

Mrs. Whitman looked at the jar in Greg's hand. "Lucky you."

"Don't be silly," he said, staring at the length of orange fuzz. "We're going to be fast friends. Leaves and butter. That makes sense."

Mrs. Whitman made a puzzled smile. "Yeah, I guess it

does. In fact, I never quite noticed the *butter* in *butter*flies before." And she laughed to herself.

"There may be a lesson here about how kids see the world."

She made a curious expression and nodded. "I guess."

Greg could have gone on chatting with Mrs. Whitman. She was easy to talk to, and he also liked looking at her as they conversed. She was beautiful, and her large expressive eyes were flecked with gold, making them appear as if in kaleidoscopic motion, drawing him dangerously in as she spoke. He opened his notebook. "I hate to downshift, but I do have some questions," he said, trying to feel cop-professional again.

"Of course." She glanced through the porch screen. Dylan was back outside eating a cookie.

"How well did you know Vanessa Watts?"

"Really, not well at all." She explained that they were members of the same country club, having seen each other only on occasion. But, yes, she had attended the party on that tragic night.

"Did you know her son?"

"I had met him once."

"Can you tell me a little about him—what he was like?"

She hesitated at first, measuring her response. "Well, as I said, I really didn't know him. But he was very smart and a talented artist." And she went on to describe his ability to create images of photographic exactness and how he had taught himself Italian and Spanish by listening to speeded-up language tapes.

"Did you know anything about his medical condition?"

Instantly her expression clouded. "Medical condition?"

"That he had epilepsy."

"No. I didn't know he was epileptic."

"Then you weren't aware that he had seizures."

"No."

"Or that he had had medical operations as a child to alleviate the condition?"

"Operations? No." Her face was full of concern. "Officer, may I ask what this is all about?"

Greg pulled out the schematic and briefly explained the circumstances of the two sets of skeletal remains. "One was six when he was kidnapped, the other about the same plus or minus a year."

"And you think they all had epilepsy?"

"That's what I'm trying to determine."

"I didn't know epilepsy was treated with surgery."

"Neither did I, but I guess a small percentage of cases necessitates the removal of lesions."

"Then how are they connected to Julian?"

"I'm not sure they are," Greg said. "I was just curious about the configurations on the skull. And why the remains of two missing children with similar drill holes showed up in Massachusetts coastal waters."

"I wish I could help you." She glanced at her watch.

"Would you know any other friends or acquaintances of the Watts family that I might speak to?"

She hesitated for a moment. "Not really."

"How about your husband?"

She made a flap of her hand. "He wouldn't know."

There was something dismissive in her gesture. "I was just wondering if he was a friend of Mr. Watts and might have some useful insights."

"No. He's very busy with work and not around much. I know he doesn't know Brad Watts and only met Julian once."

"By the way, what does your husband do?" The question had nothing to do with the investigation, and they both knew that, Greg thought.

"He has a recruitment company."

"And what do you do?"

She smiled. "I'm Dylan's mother."

"And from all appearances, doing a fine job."

"I hope so," she said, and looked into the backyard again. Dylan was on the swing singing to himself.

Greg knew the question was a long shot and out of line, but he asked anyway: "This being a small town, I'm wondering if you'd know who Julian Watts's pediatrician was."

"His pediatrician?" Her eyes suddenly took on a curious cast. "I'm sorry, but I haven't got a clue." She glanced at Dylan then her watch again.

It was Greg's cue to wrap things up. Greg got to his feet. "I know this is off the wall, but would you know if Julian was right-handed or left-handed?"

She thought for a moment. "I remember he did his pictures with his left hand."

Greg nodded. "One more question, if I may."

She hesitated. "Okay."

"Have you ever heard of the Nova Children's Center?"

Without a moment's hesitation, she answered, "No." But there was something in her eyes.

He thanked her for her time and waved good-bye and thanks to Dylan for the caterpillar.

Some time later, while he was driving back to Sagamore, Greg's cop instinct kept bringing him back to that final look in Mrs. Whitman's eyes—a look that said she was lying.

46

B rad told him Julian was treated for epilepsy," Rachel said to Martin.

"We don't know that he wasn't."

"I called Dr. Rose. Only a small percentage of epilepsy patients have surgery, and those are extreme cases."

"So?"

"It may just be a cover story."

It was later that evening, and Rachel was in the kitchen fixing a dinner of lamb shish kebab, bulgur pilaf with toasted pine nuts, and a string bean, onion, and tomato stew. She hadn't cooked Armenian for years, but meeting Officer Zakarian earlier had inspired her. She had even dug up a gift cookbook her old roommate had sent her one Christmas.

As usual, Martin had gotten home late. Dylan was in the family room watching a video of *A.I.* that Martin had picked up. Rachel had not seen the movie and asked if it was appropriate for Dylan, vaguely recalling that it was something of a downer. Martin said it that was age-appropriate, a robot version of *Pinocchio*—nothing to worry about.

"If it is a cover, it makes sense: He's honoring the nondisclosure agreement. Besides, Julian's medical history is none of the cop's business, or anyone else's."

"That's not the point. Two other children with the same holes were kidnapped and murdered."

"Rachel, that's pure coincidence. The holes were probably from being in the sea so long."

"And what if they weren't?"

"Like what?"

"What if they were enhanced also?"

"But you don't know those holes came from enhancement."

"Malenko said it was an invasive procedure using stereotaxic needles."

"Lots of people have stereotaxic surgery—kids included—and they aren't enhanced. It's an established neurological procedure to get into the brain for a thousand different reasons."

His explanation was facile and unsatisfying. Still, he may have been right—that it was all a coincidence. But what were the odds of that?

"Did the cop give you his name?"

"His card is on the counter."

Martin picked it up. "Wasn't your roommate Iranian?"

"Armenian."

"Whatever," he said. Then he lowered his voice so Dylan couldn't hear. "If he comes around again, you know nothing about Julian's enhancement. Just play dumb. It could compromise our chances if Malenko hears some cop's snooping around."

The suggestion grated on a nerve. And, yet, she had yielded to that same protective instinct earlier when Zakarian had asked her if she knew Julian's doctor or had heard of Nova Children's Center.

She had later chided herself for not being forthcoming. Yet, Malenko had made it clear that he could get into an ethical imbroglio were the procedure to become public. And, as Martin said, if a police detective showed up at his door asking about holes in the skulls of dead children, that would be it for Dylan.

And, for all her misgivings, she still kept her foot in that door.

A little before nine on Saturday morning, two hours before Dylan's baseball game and six hours before Rachel was scheduled to fly to Phoenix, Lucius Malenko telephoned.

He said he was out of town and called to wish her mother a full recovery from her operation. He expressed his condolences for the death of her friend Vanessa Watts and her son. "Unfortunately, I didn't hear until after the funeral. Otherwise, I would have gone," he said. "It was certainly shocking. Julian was a remarkably accomplished child. Such a waste."

"Yes, it is."

"I had not seen the boy for some time," he added, "but when last he came in, he was doing very well. Top in his class and giving piano recitals. I had also heard that his paintings were on exhibit at his school."

"Yes." She did not want to talk to Malenko.

Martin was still asleep. Across the kitchen, Dylan sat at the table eating a bowl of Alpen muesli and studying the photo of a missing child on the side of the milk carton.

"Have you seen me?"

Because she had to leave town, they would postpone their next meeting with Malenko until she returned—maybe the middle of next week if all went well with her mother.

Martin had marked the calendar that sat on the wall above the phone. He had circled it in black. That was when they were to give their final decision on enhancement: Friday July 3. The date hovered in her mind like some doomsday raven.

"We'll call when I return," she said, and walked over to the table where Dylan was eating. It was a little boy from New London, New Mexico. At the bottom was an 800 number and a Web address for the National Center for Missing and Exploited Children.

"That would be helpful since, as you may suspect, such a procedure requires considerable planning of material and staff."

"I understand," she said. "We'll do our best to come to a decision, but I still have reservations, as you know."

Her eyes rested on the carton photo—a little towhead with a bright smile and a missing front tooth.

And what if we go through with it and in a year he turns into a total stranger—brilliant, but no one I recognize?

"I understand, but as I've explained, we have an accomplished team and the finest equipment. And you have seen the evidence."

"Yes, but I still need time to think it over." She wanted to get off the phone. She did not want to corrupt the day with more anxiety.

"Of course. And while you do, please ask yourself what's important to you as a parent: If you want to increase your son's chances of having a full and productive life."

The man was putting pressure on her and she did not like it. "I really have to go, but we'll call when I get back."

"I don't mean to be so blunt, but don't you think your husband deserves a smart son, Mrs. Whitman?"

"That's not exactly how I view it, Dr. Malenko. In fact, I find your implication offensive."

"I apologize, but under the circumstances, I believe you owe it to him to strongly consider the option." He then said good-bye and hung up.

"you owe it to him"

The bastard. She had confided in him the most painful secret in her life, and now he was using it against her like a cattle prod.

She put the phone down and went over to Dylan and kissed him on the head.

"Who's this little boy?" he asked.

"His name is Sean Klein."

"But how come his picture's on here?"

"Well, he's missing. He got lost."

"He got lost?"

"Uh-huh."

"But, Mom, you wouldn't get me lost, would you?"

She put her arms around him. "Never, never."

"Cuz then I couldn't sing for you."

47

They came for Lilly about ten that morning.

There were three of them. Because of the sedative they had given her, she was fuzzy-headed. A man and a woman.

Vera. Her name was Vera. The man was Phillip.

Phillip had a dark mole on his cheek. Every time he came in, she could not help staring at it. Phillip also had a big head and short black hair combed straight forward.

They picked her off the bed and put her on a stretcher with wheels like the kind they use in ambulances, and they took her out of the room and down the hallway.

She was glad to be leaving that room. There were no windows, the door had no handle and it was always locked. And the lights were always on. She also didn't like all the stupid cartoons, because they kept playing over and over again. Also, the toys were old and some were broken. But she liked the big blue stuffed elephant because it had straps for your feet and hands so you could dance with it. But it was strange looking since it didn't have big blank elephant feet but actual hands like people have. And arms. Four of them. It was kind of creepy. Like an elephant centipede. His name was Mr. Nisha.

As they wheeled her into the hall, she hoped that they

were taking her outside. The day when she arrived, she had spotted some kids in a playground. She had only gotten a glimpse through the van's window, but she saw two kids on a jungle gym and two other kids at a nearby picnic table playing computer games on laptops. Which made four. She wondered who they were.

She had also noticed that they were beside a big lake with a real seaplane. *Wouldn't that be fun?* she thought. She had never been on a plane. Mom said they were too expensive. When she asked Oliver yesterday, he said he would take her for a ride in it. Tonight.

She hoped they were wheeling her outside to play with the other kids. And no more tests. Maybe somebody was going to explain what she was doing here. Maybe this was the day she would go home, and that when they took her outside, her mom and dad would be there, and Bugs, her dog. Maybe.

Eeeep, eeeep. Eeeep . . .

One of the wheels on the gurney squeaked, and she tried to look down. It sounded like mice in a cage. She once had mice in a cage at home. They weren't hers, but belonged to the school. One Christmas vacation she had volunteered to take them home for the break. Her mom didn't like the idea because they were too close to rats, and rats were mean and filthy animals, Mom had said. But Lilly convinced her that these mice were clean and cute and wouldn't be any fuss. By the end of the vacation, Mom got to like the "little critters." She also got a kick watching them run through the Styrofoam structure the kids had made in class.

The gurney squealed down a corridor that seemed to be a long bright tunnel with rows of windows with venetian blinds pulled down. That was strange.

They took a hard turn to the right and pushed their way into a big bright room.

Inside she saw lots of fancy equipment—machines with wires, dials, and lights, some computer equipment, a sink, and more drip bottles. She had not been in a real hospital since she was born, and she didn't remember that; but this looked like one of those operating rooms in the hospital shows her mom watched.

She closed her eyes again to doze off. But that did not last long because something snapped them open.

A buzzing sound.

Like the electric clippers her mom's hairdresser used. Sure enough, she felt somebody from behind run it across her scalp. For a moment, she just let the buzz fill her ears, as the cool metal mowed its way across her head. Then she looked down to see large chunks of her hair land on the ground.

"Don't take so much off," she insisted.

"Don't worry," somebody said. "It's not going to hurt."

Because there was no mirror in front of her, she couldn't tell how much they were cutting—but her head suddenly felt cool. Naked. She tried to raise her hands to feel, but they were clamped to the sides.

Hands brushed away the hairs from around her. Then the sound of somebody vacuuming the floor under her.

Then it was quiet, but for feathery-soft voices and the squeal of the wheels as she was rolled across the room.

Somebody said something, and she felt herself being lifted off the gurney and onto a table under a huge round dome with lights blazing down on her. She could feel their heat.

Then she was being cranked up a little. She looked down the length of her body and saw lots of the machines with colored lights and screens with orange squiggles going across, and some people moving about. But the light was too bright, and her mind was too fuzzy to make them out clearly. They seemed so small and far away, as if the world had gone to miniature.

Hanging over her was a large television, but there was no picture—just bright blue with what looked like ruler lines making a cross right in the center—like looking through the scope of her father's rifle. On another screen next to it were black-and-white pictures of a skull with numbers and lines drawn through it.

All around her, she heard the soft hum of the machines and the murmur of voices. She tried to move, but her hands were tied for the new IV somebody taped onto her arm. Then she felt herself lifted up as a pillow was placed under her neck.

"Lilly, how do you feel?" she asked.

She knew that voice: Vera.

She didn't like Vera. She was a fake. She would pretend to be friendly so Lilly would take her medicine or eat the food or do the tests. She said things like how they had her locked up like a jailbird—such a shame. But if she ate and took her meds, Vera would talk to Phillip to let her outside. But she lied. They brought her outside only once—to dance with Mr. Nisha.

"Fine."

"Can you tell me your name?"

Silly question, they all knew her name. "Lilly Bellingham."

"Good," Vera said. "Oh, look, it's Lilly dancing."

Lilly opened her eyes again, and there on the television was a video of her dancing with Mr. Nisha.

"And who's dancing with you, Lilly?"

"Mr. Nisha." Why were they asking such dumb questions? Nothing like the tests.

"Good girl."

Lilly kept her eyes fixed on the video, trying not to doze off. Suddenly she felt something on her head. From behind her, a hand drew marks on her scalp. Four marks—two on her forehead just above the hairline, another two at the back of her head just above the ears.

"These are where the screws will be inserted," said a man with a soft voice.

He had a funny accent—"broken English," as her mom would say.

"Since the brain itself is not sensitive to pain, only the surface requires local anesthetic."

"Lilly, how you doing?"

"Fine."

"Good girl. And when this is over, Oliver is going to take you for an airplane ride. Would you like that?"

"Yes, I would," she said. She couldn't see any faces be- cause everybody was wearing green masks and caps. Just eyes staring down at her. And hands.

"Nurse Cooper is going to put a little cream on your head so you won't feel anything," the man with the accent said. "Dermal analgesic, please."

Hands spread some cool sticky stuff to her head.

"An equal mixture of lidocaine and prilocaine," the man continued, "the substance works subcutaneously and is one hundred percent effective. We've used it for years. As you'll notice it has a strong almond odor."

Lilly could smell the stuff, although she didn't know what almonds smelled like. Then she felt some dull scratching on her head.

"We make four small incisions for the screw supports of the frame," the man said to the others.

She felt someone dab her head in places.

"This is going to keep your head still. So, make Mr. Nisha happy and don't try to move. Okay?"

"'Kay."

Movement. Lilly forced her eyes open. Gloved hands had clamped a heavy metal frame to her head while some- body turned the screws. There was no pain—just a dull squeezing across the top of her skull.

When they were through, her head was frozen in place. And all she could see was the thick metal bar across her eyes—and hands turning knobs and moving things.

For a brief spell, she closed her eyes, and . . .

She was at Crescent Lake Beach with her mom and dad. Her mother was saying not to go out into deep water.

"Lilly, don't fall asleep. We need you to be awake to talk to us, okay? Just watch the video."

"'Kay," she said. On the television monitor she was still dancing with Mr. Nisha. She looked so silly with him attached to her like that, his big fat trunk swaying with the music.

Someplace in the background she thought she heard the squealing of the gurney.

"Because the brain is completely encased in bone, reaching surgical targets is more difficult than for surgeries on other parts of the body. And the reason, of course, is that critical structures or vessels limit the choice of possible trajectories. But that's not our concern here."

Then Lilly heard another voice. "Doctor, the first target is two millimeters below the midcommissural line and twelve millimeters laterally which locates us in the subthalamic nucleus."

"Good," the doctor said. "This halo structure has major advantages over conventional stereotaxic frames for determining coordinates," he continued, although Lilly had no idea what he was saying. "It's precisely calibrated with little stopples to prevent the probes from straying or probing too far. It's one of the wonders of finely tooled machines—the ultimate in precision drilling."

She closed her eyes. Someplace in the fog she heard, "Don't be afraid. It's not going to hurt."

Small voices. Kids blurred on the beach behind her as she waded into deeper water. "Not too far." She tried to look back at the beach, to her mother sitting on the blanket. She could hear her calling her name, but because of the big metal thing on her head, she couldn't turn.

"Lilly, look at the movie and tell me your name."

"Lilly Bellingham."

"Good girl."

She closed her eyes and was back at the lake, now in waist-deep water. Voices on the shore fading, and her mother calling her name. "That's far enough." Suddenly she heard something that snapped her eyes open.

Zzzzzrrrrrrr.

She tried to turn her head, but it was anchored in place.

Zzzzzrrrrrrr.

The sound was right behind her. On top of her.

"Lilly, do you feel anything?" Miss Vera.

"Uhnnn."

"What's that?"

"No, I don't." Her words sounded clear.

"Good. What's your name?"

"I told you it's Lilly Bellingham."

The buzzing was louder, almost as if there were some kind of bug in her head trying to get out.

"How you doing, Lilly?"

"Fine."

More buzzing at the other side of her head. And a funny tingling sensation deep inside as hands worked away on the instruments.

Suddenly the drilling stopped.

"Lilly, how you doin'?"

"Fine."

She started to doze off, when the same man in the green mask said, "First hollow needle, please."

"Localization?"

"Target."

"Good."

Out of the crack of her eyes, she saw a hand with a large hypodermic needle full of cloudy pink stuff.

"Lilly, tell me your name."

"Lilly Bellingham."

She waded farther into the water up to her chest. Strange, the water was turning cloudy. She tried to look back to shore, but could not turn her head. She heard her mother's voice.

"Needle."

A little later, somebody said something. "Lilly, tell me your name."

"Lil-ly Bell-ing-ham."

"Good girl. Needle."

The water was turning pink. A milky pink. Like calamine lotion.

"Lilly, what's your name?"

"Lilbingum."

"What's that?"

"Lilbingum."

"Good girl. Needle."

Lilly moved deeper into the water which she knew was not a good idea because her mother said not to go in past her waist especially after eating, and she had just eaten a sandwich what kind she forgot but she just could not stop moving away from shore and the funny thing was that the water became cloudier as she moved deeper—cloudy pinkish-white and bright as if it were blending in with the blank white clouds on the horizon or as if the water were turning into milk which was so strange because it was dark brownish-green earlier when she walked into it and she could see her feet through it but now it was cloudy white like the sky ahead and above—just a big white mass.

"Lilly!" Her mother, calling from far away.

She opened her eyes.

"Needle."

So many needles.

"Lilly, tell me your name."

"Libum."

"What's that?"

"Lib."

"Needle."

Lilly could barely hear her mother calling her. She wanted to call back and tell her mom that she could not stop and that she had to come and bring her back before it was too late—but the strange thing was she could not answer her.

"Lilly? Are you okay? Tell me your name, Lilly."

Lilly opened her eyes.

The woman's face was right above her. And behind her on the television monitor was a picture of a little girl. She could see it clearly and she could hear her words.

"Your name, Lilly. Tell me your name."

She had no idea.

48

Saturday was a stunningly beautiful day. The air was light and sultry, the sky was a delft-blue with cumulus puffs rolling overhead, and a full face of the moon hung above like a silver wafer. The mid-morning sun lit up the Charles Tracey baseball field with stereoscopic clarity. The red clay diamond, etched into the brilliant expanse of green, seemed to blaze as if lit from within. In the distance, beyond the trees, spread the Atlantic like a vast sheet of amethyst all the way to the horizon where it merged with the sky into a seamless blue vault.

The teams were gathered along the sidelines—Dylan and his mates in their bright blue Beacons T-shirts and caps, and the Lobsters, of course, in red. It was the first day of actual intramural T-ball, and Dylan was beside himself with excitement. Last weekend and on a couple afternoons, they had practiced hitting, fielding, and running the bases. Now was the "Great Big Game," as he had called it. All week long he had been talking about it. *I'm gonna hit a big one for the ole Mama Rache,* he had promised. *The ole Mama Rache.* She didn't know where he got that from, but she loved it.

From the little grandstand along the first base line, she and Martin watched the coaches try to calm the kids for instructions. For the first time in weeks, Rachel let herself relax into the moment—a moment that she would give her life to hold on to forever.

When they were ready, the Beacons took to the field. Luckily Dylan started and was sent to left field because the coach said that he had a strong arm.

Dylan waved at Rachel and Martin as he trotted off with his glove, looking back to the coach who signaled where to stand.

The first Lobster got up to the plate holding a fat plastic bat almost as big as he was. Laughing to himself, one of the coaches brought him a smaller one and showed him how to choke up. The head coach served as pitcher, gently lobbing the balls underhand to the batter. The first boy struck out. The second sent a dribble to the third baseman who overthrew as the batter made it to first, and the crowd in the opposing grandstand cheered him on. In a less than ten minutes, the sides retired and the Beacons came in. Rachel and Martin didn't know where Dylan was in the lineup, but the inning was over with the fifth batter. And Dylan was sent back to left field.

Rachel was thoroughly enjoying the game and letting the sun soothe her spirit. Yet, observing the other parents even at this level of play, she could sense a competitive tension—one that she imagined would evolve into one of those sharp-edged things as the years progressed. While she could not imagine Hawthorne Little League parents coming to fisticuffs, something just below the surface made her uncomfortable. A nearby couple appeared to take it hard when their son struck out or when a batter from the opposing team scored. The woman two rows below cried *"Oh, shit!"* when her Clayton was tagged running home. And downbench from them people were keeping a running tally as if this were the Red Sox and Yankees.

At the bottom of the second inning, Rachel spotted Sheila MacPhearson approaching the grandstand, and her stomach tightened. Rachel didn't want to talk to Sheila.

She didn't want to be distracted from the pleasure of watching her son. She did not want to share the moment with anybody other than Martin.

Sheila waved and climbed up toward them. "I saw the blue uniforms," she said, settling next to Martin. "So I knew you guys would be here. There he is," she chortled, fluttering her hand in Dylan's direction even though he was looking the other way. "He looks adorable. I love the blue on him," she said as if she were a favorite aunt.

"Aren't you working today?" Rachel asked.

"I will be," she said and checked her watch. "So what's the score?"

"Seven to three, Beacons," Martin said.

Rachel looked at him. He too had been keeping score. Like it mattered!

"Good for them," Sheila said. "I hope they whip their butts."

"How are sales?" Martin asked.

Sheila rocked her head. "*Mezzo mezzo.* With the economy, things are slow even with price drops. People don't have the money they used to. It's gotten tough."

Rachel nudged Martin. Dylan moved up to the plate. He tapped his sneakers with the bat like the pros and took a few practice swings. Rachel's heart flooded with love.

"You're a hitter, Dylan," Martin called.

"GO DYL-AN!" Sheila shouted.

Rachel felt her insides clench. All she wanted was for him to feel good about himself, and that meant just one little hit, even if he popped out or got tagged. Just for him to feel the ball crack against the bat.

The first ball went by him almost without his notice. They weren't counting balls and strikes. Dylan let four perfect pitches go by. When the fifth one passed him and he still hadn't taken a swing, Rachel began to wonder if he was scared or wasn't sure what to do. The coaches kept up a constant litany:

"Come on, Big D!"

"You're a hitter, Dylan."

"Nice easy swing."

"Keep your eye on the ball."

"Is he okay?" Sheila asked.

Before Rachel could answer, Dylan smashed the next pitch.

Instantly she was on her feet, jumping up and down and cheering as the ball shot past the second baseman on a fly and toward center. The outfielder missed the catch and took off after it. By the time he got the ball, Dylan was bounding toward third base while the coaches waved him on and the crowd cheered.

Rachel was so excited she heard herself hooting. The second baseman threw the ball to the shortstop, backed by the kid from third. But the throw was high, and while the coaches shouted for Dylan to slow down as he rounded third, that he'd be safe, he didn't stop but made a dramatic slide home in a cloud of dust just as he had seen on TV. Instantly, the coaches and Beacons were all over him with pats and high fives.

Rachel's heart was pounding, and her eyes were wet. "Way to go, Dylan!"

Beaming at them, Dylan waved, then he pointed his finger at her. *"A big one for the ole Mama Rache."*

Thank you, God.

Now she didn't care what happened for the rest of the game.

When the shouting died, Martin leaned to Sheila. "How's Brad doing?"

"Well as can be expected, what with a double death." Then she pressed into a conspiratorial huddle with Rachel. "I don't know him well, but I think he's in shock. He went to his sister's in Oregon." She then shook her head. "She was a driven woman. And sometimes under pressure you do careless things. It's not like she was a dummy and couldn't write her own book. But there's a lot of pressure to produce, and she fell to temptation. What can I say?"

With one eye, Rachel was watching the kids below. She wished Sheila would stop yapping, but she went on.

"The humiliation was just too much for her, and she snapped. It's horrible." When Rachel looked away to watch Dylan, Sheila nudged her. "Julian was his pride and joy. And what a loss. Not just a brilliant artist, but he got a perfect score on his math PSATs, an eight hundred, and seven hundred seventy in verbal. Top sophomore at Bloomfield."

Rachel nodded.

Martin, who sat to Rachel's left, pressed closer to Sheila. "What a tragedy."

"No doubt he would have gotten a free ride through college even with their income. Absolutely brilliant, is all."

The boy's dead and she's talking about his damn PSATs, thought Rachel.

"Could have been a rocket scientist."

I don't bloody care what he could have been, Rachel shouted in her mind.

"No doubt," said Martin. "A terrible shame."

One of the kids hit a grounder past shortstop into left field. Dylan raced for it and scooped it up like a kid twice his age. He paused for a moment not sure where to throw it. One runner who had been on second was heading home. Rachel froze. The other runner was rounding first base with no intentions of stopping.

Second! Rachel screamed in her head. *Throw to second!*

People were yelling, cheering on the runner, cheering on Dylan. The coaches were shouting to Dylan to throw it. Throw it anywhere.

Rachel shot to her feet and pointed. "Second!" she shouted.

Whether or not Dylan saw or heard her, he fired the ball with all his might toward home. A giant *"Whooooa"* rose up from the stands. The ball bounded on the third base line in front of the runner and into the catcher's mitt which surprised the catcher as much as the crowd. The runner fell on top of the catcher just two feet from the plate, and was called out.

In left field, Dylan didn't know the call until he saw Rachel bouncing on her feet and cheering. Then he started yowling and jumping up and down. Rachel knew she was no doubt overreacting, but it was a glory moment for Dylan, and she just didn't give a damn.

"You know," Sheila said, when the noise died down, "Bloomfield has a terrific baseball team. They were second two years in a row in the Indy school regionals."

Rachel looked at her blankly. *Damn her,* she was stealing the moment from them. "Beg pardon?"

"The Bloomies. Maybe . . . you know, in a few years . . ."

Sheila was trying to be encouraging, but Rachel was offended. She wanted to say, *Fuck you and the Bloomies,* but she only nodded politely.

"Anything's possible," Martin said.

"Depends what's important to you as a parent," Sheila said.

"I didn't realize they were such a sports school," Martin said.

"Absolutely," Sheila said, latching onto Martin's interest. "You know what I'm saying? With his arm, he could be a superstar there. Lucinda's going to be starting two years from September. Maybe they'll be classmates." And she winked at Martin.

Martin made a promising smile. "Maybe so."

Then she dropped her voice. "By the way, if some Sagamore cop comes by asking about Julian, my advice is to tell him nothing."

"Of course," Martin said.

"Oops! Gotta go," Sheila said, checking her watch.

Rachel muttered a silent prayer of thanks.

"By the way," Martin said. "Would Lucinda want a couple of gerbils? Dylan's just had a bunch of babies. About the size of a peanut."

Sheila's face seemed to harden. "No, that's all right."

"How did the kitten work out?" Rachel asked.

"Ran away. The mailman left the back door open. *C'est la vie.* What can I say?" She slung her bag over her shoulder to go. "By the way," she said, pressing into a huddle again. "Turn on your TV Sunday night at nine. A special edition of *Who Wants to Be a Millionaire?* for kids under eighteen. I'm not supposed to tell, but a boy named Lincoln Cady's going to be a contestant."

"Who?"

"Lincoln Cady. A black boy from Detroit." She made telling wide-eyes.

"You mean . . . ?" Martin began.

Sheila nodded and winked.

Enhanced, thought Rachel.

Sheila stood up. "I know nothing about him, but he's supposed to be something else."

"We won't miss it," Martin said.

And she whispered, "And mum's the word." She fluttered a good-bye and climbed down the stand.

Rachel watched her cross to the parking lot to her car, thinking that her visit was not by accident.

49

Martin and Dylan dropped Rachel off at the Delta terminal at Logan Airport a little before two that afternoon. They pulled up to the entrance where cars and busses were double- and triple-parked.

"Why do I have the feeling that you're glad I'm going?" Rachel said as Martin waved for a redcap to take her luggage.

"Why do you say that?" He looked at her in partial dismay. Perspiration made a beaded mustache band under his nose.

"I don't know. You seem anxious. That's all."

Martin looked at Dylan. "It's just that we're going to do some guy-bonding today, right, champ?" And he tousled his son's hair.

"But you know what, Mom? Me and Dad, we go the movies."

Rachel knelt down and hugged Dylan. "That's a great idea."

"You wanna go, too?"

"I'd love to, but I have to visit Grammy. When I come back you take me, okay?"

Dylan nodded. "And you know what? I sing you a new song." And he gave her a big hug.

She held him for a long time.

"Mom, are you crying?"

"Only because I miss you already."

Dylan stared at her with a dreamy concern. Then he asked, "Mom, where are my Gummy Bears?"

"In your backpack." She opened the rear door of the car, and Dylan slid in and began to search through his backpack.

Martin checked his watch. "We'll be fine," he said. "My love to everybody."

He kissed her good-bye and started to pull away toward the car, but she caught his arm. "Martin, promise me something."

"What?"

"If Malenko calls again—"

"Rachel, he's not going to call again."

"But he may. He's pushing us, and I don't like it."

Martin sighed. "It's because he has a deadline, and you know that."

"It's not his son!" she snapped.

Dylan looked up at her from inside the car, and his eyes locked on hers.

She lowered her voice, and in a grating whisper, she said, "If he calls again, just tell him that you're not going to discuss it until I return. Not until next week. Period."

Martin made a face of exasperation. "Okay, okay."

"Promise me."

"Yeah, okay." His eyes were perfect clear orbs. "I promise."

Dylan climbed out of the car. He came up to Rachel and put some Gummy Bears in her hand.

"What are these for?"

"To make you feel better. The green ones are the best. They make you happy."

"You make me happy," Rachel said and pulled him to her. "I love you, little man." She hugged him for a brief spell, then let him get into the car. The traffic behind them was piling up.

"Love you, too."

Rachel watched as Martin strapped Dylan into the front passenger seat. "Have a nice flight," he said and walked around to the driver's side and got in. As they pulled away, Dylan waved out his window at her. "Bye, Mom."

"Bye, sweetie."

Please, dear God, let me do the right thing.

Around three-thirty, Rachel boarded the plane. She had booked a window seat because she liked the view of Boston, especially when the plane took the northwest corridor, which gave her a full shot of Cape Ann and Big Kettle Harbor just under Hawthorne. But with the low cloudbank, there would be no view today.

Because of a last-minute change of schedule, Bethany had been operated on that morning. According to her brother, the surgery went well, and her mother was on a respirator in the ICU recovery with a new biological valve made from pig tissue. Amazing what they could do in modern medicine, Rachel thought.

Inside her seat pocket was a copy of *The Miami Herald* that somebody had left. The flight had originated in Atlanta where connecting Miami passengers would have boarded. Several of the stories were about Florida affairs and politics, some directed at the elderly. There were pieces about retirement portfolios and how water bans from the latest drought were affecting South Florida golf courses. How brushfires were plaguing the state. About the latest local security measures against terrorism.

But it was the story on page 9 that caught her eye.

"Searchers Abandon Hope of Finding Okeechobee Boy."

The story went on to describe the all-out efforts of police, sheriff's deputies, scuba divers, neighbors, and other volunteers to find six-year-old Travis Valentine who was last seen nearly two weeks ago in his backyard near Little Wiggins Canal. All that was found of the boy was a shoe and his butterfly net at the water's edge. Divers had scoured the canal for over a mile, while hundreds of volunteers had searched the woods and canal banks all the way to the next town. " 'I hate to say it but my best guess is a gator got him,' " claimed the local sheriff. According to the article, there had been more than a dozen alligator attacks of children over the last eight years. " 'They hover below the surface out of sight. A dog or a child comes by, and whamo! They can shoot out of the water like a rocket.'

"Several large alligators have been killed over the last two weeks, but none containing the remains of the child."

"Just last month young Travis was among five county children who had passed a qualifying test from the University of Florida that would guarantee him a full four-year UF scholarship should he graduate high school. The program is part of the SchoolSmart campaign to encourage children to stay in school . . ."

Eaten by an alligator, Rachel thought. *God! How far removed their lives were from such horrors.*

50

Oliver banked over Casco Bay and headed straight eastward on a course that would take them to the northern end of the Gulf of Maine. Until recently, he had vectored a southerly route toward Wilkinson Basin, about eighty kilometers off the coast—a quick ride out. While Jordan Basin in the gulf was farther by fifty kilometers, the floor fell down to more than two hundred and fifty meters, twice the depth—and where storm surges couldn't reach and the currents were northeasterly toward Nova Scotia, not the other way. It was a longer flight, but less risky. And great foraging ground for bottom feeders and sharks.

The cloud ceiling was eight thousand feet, and visibility five miles. Rain was in the forecast for tomorrow, but they would have no trouble tonight. And a good thing it wasn't Sunday, or he'd miss the quiz show.

When they were about an hour out, Oliver cut the engine speed.

Below the ocean was a vast black void. Not a ship light in sight. Nor any other planes. At a hundred feet, Phillip unlocked the door. They had rigged a chute from an old plastic playground slide and fit it across the rear seats. They also had devised a crank mechanism to open the door at high speeds.

"Approaching the mark," Oliver said into his speaker-phone.

Phillip finished his beer and got into position.

"Okay."

Phillip began to crank open the door. The sound of the sucking air filled the cabin. Oliver could feel the cool rush. When it was partway open, Phillip tossed out the beer can.

Oliver steadied the plane against the turbulence, keeping his eyes on the dials.

Usually they would put them to sleep, but Phillip had forgotten the phenobarbital. It made no difference anyway. She didn't have a clue.

Lilly lay groaning under a sheet. She was naked except for the polyvinyl chord around her arms and legs and fastened to a cinder block. Her head was a scabby mess, and she struggled feebly against the ropes. Her eyes were open, but they looked dead.

"Mark," Oliver said, checking his instruments.

At one hundred feet, he would bank fifteen degrees to the right and let gravity do the trick. The sheet would stay because that was traceable. The rope they got in Florida, and wouldn't connect in a million years.

"Now!"

And Lilly slid out feet first.

51

B"ut how come they have to kill them?" Dylan asked.

Martin and Dylan were watching an animal show about elephants and ivory poachers when the telephone rang.

He had expected to hear Rachel's voice, telling him how her mother was finally out of ICU and had been moved to her own room. Yesterday when she called, Bethany was still recovering and barely alert, but the doctors said that she would soon be off the respirator and moved to her own room.

"For money," Martin said, and grabbed the portable phone.

It was Lucius Malenko.

He had called to express condolences about Vanessa Watts and Julian just as he had to Rachel yesterday. The sentiment struck Martin as a little strange since they barely knew the family. Yet it was very considerate of him.

Malenko also happened to mention that he had a friend who had graduated from MIT the same year Martin had. He didn't recognize the name. Before they said good-bye, Malenko reminded him of the time element. "This is not like having a tonsillectomy. There are considerable preparations to attend."

"I'm aware of that," Martin said.

"Even more critical are the time constraints. I'm leaving the country in a couple weeks and won't be back for a month, which means that it may be another ten weeks before we can set up another time. And, frankly, Mr. Whitman, we're running out of time."

"I understand, believe me."

"I'm not sure exactly why," Malenko added, "but your wife seems to have reservations."

"Yes, she has."

He didn't say it, of course, but Rachel had a tendency to let irrational concerns grow to paralyzing proportions. It was habitual: She'd worry things to death and end up getting nothing done. When Dylan was three, a New York textbook publisher with a Lexington office called her to say they were looking for an English editor with her experience and track record. They had hoped to woo her out of retirement with a handsome salary. For days she agonized over whether to pursue the opportunity or stay home with Dylan. Martin had pushed her to go for it. It would have been good for her; she was good at it. And they could have gotten great day care for Dylan. Not to mention how they could have used the extra salary. But no! She couldn't let go. Dylan needed her—which was a lot of bullshit guilt. So somebody else got the job, and she remained your basic hausfrau.

"We'll work on it," Martin said.

Before Malenko hung up, he said, "You know, it would be very nice, of course, if Dylan could follow in his father's footsteps. Schools don't get much better than MIT."

"I hear you, Doctor."

Dylan was still spread out on the couch. Martin went back to his chair. It was nine o'clock.

"Time for bed," Martin announced.

"But I not tired," Dylan whined. "I wanna stay up with you and watch TV."

"Well, then how about we watch *Who Wants to Be a Millionaire?*"

"I don't like that show. It's stupid."

Stupid.

"Well, Daddy wants to watch it."

"I wanna see the elephant show."

"But the elephant show is all over."

With the remote Martin switched channels. The camera closed in on Regis Philbin who announced the special show for teenage contestants, eighteen and under.

"You're mean."

Martin felt a blister of petulance rise. "I'm not mean. I just want to watch this."

"You don't like me," Dylan mumbled.

Martin muted the commercial. "What did you say?"

"You don't like me."

"Of course I like you. I even love you."

"How come I had the dream?"

"What dream?"

"The dream about you gave me away."

"Gave you away? That's silly. I wouldn't give you away."

Dylan looked at him. "Me take stupid pills, that's why."

"Don't say that."

"Lucinda says."

"Well, Lucinda is wrong."

Dylan pouted and buried his face in the pillow.

Maybe he'll fall asleep.

Martin recalled what Malenko had said about sedatives to calm him down, to minimize the trauma, to delete all memory of the event. Ketamine, or something like that.

The commercials ended, and Philbin announced the qualifying round. The camera showed ten young people, four females and six males, at their consoles with their hand controls waiting for the question. One of the boys was black.

The question was to place four foreign capitals in order from east to west. Before Martin could register the question, the buzzer went off, and five kids had gotten the correct order, the fastest time going to Lincoln Cady—in 3.8 seconds, which was nearly two seconds faster than the next fastest answer.

While the audience applauded, Cady moved to the console across from Philbin.

He was a pudgy serious-looking boy with thick glasses. He did not seem the least bit nervous. In fact, he seemed preternaturally calm.

He and Regis Philbin chatted briefly to warm him up. The boy spoke in a soft even tone, his words enunciated precisely and deliberately. He seemed like a sixteen-year-old going on forty.

The first five questions were the usual throwaways.

In no time, Lincoln Cady had reached the $32,000 mark without having to use a single lifeline.

"Do you read a lot?"

"Yes."

"Good for you. You have remarkable recall."

"Thanks."

"What do you hope to study at Cal Tech next year?"

"Computer engineering."

Regis nodded. "You did so well on the medical questions that I'd think you'd be interested in studying medicine."

Lincoln raised his eyebrows. "I'm more interested in machines than people."

Regis smiled. "I have days like that, too."

The audience laughed, and they went on to the next question, which he got, then the next.

Throughout the exchange, it struck Martin that the boy didn't appear to blink.

The next question: "What was the occupation of Albert Einstein when he published his theory of relativity: *(a)* teacher; *(b)* mathematician; *(c)* office clerk; *(d)* student.' "

The kid deliberated a bit, but Martin was certain that he had been told to draw things out in order to heighten tension. Then he said, "Office clerk."

"Is that your final answer."

"Yes."

Regis Philbin cocked his head. "You got it for a hundred and twenty-five thousand dollars."

The audience exploded. The boy smiled and fixed his glasses calmly. There was more perfunctory chitchat then the next question.

"Who hit the first Grand Slam in World Series history?" The choices were: *(a)* Charlie Peck; *(b)* Eddie Collins; *(c)* Frank Baker; and *(d)* Elmer Smith.

Martin had no idea what the answer was, and Lincoln Cady said he did not know sports and would have to call a friend, a classmate at his school named Robert. Philbin called, Cady read the question, and the young male voice at the other end said, "Elmer Smith." Cady offered that for his final answer, and Philbin congratulated him for reaching the $250,000 mark.

After the applause and more small talk, they moved to the half-million-dollar question. When Philbin asked him what he was planning to do with whatever money he won, Cady said he would give it to his parents to help pay off some debts, then put the rest toward college. Philbin liked that, and the audience approved.

The next question lit the screen: "When three celestial bodies form a straight line, what is the phenomenon called?" And the answers listed were *(a)* syzygy; *(b)* string theory; *(c)* Lineation; *(d)* synapogee.

Cady still had two lifelines left, but he said he didn't need them.

Syzygy, thought Martin.

"Syzygy," said Lincoln.

"Is that your final answer?"

"Yes, it is."

"You just won yourself half a million dollars."

"YES!" shouted Martin, and the audience went crazy.

There was a cut for a commercial break, and Martin turned off the audio, thinking how in grade school he was a stutterer. He remembered vividly all the shit—how they had called him "Muh-Muh." The running joke was: Hey, Martin, try to answer this in under an hour: "What's your name?" In English class when they got to poetry, they said Martin was an expert on alliterations.

He supposed it was funny, looking back. But at the time it was hell. People thought that stuttering meant you were stupid. He could still recall the raw humiliation, the mortification he felt when he couldn't get out what he wanted to say, just a vicious staccato of syllables—"*Wha-wha-wha-wha . . .*" At that age, kids are brutal. Once they see a spot of blood, they will peck at it until you're bled of self-esteem.

He was not going to put his own son through that. *Life's hard enough . . . but . . .*

(*go ahead! Say it . . .*

it's harder when you're stupid)

Suddenly his mind was a fugue.

He heard Rachel: *But he won't be the same person.*

Then another voice: *Maybe not, but he's not the same person he was with pigeon-toes. He's better, more capable. Look how high he was when he slid home yesterday. Imagine his ego growing up without a mental handicap.*

And Rachel again: *What about accepting him as he is?*

Not if we can do better for him.

But what if he loses his interest in music and sports? Or if his personality changes?

Not going to happen. Malenko said so. Look at Lucinda. Look at all the nameless enhanced kids in Harvard at fifteen. Look at this kid on the screen. Calm, cool, collected. Brilliant.

Martin glanced at Dylan lying on the couch, his eyes drooping. He hated that mushroom haircut. It made him look like a young Bluto. But it was what all the kids on the team sported. And Dylan wanted to be like them.

We can change that for him. A chance of lifetime.

It was time for the million-dollar question. Philbin and the audience were charged. Lincoln Cady looked as if he might start yawning. The kid was remarkably impressive. *Cool incandescence.*

"Okay, here goes. For one million dollars."

The screen lit up with the question and the four choices: "What 1959 novella was the basis for the 1968 movie *Charly*?"

The four answers given were: *(a) Odd Man Out, (b) A Case of Conscience, (c) Flowers for Algernon, (d) The Duplicated Man.*

Cady nodded as he scanned the answers. He hesitated as the music played up the tension. Then, after several seconds, he said: "The answer is *(c) Flowers for Algernon.* Final answer."

Regis Philbin looked teasingly at the camera then back to Cady. Then he beamed: "You just won yourself one *million* dollars."

And the audience went wild. Lincoln Cady smiled thinly and shook Philbin's hand as the applause continued and confetti rained down on the set.

Dylan had slept through the whole drama.

Martin muted the set and dialed Rachel on her cell phone. She answered on the third ring. "Did you see the show?"

"Some of it. The nurses had it on. And in case you're interested, my mother's doing fine."

"Great. Give her my love. Jack, too. So, what did you think? I mean the kid—Lincoln Cady. Is he a whiz, or what? I mean, talk about photographic memory."

"He was very impressive," Rachel said.

"Impressive? That doesn't come close." Her lack of enthusiasm was so typical.

"He also looked as if someone had shot him with a tranquilizer dart."

"What does that mean?" Martin couldn't disguise his defensiveness.

"Just what I said. He looked stiff, robotic."

She was purposely downplaying a spectacular performance, and Martin was getting more irritated by the second. "How about it was just cool confidence. I mean, the kid's a genius."

"Martin, can we change the subject, please?"

Christ! he thought.

"Because she's doing so well, I'll probably be coming home Tuesday. How's Dylan?"

"He's fine." There was a pause. "Rachel, you're aware that Dr. Malenko has got to know pretty soon."

"I know that," she snapped. "We'll talk about it when I get back."

"Well, I'm just saying. He's pressed for time."

"Look, stop pressuring me. This isn't something I'm going to rush into."

"We've been thinking about it for weeks. I mean, how much more time do we need?"

Her voice tightened. "I don't want to talk about it right now. I've got enough on my mind."

Shit! "Well, think fast because he's leaving the country in a couple weeks."

He looked across the room at the sleeping figure of his son. It struck Martin just how much he looked like him when he was young. In fact, he could have passed for seven-year-old Martin on a pony in the photograph sitting on the fireplace mantel.

"Then if we do it, it'll have to be when he gets back."

Martin did not say anything more about it.

According to Malenko there would be a three-to-four-week recovery period, which meant that if they waited too long, Dylan would miss the first weeks of school in the fall. But if they did it soon, he could stabilize and miss nothing. Then over the next few months, he would begin to show signs of improved cognition. It would be subtle and progressive, which meant that by next year at this time, Dylan would have begun to plateau. Then by the fall of that year, they could enroll him in a different school where no-body would know his academic history, which, in this state, was confidential—a fancy private school whose en-trance exam he'd ace. Not like what he did on the Beaver Hill qualifiers.

As Malenko had said, he would by then have grown into his own new mind.

And what happens when he's suddenly brilliant and Un-cle Jack, Aunt Alice, and Granny come to visit? How are you going explain the fact that Dylan's a little whip? How he's reading Dr. Seuss on his own when just last year he couldn't get through the alphabet? Whatcha gonna tell them, huh? That his new tutor is something else? Or that the school he's attending has some great new breakthrough strategies on learning? Or that they put him on an all–ginkgo biloba diet?

None of that.

Well, you see, we found out about this secret little brain operation that jacks up IQs?

Not that either, because Dylan was still young. And be-cause Jack and Aunt Alice and Granny knew little about his cognitive status. Rachel had mentioned how Dylan hadn't passed the Beaver Hill entrance exams, but she hadn't gone into detail. She had not told anyone his IQ. It wasn't anybody else's business, even family. So all they knew was that Dylan was a sweet, handsome little boy who hit a mean T-ball and who sang like a bird. Sure, he had some language problems, but many kids do. And he just grew out of them like millions of other slow starters, that's all. Like his old man, for instance.

After they hung up, Martin walked over to the couch and looked at his sleeping son for a long moment. Even his profile resembled Martin's. Like father, like son.

Yep, just grew into his own mind.

52

It was almost too easy how Greg found the Nova Children's Center.

He got the name from information and discovered that it
was located in Myrtle, Massachusetts, just twenty minutes
northwest of Hawthorne.

Around noon on Monday, he drove to the place, which
was a grand old Gothic Revival building with turrets, a
dunce-cap roof, and fish-scale slate shingles. He wouldn't
have known that from Disney, except that Lindsay had
been interested in architecture.

He went inside, uncertain what he was looking for, uncertain if he was pursuing a bona fide lead or more white
rabbits. His only certainty was his suspension if Lieutenant
Gelford learned he was here. And that was the reason he
didn't contact the local police. If he asked the investigator
on the Watts case to keep their exchange quiet, that would
make the officer suspicious of Greg's credibility.

The receptionist said the person to speak to was Dr.
Denise Samson. However, she wouldn't be back until after
lunch, about one. That was cutting it close, since it would
take him almost two hours to get back to the office, and for
this week he'd been rescheduled to start at three because of

vacation absentees. Unfortunately, he'd be about half an hour late.

So he sat in the waiting room and thumbed through magazines. At one-thirty, Dr. Samson called the secretary to say she'd be late. That made Greg's stomach leak acid. With the traffic, he wouldn't get to the department until after four. That would not look good.

At two-fifteen, Dr. Samson came up the stairs. She was a tall stately woman with short reddish hair and dressed in a moss-green dress. He asked to speak with her in private, and she led him to her office.

He did not tell her about the skulls. Instead, he mentioned how one of his cases involved a child who had been evaluated on a SchoolSmart test, and wanted to know about that.

"Well, in addition to offering tailored learning programs, we have a diagnostic service that designs, administers, and evaluates tests used in different school systems nationally. SchoolSmart is one of them and is sponsored by private benefactor organizations as well as some colleges and universities that offer scholarship incentives to extremely gifted children from low-income families."

Greg noted that on his pad.

"As you can imagine, many such kids either quit school at sixteen to work or, if they graduate, they take the first job that comes along and almost never go on. What School Smart offers is full-tuition scholarships for select students if they remain in school through the twelfth grade. And we administer the tests as early as the first grade."

"An incentive to remain in school."

"Exactly, and a just reward."

"And the only qualifications are smart and poor."

Dr. Samson smiled. "That's putting it bluntly, but yes. And that they complete their schooling," she said. "But I should add that our tests are not the standardized group intelligence tests, but ones specially designed as individualized evaluations for young children identified by their teachers as gifted. They're more accurate, and we make certain they're administered by licensed psychologists."

She would have gone on, but Greg cut to the chase. "I'm wondering if you could check your database for a Grady Dixon."

Her fingers flew across the keys. "Grady Dixon . . . Yes, from Cold Spring, Tennessee." And she gave the date of his evaluation.

Greg felt a little electric thrill run through him. He was tested just three months before he was kidnapped. "Can you tell me where exactly he was tested and who administered the test?"

The woman looked a little flustered. "Well, I can tell you he was tested at his school, the Michael Lowry Regional, and the local psychometrician was Dr. Maxwell Barnard from Signal Mountain, Tennessee."

That did not seem helpful. "Can you run a database cross-reference to see if this Dr. Maxwell Barnard conducted tests on any other SchoolSmart candidates?"

Dr. Samson started the search when she suddenly stopped. "I can do that, Officer, but I'd like to know why you're asking. I'm concerned that we're going to violate a contractual agreement with our clients."

He saw that coming. "Dr. Samson, I'm looking into a possible connection between some past kidnappings and children who might have been tested by your organization."

Dr. Samson looked worried all of a sudden. "You mean a criminal investigation?"

"Yes."

"Well, I'm sure you understand, but I would have to consult with the directors before I can divulge any more information—unless, of course, you have a court order."

He didn't, and he had her against a wall. Without a warrant, any more nudges could push her behind a legal blind. "Of course, but maybe you can tell me if his files contain any record of neurosurgery?"

She seemed tentative. "Well . . ." she began.

"Doctor, Grady Dixon has been dead for three years and it's presumed he was kidnapped and murdered." He was hoping the drama of that would override protocol.

"I see. Neurosurgery?" She glanced at the screen. "Well, no, nor would we have any record of that sort unless he had been a patient of ours. That's a completely separate entity from what we do on site. Besides, I'd imagine the parents would have consulted neurospecialists in Tennessee."

"Of course. And just who are the neurosurgeons here?"

"Actually, we have two: Dr. Stephen Kane and Dr. John Lubeck."

He took down the names. "Is there a Julian Watts in your database?"

"Julian Watts. Why is that name familiar?" she asked. Then her expression contorted. "He wasn't the boy murdered by his mother last week, was he?"

"I'm afraid so."

"Oh, how horrible. I read about that."

"Can you check if he had taken a SchoolSmart test?"

She slowly turned to the computer again and tapped a few more keys. "Oh, my! He's in the database . . . but he was not a SchoolSmart candidate." She hit a few more keys. Then she sat back and stared at the screen, a look of surprise on her face. "He's listed as a patient of Dr. Malenko."

"Dr. Malenko?"

"Yes, he's one of our neurologists. Dr. Lucius Malenko."

"Do you have any idea why Julian was seeing Dr. Malenko?"

"I don't, but even if I knew I couldn't give you that information. Besides, Julian was one of his private patients."

"Private patients?"

"From his private practice." Then she glanced back at the screen. "I'm just surprised he didn't mention the boy's . . . what happened."

Greg filed that away. Then he pulled out the schematic and showed her. "Any idea what kind of neurological procedure would have produced these holes?" He briefly explained the origin of the drawing.

She shook her head. "I'm a psychologist, not a neurologist."

"Could they have been the results of some surgical treatment of epilepsy?"

"I suppose."

The woman looked as is she were becoming uncomfortable with the interrogation, knowing full well that she didn't have to proceed without a warrant. "One more question, if you don't mind," he said, without giving her a chance to respond. "How many people here have access to your database?"

"The entire professional staff."

"I see." He thanked her and left.

On the way out, he stopped at the reception desk again. "I'm wondering if I could speak to Dr. Malenko."

"I'm afraid he'll be out of town for a few days. Would you like to make an appointment?"

"When do you expect him back?"

"Next Thursday."

"Do you have a number I can reach him at?"

"I can give you his other office. You can leave a voice message."

"That'll be fine."

She jotted down the address and number on the back of the center's card and handed it to him.

As he returned to his car, he noticed the slot for L. Malenko. Greg wasn't sure what he had: two dead six-year-olds—one from Tennessee, the other from parts unknown. Two teenagers—one dead known teenager, one alive unknown teenager—both from the North Shore of Massachusetts. Except for the live one, they were all murder victims, one by his mother. The only commonality was their gender and the fact that each had neurosurgical bore holes in the skull. Two were connected to Nova Children's Center. And two points determine a straight line.

He looked at the little white reserved parking sign. L. MALENKO.

Greg didn't know why, but he had the prowling suspicion that this L. Malenko might connect a couple more points.

53

Going back up there is outright insubordination, and you know that, Greg."

Because of the traffic, he didn't return to the office until nearly five. And the dispatcher said that Gelford wanted to see him in his office immediately.

Again, Gelford was not alone, but flanked by Chief Norm Adler and Internal Affairs Officer Rick Bolduk. Something told Greg that they were not here because of tardiness.

Gelford, of course, was ripped because Greg had gone against his notice to drop the Sagamore Boy case—which meant that this was a *mano a mano* thing—a personal offense against his supervisor who prided himself on running his ship on uncompromised discipline. But Gelford would hear him out first.

"I realize that, but I'm telling you, there's a connection. What I need is a court order for that database."

"And what's that going to do?"

"It's going to let me cross-reference missing children from three and four years ago with kids who were part of the SchoolSmart program."

"Because one of your skull kids happened to take a test?"

"Yeah, and because three dead kids had similar holes in

their skulls and two of them are linked to the Nova Children's Center. And two of the three kids were very smart, and a fourth unknown and still alive has the same kind of holes. And I want a court order to obtain his identity and check his medical records. He too could be in their files."

"Before you go banging on some judge's door, you've got to have evidence that a crime's been committed," Rick Bolduk said. "All I'm hearing is circumstantial evidence."

"I've got the testimony from two doctors who are convinced that these kids might have undergone some experimental procedure. And one of those kids, Grady Dixon, was kidnapped and possibly murdered. So was the Sagamore kid. That's evidence enough for me."

"They're not our jurisdiction. None of them. We don't own them," Gelford said, his face turning red again. "One kid's from Tennessee. The Sagamore kid is from God knows where." He picked up the schematic of the North Shore boy's X rays. "And this kid's still wearing his head. There's no goddamn crime."

"There's one more thing," Greg said. "Two neurophysicians say that these patterns trace the areas of the brain associated with intelligence and memory."

"So?"

"It's possible some kind of experiment is being done on kids' brains, maybe tampering with intelligence or memory. I don't know, but I think it's something nasty and should be investigated."

All three of them stared at Greg as if he had just reported the landing of Martian spaceships.

Gelford, who was nearsighted, removed his glasses and picked up a fax lying on some other papers. "While you were gallivanting around the North Shore today, a Reed Callahan was severely beaten up and hospitalized by Mr. Ethan Cox. And in case you don't recognize the latter's name, he was assigned to you last week on the school break-in, and had you done your job and questioned these kids and brought him in as you were supposed to, Cox would have been behind bars before he tried to shut up the Callahan boy who's now in the ICU of Cape Cod Hospital with a fucking concussion." Gelford's face was purple with rage.

"I got held up in traffic."

"Maybe you were, but something tells me your distraction with this skull shit has compromised your attention, your efforts, and your abilities to fulfill your assigned duties. This Callahan kid may not come out of his coma. He might also die because Cox took a baseball bat to him, and you could have stopped him because he's got three previous assaults on his record and two B and Es. He's a fucking animal, and you didn't go after him but flew off to Cape Ann to look for skulls."

"I'm sorry."

"Not as sorry as I am, because you've disobeyed orders and turned a blind eye to everything else on your desk, and a kid's in a coma as a result."

Gelford then opened his desk drawer and pulled out a letter and handed it to Greg.

Greg felt his heart slump. He didn't have to ask its contents. He was being suspended.

"I wish it didn't have to come to this," Gelford said. "But you were put on notice, you were given a verbal and written reprimand, and you chose to violate department policies."

"How long?"

"One month with pay until a hearing on a determination of guilt." Then Gelford added, "As corny as it may sound, we live by discipline in this department, and you pissed on it."

Greg looked at the letter, aware that they probably viewed him as a crazy man on a mission, a cop who saw things that they discounted as patently foolish. It was possible that they even suspected that he had made it all up about the doctors and Nova Children's Center.

Technically, Gelford was right: They were not bound to

crimes in another jurisdiction, especially when it was questionable that a crime had been committed. His lone hunches weren't enough. The long and the short of it was that he was no longer credible or reliable in their eyes. Possibly even psychotic.

"Sorry, Greg," said Chief Adler. "You have a right to a hearing, of course, but in the meantime I must ask you to clean out your locker and turn in your badge and weapon."

Greg got up. He unstrapped his weapon and his badge and laid them on the desk. He felt half-naked.

Gelford rose to his feet. "I think this might be for the best," he said. "I think you need to decompress, maybe get away for a while. Get off this thing. Chill out."

Greg nodded.

"And I think in the meantime you should see somebody—a professional. It's nothing to be ashamed of."

Greg nodded again and headed for the door with his suspension letter in hand.

"One more thing," Gelford said. "I need not tell you there are laws against impersonating a police officer. Furthermore, if you keep bothering those people up there, you could be arrested for harassment and disturbing the peace."

Maybe that's how it would end, Greg thought. He thanked them and left.

54

Brendan was thinking about love and death when the phone rang.

"I have to see you." It was Nicole.

Brendan felt mildly shocked. The last time he saw her, she all but wished him to disappear. "What's up?"

"I'll tell you when I see you," she said. Her voice was its familiar neutral.

"C-can't it wait? I'm in the middle of something."

"I'm going back to camp tomorrow. It's about the stuff you told me last week. We have to talk."

"Can't you tell me over the phone?"

"No. It's too important. Please."

Please was not a Nicole word. Brendan felt his resolve slip. "W-w-where you want to meet?"

"In the parking lot on Shoreline Drive at eleven."

That was just outside Hawthorne, about eighteen miles from Brendan's house. He had no desire to jump in his truck and drive all that way. Maybe she had some information about all this. Maybe she remembered stuff. Maybe she had decided to fess up.

"Okay."

He hung up and stared at his hands for a long moment.

"Death is the mother of beauty." Wallace Stevens again.

The line had hummed in his head all evening. Even before Richard had gone to bed.

Brendan got up and stepped out of his room to the second-floor landing. There was a wall mirror hanging between his room and Richard's. In the overhead light he studied his face.

I'm going to kill my grandfather, he said to himself.

Nothing.

Time to get off the bus.

He pressed his face closer. No change of expression. No dilation of pupils. No look of horror. No shock. No fear. No pleasure. No pounding of his chest.

Nothing.

He had hoped to detect some shift in his features, some microexpression to betray the flat featureless landscape of his face. Yes, he had been prepping for this for weeks, so it was no surprise. But still. Murder.

God! I could be a terrorist, he thought. *Except even terrorists have passion, misdirected as it is.*

I'm half-dead. A zombie.

He had no intention of hurting Richard. This was not an act of cruelty. In fact, he knew he was not a cruel person. He never entertained fantasies of hurting anyone. He was not into torturing animals. He did not get off looking at pictures of train wrecks or dead people.

In fact, he liked Richard. And he knew murder was a morally wrong act, but Richard was near death anyway. Why prolong his misery, and he suffered daily debilitation and pain. Euthanasia is not murder. He'd be Richard's own Jack Kevorkian.

An act of mercy. I'm a moral being.

Then another voice cut in: *You're twisting logic to arrive at a preordained conclusion.*

No.

Brendan had worked out all the details, thought through the consequences of Richard's death. Because he was a legal eighteen, Brendan would not have to contend with guardians or foster homes. And because he was sole beneficiary of Richard's estate, he would inherit the house, the contents, the truck; the old man's meager savings would be his; and he would collect on a small life insurance policy. With his job at the Dells, he could support himself just fine.

As for Richard's death, there'd be no telltale signs. Richard had a long history of heart disease, so the coroner's report would be *pro forma*: heart failure. Brendan had read someplace that unless there were suspicious circumstances, people who die over the age of seventy-five are almost never autopsied. And there would be no suspicious circumstances.

Besides, he had an alibi. He spent the evening with Nicole DaFoe.

He tilted the mirror to change angles.

Am I insane?

Richard was near death anyway. Why not wait?

Because he could linger for months. Wasn't that more cruel?

Brendan knew full well why he was doing this: He simply hoped that Richard's death would release the emotional blockage. To let him know love and sorrow.

And what if there's nothing? a voice asked. *What if you kill him and you're still made of wood?*

There's the shotgun in the cellar.

Brendan took a deep breath and closed his eyes. He tensed his muscles into a tight crouch and squeezed with all his might against the maelstrom raging in his brain. He held firm and pressed until it swirled into a pinpoint and blinked itself out.

Silence.

Brendan straightened up and opened Richard's door.

The hinges let out a rusty squeal, but Richard did not stir.

The interior of the room was very still. The hump of Richard was slashed with moonlight through the blinds. Because of the arthritis, Richard always slept flat on his back.

Brendan moved closer. Richard's mouth was slightly

open and a hand rested under his chin. His eyes looked fused.

A pillow had fallen to the floor. He picked it up. It was thick enough to do the job.

Without an autopsy, suffocation would pass as heart failure.

In his head, Brendan ran through the moves, almost feeling the old man's bony frail frame under him. He wondered how much Richard would struggle. That would be the hardest part. He hoped not much. He might even die of fright.

Brendan stood over Richard's sleeping body, the pillow in his hands.

He felt as if he were trapped in a tale by Edgar Allan Poe.

I can do this.

I can.

He stopped for a moment to gauge his feelings, putting his finger to his own carotid artery to feel his pulse. He checked his watch. Sixty beats per minute. Normal. Cold-blooded normal.

His eye fell on the contents of the bed stand: a glass half-full of water and three prescription vials. Old-man meds. Crazy-boy meds. The same amber vials.

Richard's disheveled white hair looked like a scattered cloud above his head. Brendan bent over him until he could smell the mustiness. Brendan held his breath.

Richard was not breathing.

Brendan lowered his ear to Richard's mouth. No wheezing. No scrapping air. No flutter of his uvula.

Brendan peeled back the covers to see if he could detect movement of his chest. Nothing.

Jesus! He's already dead. He had not expected this.

A sensation rippled inside his breast and he dropped down on his knees.

"Richard?"

Nothing.

He put his hand on the old man's shoulder and gave a little shake. "Richard!"

Still nothing.

"Richard?"

Richard's body jolted. "Wha-what? What's the matter? What're you doing?" His eyes were no longer gummed with sleep but huge with alarm. "Why you holding that pillow? What the hell's going on?"

"It f-f-fell off the bed. It's okay," Brendan said. "I d-d-didn't think you were breathing."

Richard was now fully awake. "Well, I am . . . for what it's worth." Richard rubbed his eyes and pushed himself up onto his pillow. "Why, you worried I wasn't?"

"I guess."

Richard humpfed. "Hell, I've got a few breaths left in me still."

Brendan was full of words, but he could only nod.

Richard looked around the room. "So, what are you doing in here? Is something wrong?"

To see if I'm human.

To see if Death is the mother of beauty.

"To g-g-get the truck keys. You left them in your p-pants when you moved it."

Richard craned his neck to see the clock radio. "Jeez, it's after ten. Where the hell you going at this hour?"

"To g-g-get some air."

Richard humpfed again. "Well, I hope it's female air." Then Richard gave Brendan an odd look. "You were really worried about me, huh?"

Brendan nodded and moved toward the doorway. In the light he could see Richard smiling.

"Be back before midnight. And careful driving, for cryin' out loud. Lotta drunks on the road at this hour."

"Yeah."

"You take your meds?"

"Yes, I did."

Another thing he was always after him about. That, eating right, and going back to school. What was left of his life's checklist.

"Good boy. You need some money?"

"No, I'm fine."

Before Brendan stepped out, he looked back at his grandfather with his cotton-wispy white hair and face so pale it seemed to glow in the dark. "Good night, Richard."

"Good night, kiddo. And thanks for looking out for me."

"Mmm."

Then as the door was closing, Richard added, "Hey!"

Brendan stopped. "Yeah?"

In the strip of light, Brendan could see Richard's mouth lopsided with emotion.

"I love you, Brendy Bear."

Brendan could hear the catch in his grandfather's throat. And for a moment, he was unable to breathe for the small glow in his chest. Then in a barely audible voice he muttered, "Thanks." And he clicked the door shut.

But Brendan did not bound down the stairs as usual. Instead, he put his hand on his chest and gazed into the mirror again.

His heart was pounding. And his eyes were wet.

It was about eleven-thirty when Brendan pulled into the lot—a small tar-topped parking area on the bluff hanging over the town beach. The only other car was Nicole's mother's SUV. She swung open the passenger door to let him in.

"W-w-what's up?"

Nicole was dressed in white jeans and a Harvard sweatshirt. "I want to go down to the beach." With that, she got out of the car, tugging a shoulder bag.

Brendan didn't like beaches. He couldn't swim. He didn't like trudging in sand. He didn't like the fishy brine. In the daytime, it was too hot and bright, at night it was dark and forbidding. But he followed her down the serpentine steps to the sand.

There were no lights on the beach, and the nearest residents were a mile away. The only illumination was a white crescent moon, which rocked in the sky about thirty degrees above the eastern horizon like a rib bone.

"I'm sorry for being such a bitch."

It was a night of surprises. Brendan could not believe she was actually apologizing. Such a sentiment seemed antithetical to her nature. "N-no problem."

"It's just that what you said about getting a head operation freaked me out."

Nicole didn't freak out, he thought. "Your parents knew my parents. That's what got to me—that note."

"Did you ask them?"

"My mother said I got seizures when I was small. Maybe that's what it was all about. I had chicken pox too. I don't know." She turned her face toward him so that the moon cast shadows across her eyes. "Do you really think they made you smarter?"

"I'm n-not sure, but that's what the tests and the X rays s-suggest. Maybe I was au-autistic or had a t-tumor or something and they got me fixed. That's what I don't know. Whatever they did, I think it s-s-screwed me up big time. And I'd like to find the people who did it to me."

Nicole said nothing.

"Did you ask them about that doctor—Lucius Malenko?" The name meant nothing to Brendan.

"Just that he's some kind of specialist. I don't want to talk about it."

She took his hand.

"Don't be afraid, I'm not going to jump on you."

He was grateful for that.

"And I don't think you're a fag." She brushed the hair out of his eyes. "It's just that I wish I turned you on."

"Sorry, b-but it's not you."

They were quiet for a while; still holding his hand, she pulled him up.

"How's camp?"

"It's okay. We just play a lot of head games."

"It's a g-g-genius camp, right?"

"There are lots of geeky kids there, if that's what you mean."

"What kinds of things do they have?"

"Computer workshops, physics, astronomy, math workshops, bio lab—stuff like that. It's fun. Besides," she added, "I want to go to med school someday, so it looks good on my record."

"I'm s-sure you won't have any p-p-problems there."

"Whatever," she said, then tugged on his hand. "I want to go swimming."

"S-s-swimming?"

"Yeah, I'm warm." She slipped off her sandals.

He watched her, but said nothing. He wanted to tell her that he couldn't swim, but decided against it. She peeled out of her clothes, and, thankfully, she was wearing a bathing suit. A black one-piece.

"Come on."

"Nah. I'm fine."

"Don't be a pussy."

"I d-d-don't have a bathing suit."

"You don't need one. Nobody's around for miles. Or go in your underwear if you're so modest."

"No, that's okay."

But she wouldn't take no for an answer, and began to pull his shirt over his head. But he stopped her and took it off himself.

"Come on, the rest of it."

Reluctantly he lowered his pants to his boxers. He did not like this. He did not want to get wet, but she was pushing him. It crossed his mind that she might have been nervous about going in the water alone. The waves weren't very high, and were breaking a good distance out.

She pulled him into shallows, the initial shock, sending

spikes through his body. It was also not a smooth sandy bottom, but one carpeted with large round rocks that made the footing precarious. He could feel sharp things between slimed rocks—shell fragments and seaweed clumps. They felt awful, especially to his tender feet.

But that did not seem to bother Nicole who bounded ahead, kicking up her long muscle-tight legs.

"This is as far as I go," he announced.

"You're being a wimp." And she turned and splashed him.

The chill cut through him. "There m-might be an undertow, r-r-rip currents."

"Not here," she said, then dove in and came up in the foam of a breaker. With her slicked-back hair and black suit she looked like a seal.

She dove in again and surfaced beside him. "Come on," she said, and grabbed his hand and pulled him in to his waist.

He began to feel nervous. It was deeper than he liked and he could swear he felt a current pull against his legs.

He stood in place with his feet firmly planted and watched Nicole cavort in the waves ahead of him. The cool air made his skin a sheet of goose rash, and he began to shiver.

The wind had picked up, and the breakers came in long even rows, cresting and crashing maybe thirty feet ahead of him in lines of foam running down the shore.

He tried not to think of what the water looked like from underneath. He tried not to think of the kinds of creatures that lurked just below the surface—schools of blues and leg-sized stripers. He tried not to think of those opening scenes from *Jaws*. He wished he were back on shore. He wished he had never answered the phone.

He turned, and his truck in the lot looked so far away; and on shore, in the dim glow of the sky, he could see his pants lying on the sand, the leg holes still opened, as he had left them, beckoning him to step in and pull them back up.

Behind him, another long breaker arched against the

gloom like a small tsunami and crashed no more than twenty feet ahead. The rush of foam rose up his chest and sprayed him about the neck and face. They were coming closer and growing higher with the incoming tide. With each wave, he could feel the tug at his legs—the push toward shore, then the brief slack followed by an unnerving pull outward as the next wave sucked itself up into a black hump coming down at him like some faceless predator.

Nicole.

She was nowhere in sight.

"Nicole!" he said.

He looked upbeach and saw only the black water and whitecaps—downbeach, more of the same. No long slick body. No head bobbing at the surface. No body flying in with the surf.

"Nicole?"

Nothing but the crash and grating roar of the waves against the pebbles.

"Nicole!"

Nothing.

"Oh God, no."

He moved out a little farther, scanning the surface in all directions. "Oh, please," he muttered to himself, feeling an electric wire of panic begin to glow in his chest.

He turned back toward shore. The beach was an unbroken stretch of sand—not a soul in sight.

She could have gotten sucked under or driven headfirst into the rocks by a crashing wave, he told himself.

What the hell would he do? What would he tell her parents? That they came out for a midnight swim and that she just drowned while he wasn't looking?

Out of the corner of his eye, he saw a line of foam cresting behind him. He was about to turn when a huge wave crashed over him, pushing him off his feet and curling him under.

Suddenly he was completely disoriented, being rolled and punched into the stone-cased sandbar. When he finally got a foot planted, he pushed up, panic bursting inside. But instead of shooting to the surface, he felt himself suddenly gripped from behind and pulled under.

Reflexively he sucked in air, only to take in a throatful of water.

He spasmed instantly, choking and coughing, and sucking in more water.

Legs.

Nicole's tight muscular legs had clamped around him like an anaconda, and the weight of her body pulled him back so he could not get his head above water.

His mind shut down for an explanation because he was too busy trying to catch his breath and uncurl her legs, which were locked in a death hold and making it impossible to right himself.

But he could not get leverage. And the more he flailed his arms, the more he spent himself, all the while trying to hold his breath until he could get his face out of the water.

She must have needed air herself, because for a split second Brendan felt her grip slacken as she rode up his body from behind. But instantly she relocked her legs around his chest and gripped him in a headlock with her arms. She was choking him and trying to keep his head underwater.

With panic flooding his brain, his neck feeling crushed, and his diaphragm wracking for air, Brendan concentrated every scintilla of awareness on Nicole's arms, found a hand, and sank his teeth into her thumb.

Instantly her limbs flew up, but not before she horse-kicked him in the spine.

He shot to the surface in chest-deep water, coughing and choking and trying to open an air passage before he passed out.

Vaguely he sensed where Nicole was, and he turned toward her in case she tried to jump him again.

She had surfaced maybe fifteen feet in front of him. She was holding up her hand. "It's bleeding."

He bobbed in place not taking his eyes off her, madly sucking in air as if he'd drain the atmosphere. He could not talk and could barely see, but he kept her before him, struggling to suppress coughing while filling the air-starved pockets of his lungs.

"I can't bend it," she said in dismay. "I can't bend it."

"Y-y-y-y-you—" he began.

"I'm going to need stitches."

"—tried to drown me."

She continued to study her thumb, as if he weren't even there. "Maybe a cast." Her voice was a little-girl high, thin whine. "Wha-wha-what did you d-do that for?"

In the moonlight, he could see her eyes saucer and a strange look contort her face. Without another word or a glance his way, she turned and plowed her way to shore as fast as she could.

Brendan trudged his way across the stones, still gasping for air, his throat constricted, his windpipe feeling as if it had been permanently pinched.

He barely noticed Nicole get dressed and run off. He just flopped down when he hit the beach, his diaphragm still fluttering like a small trapped animal. He rolled onto his knees and regurgitated a bellyful of brine and most of his dinner.

For several minutes he remained on all fours with his head down, strings of bile hanging from his mouth, his heart throbbing at an impossible rate, the air scraping into his lungs in little yelps.

Someplace in the distance he heard the sound of a car engine.

Still panting he looked up to see Nicole peel out of the parking lot.

When his head cleared, he stood up and stumbled up the sand to his clothes. He flopped down beside them. The towel she had brought was gone, as were her clothes.

While he worked at catching his breath, all he could think, while staring blankly out to sea, was: *Why does Nicole DaFoe want me dead?*

55

Y ou *what*?" Rachel wasn't sure Martin had actually uttered the words or that she was stuck in a nightmare
from last night.

"It's the best thing."

"Where is he? WHERE IS HE?"

"Stop getting hysterical. I dropped him off with Dr.
Malenko."

"Oh, God! Where did you drop him off?"

"His office."

"When?"

"Yesterday."

Out of sheer reflex, she pounded him on the chest.
"Goddamn you!" She felt so disoriented that she couldn't
find words for her outrage and horror. She had just been
dropped off by the taxi and walked in the house only to discover Dylan was gone.

"We've already been through this."

"You just dropped him off? You didn't stay with him?"
She suddenly felt faint from the thought of Dylan trauma-
tized by strange people in some clandestine medical facility.

"We weren't allowed to stay with him. You know that.
We'll pick him up in a few days. It's no big deal."

"No big deal? I don't want him operated on," she said, trying to steady herself. "I decided against it."

"Well, I haven't," Martin shot back. "If there was nothing we could do, that would be different. We would raise him as he is and love him unconditionally. But there is something we can do to make his life better."

"I want him back the way he is. Do you understand? *I want my son back.*"

"Rachel, calm down. You're going to get your son back, and he'll be better for it."

She ran to the desk in the kitchen and snapped open the address file box. Sitting in the mail inbox on the desk was a pink receipt for a bank check. Five hundred thousand dollars. What he had paid Malenko. While she was gone, he had cashed in mutual funds, sold stocks, and God knows what else so he could put a down payment on his son's IQ.

But money was the least of her concerns.

Her mind was so jammed, that for a moment she didn't know what name she was looking up. She just kept fumbling for the *M* tab, then couldn't remember if she had filed it under *Malenko* or *Nova Children's Center*. When at last she found it, the number looked nonsensical—like hieroglyphics—as her mind fought off images of Dylan someplace—*God knows where!*—having his head shaved.

Martin came in to help her, but she hissed at him and punched the number.

When the secretary answered, she took a deep breath to get her center. "This is Rachel Whitman. I need to speak to Dr. Malenko. It's an emergency."

"I'm sorry, but Dr. Malenko isn't in today. May I take a message?"

"How can I reach him?"

"I'm not sure. He's out of town for the next few days."

Another bolt of horror crashed through her. "Out of town?" Martin was flashing her hand signs, warning her not to mention enhancement. She turned her back to him.

"He'll be back next Thursday," the secretary said.

"But I have to speak to him. It's urgent."

"Well, I can take your number, and when he checks in I can have him call you."

"Can't you contact him directly? He's a doctor. You must have some emergency number."

There was a pause at the other end. "I can give you his voice mail and you can leave him a message."

Martin made a move to take the phone from her, but she backhanded his arm.

"I don't want his voice mail." She was about to say *"He's going to operate on my son!"* when Martin pulled the phone cord out of the wall.

"What are you doing?" she screamed.

"You're getting hysterical, Rachel. Now cool it!"

By reflex she swatted his hands away.

"Rachel, you're just keyed up because of your mother's condition."

"My mother's condition has nothing to do with it. He's going to operate on our son's brain—"

"It's what we agreed on."

"We didn't agree on anything. I DIDN'T AGREE." She was almost blind with rage. "We were going to talk about it when I got back. You took him without telling me."

"And I wouldn't have, if you hadn't done all that shit."

Rachel's mouth dropped open.

"Yeah. He told me. 'TNT for dynamite sex. Get off with a bang.' "

"That bastard."

"Yeah, well, that bastard's a godsend. He's going to undo the damage you did, and he's going to do it before it's too late."

"You don't know that. YOU DON'T KNOW THAT."

"He showed me the studies—a forty percent chance. We're just lucky he wasn't born brain-dead," Martin said. "Whatever, next year at this time we'll be burning candles to Lucius Malenko."

Without a word, Rachel grabbed her purse.

"Where are you going?"

But she didn't answer. All she could think was how she hated Martin at that moment. And herself.

She dashed into her car and shot down the street. Martin did not follow her. He wouldn't. He'd wait until she cooled off and came whimpering back.

She drove without direction, telling herself not to panic. To get a bearing. That such a procedure would need several days of preop preparation.

Preop. Jesus Christ! And she fought down images of what they might be doing to him.

It was twenty after four, and the offices of Nova Children's Center closed at five. Because of the rain, the traffic was thick and slow, and there were no shortcuts. She kept one eye on the road, the other on the digital clock readout, watching the numbers tick by, feeling the pressure building in her chest—hoping that she would not have a stroke before she reached the place—thinking if she found it closed, she'd probably smash the windows in.

It was five minutes to five when she pulled into the lot. No red Porsche, of course.

But there were a few staff cars.

She parked and dashed around to the front entrance, the rain soaking her. The receptionist was the same woman, Marie, who had answered the phone. "I called you earlier. I have to reach Dr. Malenko. It's an emergency."

"Yes, Mrs. Whitman. I'm sorry, but he still hasn't called in."

"Is Dr. Samson here?"

"No, she's out, too."

"Isn't there anybody here who knows where he is?"

"Lemme check," she said, and she punched a few numbers. "Hi, it's Marie. Yeah, I know, it's really coming down. Well, I have Mrs. Whitman here and she needs to speak to Dr. Malenko. Any idea where he might be reached? Oh, okay. Thanks. Yeah, you, too." She hung up and looked at Rachel. "Sorry. He's gone for the week."

"You must have some emergency number, a cell phone or some way to reach him."

"Unfortunately, he doesn't believe in cell phones—he thinks they're dangerous. But he calls in frequently for messages."

"Maybe you can tell me if Dr. Malenko has any surgeries scheduled within the next few days?"

The woman gave her an incredulous look. "Any *surgeries*?"

"My son is supposed to have a neuro procedure done, and I'm just wondering when Dr. Malenko will be doing it." It was an outside shot since maybe nobody here knew about enhancement.

"What kind of procedure?"

For an instant she could hear all the caveats about secrecy. But *fuck it.* "Enhancement."

"Enhancement?" The woman's face scrunched up. "What's that?"

Rachel studied the woman. There was no sign of guile in her manner. She really had not heard the term. "Some kind of surgical procedure."

"With Dr. Malenko?"

Rachel was on the verge of screaming. "Yes, *with Dr. Malenko.*"

Marie made a grimace of dismay. "There must be some mistake. Dr. Malenko doesn't do surgery."

"What?" For a split instant Rachel felt as if she had passed into some demented *Alice in Wonderland* dimension. "He's got plaques on the wall from the American Neurosurgery Society."

"Well, those are kind of old, frankly." Her voice dropped to a whisper. "He's retired from surgery. In fact, he hasn't done surgery for over ten years." The woman made a kind of self-conscious expression and raised her fingers to her face. "His vision."

"His vision?"

"He's blind in one eye."

Rachel looked at her blankly, exerting every ounce of will to prevent herself from cracking. "What about the other neurosurgeons here?"

"There's Dr. Kane and Dr. Lubeck," she said, checking a folder. "But they're not scheduled for any medical procedures with your son."

Rachel nodded. She didn't know the names.

"Would you like me to make an appointment with Dr. Malenko when he returns?"

"I have to find him now."

"Sorry. But you can leave a message with his answering machine."

Rachel nodded and wrote down her cell phone number in case Malenko called. She then headed out, thinking that if Malenko didn't perform the surgery, who did? Who was his staff? And where were they?

And where is my son?

As she headed for her car, it crossed her mind to go to the police, but what would she report? What was the crime? Martin had dropped off his own son to the man.

Then a darker thought cut across her mind: If she called the police and Malenko found out, he might hurt Dylan. Or deny he had him.

He wouldn't do that, a voice in her head protested. *You're working yourself into a full-blown panic.*

Halfway down Main Street, she pulled over and dialed Sheila on her cell phone. She got the answering service and left a message to call her ASAP. She then called Sheila's office, getting the number from information because her mind was too chaotic to remember it. Sheila was on the road, her officemate said.

"SHIT!"

Who was left? Suddenly, all her deepest fears about this whole bloody thing rushed up: There was nobody else to contact. They had put their trust in people she didn't know and turned over their son to some clandestine medical operation that was outside the circle of professional ethics and practice—*and this was the conse-quence.*

She turned down Magnolia and headed north to Cobbsville. She was halfway there when her phone rang. It was Martin, who wanted her to come home.

"When you dropped him off, what did he say about contacting him?"

"Nothing, just that he'd call when it was over."

"Jesus! He didn't give you a number?"

"No."

"How long would it take?" she shouted.

"Three or four days. Rachel, cool it. Everything's going to be okay."

He had dropped him off yesterday. "I don't care. I don't want him to have this. I don't want him changed."

"But it's the best thing for him. You said so yourself."

"I've changed my mind." Before he could argue back, she said: "Do you know where they brought him?"

"No, but he said he'll call—"

Rachel clicked him off. The sky had darkened over the highway, and storm clouds looked like bundles of steel mesh rolling in.

A few minutes later, her phone rang again. She braced herself for Martin's insistence that she cool it and return home. But it was Marie, the receptionist at Nova. "Dr. Malenko called and left a number for you," she said.

Thank God.

Rachel fumbled in her purse for a pen and wrote it down on her hand. She then dialed the number and held her breath.

On the third ring, she heard a click. Then: "Hello, Mrs. Whitman. This is Lucius Malenko. Your husband informed me that the bypass surgery for your mother was successful and that she's recovering nicely, I am happy to hear. Dylan is doing fine and will be coming home in a few days. Enjoy your weekend."

Click. Then the hum of the dial tone.

She redialed the number, but got no answer. No outgoing voice message. Nothing but endless ringing. The message automatically erased itself so as not to leave evidence.

Rachel let out a groan and drove on.

It was after six when she reached the small white ranch. The place was dark as if abandoned. Except for a couple of vehicles parked along the street, the area looked deserted. The driveway beside the house was empty. No Porsche. No lights in the windows.

She went up to the entrance. The interior was dark, but she rang the bell nonetheless. Nothing.

She felt frantic. "DYLAN!"

She cut around the back, knowing she would find nobody. The rain was in a steady downpour. She pulled open the storm door and went inside the small rear foyer and banged on the door. Of course, there was nobody inside. She thought about kicking in the door, but if the guy had a secret locale where he did his enhancements, it wouldn't be tacked to the wall. Nor would it be in any of his files. He was too smart for that.

The rain pelted her face as she dashed around front to her car.

She drove northward on the main road that cut through small rural towns this side of the New Hampshire border. But after a couple miles, she realized that she had no idea where she was heading. Soon she came to a sign that said that she was entering Carleton Junction. She had never been to Carleton Junction.

She pulled over, and as the rain pattered dismally against her car, she opened her glove compartment for the map. In the light, she saw a small silver tape recorder. She had never seen it before. She was sure it wasn't Martin's; besides, he almost never used her car. She opened it up and there was a tape inside, rewound. She pushed the play button and turned up the volume wheel.

"Rachel, this is Vanessa Watts. I don't know what condition I'll be in when you get this, but I could not live with myself if I didn't tell you that you'd be making a mistake if

you bring your son to Lucius Malenko. I'm sure his intentions were noble enough, but he ruined my Julian's mind. Yes, he's smart, but he's very troubled. He's been diagnosed as obsessive-compulsive. But that doesn't come close to the horror of his condition. He's possessed by his rituals—his painting and music and science projects. He has no other existence. He barely sleeps. He doesn't have any social life or friends. He spends his days and nights working—and counting. He counts everything he does— every bite of his food, the steps he takes throughout the day, every point he taps on a picture. It's horrible, but he can't help it. He's been on a dozen different kinds of medication for years, and his condition is getting worse. They tell me he would have been this way without the operation. But I don't believe them—not for a minute. They did something to his brain when they stuck that shit in. I don't know what, and they're not talking. But don't do it to your son. It's not worth the chance. Julian's not the boy I gave birth to. He's not my son . . ."

Her voice cracked.

"There's something else. Julian remembers something about the operation . . . something about another . . . I have to tell you in person. It's just too . . . I'll call you."

Then she clicked off.

"Oh, sweet Jesus," Rachel said aloud. These might have been the last words Vanessa had spoken before taking their lives.

Rachel dialed home, but she got the answering machine. She called Martin's cell phone and got another voice message saying that the party was not responding. She left him a message to call her immediately—that it was urgent— and she summarized what Vanessa had said on the tape. About the last unstated bit, she only said that Vanessa wanted to tell her something that might have been too alarming even for a tape message.

She continued driving, still not certain where she was heading. The rain kept coming down hard. She had no idea where Martin was. Again, she thought about going to the police, but what could she tell them?

She passed through the center of Carleton Junction, following a sign to I-95 South that would take her back to Hawthorne. Maybe Martin would be back.

As she rounded a bend in the road, headlights filled her rearview mirror. She pulled over to let the car pass, but it stayed on her tail. Because of the rain and dimming light, she could not make out the driver, but she was beginning to think that he was playing some kind of game with her.

She took the next turn, still following signs for I-95. But the car stayed right behind her.

A coincidence, she told herself.

At the next juncture, she took a right onto a wooded road, hoping to shake the tailgater. But the vehicle stayed with her. With a shock, she realized she was being followed. Out of instinct, she accelerated—and so did the car behind her, filling the mirror with lights.

Goddamn it! her mind screamed. She put her hand behind her seat and pulled up the club wheel lock. She wasn't going to be intimidated. She had no idea who'd be following her or why, and she didn't know the road or where the next gas station might be, or how much farther to the interstate. So with a sharp turn of the wheel, she pulled over and grabbed the steel rod.

But in the rain she didn't see that the cut in the side brush was a washout, and the car slid down the bank and hit a tree with a jarring thud. The engine died, but she was not hurt. She looked back. The truck had pulled over.

The same truck that was outside Malenko's house.

Before she knew it, a large man in black pulled open her door just as she reached back to lock it. But that made little difference since he could easily have smashed the window.

Because of the tightness of the interior, she couldn't swing the rod, so she held it in front of her like a small lance ready to drive it into the man's face.

It was Brendan LaMotte.

A blinding rain was coming down when Greg found Lucius Malenko's Cobbsville office. It was not what he had expected, which was some kind of fancy complex of physicians' quarters. Instead, the man's private practice was housed in a small, nondescript ranch with no shingle distinguishing it from any other of the modest residences on the street.

The place looked closed. No light burning in any of the front windows. No cars parked in the driveway. A black pickup truck was parked across the street.

From his cell phone, Greg had called the number the receptionist had given him yesterday. But he only got an answering machine and an accented male voice asking for the caller to leave a message. He didn't do that.

It was about five-thirty, and he didn't have to be at work for another month. And here he was sitting in the rain waiting for nothing and wondering at what a mess he had made of his life, not to mention some kid lying in a coma. How he had followed one hunch behind another into a suspension, humiliation, and a burning urge to get blinding drunk.

Just as he was thinking about the taste of beer and heading home to do something about it, a gold Maxima pulled up in front of the Malenko place and out jumped Mrs. Rachel Whitman.

She was alone.

Without bothering with an umbrella, she dashed to the front door of the ranch house and rang the bell then started banging the knocker. She looked frantic. Not getting any response, she ran around back. He heard her calling. A few moments later, she came around then got back into her car and screeched down the road.

Greg started the car. Maybe it was something, maybe not. But it was more interesting than watching the rain make streaks down his windows.

As he pulled onto the road thinking about T. J. Gelford's

warning about impersonating an officer of the law, it occurred to him what name the Whitman woman was yelling. *Dylan.*

Her six-year-old son.

The huge body filled the door opening.

"Brendan!"

He didn't respond.

"Why are you following me?"

Brendan's hair was plastered to his head from the rain and his eyes looked wild. His mouth was moving as if he were reciting something without sound. *Crazy. This kid is crazy.* She knew the rod was useless with the roof and steering wheel blocking an effective swing. But, she told herself, if he reaches for me, I'll claw his damn eyes out, so help me God.

"I know where your son is."

"What?"

"I heard you c-call his name back in Cobbsville," he said. "C-can I get in?" The rain was pouring off him.

"Yes, yes." She tossed the rod in the back seat and watched him come around. The car dipped as his big body settled in the passenger seat. He wiped his face staring straight ahead.

He was muttering something rapid-fire under his breath . . . something she couldn't catch. A crazed rambling as if he had lapsed into a weird trance.

What if this was some kind of hideous trick? she wondered. Get her to let him in then work himself up to attack her.

"Wind and rain and little boy lost . . ."

She caught a scrap of verse of some kind.

"Brendan!"

He snapped out of it and looked at her.

"My son. What do you know about my son?"

Before he could answer, the figure of a man came down the banks to the car. "Is everything okay here?"

For a second, Rachel could not place the man's face. "Officer Zakarian."

He came up to the window.

Rachel instantly felt on guard. "Yes, everything is fine," she began. "My car just skidded off the road."

"So it appears." He looked at Brendan suspiciously.

"This is Brendan LaMotte," she said, trying to affect an air of control. Although he seemed liked a nice man, she did not need him or the police involved in this. All she wanted was for him to go so Brendan could tell her where Dylan was.

Zakarian reached across her and shook Brendan's hand, no doubt wondering what he was doing tailing her up here in the woods. "I was just leading Brendan to the highway back home. He's not familiar with these roads."

Brendan gave her a quick look. "I'll g-g-get the chain," he said and dashed back to his truck.

Zakarian walked around her car in the rain to assess the situation while she waited inside trembling. He stuck his head in the window. "I don't see any damage. Try starting it."

She turned the key, and the car started up.

"You're sure everything is okay, Mrs. Whitman?"

"Just a little rattled, but I didn't get hurt. I'm fine, thank you," she said. "I just want to get back on the road is all." She felt that at any moment she would begin to scream.

"We'll get you back," he said.

Brendan returned with the chain, one end of which Zakarian attached to the underside of the Maxima, while Brendan connected the other end to the hitch. Then Brendan maneuvered the truck into position and pulled the car back up onto the road with Rachel still inside.

"Thank you, Officer," she said, trying to force a smile. "That was very considerate of you." He was soaked from the rain. "We'll be on our way now." She hoped he would take the hint.

His head was at her window, and the rain was pouring

off him onto his yellow Sagamore PD slicker. Again he asked, "You're sure everything's okay?" This time he looked back at Brendan who was out of earshot. He was asking if she felt threatened by the boy.

"Yes, I'm fine, thank you. Brendan's a family friend. I'm just leading him back to Hawthorne." She could hear the edge in her response.

"Well, you showed up at Dr. Malenko's office looking pretty upset earlier."

Her mind went numb for a moment. How had he seen her? And what was he doing at Malenko's? And why was he following her? She had to play down the connection—play it cool. "My husband brought my son for a five o'clock appointment, but I got there late—the weather and all." She knew it was a feeble answer. She couldn't tell if he believed her or not, and at the moment, she really didn't care. She just wanted him to leave.

"Your son's a patient of his?"

"Yes. Look, Officer, I appreciate your help, but I really have to get home." Her heart was pounding so hard, she was certain she'd go into cardiac arrest.

"I was waiting to see him because I had some questions to ask about the Nova Children's Center. Julian Watts was a patient of his also."

"I see."

Brendan sat waiting for her in his truck. Zakarian's hands still rested on her door. She stared at them to ask if he was going to let her go. If he didn't, she knew she would lose it.

He studied her for a brief instant, trying to read her manner. Then he backed away. "Okay. Maybe we can talk soon."

She nodded and put the car into gear.

Through her rearview mirrors, she watched Zakarian move to his car, which was a black SUV—which, for a split instant, struck her as odd. Didn't police use squad cars?

"By the way," he called back. "The highway is that way," he said, pointing north. Her car was facing south.

Then he waved to Brendan in his truck and got back into his own car and drove off, heading south.

Rachel nearly broke down with relief as she watched the car disappear into the distance. When he was gone, Brendan got back into Rachel's car. "If he's a c-c-cop, how come he d-didn't have a badge or gun?"

"I don't know. I don't know. Maybe he's off duty," she snapped. "Where's my son?" Her voice was trembling.

"In Maine near Lake Tarabec."

"Maine? How do you know?"

"Because I followed him there. I saw your husband come to the doctor's office with your son yesterday. Thirteen minutes later he left. Twenty-two minutes after that, Dr. Malenko left with your son in his car, a red Porsche, New Hampshire plates, WMD 919. I followed them for three and a half hours."

"Do you remember the way?"

"Yes."

Thank God, she whispered silently. "Brendan, I want you to take me there. I'll pay you anything you ask—but I must find my son." She did not want to go up there on her own.

He nodded that he would.

She tore open the glove compartment for a pad and pen. Brendan wrote down directions to Camp Tarabec from memory just in case they got separated. He put his hand on the door to go to his truck. "Were you waiting for me there?"

"No, Dr. Malenko. Since this morning. He's supposed to have office hours here today."

"Why did you want to see him?"

"Because I w-w-want to know what he did to me."

"What?"

He took off his cap and clicked on the interior light. Then he lowered his head, parted his hair, and showed her a cluster of small round scars under his hair on both sides of his head and above his ear.

They looked like drill holes.

Then he told her his story.

When she was on the road, she called Martin. He still wasn't home, so she left a message about how she had found out where Malenko had taken Dylan and recited the directions. Then she followed Brendan to the center of Carle-ton Junction where, gratefully, there were signs to I-95 northbound. She had just crossed the state line when her cell phone rang. It was Martin. "What do you mean you're going to get him?"

"I told you what Vanessa said—they ruined her son."

"How do we know he wouldn't have been that way without enhancement? We don't."

"That's right, and I'm not going to take that chance," she said.

"What the hell does Brendan have to do with this?"

"He had the procedure ten years ago, and he now wants to know what they did to him. He wants help. Don't you get it? This thing has problems Malenko never told us about."

"So you're saying he lied to us?"

"Or he didn't tell us the whole truth."

"Talk about the pot calling the kettle black," he said.

"Fuck off," she said. He was rubbing her nose in it. "Are you with me or not?" she screamed.

"Rachel, Dr. Malenko is not lying or covering up failures or whatever. He explained to me that it's the only thing that can be done for him—grafting new cells where the damage is. It's done all the time with brain disorders. He said that his particular malformation makes him a perfect candidate for the procedure. Besides," he added, "we already paid for it."

"I don't give a damn about the money," she screamed. Suddenly electronic crackling filled the phone. "Goddamn it, I'm losing you," she shouted. "Can you hear me?"

"Yes, I can hear you." His voice was distant and fragmented.

"I'm going to get him with or without you," she shouted.

"Rachel, don't—" he began, but the connection was lost.

She put the cell phone on the console next to her, feeling more alone than ever.

Greg drove in the rain, thinking about Mrs. Whitman.

At Malenko's place, she had appeared frantic, banging on the doors and calling for her son. Half an hour later he found her stuck in a ditch, looking as if she were about to explode while claiming everything was just dandy, that she had just slid off the road while leading home the big ponytailed kid Greg had spotted in the cemetery the other day with the good-looking blond girl—the same kid who was currently driving a black Ford pickup—the same black pickup that had followed her from Malenko's Cobbsville office.

Points were connecting.

And he smelled the proverbial rat.

Clearly something else was going on with Rachel Whitman—something she did not want to share with the police. Certainly, there was no crime in that, and he was convinced that the LaMotte kid posed no threat to her since Greg detected no equivocation in her denial, nor did the boy project an aura of aggression or offense. But the woman was noticeably at the edge, and Greg was positive that it had nothing to do with sliding off the road or getting home late for supper.

Although he admired her, Greg did not, of course, know Rachel Whitman, having spent only half an hour with her the other day. But he could swear that those golden-brown eyes staring up at him from the driver's seat were dilated with fear.

Greg reached over to his jacket and removed his cell phone. Because it was after six, he punched Joe Steiner's home number. His wife answered on the third ring and gave the phone to her husband.

"Joe, I need a favor," Greg said.

"Why should you be any different?" he said. "Can it wait until I finish dinner?"

"Unfortunately, no."

"Greg, you make me yearn for telemarketers."

Greg chuckled. "Sorry. But as you know, I've been granted thirty consecutive personal days."

"And unsolicited, I understand."

"Yes, how considerate of them."

"And you're calling to ask for a list of good books and videos to fill your time."

"That and a rundown on somebody: an eighteen-year-old male from Barton. His name's Brendan LaMotte. Anything you can find on him—criminal record, school activities, employment—"

"Any known terrorist ties," Joe said, cutting him off, "plus his favorite color, books, dog names, TV sitcoms . . ."

"You got it," Greg said.

"And all within the next ten minutes."

"No rush—take fifteen." He could hear Joe snicker. "One more thing while you're at it: any recent hospital admissions."

"Uh-huh. And where exactly are you enjoying your persona-non-gratahood?"

"Having high tea at the Ritz."

"Well, don't let me keep you."

Greg gave Joe his cell phone number and told him where exactly he was on 95. But before he hung up he asked, "How's Sarah doing with the driving?"

"Eleven days, and nobody's revoked her license yet. Yippeee!"

"And did we find her a car?"

"My wife's was falling apart, so we tried to find one that would also be safe for Sarah. Unfortunately, everybody was out of used Sherman tanks, so we settled on a ninety-eight Volvo. But I'm saying kaddish for it, in advance."

Greg laughed, and they clicked off.

About forty minutes later Joe called back. Greg was still on the highway. The traffic was moderate. The rain was beginning to let up, and the sky ahead looked bleached under shredded clouds.

"What do you have?"

"The kid lives in Barton with his grandfather." Joe gave the address and telephone number and said that Brendan LaMotte had quit school and was working at the Dells Country Club as a waiter. He also said that his parents were dead, that he was very bright and had some serious personal problems—information he had gotten from the boy's high school guidance counselor. Joe had also called the Dells, the Barton PD, the state police, the local newspaper, and other places.

"All that in less than an hour. You're pure magic, pal."

"It was worth it. I love cold chicken." Then Joe added, "One more thing I think you'll find interesting: On the evening of June twenty-three, he was brought into the Essex Medical Center ER with a head injury. Apparently he slipped and fell headfirst into a glass door. He was released two hours later after cleanup and X rays."

"My, my."

56

Nearly three hours later, Brendan pulled over.

He had led Rachel to a heavily tree-lined dirt road. A small sign on a post said: CAMP TARABEC—PRIVATE PROPERTY.

Brendan got out and came around to her window. "This is the place," he said. "He t-turned down there, but I didn't follow him."

It was the understated entrance to a campsite. "How long did you wait?"

"A f-few minutes because the security guard came and told me to leave. I d-d-didn't have official business."

"We have now," she said. "Get in."

Brendan looked hesitant, but he got in. "There are s-security cameras in the trees."

She nodded and drove down the drive through the woods. After about a quarter mile she came to a crossroad, also dirt. Signs with arrows pointed right to THE BEACH, THE DOCK, and BOATHOUSE; left to THE LODGE, CHAPEL, CABINS among other places.

She turned right. The rain had stopped miles back and there was enough light left to make out some cabins with the lake in the background through the trees. At the end of the road was a boathouse and a small dock with a large white outboard and two smaller boats. But no people or cars.

She turned around and returned to the intersection but proceeded straight, this time passing an open area with more log cabins on the right and playing fields and a tennis court to the left. On the far side of the fields, she spotted some kids at a picnic table with an adult. None looked like Dylan, but the sight of them made her feel better—all so normal and innocent. But her mind was racing trying to connect all this to Malenko. *Why a campsite? Is this the right place? Where is my son?*

The lodge was a handsome log structure with a porch and steps and screen door with a WELCOME sign next to it.

Brendan waited on the porch while Rachel went inside.

At a reception counter was a man in his forties dressed in a bright green pullover with a monogram saying CAMP TARABEC and a name tag saying KARL. A computer sat on the desk next to him. On the wall were camp notices and group photos of smiling teenage campers. To the side was a small private office. Again all normal and innocent looking. The man appeared to be alone in the building.

He looked up. "Hi, there. What can I do for you?"

"My name is Rachel Whitman, and I'm looking for my son, Dylan. He was brought here yesterday by Dr. Lucius Malenko."

The man stared at her blankly, then slowly shook his head. Without taking his eyes off her he said, "What's your son's name again?"

"Dylan. Dylan Whitman."

"That's not a name I recognize." He made no effort to check his computer or a printout list.

"Are you sure?"

"Yes, I'm sure," he said. "Nobody here by that name."

"But you didn't check."

"I don't have to check. I know all the children here by name. There's no Dylan Whitman. Sorry."

Rachel was feeling faint. "What about Dr. Lucius Malenko?"

"Nope."

The flat abruptness of his answer said that she could leave now. After a few blank seconds, she turned to leave.

"By the way, how old is your son?"

"Six."

The man's face softened. "Well, you've definitely got the wrong place. We have twelve-year-olds and up. You might check Camp Ossipago about ten miles up 123."

She shot a look to Brendan outside. God, was it the wrong place? How could that be? The kid was supposed to have a flawless memory. Or maybe Malenko didn't come here after all. Maybe he just turned off the road to relieve himself in the woods.

On the wall hung a bulletin board with large letters: CAMP DISCOVERY: HANDS-ON WORKSHOPS. Memos and notices were tacked up as well as a sign-up list for classes on computer programming, Web design, robotics, and interfacing ergonomics. There were announcements about lectures on cloning, stem cells, black holes, and observational astronomy. The place was a summer camp for child geniuses.

Rachel thanked the man and headed outside, feeling the panic rise again. "It's the wrong place," she said to Brendan, as they headed back to the car. "They never heard of Dylan or Lucius Malenko."

"It's n-n-not the wrong place," Brendan insisted. "I saw him drive down the road with him. He brought him down here."

There was nothing in his manner that suggested doubt.

Rachel looked around. It was a bona fide camp with climbing structures, playing fields, tennis courts, water activities, et cetera—and clearly for very bright older children. So, what would Malenko be doing here with Dylan? Unless he just made a short stop for some reason.

"Wait a minute," she said as Brendan opened the car

door. Across the road was a building with a sign: INFIR-MARY/FIRST AID. She headed for it.

She entered a small foyer to an examination room. A young woman stepped out in a white smock. A name tag said MARYELLEN STAFF NURSE.

"May I help you?"

Rachel explained that she was looking for her son.

"We have nobody here by that name. Did you check with Karl at the lodge?"

Rachel nodded. "Does the name Dr. Lucius Malenko mean anything to you?"

The woman repeated the name and shook her head. "Our camp doctor is Mark Walsh," she added pleasantly. "May I ask what this is all about?"

Rachel shook her head. "Are there any other medical facilities around here? An infirmary, hospital, clinic?"

"This is the only infirmary we have. What are you looking for?"

Rachel took a deep breath to steady herself. "If a child got seriously injured—say a concussion or worse, where would you send him?"

The woman gave her a puzzled look. "Well, there's the Coburn Medical Center in Barnstead about eight miles from here." And she rattled off the directions.

"That's the closest?"

"Yeah. If we have a serious problem, that's where we'd take them. May I ask . . . ?"

Rachel thanked the woman and left.

She stood on the porch for a moment. It had begun to drizzle, and the sky was darkening. In an hour, it would be night. She had been up since early that morning, exhausted from the flight, then the ride up here. On top of that, fear and despair were filling her up.

Brendan was in the car. She started toward it, her mind racing to decide what she should do. She cut across the road to the parking lot, when out of the gloom she heard a child's voice.

"Mommy!"

Rachel turned around, and before she knew it a little boy wrapped his arms around her middle.

"Mommy! Mommy!"

For a split instant Rachel's heart swelled with joy. Suddenly she gasped in horror. It was not Dylan.

Still clinging to her, the child said, "I love you, Mommy! I love you, Mommy! I love you, Mommy!"

A woman rushed up to her. "I'm terribly sorry," she said and tried to peel the child off Rachel. But he would not let go, and Rachel struggled to keep from being toppled.

Suddenly the boy began to wail as the woman tugged at his arms.

"Daniel, no! Let the lady go. She's not your mommy."

But the child fought her, pulling with one hand at Rachel's blouse. Finally, the woman grabbed both of Daniel's hands and yanked him free.

He continued to blubber and grasp at Rachel. As the woman apologized and pulled him away, Rachel noticed that the boy was wearing a red plastic band on his left wrist. And there was an awful vacant look in his eyes as the woman held him back, explaining that Rachel was not his mother. In the confusion, the baseball cap he had been wearing fell off, and instantly the woman put it back on his head. But before she did, Rachel noticed the boy had no hair.

Cancer, she thought. *The poor child has cancer. He is also clearly retarded.*

"Sorry," the woman said, and led the little boy to a dark van.

Rachel returned to her car, and through the windshield she watched the woman put the child inside. She was probably an aunt or guardian, and they were up here to visit an older sibling, Rachel told herself.

For a brief moment before she got in herself, the woman looked over her shoulder at Rachel. For a second, Rachel felt something pass between them. Then the woman got in and drove away.

Rachel started the car, shaking as if the drizzle had turned to sleet. "Brendan, think again. Are you sure this is where you followed him? Are you sure this is the road he turned down, not some other dirt road?" From the main road, they all looked alike.

Brendan looked at her solemnly. "It's the right road. I r-r-remember the sign."

She pulled out of the campsite and up the drive to the main road.

"Where we going?"

"I don't know," she said. *God, help me find him.*

"You're almost out of gas." The dashboard warning light was on. "There's a self-serve M-Mobil station we passed about two miles up the road."

Brendan was right about the gas station. After a few minutes Rachel pulled up to the pumps. While Brendan got out and pumped the gas, she called the number for the Coburn Medical Center. When the operator answered, Rachel asked if they had a recent admission named Dylan Whitman or a Dr. Lucius Malenko on staff. There was a promising pause, then the operator said there was no record for either name.

Her body began to shake again, and tears flooded her eyes. Any moment she might begin screaming and not stop.

"Mrs. Whitman?" Brendan's head was at her window.

She rolled down the window and handed him a wad of money then began to raise the window.

"Mrs. Whitman, I think Dr. M-M-Malenko just drove by."

"What?"

He nodded in the direction they had come. "It was hard to tell, but a red Porsche j-just went by."

"Get in! Get in."

"B-but . . . the g-gas?"

He had only put in a couple dollars' worth. "We've got enough."

Brendan lumbered into the station to pay as she turned the car around.

In a few seconds, they were on the road racing through the rain in the direction of the Porsche.

Brendan didn't know if it was Malenko, but how many red Porsches were there in this part of Maine? And if it was Malenko, she prayed he wasn't driving far, because she had barely a quarter tank of gas.

The pavement was slick, and she had to take care rounding the corners. After several miles, she still had not caught up, and less than a mile ahead was the cutoff for Camp Tarabec.

When she came to the entrance, she began to turn down when Brendan stopped her. "No. Straight. There aren't any tire tracks in the mud."

He was right. She backed up, leaving clear tracks, but the rest of the dirt road was unrutted mud. She shot back onto the street. Thankfully, there were no other driveways or side roads for a couple miles. But there would be more, so she accelerated in case he turned off.

After maybe another two miles of black woods, she saw red taillights flicker ahead of her. They passed a sign saying MARLON'S HEAD BEACH—3 MILES. They were heading for the coast.

"That's him," Brendan said.

A red Porsche.

The road opened up on either side, as the woods gave way to fields then to saltwater marshlands. In the distance, she could see the Porsche pull behind more cars, and just beyond it, about half a mile, was a bridge.

Suddenly, red and yellow lights began flashing ahead as bells clanged.

"Oh, God, no!"

Maybe a quarter mile ahead, the Porsche shot onto the bridge just as the gate came down. It was a drawbridge, which had opened to let sailboats pass. In the distance was the ocean.

Rachel came to a screeching halt before the gate. Three

mast vessels lined up to pass through. It could take fifteen minutes before the bridge was passable again.

While the lights blinked, the first sailboat slowly glided through the opening. Holding her breath, Rachel watched the Porsche take off toward the shore road. In a matter of seconds, he would turn one way or the other and be gone.

But instead of proceeding to the beach, the car turned right into a parking lot maybe half a mile away. The taillights flared as it came to a stop.

Brendan got out. A moment later he stuck his head into the window. "Mrs. Whitman?" He handed her a large black pair of binoculars.

She got out and came around to his side. The rain was thin but steady.

Brendan pointed in the direction of the red car.

Rachel raised the glasses to her eyes, having to adjust one lens then the next. Rain had smudged the front piece, but through the dimming light she could make out the red car. There were two men, shaking hands. One with white hair. Lucius Malenko.

The other was Martin.

While the last of the three boats drifted through the channel, Rachel watched in disbelief as Martin waved good-bye to Malenko and headed for his Miata. Then Malenko took off toward the shore road with Martin behind him. They came to the stop sign at the end, the beach and the ocean spreading beyond them. The Porsche turned left, and the Miata turned right.

Shortly, the bells began to ring and the lights flashed as the gate was raised. Rachel and Brendan shot across the bridge and down the strip to the shore road. In the distance to the right, she saw the taillights of Martin's car. To the left and rapidly disappearing was the Porsche's lights.

For a frozen moment, she didn't know which way to

turn. Martin had probably tried to call Malenko to alert him that she was heading up here for Dylan. When that failed, he drove up here following the directions she'd left on the answering machine. Maybe by the time he arrived, Malenko had gotten his message and called him back. And this was their rendezvous. But she didn't care about that. Malenko may or may not lead her to Dylan, and if she caught up to him he could stonewall her.

She turned right, not taking her eyes off Martin's car, thinking how he had betrayed her.

About a mile down the shore road, they passed a sign to the Maine Turnpike. Martin's business with Malenko was over; he was heading back home.

The Maxima growled after him. At about a quarter mile behind him, she began flashing her lights. At about a hundred yards, he slowed down probably thinking it was Malenko in his mirror. When he recognized her car, he pulled over and got out.

"What the hell are you doing?" Then he noticed Brendan in the car. "What's he doing here?'

She got out. "He's helping me find Dylan. Where is he?"

"Rachel . . ." he began.

She lurched at him and grabbed his shirt, ready to claw his face if he resisted her. "Where did they take him?"

"To his clinic."

"Where? Where is his clinic?"

Martin looked startled by the intensity on her face. "I don't know. He wouldn't say."

"What were you doing in his car?"

"That's where we met. He called me from the road and said to meet him."

"You came up here to warn him about me."

"Yeah, and to give him the rest of the money."

"*Christ!* Get in. GET IN."

"But my car."

"GET IN!" she screamed.

Brendan jumped into the back seat as Martin got in front. Rachel squealed into a fast U-turn and raced back upshore. The lights of two cars burned in the distance.

Martin had no idea where they were performing the procedure, but it would happen within a few hours. "Rachel, I think we should talk, and talk privately."

In the back seat Brendan had the map out. "The shore road connects back to 123," he said to Rachel.

Highway 123. That leads back toward the camp, she thought.

If they didn't intercept Lucius Malenko there, she'd call the police no matter what.

"Rachel, we've been through this. It's the best thing."

"Martin, I don't want them to lay a finger on him, do you understand? It's bad, it's wrong, it's lousy with problems." Then she reached over and pushed the tape recorder from Vanessa Watts in his hands. "Listen to her. And when you're through, listen to Brendan."

Reluctantly Martin raised the tape recorder to his ear. After listening he said, "But she was half-crazed when she made that."

"Goddamn you, Martin!" Rachel screamed. "She wasn't crazed. She was pouring her heart out." She looked into the rearview mirror. "Brendan, tell him what they did to you."

And while she drove trying to keep from backhanding Martin, Brendan told him about his condition, about the torment of living in his own mind. About wanting to end his life. "Maybe I w-would have been screwed up anyway, m-maybe not. But I think I lost more than I g-gained."

Martin listened, the skin of his face looking as if it had been stretched. "I'm sorry," he muttered. "I didn't know."

Rachel was too numb to respond. She raced back to Camp Tarabec. At one point, Martin said half to himself, "Maybe we can still get our money back."

"Is that your only concern?" she asked.

"Of course not, but still . . ."

Nothing else was said, and twenty minutes later they arrived at the camp. By then, the sky was black.

Rachel stopped at the crossroad where the signs pointed left and right. She turned left toward the lodge. The lights were still on, but in the dark and rain nobody was outside. Slowly, she passed the lodge toward a small service road that led to some rear cabins and to the dead end. No red Porsche in sight. She turned around and headed back, passing the lodge.

Instead of taking a right back onto the entrance road, she continued straight toward the dock. Cabin lights glowed. But nobody was about. And no cars. Rachel continued all the way to the dock, the lightless boathouse on the left.

"There's nobody here," Martin said.

But Rachel wasn't satisfied. She jumped out of the car and ran to the dock. Two small runabout outboards were moored alongside. The boathouse was black, so was the nearby dock shack. But for two exterior lights, the place was dead.

Under an opaque sky, the water spread before her like corrugated lava. In the distance, where the island sat, a dim yellow light glowed. She started back toward the car, when she stopped in her tracks. The large black structure of the boathouse pulled at her. She crossed to the front. The door was locked, but in the headlights from her car she could make out the interior. The red Porsche.

"He's here," she said.

"He is?" Martin walked over to her as Brendan headed to the dock. "So what are we going to do? There must be fifty cabins here."

Rachel's mind raced. Malenko had warned them that he wouldn't tolerate any breach of confidentiality—which was probably why his people at the lodge back there denied recognizing his name. And Dylan's. If they called the local police, what would they say—that their son was being illegally operated on by a neurosurgeon they had hired and paid and with whom they dropped off their son? Or that they changed their mind at the last minute? And what was the crime but their own foolishness? Besides, if the police showed up and word got out to Malenko wherever he was, he might harm Dylan. Or deny he had him?

Besides, the nearest police station could be miles from here. And they had no idea where Malenko had gone or where Dylan was.

"He t-t-took the boat."

Rachel looked over to Brendan. "What?"

"There was a boat here earlier. A big white p-power boat with twin Mercury engines."

Rachel glanced out over the water to the yellow light burning in the gloom. She could not hear any sound but the wind.

She moved to the dock. "What about one of those?" Two skiffs with small outboards attached to the transoms.

"We can't just take it," Martin said.

She got in and began to feel around the motor. "Does it need a key?"

"N-n-no. It's got a p-pull cord."

Martin stood frozen for a moment. "What are you doing? That's private property."

"Untie it, goddamn it," Rachel snapped.

"This is crazy."

"Then stay here."

Martin looked at them for a moment, then removed the rope from the dock cleat. Rachel found the cord, hoping to get away before somebody discovered them. At the moment, nobody was around, and the nearest cabin was a hundred yards away.

But in the distance, she heard a car approach.

"Hurry."

Brendan pumped the fuel bulb on the line a few times then pulled the cord. The engine started up instantly. And Rachel whispered a prayer of thanks and sat beside Brendan at the throttle arm.

From her bag she found her small penlight and gave it to

Martin to guide them through to open water. He no longer protested and kept the flash low, as Brendan pulled them away from the dock.

They were maybe a hundred feet into the water, when the headlights of a car flickered through the trees to the dock. Suddenly its lights went out.

Martin killed the flash, though the sound of the motor filled the air. Brendan cut the motor.

But Rachel said, "No," and took the throttle, pulling them into the black water, guided by the dim yellow light on the island and the pulse of her own heart.

57

They were soaked and cold by the time they reached the island.

Rachel throttled down to a low putter as they rounded the thick eastern flank. Through the growth, they could see lights from a small dock at the water's edge. Roped alongside of it was the long white powerboat they had seen earlier at the camp dock. In the shadows beyond sat a twin-engine floatplane.

Rachel killed the motor as Brendan and Martin paddled to the dock.

Set back on a rise under a canopy of trees was a large two-story building, the interior lights burning. Every instinct told her that her son was here.

God, let us be in time.

They tied up to the dock then got out. Except for the wind in the trees, the only other sound was the water slurping under the dock like some demon beast licking its chops.

Slowly they moved to the house—a dark sprawling structure that was probably an old fishing lodge. A deep porch wrapped around the front with chairs and tables; a set of stairs led to the front entrance. In the open yard to the right was a small playground area with a set of swings, climbing structures, and a sandbox. Nearby sat what looked like a length of a child's slide against a pile of cinder blocks.

As they approached the front stairs, twin spotlights snapped on from above, catching them in full glare.

"That's far enough."

A man stood in the shadows.

Because of the blinding lights, he appeared a clotted shadow. But as he got closer, Rachel could see he was tall. "This is private property." He held a shotgun on them.

"We're looking for Lucius Malenko," Rachel said, hoping that the man would recognize the name and let them in. But he said nothing, nor did he move.

"He has our son."

Still no response. And the only sound was the high wind and the rain pelting the building.

"Do you understand me?" she said. "Dr. Malenko knows us. We're here to get our son."

The man leaned the shotgun against a tree, then removed a pistol from his hip holster. He came up to Martin and poked the gun at him. "Turn around," he said and snapped open a pair of handcuffs.

"Look, this isn't necessary," Martin protested. "Just tell the doctor that we're here. The name's Whitman. Martin Whitman."

"Turn around."

"Please, we're friends," Martin pleaded. "I was with him just an hour ago."

"If I tell you again, I'm going to hurt you."

Martin looked at Rachel and slowly turned around.

"Please, we didn't mean to intrude," Rachel said. "We're just here for our son."

But the man disregarded her and began to fix a cuff onto Martin's wrist.

Suddenly there was the sound of movement, then a dull *thwack*—and the man plunged forward onto Martin, knocking them both onto the ground.

Rachel turned in disbelief. From out of shadows, someone had sprung on the guy and whacked him across the base of the skull with an oar.

Officer Greg Zakarian.

Martin pushed the guy off him. And Zakarian came down on the man's back with his knee and snapped the cuffs on him. The man groaned half-consciously.

"Is Malenko here?" Zakarian asked.

"Yes. And he has our son."

Zakarian removed the pistol from the guard's grip then found some shotgun cartridges in his vest and stuffed them into his own pocket. He then rolled the guy over and found a set of keys in another pocket as well as a long metal tube.

"What's that?" Rachel asked.

He sniffed it, then looked through the hole at the end. "A silencer."

A silencer? Rachel thought. The man was prepared to shoot people and not be heard. *And why out here on a remote island?* She wondered. *What the hell kind of people were they dealing with?*

Brendan helped Zakarian drag the man to the swing set. With one of the keys, they recuffed him to one of the steel support poles. When he was finished, Zakarian took the shotgun from Martin. He opened the chamber to see if it was loaded. It was.

"Why do they have your son?"

"They're going to do a brain operation."

Zakarian nodded without surprise.

"Why did you follow me?" Rachel asked.

"Because I think this Malenko can tell us about some missing children."

A shudder passed through Rachel. She wasn't sure what he knew, but she said a silent prayer of thanks that he was here.

Zakarian pulled out his cell phone from a hip case and punched 911. But out here on an island surrounded by water and woods, he had difficulty making a connection. Several times he repeated his message, identifying himself as a Massachusetts police officer in an emergency situation. He gave their location—an island in Lake Tarabec offshore from the camp—and asked for backup. When he got off, he shook his head. "I don't think I got through." He cocked the shotgun. "I'm going to go in. The rest of you stay here."

"Sure," Martin said.

"Like hell," Rachel said. Zakarian began to tuck the gunman's pistol into his belt. "Let me have that."

"I can't do that, ma'am," Zakarian said.

But she yanked it out of his belt. "My son is in there." She held the gun with the barrel aimed at him.

He studied her face for a moment. "Have you ever fired a pistol before?"

"No."

He looked to Martin and Brendan. "What about you?"

Martin shook his head, but Brendan said he had done some skeet shooting a couple times with his grandfather.

He nodded and gauged the look on Rachel's face. "Let's hope it doesn't get to that, but if it does: two hands, aim, and squeeze." And he showed her the stance.

She nodded and started up the steps, but Zakarian pulled them to the side of the building. Inside lamps glowed, but there was no sign of life—nobody peering out the windows, no shadows moving against the walls. But for the wind and light rain, the place was dead silent.

They cut around to a door at the rear of the building. They could see nobody inside. Martin opened the door as Zakarian led the way shotgun first.

They had entered an empty kitchen.

What immediately struck Rachel were all the children's effects—plastic drinking cups with cartoon animals, a bunch of small toys and figurines in a box on the floor, cartons of kids' cereal on the shelves, packages of cookies. But they all seemed like stagecraft. No crayon art on the fridge, no happy kids' photos tacked up.

Off the kitchen to their left was a hallway leading to the front of the lodge, a dining room on one side, a library of sorts on the other, the living room making up the whole front of the house.

Zakarian led the way, with Rachel behind him and Martin and Brendan behind her. As they moved into the interior, Rachel could hear a deep hum, just above the threshold of awareness. It seemed to emanate from under the building.

Zakarian pointed the shotgun toward the back room. Rachel turned the knob, and he nodded her back, then kicked the door open. An empty mud room, but with another door that could only lead downstairs. It was locked. With the keys he had taken off the guard, Zakarian got the door to open.

Rachel's heart was pounding so hard she half-expected her ribs to crack. Every fiber of her being told her that Dylan was here. And on some instinctive level she was drawn not into the house or upstairs but toward the source of that deep-bellied hum from below.

Zakarian slowly pulled open the door. A quick look with the shotgun. Nobody.

A dozen stairs led down to the bright interior below. Zakarian began to descend with Rachel, Martin, and Brendan in tow.

The humming became louder and the air became cooler as they descended.

The sight at the bottom was startling. In contrast to the dark, rustic interior of the lodge, they were in a large underground complex that ran off a brightly lit corridor with a clean tiled floor and fluorescent lights running the length of the place. At intervals along the corridor were dormitorylike rooms—twelve, six on a side—each with its own numbered door and viewing window, some with venetian blinds up, some down. Like diorama exhibits in a museum.

Slowly they made their way, following the steady low-grade electronic groan emanating from someplace at the corridor's end.

The first room on the right was empty, but it was clearly designed for children. The walls were painted with cartoon figures, toys were scattered all over the place, and a TV monitor was playing some animal show, with no sound.

Brendan stopped for a moment at the first window, staring at a large stuffed elephant doll sitting on a beanbag chair. He seemed transfixed. "Mr. Nisha," he muttered to himself.

Martin nudged Rachel. In the room across the hall was a little girl. She was sitting on the floor, her head bobbing. Although the door was closed, Rachel could faintly hear the girl grunting as she rocked in place staring blankly at the wall. She was tethered by one foot to a metal clip on the floor. On her shirt was a name tag: TANYA. Her head, which had been shaved, was speckled with scabs along the sides. She wore a red wristband.

Rachel wasn't certain the child could see her, or if the glass was one-way, but for a brief moment, the child stared at Rachel. Her eyes were like burnt-out fuses.

"My God," Zakarian whispered.

Across the hall, Brendan was looking at another child, a little boy whose head was also shaved and scabbed. Blood ran down the side of his face where he had picked. Like the girl, he wore a red wristband. He was sitting in the corner looking at a spot on the floor. His body was twitching and he was drooling on himself. It was not Dylan.

Rachel held her breath and moved down the hall beside Zakarian with Brendan and Martin behind.

The next four rooms were empty. But the last two rooms had a child in each. Through the window on the right, a little girl was staring blankly at the TV monitor. She wore a green wristband. In the room across the hall, a little boy was curled up asleep on the floor in his underpants. His head had been shaved, but it was not Dylan. A red wristband was fastened around his wrist. They were color-coded. A name tag lay on the table. DANIEL. The little boy from earlier this evening—the one who mistook Rachel for his mother.

Rachel groaned, feeling as if she were in the midst of something unspeakable.

The humming at the very end of the corridor pulled her away. Its source was on the right behind two swinging doors with narrow glass panels through which they could see bright lights.

"Stay behind me," Zakarian said.

With the pistol firmly gripped and Martin and Brendan beside her, Rachel held her breath as Zakarian pushed their way through, shotgun poised.

They froze.

They had entered an operating room, humming with electronic equipment. Clustered under two separate domes of lights were two groups of people in green scrubs standing around twin operating tables, each supporting a body whose head was locked in heavy metal frames, above which were television monitors casting scans of their brains with coordinates and lines indicating the paths of the stereotaxic probes. A man in street clothes sat at one of the computers.

Rachel could not tell if the patients were boys or if one of them was Dylan because the faces were blocked by the apparatus attached to their skulls. But the child on the right was wearing a green wristband, the other a red one.

Besides the deep hum, the only other sound was a kind of high-pitched whirring—like that of a dentist's drill. Two of them were positioned on stands with metal arcs, viewing scopes, and long probes aimed at the children's heads.

Zzzzzrrrrrrr.

The sound of the drills shot through Rachel.

"Police! Don't anybody move," Zakarian shouted.

The team of people under the lights looked up. And standing by the monitors of the brain scans, directing the operations, was a large man in street clothes.

Lucius Malenko.

Seeing the four of them standing there in horrid disbelief, Malenko coolly announced, "We seem to have uninvited company."

"Drop the masks and keep your hands high," Zakarian said, fanning them with the shotgun.

The surgical team was made up of six people—two teams of three and dressed in scrubs, caps, and masks. But nobody moved.

"NOW!" he growled.

Malenko nodded to them, and slowly one by one they began to remove their masks.

Rachel let out a gasp. They were children.

The surgical operating teams were all children—kids in their teens.

One was so short that he had to stand on a low footstool to adjust some instrument affixed to the head of one patient.

"What are you doing?" Martin said, stunned.

"If you weren't so impatient, your son might have had the opportunity to join us someday."

"They're kids."

"Only chronologically speaking," he said. Then he turned to Zakarian. "Officer, this is not a police matter. There's no need for guns. Please," he said, waving to lower the weapons.

"I don't think so," Zakarian said. "Hands high. All of you."

One of the masked children was holding a large syringe, one of several on a tray, ready to be inserted into the brain probe of the child on the left table—the one with the red wristband. Two others were manning the drill probes, the high-whining motor still cutting the air.

"Drop it and hands in the air."

Rachel moved closer to the child banded with green.

It was Dylan.

Rachel groaned. He was breathing through a respirator. His head had been shaved and slathered with some bitter-smelling jelly-stuff—like burnt almonds. Clamped to his skull was a metal frame that looked like some medieval torture device. No probes had yet been inserted into his head, but a high-speed drill was poised to bore its way through his skull above his left ear. On the stainless steel tray beside Dylan's head lay surgical knives, drill bits, and other glistening steel tools.

Unconscious beside him was some hapless child whose brain matter they were ready to harvest. Several probes aligned at his skull at different angles were poised for insertions. Beside his head were half a dozen large syringes for extraction.

"Turn off that drill," she growled to one of the kids, who looked about twelve.

He shot a look to Malenko for help.

With both hands Rachel raised the pistol. "Turn it off, or I'll blow your fucking head off!"

He turned it off.

"But isn't this what you wanted, Mrs. Whitman?" Malenko asked. "To undo the damage you'd done? To make him a brilliant little boy so he could learn to love literature like that of the poet whose name he carries? Isn't that what you wanted, Mrs. Whitman? Wasn't that your dream—the scientifically correct child?"

"You son of a bitch," she hissed.

Malenko looked at Martin. "And wasn't it you who wanted a son to follow in Daddy's footsteps?"

"But you're harvesting other kids," Martin said in utter disbelief.

"And where do you think incandescence comes from— battery implants? Just ask him," he said, flashing his grin at Brendan LaMotte.

Brendan looked in shock.

"Oh, yes, I remember you," Malenko continued. "When they brought you to us, you had little more language capabilities than the domestic cat. But we fixed you, didn't we, Brendan? Perhaps a bit too much, I hear. But we solved your language deficiencies, no?"

"Y-y-you messed me up."

"Messed you up? If it weren't for me, you'd still be working on your ABCs."

"You made me a f-f-freak."

"No system's perfect, but we're getting there."

Malenko did not seem the least bit intimidated by Zakarian or their weapons. He looked over Rachel's shoulder.

Zakarian shouted to the other man behind the computer
terminal. "Over here and hands high."

Rachel looked at the child beside Dylan. "But you're
killing them."

"Not technically," Malenko said. "Just a little . . . sim-
plified." Then he smiled, showing that row of white teeth
and sugary pink gums. "The universe loves a balance."

"You monster."

"Monster? But you hired me, Mrs. Whitman. What does
that make you? Or all the other good earnest parents who
want their supertots. Should I be crucified because I've
raised the dead?"

"We didn't know."

"And now you do."

*Why was he confessing all this with a police officer here
and the guns on him?* They had to get Dylan out of here.
"Take that thing off his head *now*!"

Malenko looked at her without expression for a moment. "Ahh," he sighed. "About time."

A voice behind them: "Freeze!"

Behind them stood a woman holding a pistol, which she
moved between Rachel and Zakarian. Martin raised his
hands, Brendan was frozen in place. The woman she had
seen earlier at the camp. With little Daniel and Tanya, the
girl in the room.

"You too, asshole!" A man's voice. Coming up from
behind the woman was the guard they had encountered
outside. He too had a pistol. The woman had freed him.
He and the other man were closing in on Rachel and Zakarian.

"Is there a safety on this?" she said under her breath.

Zakarian looked. "It's off."

"Drop them," the guard shouted.

"Get them out of here," Malenko bellowed. "Immediately. Outside, and get rid of them."

In a flash, Zakarian spun around and dropped to his knees and fired. The huge explosion reverberated in the closed structure. Rachel fell to the ground. When she looked, the woman was on the floor half in and half out of the swinging doors, the front of her blasted in red.

The guard shouted something to the other man, and fired his pistol. People scattered everywhere as the shots rang out.

But all Rachel could think was that a stray bullet would hit Dylan and the other boy. She held her breath and took aim with both hands as she had seen in movies . . .

Just squeeze

. . . and she did. The explosion instantly jolted her backward. But the guard was hit, because he fell backward against some equipment. His left sleeve had been torn away and was turning red.

The next instant erupted into frenzied and deafening commotion. The guard began firing with his good hand. The operating-team kids were hollering and scattering for cover. From behind computer terminals, the other man had scrambled over for the dead woman's pistol. On his knees with the shotgun, Zakarian shot at the man, who collapsed to his knees, bleeding in the hand and side. The air filled with sulfurous smoke, and Rachel was nearly deaf from the gunfire. Her only thought was Dylan and the other child on the operating tables.

But the guard was up with his gun taking aim. Rachel took one look and squeezed off another shot.

The explosion rocked the room again, and when she opened her eyes, the guard was on the floor clutching his leg. And Zakarian was upon him.

With Martin scrambling on the floor, Rachel dashed to the operating tables. Neither of the children had been hit by the gunfire.

Dylan was still breathing through the respirator, his vital

functions pulsing on the monitor overhead. His skull had been marked with black ink, long evil-looking metal probes poised for insertion into his head, calibrated brain scans on the screen above. All she could think was: *God, what have we done to you?*

She flashed the gun at a female in a mask cowering behind the surgical table. She still wore her mask and cap. There was a bandage on one of her thumbs. "Take that off his head."

The girl stood up. A tall girl.

From behind her, Brendan suddenly snapped off her mask. "Nicole!"

That girl. Rachel knew that girl. At Bloomfield. *The girl in the psych lab.*

"You asshole! You just wouldn't let go, would you?" Nicole said to Brendan. "Now you ruined everything."

She lunged toward him, but Rachel whacked her in the chest with her left arm. She raised the pistol to Nicole's face. "Take that off him or I'll fucking kill you."

Nicole regarded the fury in Rachel's face and the gun trained at a spot between her eyes, and she began to unfasten the screws.

On the floor the other kids were huddled together. Rachel flashed the pistol at them. "Help her. NOW!"

They shot up and began to remove the head frame apparatus from Dylan while Martin started to disconnect the IVs.

"NO!" Brendan shouted.

Before Rachel could turn, Nicole had grabbed a scalpel and lunged for her. By reflex, Rachel threw herself between Nicole and Dylan to block her aim. But in the scurry, she dropped the pistol to stop Nicole's hand, which came down, catching Rachel across the forearm.

To keep Nicole from Dylan, Rachel pushed the gurney out of her reach with her back, blood spurting from the gash. But Dylan had not been touched.

As Rachel got her balance again, Nicole raised the blade again and brought it down on Martin's neck.

Rachel let out a scream as he fell to his knees.

The next moment passed in a flurried haze. Brendan grabbed Nicole from behind and flung her across the room to where Officer Zakarian was cuffing the other two men. Then he dashed toward the rear, snatching the shotgun off the floor behind the officer, and ran out the door.

Malenko was nowhere in sight. But that did not register on Rachel. Only the fact that Dylan was safe and that Martin lay in a pool of blood.

Brendan ran down the corridor, checking all the rooms as he did. Only the children he had seen before. No Malenko.

His head was a wild cacophony of voices—a continuous tape of scraps that kept pulsing with the rhythm of his feet pounding the floor.

He raced upstairs and ran through the house. He was halfway up to the second floor when he heard the sound of an engine outside.

He dashed back down and out the front door.

The dock.

He bounded down the path half-expecting to see Malenko cutting across the lake in the boat. Instead, the floatplane pulled away from its mooring, its props driving it into the black open water, the red and yellow safety lights blinking on the wings, a small cabin light illuminating Malenko's white hair. The plane made a U-turn in the water to the left to take off toward the southeast and over the ocean.

"No!" Brendan shouted.

The engines revved as the plane picked up speed in the distance.

Brendan dropped to his knees and braced himself against a mooring pole with the shotgun. As the plane lifted off the water maybe a hundred feet ahead of him, he squeezed off a shot just ahead of the plane's exterior lights, pumped another shell into the chamber and fired a second.

He barely registered the recoil.

For a moment, he had no idea if the shots would even reach at this distance, or merely pepper the fuselage.

But at about thirty feet off the water the nose of the plane suddenly lit up in flames, as one of the engines streamed fuel back over the windshield. The engines roared in protest as they tried to gain altitude. The plane made a tipsy roll to the right and headed back toward the dock. As it came closer, Brendan could see the interior of the cabin awash in flames, and the figure of Malenko frantically flailing his arms. From fuel spraying through the shattered windshield, his head was on fire.

The plane sputtered and rocked, and for one last moment shot up as if taking off to the stars. Then it made a deep curtsy and came down in a flaming streak into the lake no more than fifty feet away.

Fuel and debris burned on the surface for a few minutes and mushrooms of air belched from below, then all was black again, as the night returned to silence. Overhead the sky had opened, and a new moon set the clouds in motion.

Brendan tossed the shotgun on the dock and stood there staring out over the opaque water. He trembled against the cold air, but inside he felt as if something had opened up— like a sac of warm fluid bursting.

He wrapped his arms around himself and cried.

EPILOGUE

SIX MONTHS LATER
BOSTON

The auditorium blazed in colored lights.

The stage was set with Christmas trees, giant candles, and nutcracker soldiers. Large shiny ornaments hung from the rafters. The orchestra, formally attired in black and white, was warming up as the children filed in to take their places on the dais.

It was the Children's Yuletide Pageant at Symphony Hall, and from all over the commonwealth, young people had been selected to make up the special holiday choir.

Dylan was in the second row dressed like all the rest in a white robe.

Rachel had managed to get tickets in the orchestra, middle section, ten rows back, so that Dylan could see them from the stage. When he spotted them, he broke into a wide grin and waved.

And Rachel's heart flooded with love.

While the performers got settled, her mind rumbled back to that awful night six months ago.

They had seen things almost too sordid to imagine, and it still sickened her that they had been unwitting parties to it all. Over the course of a decade, Malenko had enhanced over eighty children, kidnapping as many from randomly scattered locales across the country so as not to establish any coherence. He had apparently had a small but organized network of people who did freelance kidnappings almost always from poor rural families where the authorities had neither the resources nor the wherewithal for deep investigations. They were diabolically clever, often staging the disappearances as fatal accidents. On a few occasions they had crossed the border into Mexico and bought snatched street kids from local criminals. They never left tracks or telltale clues connecting the disappearances.

Luckily, the little boy who had been the harvest for Dylan had suffered no brain damage. His name was Travis Valentine, a gifted child with a love of butterflies, who had been safely returned to his mother in Florida.

As for the enhanced kids, some were Malenko's clients from the Nova Children's Center. But neither the parents nor other Nova clinicians had any idea of Malenko's secret practice nor how he had scanned the database for prospective harvests—nor the fact that those children had been stolen, rendered brain-damaged, and disposed of at sea.

As one reporter had written: "The brain is the most wondrous creation in the universe—and, as Lucius Malenko had confirmed, the most frightening."

The media had dubbed him a latter-day Josef Mengele.

And like his Nazi counterparts, Malenko kept extensive records of his practice. He even had a photo album and full medical report on each enhanced child, allowing authorities to contact the parents. None claimed any knowledge of the harvesting. While nearly all the treated children were exceptionally bright, some suffered serious behavioral problems that were being treated by medication and counseling.

The kids who had made up the surgical team were turned over to juvenile courts. Nicole DaFoe was arrested for the murder of Martin and was awaiting trial as an adult. The surviving cronies of Malenko were indicted for serial kidnappings and murder.

Rachel wore a permanent scar on her arm from the scalpel attack.

Because of the awful associations, Rachel sold her house in Hawthorne and moved to Arlington, which bordered Cambridge and which had a more diversified population. In the fall, Dylan was enrolled in a local school where they had a well-trained support system for LD children. And, most importantly, he was very happy.

When it was discovered that Sheila had recruited Rachel and Martin on the promise of a commission from Malenko, she was arrested for being an accessory to crimes—although her lawyers would probably get her off on a lighter sentence of abetting medical malpractice rather than kidnapping and murder. It was also discovered that she had switched videocassettes the night of Vanessa Watts's death, having been spotted by one of the waiters.

Brendan LaMotte was put in the care of neurologists at Children's Hospital. When he had visited Rachel last weekend, he seemed to be doing much better and was back in school. To the delight of his grandfather, he was talking about going to college next year.

A burst of applause brought Rachel back to the moment. The conductor had entered the stage.

Shortly the program began, and Rachel took Greg Zakarian's hand and settled back.

She had, of course, gone through the Kübler-Ross stages of dealing with Martin's death—denial, anger, a sense of sadness and grief. She even still harbored guilt for the loss of him. And, yet, with Greg's help she had come to believe that what she had done was necessary to save her son's life.

Of course, Dylan missed Martin. He sometimes spoke of him, recalling some of the things they had done together. And for a few weeks, he wore his father's college ring on a chain around his neck. But that soon ended up in a bureau drawer. And that sometimes-miraculous healing process possessed by children had begun to take over.

It helped that Greg was beginning to fill the void in Dylan's life. He came up every weekend from the Cape, or they went down there. He was back on the police force and had been promoted to detective sergeant. During Sagamore's Town Day celebration in September, his superior officer, Lieutenant T. J. Gelford had presented Greg with a medal of commendation for his actions that night in July. Rachel and Dylan attended the ceremony. Rachel cried, and Dylan gave Greg a standing O.

After weeks of cross-checking Malenko's files with those of missing children, Greg had determined the identity of the Sagamore Boy. His name was Emilio Cruz from Clayton, Alabama. His father was a farm worker, his mother cleaned other people's homes. The boy, who was kidnapped just a week before his sixth birthday, had tested brilliantly.

Greg had accompanied Emilio's remains to his parents. A private funeral was held at a local Catholic church, attended by Emilio's family and many classmates from the local elementary school that Emilio had attended. With the aid of local residents and business people, Greg established the Emilio Cruz Scholarship Fund for rural Alabama children. Even from afar, he continued to raise money, and not just to help bring emotional closure for himself, but to keep alive the memory of that little boy.

About forty minutes into the program, Rachel felt a flutter of anxiety. They had reached the last vocal number before the intermission: "What Child Is This?" And, as written in the program, the piece featured a solo by Dylan Whitman.

Rachel squeezed Greg's hand as she naturally tensed up. But there really was no cause for apprehension. Dylan sang like an angel.

Carnival Elation

7 Day Exotic Western Caribbean Itinerary

DAY	PORT	ARRIVE	DEPART
Sun	Galveston		4:00 P.M.
Mon	"Fun Day" at Sea		
Tue	Progreso/Merida	8:00 A.M.	4:00 P.M.
Wed	Cozumel	9:00 A.M.	5:00 P.M.
Thu	Belize	8:00 A.M.	6:00 P.M.
Fri	"Fun Day" at Sea		
Sat	"Fun Day" at Sea		
Sun	Galveston	8:00 A.M.	

TERMS AND CONDITIONS

PAYMENT SCHEDULE:
50% due upon booking
Full and final payment due by July 26, 2004

Acceptable forms of payment are Visa, MasterCard, American Express, Discover and checks. The cardholder must be one of the passengers traveling. A fee of $25 will apply for all returned checks. Check payments must be made payable to **Advantage International, LLC** and sent to: Advantage International, LLC, 195 North Harbor Drive, Suite 4206, Chicago, IL 60601

CHANGE/CANCELLATION:
Notice of change/cancellation must be made in writing to Advantage International, LLC.

Change:
Changes in cabin category may be requested and can result in increased rate and penalties. A name change is permitted 60 days or more prior to departure and will incur a penalty of $50 per name change. Deviation from the group schedule and package is a cancellation.

Cancellation:

181 days or more prior to departure	$250 per person
121 - 180 days or more prior to departure	50% of the package price
120 - 61 days prior to departure	75% of the package price
60 days or less prior to departure	100% of the package price (nonrefundable)

US and Canadian citizens are required to present a valid passport or the original birth certificate and state issued photo ID (drivers license). All other nationalities must contact the consulate of the various ports that are visited for verification of documentation.

<u>We strongly recommend trip cancellation insurance!</u>

For further details call 1-877-ADV-NTGE or visit www.GetCaughtReadingatSea.com

----

This coupon does not constitute an offer from Tom Doherty Associates, LLC.

For booking form and complete information
go to <u>www.getcaughtreadingatsea.com</u> or call 1-877-ADV-NTGE

Complete coupon and booking form and mail both to:
**Advantage International, LLC,
195 North Harbor Drive, Suite 4206, Chicago, IL 60601**